HAPPINESS

HAPPINESS

Theodore Zeldin

COLLINS HARVILL
8 Grafton Street, London W1
1988

William Collins Sons and Co Ltd
London · Glasgow · Sydney · Auckland
Toronto · Johannesburg

BRITISH LIBRARY CATALOGUING IN PUBLICATION DATA

Zeldin, Theodore
Happiness.
I. Title
823′.914[F]

ISBN 0–00–271302–0

First published by Collins Harvill 1988
© Theodore Zeldin 1988

Photoset in Itek Bembo by
Ace Filmsetting Ltd, Frome, Somerset
Printed and bound in Great Britain by
T.J. Press (Padstow) Ltd, Padstow, Cornwall

To
A. and O.

CHAPTER ONE

The history of Paradise begins on the day its gates were shut for the last time. Until then, Paradise had no history. Nothing ever happened: everybody was happy: there was no more to be said. But then perfection turned sour and curdled.

A shock now awaits the new arrivals. The old residents had been spared it: they say that they reached Paradise by a tempestuous route that left them haggard and heavy eyed, but the very first glimpse of the beauty of the place was enough to fill them, however shaken, however terrified, with a warm glow of recognition, a certainty that they had reached home. They used to land from small boats, in groups of half a dozen at most, at a sunny, sleepy, quaintly ornate port, where the waves gave the impression of licking the hulls in welcome, and where seemingly toilet-trained birds paused from their gossip to sing a madrigal of greeting, and to fan the still, balmy air. Every detail was reassuring: this was a haven of peace. They forgot the very meaning of words like pneumonia and cancer, which had so recently obsessed them, and which they could rediscover only with the aid of dictionaries, marked "obsolete". They stared uncomprehendingly at the germs displayed in the museum, next to the pterodactyls and the antique devil masks. The battle against old age and decay was over. They had no need any more to watch the clocks, which told only the time they wanted to see. Plumbers were not called out at all hours to mend leaks in a hurry, but took their ease constructing bizarre works of art out of pipes, vent-holes, inlets, grilles and plugs. Even the wasps at last learnt to kiss, not sting.

But today, as the immigrants approach from the air, they see the port, though still sunny, surrounded by dark country-side, and as they come to land they realise that it is not cov-ered with olive trees or vines, but with an endless succession of human anthills. Each new load of passengers is disgorged, exhausted and dizzy, into a maze of turnstiles, like a drunken football crowd trying in vain to disband. The megaphones blare unintelligible instructions. The faces wear a blank, orphaned look, as they search anxiously for friends or family. When they recognise public figures or distant neighbours, they are stunned: "How did you get here?" It is painful for them to discover that they are members of a club far less exclusive than they had expected. Each day, a million people, no less, become eligible to enter Paradise, and it was not built for such crowds.

Do they really arrive by boat or plane? They imagine they do, and that is all that matters. In Paradise you are what you imagine yourself to be.

The gates of Paradise are a historical monument now, des-erted except for the occasional sighing tourist. The massive stone pillars have been defaced by scribblings that the archae-ologists prefer not to decipher. The mosaic is crumbling in the once splendid baths nearby, unequalled masterpieces of perfumed, drowsy relaxation. The archives beyond, which housed the files of every visitor, and grotesque drawings of their sins and death wishes, are empty. Old Ismail no longer sits in his sentry box, and no longer sprinkles the lawns in front of it with his jovial patter. His passion for new company, his delight in conversation, his skill at prolonging the process of admission over bottomless cups of coffee, used to make it clear that here, at last, you could take things easily, and that time would for ever be your slave. He memorised the names of newcomers in advance, making them feel not just expected, but appreciated, honoured. And nothing could upset his good humour. He loved to put on a pretence of severity, to issue enigmatic warnings about the rules you were supposed to observe – absurd rules he invented to show his wit and to loosen yours; he used language you had not expected to hear in such a place, teasing you with prophecies of the mischief you would be getting up to. But now Ismail has retired to a small house some miles away and he has lost the glint of a smile in his eye that told you he was on your side. He spends his day mourning that Paradise is not what it used to be. He explains this with one reason only: there are too many people. He has grown discreet, taciturn. For long, he was careful to say nothing more, nothing that could be argued about. The traces of his old ingenuity were to be spotted only in the variations he played on his good morning greetings.

What led him to close the gates and withdraw in this way? There are many guesses on the subject: only recently has he given his side of the story, or part of it. Pressed by a curious visitor, to whom he took a liking, he suddenly unburdened himself, and his indignation came pouring out. They are not the same class of people who come his way these days, he said. Standards have fallen. Anyone, or almost, can get into Paradise today. And their expectations are so different. In the old time, they came for a rest, a long, sleepy basking in

9

nothingness. They had worked hard and suffered extremes of pain: they were worn out. But now rest was the last thing they wanted. They chased around for new adventures and new entertainments like irritated, irritating flies; considering themselves experts in leisure, they could barely conceal their contempt for the kinds of relaxation that were offered to them. Moreover – Ismail spat in horror – they looked on eternal bliss as their due, they had passed the test, they were entitled to it as a fair exchange for having been virtuous, or for having repented. Paradise was a kind of promotion for them, they expected it to be like a more powerful, more luxurious car than their last. Niggling, complaining of imperfections, proud of having already tasted so many forms of happiness in the world, they arrived defiant: they seemed to challenge Paradise to produce something quite unimaginable to surprise, titillate or satisfy them. But – Ismail sneered – they were also worried. How would they fight boredom? What were they going to do, stuck in the same place for ever and ever? Their pompous statements that happiness is something you must under no circumstances seek, it just comes if you interest yourself in absorbing pursuits, did not seem to convince them. For what was there to do? Singing hymns of praise weighed on them as an intolerable chore; they mouthed them sheepishly and mechanically, as though they were paying a bus fare, but felt cheated because the bus was not travelling fast enough and there were not enough seats.

Ismail's complaints do not go to the root of the trouble. He is not wholly reliable; an old man who has done the same job for a very, very long time and who, in any case, had himself caught the very disease he was protesting about: the newcomers had, without anyone realising it, infected the old hands with an irresistible itch, the need to complain. But revolutions do not happen just because people complain: much satisfaction can be derived from complaining.

When Ismail closed the gates, they had already outlived their purpose. The invading hordes had surmounted the walls and had got in without waiting to be admitted, or to be initiated, or to be put in touch with their guardian angel. It was said that there were no longer enough angels to go round. Paradise was filled with people who had to work out for themselves how to find their way around, how to enjoy it.

There had been no news from Paradise for many centuries when a young woman, then unknown to the public, set out to explore it, and understand it, in a way no one had tried to do before. Sumdy – that was how she spelt or shortened the name Somebody which she adopted – did not emigrate to Paradise with the normal expectation of remaining there. The unique feature of the place is that people try to postpone their journey to it as long as they can, and go only when they are forced, even though they speak in terms of rapture about its charms. Sumdy went there not because she wished to end her life on earth, but because she wished to enjoy it more, to discover what it is that everyone was so admiring of, and yet so terrified of approaching.

She took her passport to the Paradise Consulate and asked for a Tourist visa. That caused consternation. No one had made such a request before. She was sent from office to office. Men in black, always in black, always men, rushed in and out, ignoring her, clutching documents, without a smile, without a thank you. Everybody else knew exactly what needed to be done. But the right application form for Sumdy to fill in just could not be found. They tried to convince her that she should be content to obtain an entry visa, like everybody else. But no, she insisted she wanted to come back. Unimpressed by their assurance that the exit visa could always be obtained once she got there, she asked to see the

11

consul himself. That was impossible: he never gave interviews, and besides what she wanted was "irregular". Finally, however, he yielded to her persistence, and sent word that she had better write him a letter, since there were no forms, and since nothing could be decided unless it was put on paper.

"I want to visit Paradise," Sumdy wrote, "because I want to know what happiness is. Not because I am unhappy. But because I want to know what becomes of people when they are happy.

I realise you do not want noisy living humans snooping around, taking photographs, asking silly questions; the seraphim and cherubim, I know, tend to go around almost naked and might be embarrassed by strangers staring at them. But I assure you I do not wish to make trouble.

I enclose my photograph, from which you will see that there is a great smile all over my face. It is always there, or at least most of the time. You will find me a friendly person. But I confess that smile has been a problem. It just happens to be a smile of the wrong kind, not empty-headed enough to appear harmless, not sweet enough for me always to get my way. There are some people who suspect that I smile because I am secretly playing the fool, or because I do not take life seriously enough. A girl who cannot get rid of her smile is in trouble; it is like being the wrong shape, or the wrong colour. There is a lot of prejudice against too much laughter on earth; it has to be in its proper place. Do they laugh in Paradise? I should like to know how.

I think I am happy, but the experts have told me that I am not. They say I have got to change. I am curious to know how one does change, how all those grumpy, scowling, angry people who somehow get into Paradise are transformed into complacent, angelic beings, wearing just the right kind of beatific smile. What kind of training do you give them?

12

So far no one has been able to tell me what exactly it means to be happy. The experts say it is what everybody wants, it is normal, the very purpose of life, but they seem neither happy nor normal themselves. I'd like to hear what the angels have to say.

As further proof of my goodwill, I could point out that I have done my best to prepare myself for this visit, which I very much hope you will allow. Last year, on my holiday to the USA, I bought lots of paperbacks to give me some useful tips. Americans, as you must know, have studied happiness more than any other people, and have, in their constitution, made its pursuit one of their fundamental aims: how to succeed, how to compete, how to feel good, how to look good, how to eat the right amount. But they obviously find it difficult. I wondered whether the people in Paradise also found it difficult: it must take some effort learning to be happy if you are not used to it.

I wish to be allowed to take my dog Jolly with me, aged five and a half years, black with white paws, tail and left ear, vaguely related to the Shetland sheepdog breed. He is much wiser than his youth may suggest, and will give no trouble at all. I ask this permission not just because I would miss him if I left him behind, but because he knows me very well, and if I undergo strange transformations in Paradise, he will always be able to recognise me, and tell me that I am still the same person. Besides, his tail is the nearest thing I know to a litmus test for happiness; the trouble is I cannot quite understand why it wags when it does; perhaps I may discover that if we are faced by experiences new to both of us.''

It is quite possible that it was the plea for Jolly that won Sumdy her visa. They must have been impressed by her intuitive guess at the sort of place that Paradise was. The early explorers of it had seen only very small parts of it, or what there was of it when they visited. They have bequeathed a picture that has become outdated, even misleading. Is Paradise only a marvellous, unending garden? That is what the first travellers believed; to show how beautiful it was, they borrowed the exotic Persian word for garden to suggest the mystery and awe they felt when confronted by nature more lush and more generous than they had ever known. Infinite wealth was what most of them were obsessed by, and they found it: they could compare the riches of Paradise only to the goldmines of Abyssinia; they were enchanted by the fruit trees, and above all by the water, the real gold of the desert from which they came: one counted with glee no less than forty-one rivers, another marvelled that there were eight hundred thousand trees which gave shade and rest. Tables made of precious stones, laden with bread, milk and honey, perfumed with incense, that was what another saw; the inhabitants always ate their fill, there was singing and dancing, too, of a sort, with each reveller holding high his myrtle branch. An eminent witness, worthy of profound respect, reported that each of the first Caliphs who lived there had seventy houses, covered in gold and jewels, each house having seven hundred beds and seven hundred houris with ravishing eyes. But the Fathers of the Christian Church seem to have landed in a different part of Paradise, for they found it totally bare. How hard did they look? They enjoyed contemplation above all else, and they found it a wonderful place for that; so they built their hermits' hovels and looked no further. The music-lovers among them heard six hundred thousand angels singing the praises of God. Another estimate talks of twelve thousand choirs, each composed of twelve thousand angels. A different source calls these not choirs but armies. But even the most recent account is many hundreds of years old, and no two are in agreement.

Sumdy indeed was unable to find an up-to-date guide book: she was like a tourist going to a modern city clutching not even a hundred year old Baedeker, but only some ancient manuscript that led her to expect dancing nymphs to accost her in the street. Each century, each generation, each person finds in Paradise what they are looking for. That is the best reason for visiting Paradise, to discover what it is that one is looking for. Most people unfortunately arrive too late in life, when they have stopped looking.

Sumdy's account of her journey is brief, perhaps because it shook her so badly. It was not jet-lag, nausea, exhaustion that disturbed her. Those feelings she could recognise, she could accept them because she could hope to recover from them. What frightened, and astonished, her was something far more eerie. Neither she, nor any of her fellow travellers, had any idea of what kind of journey to expect. The theologians, like travel agents whose knowledge of lush destinations is derived from railway timetables, have been miserably vague. The only detailed descriptions available to her were from the victims of accidents, or illness, who have been pronounced dead but later recover. Their journey, they say with remarkable unanimity, begins with a strange noise, which they describe variously as a buzzing or clicking or roaring or banging or whirling or whistling. This upsets them at first. But then a wonderful sense of quiet and peace comes over them, even as their doctors are trying to revive them or lamenting their departure. All pain vanishes; they feel themselves weightless as a feather, moving through a dark tunnel or void or sewer towards a brilliant, welcoming light, brighter than they have ever seen, to which like moths they are irresistibly attracted. They pass through a door or field or mist, and they become

15

so pleased with their experience, so conscious of being liberated, that they are reluctant to go back to earth; their attachment to their surviving family ceases to preoccupy them. Restored to life, they emerge cured of all fear of death. Of course, they are not believed: they have no proof. It is all in the imagination, they are told. That is an insult on earth, where the imagination does not have the same status as in Paradise. It is looked on as a banana-skin, bound to trip you up. On earth only children are allowed to play with it freely; it is a sign of their incompetence; they do not mind falling, because they can pick themselves up again without loss of dignity. But sensible, grown-up adults are taught that experience is more valuable than the imagination. That is natural, because on earth it is time that matters more than anything else. Old men are proud to use experience as walking sticks to prop up their authority; experience is the pension everyone can look forward to, even if it is not guaranteed against inflation. Having to use one's imagination is the first great source of stress that Paradise imposes.

Sumdy's account of her journey does not conflict with that of these accident victims, except that it shows that they did not get very far. She too heard noises, but they were only, as she soon discovered, the preparations for departure. She too felt herself go lighter than air, but soon her body became noticeable in a different way: all that she had taken for granted about it became suddenly interesting: she became aware of the sound of blood coursing in her veins, her intestines churning, the tiny hairs in her eardrums vibrating. And then she passed right through the tunnel or sewer or void, and beyond the bright light, to find herself in the middle of an immense crowd of blinking, bewildered people, looking unbelievingly at themselves. Were these the same bodies they had left behind? The rapid succession of contradictory

16

emotions made them speechless. There was something peculiar even about the quality of the silence: there was bustling movement, but they could not hear it, because they were so absorbed by their own fate. The most remarkable point on which the accident victims' accounts agree with that of Sumdy is the overwhelming feeling of loneliness. Both they and she say they had never experienced such a total sense of being terrifyingly on their own. Were they on the right flight? Is this going to Paradise? They asked the questions but nobody answered them. That was what puzzled them. They forgot what they had left behind, they had no room for regret about the debts they had not paid or collected, or for worrying about what would happen to their possessions, who would feed the cat, how the office would get on without them, who would be promoted to their job, or whether their last words had been understood. They were shaken by becoming aware that they were totally independent souls, unable to lean on others, on family or friends. They did not know how to be souls. Sumdy felt the loneliness penetrating into her like a frost, she could see those around her growing numb too, even the few who pretended to be cheerful, celebrating their safe arrival or uttering inane comments on the weather. The weather was not something they could understand either: it was both warm and cold, warm to the skin and cold to the heart.

Even the rare couples or families who had set out together found themselves separated, like scraps of paper dispersed in the wind. Alone, they could not chatter, fight, be jealous, or rage with anger, for if they did, no one paid any attention. What was the meaning of all this? On earth, you took the meaninglessness of life for granted, you were never disturbed by it for very long, never went on strike to protest against it. Or if you found a meaning in life, it was too obvious to think about: life, the perpetuation of life, is the meaning of life. But here questions were more puzzling. There is no reason, in Paradise, why you should do one thing rather than another. You have all eternity to make up your mind. You are free. That grows into a nightmare. You are not used to it. You search around for someone to tell you what you are supposed to do, as a child does when it enters the world. Then the terrible truth dawns: you have to find out for yourself. Everybody is equally lost. But when everybody shares the same feeling, it is considered vulgar; so you dare not reveal how eager you are for guidance and advice, how maddened you are by any polite smile around you, even if you soon learn to wear one also. Even the telephones have learned a kind of politeness: they have the habit of going dead when you get too excited speaking on them, or too demanding, when you send more than the right amount of electricity down the line.

It was rumoured that perhaps the freezing welcome might be a test, a way of teaching you to discover yourself. But how could anyone discover himself except through others, that was the only way one knew. Alone, the new arrivals felt like prisoners in an isolation block; their voices faded away when they spoke, as though evaporating into an infinite void; they were never sure whether the people they spoke to heard what they said, were listening, or cared. Many just sat down on their battered suitcases and wept. Depending on where they came from, they blamed themselves for arriving unprepared, or cursed the demons that had pursued them, or reflected on their inherited inadequacies, or dreamed up memoranda formulating new strategies for making friends with the influential people they were bound to need. But they were as helpless as if they were back in their baby cots, unable to understand or be understood by those around them.

Only Jolly was unaffected by the freeze. He wagged his tail without stop as he trotted around with a pleased look on his face, vaulting over obstacles, crawling between people's legs, poking his nose into every corner as though searching for a vanished object that was playing hide-and-seek with him. He sniffed at the new smells, his eyes wide with wonder; even when doubt or fear made him hesitate, he could not control his excitement. The morosity around him was just one more unsolved problem. He was used to being ignored; if no one could be bothered to stroke him, or to talk to him, he simply distributed his little greetings, and moved on. Sumdy could not guess what secret Jolly had that she could not fathom; she could see that the great difference between him and everyone else was that he was bursting with curiosity, and loving it. But she did not find that to be quite a solution for her: if curiosity was a necessary condition for happiness, happiness was also a necessary condition for curiosity; she could not take pleasure in others when enveloped in a fog of gloom. That was the trouble with the happiness she had tasted on earth: it was made up of vicious circles.

Jolly was not just rejoicing that he was not being locked up in quarantine, a punishment he had always bitterly resented. (It was not that Paradise was too old fashioned to have adopted this measure of hygiene, for originally quarantine had been invented for humans; as late as the nineteenth century, travellers in the Middle East were confined – for strangers were by definition just objects of suspicion – but no one used to bother dogs or camels, who got the respect they deserved. Paradise had to be different if it was to be attractive: being composed entirely of strangers, it could not discriminate against them.) Nor was Jolly merely expressing his satisfaction that no customs officer had refused him permission to land. There were no notices saying No Dogs

Allowed – a mixed blessing for him, because there was nothing he enjoyed more than raising his paw over notices. The customs officers were in fact the only people who seemed pleased to see him. There was a shortage of dogs, and indeed of animals, in Paradise, just as there was a surplus of humans. The myth that animals were not admitted, the absurd notion that they had no souls, was a slander, but it was enough to dissuade many of them from coming. Anybody who had read his Scriptures should have known that Abraham's ram, Eli's camel, Jonah's whale, Birak's mare, Solomon's ant were long-time residents of Paradise, who had behaved themselves admirably and were much loved.

Sumdy brought not only Jolly with her, for whom she had a visa, but also her pet cockroach, Forgetmenot, in a jam jar, for whom she had no visa. She made no effort to conceal this. It may be that she was attempting to test the tolerance of Paradise; it may be that she was trying to be provocative. There were no cockroaches in Paradise, that was one thing everybody was certain about. There were no regulations forbidding cockroaches from entering, just as there were no regulations forbidding anything else. It is a myth that you cannot take your possessions with you when you leave earth – a myth invented by greedy heirs in ancient times, when society was obsessed by property and inheritance, before prosperity created too much property. It would not have worked for each generation to run off with their wealth, leaving their descendants to start all over again. But now that is what the descendants long for, and they vie in inventing inducements to encourage their elders to clear off with all the junk they manufacture. Slowly the word spread that there were no customs officers to stop you taking what you pleased into Paradise. Sensible French peasants got into the habit of having a few loaves of bread and a bottle of wine packed into

20

their graves, so that at least they would not be hungry while they looked round for a good restaurant. Rich kings had regularly insisted that they be buried with their treasure, though they forgot that their dignity forbade them to carry money themselves: pride often prevented them from arriving at the Gates with a purse in their pocket.

But recently the system has changed. Paradise does have a sort of customs service now, though it is run on a voluntary basis. The old residents pretend it is their contribution to cheering up the miserable newcomers, who seem so desperate to have someone care about them, even if only by pestering them with prohibitions. They have put up quite a good parody of meddlesome arrogance, officiousness and corruption. The new arrivals are kept waiting for hours to destroy whatever morale they have left; when they are at last summoned to be questioned, they submit with relief to every humiliation: they undress obediently, they answer intimate questions, they blush and feel guilty. It is a schoolboy prank, a form of false humour that gives its perpetrators the illusion that they are still young.

However, the customs officer who interrogated Sumdy was not amused by Forgetmenot. He was not prepared to joke about that. Grasshoppers, crickets, they were acceptable, if you argued long enough, but cockroaches were surely one of God's mistakes. How naive, how out of date could customs officers be! Sumdy protested that the cockroach was one of the most blessed of all His creatures. To how many others had He given the privilege of begetting 970 children each?

Sumdy was not experienced enough to know that it is a mistake to argue with a customs officer, who prides himself on the insight that enables him to spot the delinquent with a glance, to read the guilt in every heart; or that it is an even worse mistake to plead for mercy. She said that the cockroach

21

was the creature most deserving of compassion, for what had been more insulted than it? No one even deigned to call it by its proper name. The English accused it of being a monster half fowl, half fish. The French had heaped a ratatouille of verbal insult on it, borrowing for it the Arab word for renegade, they named it a *cafard* – and spooned into the mixture sneak, bigot and melancholy too. The West Germans referred to it as the *Franzose*, and the East Germans as *Russe*. The Bavarians insisted it came from Prussia, the Canadians' nickname for it was Yankee Settler, and the American Navy called it the Bombay Canary. Only the Portuguese could see an ambiguous virtue in Cacalaccas – "the insect with the lacquered excrement". The cockroach was the universal foreigner. Surely Paradise was the one place where all foreigners could at last feel at home? This was a test case.

And now Sumdy came to realise that she had to do not with a normal customs officer, but someone acting that role, who was not playing this prank just for fun. This was the first old settler she had talked to, who had been there for several generations, and not the least of the problems of Paradise was that all the generations that had ever lived had to live there side by side, in some kind of harmony. In the ordinary way, they solved the problem by ignoring each other, inhabiting different suburbs, going to their own shops and clubs, behaving as if the others did not exist. But that policy could not continue to work: the most unlikely meetings began to take place, and that was another of the reasons for the crisis in Paradise.

By great misfortune, the customs officer who picked Sumdy was the Archduke Francis Ferdinand, who had been assassinated at Sarajevo in 1914, and who is remembered on earth

22

for one thing only, having started the First World War without meaning to. On every other account, people had no desire to remember this once great man, heir to the faltering Hapsburg empire of Austria-Hungary. The best anyone who had worked for him could say of him after his death was that he was not stupid. His own doctor called him one of the most hated men of his time. He had an exceptional capacity for making enemies: he was a master at uttering cutting comments which left wounds that were impossible to heal. "When I first meet a person," he once explained, "I take it for granted that he is a brute; it is only little by little that I allow a more favourable opinion to be forced out of me." Francis Ferdinand despised almost all humans because they were not *well born*, that is to say aristocratically born. He feared popularity: "I am being applauded: have I done something silly?" Of the Magyars, whose King he was destined to become, he said: "It was an act of bad taste on the part of these gentlemen ever to have come to Europe." After a tour of the world, he decided that it too did not meet with his expectations; he was particularly damning about the Americans; their countryside was inferior to that of his native Austria, even the hunting there was inadequate, he was furious at having to content himself with shooting squirrels, skunk and porcupine in Yellowstone Park. For hunting was his passion, or more exactly massacring animals: in one day he shot two thousand one hundred and forty birds; shortly before his death, he celebrated having killed five thousand stags. Did he hate animals as much as humans? No, he was a frustrated soldier, who longed to be a Napoleon, and since he was spared that fate, he was forced to amuse himself shooting where he could: he even developed great skill shooting flies with a revolver. No one wept for him when he was assassinated (except his wife and children, to whom he was devoted, he

23

was the model family man). No one was keen to admit him to Paradise. But he had worshipped St George as the patron saint of hunters and had collected three thousand seven hundred and fifty statues of the famous dragon killer. The Archduke and the Saint had a rather curious interest in common. The Archduke's private museum included a collection of instruments of torture. St George had been tortured for seven years for being a Christian before being finally martyred. St George decided he would like to meet this strange disciple, and it was as a favour to him that the Archduke was admitted. St George thought he could make friends with almost anyone, if he only found the goodness in his heart; he overflowed with hospitality, conscious that he himself had been the recipient of hospitality that went beyond courtesy or generosity, appointed patron saint of England, where no one knew anything much about him (he came from Lydda, where Tel Aviv Airport now stands). But the Archduke did not respond, for he got his happiness from being furious; having lost his throne, he became a customs officer to defend Paradise against undesirable aliens. That is how chance brought together the most hated of humans and the most hated of insects.

The Archduke had probing questions to ask. What was this cockroach's nationality? He would need to see its curriculum vitae. Who was its next of kin? Who could speak for it? What was the source of its income, could it support itself? There were rumours that it was by instinct, by its very nature, a professional thief, living entirely by stealing. Had it strong political views? Could a case be made for its admission on the ground that Paradise had need for its services, which no other creature could provide? Since the Archduke had had such difficulty in getting to Paradise, he was not going to make it easier for anyone else.

The case of the cockroach aroused wide interest and much debate. Sumdy won an instant reputation by her defence of her pet. Forgetmenot's national allegiance, she explained, was not simple. The cockroach was the world's most successful commercial traveller, following man wherever he went, developing new habits, assuming new identities with rare versatility; no ship had sailed without its representatives aboard, where they acted as unpaid, uncomplaining stewards, eating up the crumbs and refuse that man disgustingly dropped wherever he went. It had adapted itself to every climate, formed three thousand five hundred different species; there were roughly as many human tribes. Like man, it had formed great power blocks, and their fate was not without interest to man. Originally it was the American cockroach that had dominated the world, with a foothold in nearly every home, from Africa to India and the Far East. It even lived in South Wales coal mines. This species had become a pillar of science, not just a greedy imperialist; it was the insect most used in schools and colleges to teach entomology; its mouth had been examined under the microscope with more care than any other, bar those of Hollywood stars. The golden age of the cockroach's coexistence with man came in the period 1900–1940: it was almost accepted. But then the Pesticide War started. Now the German cockroach emerged as the most resistant; and it became the world's fastest growing species, spotting new opportunities in restaurants, cafés, public houses, where it reigns supreme; it loves beer, and seldom allows a beer cask to travel unaccompanied; it occupies new buildings as soon as the cement is dry. Then a third species, the Oriental cockroach, moved into the less fashionable flats, older buildings, shabby offices where clerks dribbled their sandwiches on the floor. In Britain, the Oriental cockroach outnumbers the German by four to one, but the

German is twice as common in modern buildings; it is the cockroach of the future. Was Forgetmenot American, Oriental, German, or even the Australian kind, which wisely preferred to live in warm climates? Was it perhaps from Texas, the state that has the largest variety of different species? Sumdy left the Archduke the task of identifying it.

The Archduke was debating whether to squash it or to shoot it, or to use it to torment his enemies, when, once more, accident decided for him. Forgetmenot jumped out of the jam jar and disappeared into Jolly's fur. Jolly, as though fearing the worst, rushed off as fast as he could, but when he was recaptured there was no trace of Forgetmenot on him. That is how a cockroach got into Paradise. Henceforth, to catch it was to be the Archduke's mission, passion, purpose in Paradise. And it was in this way that Sumdy entered with both a black mark and a certain amount of ambiguous fame.

The brawl in the customs house was more than misadventure. The Archduke was exceptional, but he only presented in caricature the worry that people like Sumdy were causing.

The early settlers have found the new arrivals more and more irksome, difficult, indeed incomprehensible. Since time immemorial they have regarded life as a journey along well signposted roads, at every stage of which they paid more or less predictable tolls; they did not suppose that they had any alternatives; they accepted that traditional wisdom and proverbs were the best guides for their conduct. Of course, there were occasionally a few eccentrics among them, but these were seen as inevitable accidents, like the lame and the hunchbacked. To think for oneself was a feat of daring, as dangerous as going out in the dark of night, when evil spirits lay in wait to pounce on those who broke the rules. Among the new immigrants, there were certainly plenty who saw their prospects in the same light, and caused no trouble. But there was a new breed arriving, who came to be known as the Modern Person. At first, they received condolences for being modern; they could not help that; they would soon get over it; no one remains modern for ever. Then it became clear that some were incurable, whose peculiarity was not so much that they had arrived recently but that they were hardly persons in the sense that word used to be understood. No two of them seemed capable of ever reaching the same conclusion on any issue, or making quite the same choice. This was not just the spread of old-fashioned individualism. The Modern Person had been bombarded by such a variety of choice that the business of living had been transformed. Instead of paying agreed tolls, Modern Persons debated endlessly as to which by-road or shortcut to take, and they saw new paths everywhere. Even when they tried to follow the example of others, they seldom succeeded; they no longer knew how to imitate accurately; even if they wanted to be conformists, they found it difficult to know what to conform to, or how to conform. They were unpredictable. No amount of education could inculcate accepted standards into them. On the contrary, the more information was crammed into their brains, the more erratic they became. They grew immune to influence, even as the number of specialists in the art of influencing them increased, rather like insects becoming immune to pesticides. They resisted the experts not just from obstinacy, but also because they were too complex to interpret the messages they received in a straightforward way. Each Modern Person was unique; it was not possible to guess how he (or she) would behave. They did not know themselves, for they found it unbearable to believe that they were unique; they persisted in trying to conceal the fact as though it was a shameful fault, and put up a pretence of living just like their neighbours. But when they had a phase of confidence, they asserted that they were what adult humans should aim to be, in the divine image, which meant being a creator and not an imitator, and no two creators could be alike. When they felt low, they admitted that they could not even stand properly on their own feet, any more than infants, they needed to be held up by the good opinion of their neighbours, and that was hard to obtain. The freezing loneliness was the outward sign of their dilemma. The old settlers were right to be worried by them; they were faced not by the traditional conflict of generations, but by something quite new, individuals who really were different from them. For the extreme cases, somebody invented the name Plus Person.

The shutting of the Gates of Paradise was a gesture of despair, because the old residents had no answer. The Cockroach Scandal was the last of many straws.

Sumdy sent a postcard home, to reassure her parents that she had arrived safely. Forgetmenot's disappearance was not worrying; it always came back; squeezing itself into small crevices was its pleasure. Doubtless it had discovered some unsuspected fissure among the souls in which to hide. On the other hand Jolly, who seldom went out of his way to seek the company of any creature that was not a dog, and who had never shown the least interest in the cockroach, now looked as though he was troubled by Forgetmenot's fate. He was sniffing the jam jar, and throwing pathetic glances around, in a quite unaccustomed way.

Sumdy herself felt that she could not react to what she saw as she habitually did. It was as though eternity demanded that she should pause after every observation, as though every event should be treated like a piece of music needing to be listened to over and over again, until it grew slower and softer, leaving a haunting doubt as it died away. Everything seemed to be saying, go gently, at last there is time to reflect, things are not what they appear to be at first sight. In this place one has to think for ever. The most elusive quality of Paradise was perhaps that it was full of thoughts, of thoughts waiting to breed more thoughts, waiting.

CHAPTER TWO

There was no official in a suit waiting for Sumdy outside the airport, no offer of a conducted tour of happy souls, with explanations of why everyone in Paradise was happy, and had to be so, no tasting of the different vintages of bliss. She was relieved. She had her own plans, to make friends with her guardian angel, to be allowed to eavesdrop on the secret confessions of the residents, to be taught to jump over the hurdles that stood in the way of happiness, to be warned of the dangers and the omens, to get a peep at the truth concealed behind the pageantry and the reticence. What sort of people, she wanted to know, were most successful here: what kind of success did they fight for?

To recognise an angel, she realised, would not be easy. Angels doubtless wore their ceremonial white robes, and their golden belts, only when they were singing around the throne of God. There might have been a time when they could be seen in these clothes, going to choir practice or relaxing after a performance. However, Paradise had become a different place now that there was little chance, when one walked its streets, of bumping into them, merry or exhausted. On earth angels prefer to disguise themselves, as though their

30

favourite relaxation is to invent surprises and riddles, and so it is impossible to know in advance what kind of creature to look out for. The general opinion in Paradise is that they appear only when they see fit to do so, and when they have something very special to say. Greeting new arrivals is not one of their concerns. Where have they gone? What are they up to? People wanted to know, and they feared the worst, some terrible revenge.

There was thus no word of welcome for Sumdy from any guardian angel. How to set about finding him, her, it? That became her first preoccupation, and not just to satisfy her curiosity. She was no ordinary immigrant with all the time in the world to wait for a meeting. A quite unexpected frenetic sense of urgency seized her. The loneliness of Paradise was crystallising in her as a feeling of being dirty, coarse, heavy, ugly. So ugly that she was disgusted whenever she caught sight of her reflection, however vaguely, in a polished surface: no feature seemed to be in quite the proper place, or quite the proper size. She was torn between a desire to hide, convinced that she could have no place in Paradise looking as she did, and a yearning for help, for a guide; but she must also make herself worthy of being seen by her guide. Her own looks, her beauty, began to worry her as they had never before.

Nowadays, the old gatekeeper Ismail laments, they often feel ugly. It surprises them. They never expect to have to think about their bodies.

But there are no bodies in Paradise, say all the Christian saints who have visited it, just as they insist there are no marriages there, certainly no sordid clandestine affairs. According to these saints, beauty of the soul is all that counts. What would be the point of a beautiful appearance: for whose benefit? But these saints are bachelors, after only one

31

thing, purity. They are so single-minded, so absent-minded, they would hardly notice being blown up in an explosion, which is almost what moving to Paradise is like. It is certainly possible to have the impression that one has lost one's body, an experience that can be as terrifying as losing one's mind on earth. But the body does not vanish. The best way to understand what happens to it is to compare a living person who has a limb amputated. The limb is gone, but he can still sense it very clearly. So too when the body dies, it still seems to be there. After an amputation, the lost limb may feel normal in size and shape, to the extent that the victim may reach out for objects with a phantom hand, or try to get out of bed onto a phantom leg. With time, the sense of the limb may alter, become less distinct; sometimes a hand or a foot may seem to be hanging in mid air; sometimes the limb telescopes, so that only a hand or a foot remains, growing out of the stump of shoulder or thigh. Then the phantom limb takes on a life of its own, which its former proprietor cannot control; the fingers may feel tightly clenched, the nails digging into the palms, the cramp is impossible to relax, the whole arm may seem to be on fire, or be mummified with cold. It may scream with pain. He must learn to live with it as though it is a Siamese twin whose sufferings he must share. The difference between the amputated limb and the body in Paradise is that the former is completely out of control; it takes a long time for people in Paradise to realise that their new body is not as independent as it seems, that it is not a sort of importunate, irritating ghost following them around. Meanwhile, though they know they are supposed to be concentrating on matters spiritual, their minds wander; they want to know what they look like, what others think of them. The Scriptures promised they would all be beautiful in the eyes of God, but said nothing about them being beautiful to each other.

The ability to imagine one's body to be what one pleases can be exhilarating for those who have the courage to let go their fantasy, and who have a gift for transmitting or radiating that vision to those around them, but it can also have a catastrophic effect on the relations between souls, widening the gap between them, because how souls see themselves can be very different from how they are seen by others. So they often feel even less understood and appreciated than on earth. That is one of the causes of the worry about ugliness. Fantasy can turn into hallucination, if souls forget that they are only fantasising. The unprepared visitor who meets them in that condition may sometimes wonder if he has walked into some strange asylum. Most souls are careful to avoid shocking their neighbours; they continue to regard their bodies as solid lumps of flesh. It is only a few who have delusions of grandeur, inspired by the memory of chemists who can change the appearance of solid lumps, turning trees into paper, and sand into transparent window panes; flesh, like all material objects, is never a solid lump of anything, but an illusion created by troupes of little dancing wizards, who, according to the way they form up, according to whether they dance waltzes, minuets or tangos, can appear as a piece of coal one moment, as a gauzy bridal gown at another moment, be the sole of a shoe or a pair of spectacles, and then explode into smoke, or become the sweet scent in a perfume bottle. It takes time for souls to learn the dances of Paradise.

A body that plays tricks on its owner can make a timid soul disturbingly uncertain as to who he is. An immigrant arriving weighed down by uncertainty about his qualities and his importance, heaves a sigh of relief, expecting that at last his ignorance of himself, his self-doubt, will come to an end, and that he will be in the position of an actor who has the privilege of meeting the author of the play, and learns, finally and authoritatively, how the part should be acted, what the character is really like. But it does not happen that way, and instead his uncertainties can easily be multiplied if he is not careful. One of the great merits of the place, for which it has been much admired, is that when it admits a new citizen, it does not hold his past against him: it does not say to the carpenter that his experience entitles him to devote eternity to repairing the broken wooden benches in its parks, nor to the repentant drunkard criminal that everyone has been instructed to feel sorry for him. It asks no questions about what anyone did on earth. But that creates a terrible problem. Without a past, who are you? Most immigrants have found that too difficult, an impossible question. They have tried to avoid it by clinging to their old image of themselves and by rebuilding at least parts of their old lives around them.

Sumdy's first, mistaken, impression was therefore that Paradise was much like earth. There are suburbs of prim retirement bungalows, terraces with peeling paint, cities recreated as though in a film studio, and also a copy of virtually every little town that has ever existed, even those in bogs and deserts universally agreed to be God-forsaken. Everything possible is done to re-establish the familiar sights; and the postmen do not complain that so many cottages are called Mon Repos and Cosy Nook, thankful that every single one does not have the name Déjà Vu. It could not be otherwise. Paradise is what its inhabitants make it, and they like what they are used to, or at least most of them do. But Sumdy had not come all this way to admire bogus period architecture, or last year's fashions; and she trembled at the thought that the more they turned Paradise into a boring copy of earth, the less likely was it that she would meet beautiful angels and exotic cherubim, and hèar the true music of the heavens. But it was clear that there were two well-entrenched rules that kept Paradise immobile. One was: Know your place. That was a Holy Commandment to the vast majority who tried to go on existing and looking as they had always done. The other rule was: Do as your Neighbour does. Imitation was held in high esteem because it seemed a guarantee of harmony, eliminating surprises.

The new kind of immigrant, scathingly called a Plus Person, cannot easily acclimatise himself (or herself) to either of these rules. He does not want to model himself on his betters; he hates being like anybody else. He is an individual. His aim is to discover himself. He looks inside, into his own heart, for his identity. He feels that his face and body give a false impression of his real nature. He is loath to admit that other people might be in the same predicament, and so he is nervous, sensitive to criticism, capricious. He is not simply a frail plant that needs to be staked: he is too uncertain of himself to be sure whether he is going to grow at all or into what shape. He tries hard to be true to himself, but he is not sure how to do this. Above all he needs constant encouragement, approval, admiration. That is the great object of his hunger. He is obsessed by the need for beauty, and he is slow to realise that beauty cannot mean the same thing in Paradise as it does on earth: it is no longer a weapon in the war of the sexes; there is no pressure in eternity to look young. He has to discover beauty all over again. The frustration at not knowing exactly how to change himself, instantly, despite the opportunities, makes him wonder whether he is tied up, contorted, in invisible chains. That is also the meaning of the feeling of ugliness and heaviness.

If Sumdy had arrived thinking only about a good meal and a warm bed, she would have had few worries. But she was tense and self-conscious, despite herself. She too had something of the Plus Person in her. Her body was a burden: vulnerable, awkward, sensitive. The coffee bars, the clothes boutiques, the bookstores and the cinemas outside the airport took on a new meaning. Souls were obviously in danger of crumbling to pieces without the help of such props. When she wandered hesitantly through the shops, she was not pressed to buy; no one seemed interested in her. Was it because her face was losing its shape, because her gooseflesh was turning into permanent pustules all over her body? She felt dizzy, faint. She asked the way to the guardian angels, but could not get even a hint of the direction to look. There seemed general agreement that angels were not easy to meet. It was only when she stopped at an old fashioned herbalist's shop in search of some tea to revive her, that she came upon an answer. Amid the hundreds of jars on the shelves, she spotted one labelled: Perfume of the Angels. It was firmly sealed with red wax to keep it from prying noses, but Jolly sniffed it, and his nose was keen enough to detect its unique fragrance, which those who have encountered angels always remember as a major, numbing part of the impression they make. It was thanks to Jolly picking up this scent, and smelling his way through street and suburb, into the hills, and out to the ocean, that Sumdy finally came to a signpost that read: Village of the Angels: Angels only beyond this point.

They were miles from any other habitation. Before them stood a cluster of some seventy or eighty little palaces, some with minarets, some with cupolas, each in a different style, some bizarre, all of them flaunting luxury. The gardens, once spectacular, seemed neglected, vegetables were growing amid the flower beds, but the sandy beach and the peacock blue ocean beyond made this look like a true paradise in Paradise, the perfect summer residence for overworked angels in search both of peace, and of something different. The village was enclosed by a high wall, but without any attempt to conceal that the angels lived here. On the gate that led into it, Sumdy read their awe-inspiring names, unfamiliar ones, because the meetings between humans and God's messengers are so infrequent. She had heard of none of them except Kal, guardian angel to Nebuchadnezzar: it would be a real catch to have his protection. There was no sign of Baruch, master of ceremonies, in charge of visitors, remembered for having shown several eminent sages around the wonders of Paradise; but she was intrigued by Mihr the angel of friendship, Liwet the angel of invention, Theliel the angel of love, Poteh the angel of forgetting, Zadkiel the angel of mercy, Sofiel the angel of vegetables, Metatron, angel of the face, and Ergediel, angel of the twenty-eight mansions of the moon. She knocked at one door after another, rang bells, pulled clanging chains: there was no answer. Either visitors were not expected, or they were ignored, or else angels were invisible.

On the beach, however, sunning themselves, lost in reverie, some strumming guitars, some staring into space, some singing quietly to themselves, were several score of men and women; and what was most noticeable about them was the sadness in their eyes. The angels had abandoned their homes: no-one would tell Sumdy how exactly, or why. The Village of the Angels was now inhabited by squatters. It had become a refuge for the discontented. Of course everyone is discontented in some way. But most do not like to think of themselves in that light, or to advertise themselves as such. Congregated here were people who openly admitted it, who were so modest that they thought themselves unworthy of a place in Paradise, who came with expectations so high that they felt inadequate the minute they landed, or who were so pessimistic that they could not believe that Paradise could do anything for them. Though Paradise can accommodate every sort, it does not suit everybody. It is not uncommon for new arrivals to get angry, and to protest that they have been treated like package tourists dumped in a supposedly idyllic tropical island, who find, too late, that they cannot stand the scorching, humid heat, and who are appalled that the holiday will never end. News of this village spread, as though telepathically, among immigrants who were tuned in to a certain sort of discontent. For example, a pair of Japanese Kamikaze pilots, in their early twenties, came to recuperate from the shock of realising that their sacrifice had not produced what they expected; not believing that there was a paradise, it was a terrible blow to discover that they had not ended up in nothingness: now they were engrossed in plotting to escape, as soon as they could find where to go, a place that was really nowhere. That was an obsession among all the residents here: where to go next. They wanted to move on, and Paradise seemingly did not provide for that. For them, it was a crucial fault.

They were not the only misfits who had colonised the home of the angels. Here and there among the reclining bodies, little crabs and octopuses were wandering around, coming out of the sea and then running back, sometimes entwining their arms around the bodies they stumbled on, sometimes performing little dances, turning their arms into legs, sometimes gesticulating like a windmill of orchestra conductors unable to get their meaning across. The human souls seemed not to notice them. Sumdy asked herself whether there was discontent among the fish of the sea also. If fish could not fly here, Paradise hardly deserved its name; if the octopus, the most human and most intelligent of the creatures who lived in water, could not realise its ambition to move out onto dry land, there might well be more than a storm gathering on the shores of Paradise.

To discover that Paradise does not cure the weaknesses a person brings with him is heart-rending, as is the thought that there may be yet more skills to be learned if one wants to exist in it in a manner that does it justice. Sumdy was struck by the fact that the most recent arrivals seemed least able to profit from its facilities. So instead of questioning them directly, she sought the true character of the place through its gossip. She decided to visit the village hairdresser. At the same time, she could improve her appearance. However, the salon she found showed how heavy, for many, is the strain of being in Paradise, and what feeling eternally ugly can do to a soul. Wash basins had been replaced by fish bowls, driers by birdcages; the walls had fishermen's nets displayed all over them, instead of photographs of film stars, along which several magnificent octopuses were clambering about, twirling their arms as though in a private argument of their own, moving from one bowl to another. The hairdresser greeted her politely, but made no apology, gave no explanation of the unusual furniture. He had not abandoned his trade. This zoo was there with a purpose.

He introduced himself as the celebrated Saturnin, once one of the most admired coiffeurs of Paris. He said that he could detect at once why she had come to him, for he shared her unease; he knew just how shocking the experience of coming to Paradise could be. Though famous in his day, here he was – he sighed with resignation – a failure, like everyone else in the village. Delighted to have a visitor to whom he could pour out his life history, he told her that he had put his foot wrong the minute he landed. Arriving with his French identity card clutched in his hand, in accordance with the advice of his government, which took a dim view of people who forgot who they were, he hoped it would ensure the kind of reception he deserved; but he had been hurt and dispirited when there had been no one to meet him. Was he expected to keep his mouth shut and just get lost in the crowds? That was impossible. The need to make a little speech was important to him, naturally, because an identity card creates such a false impression, giving no hint of the sort of person one is, of one's dreams, of one's human qualities. He wanted to explain his claim to respect and attention, to reveal the full extent of his achievements and the complexity of his soul. In the fluster of the moment, the heat, the excitement, he could not find the right words, and even less so when, on some unreasoned impulse, he tried to talk in English, which made him incomprehensible. That was the kind of humiliation that struck many others who arrived haunted by the thought that the wrong ideas might be formed about them. However successful people are on earth, they hardly ever feel that they have been properly understood, and they are desperate to have that remedied, at last, in Paradise. Many, in addition, are worried that their job had been unworthy of them, or at least not accorded the esteem it deserved. Saturnin feared that he would be misjudged because of his own profession, that he might be tainted more than most, because he had ministered to human vanity. Nowhere are there history books that hold up hairdressers as heroes for little boys to admire, and he did not expect there would be any in Paradise. Who would appreciate that he was no mere weathervane of frivolity, and not just the typical talkative barber? He had thought a lot about the world, and about himself.

That made his inability to explain himself all the more frustrating. He had not only earned a fair amount of money, and bought a certain amount of property, he had also acquired a philosophy. Female psychology was his forte: on that topic, modesty deserted him. In his euphoric moments he used to say "Women need security. It is men who make them flower." But then, in Paradise, he became aware that he had spent his life seeking that same security, and he needed it now; the formulae that guided his conduct, that made him appear sure of himself, no longer worked. He had never failed to greet his customers with disconcerting quotations from favourite authors like Baudelaire: I searched for beauty, I found it, I did not find it beautiful. With a seemingly endless supply of such enigmatic utterances to create pauses in the conversation, he had acquired a reputation as a true artist. But now his whole existence was a pause with no end.

To give someone a good haircut never meant just that to him, and even less did it involve just reproducing a fashionable style. Saturnin always said to his customers: "My style is that I do not offer the same style. My pleasure is to discover the personality of my client and lead her to accentuate or develop her personality. If a client with long hair asks to have it cut short, I hesitate. I do not want to violate her." He always urged women to find something to distinguish themselves from others. That was the basis of the creed of every Plus Person, and Saturnin was proud to be one of them. He had respected himself because he had helped people to become beautiful by becoming true to themselves. "Beauty is to radiate a personality." Ugliness, he was confident, would vanish once every woman had found her personality and learnt to be herself. Ugliness returned only when evil thoughts, or a nasty expression, turned beauty sour. Be yourself, that was his secret to the good life. He had worn many masks in his time, he used to say, and finally he had been able to take them off. His work had enabled him to understand himself, because it required him to understand others.

"Be yourself." That seemed good advice to give to others, but when faced with the prospect of having to start all over again in a new world, Saturnin was not sure that the life he had led on earth had expressed his innermost, profound self. He had wanted to be a hairdresser since the age of nine, he did not know why, perhaps from sheer contrariness, his parents were so admiring and envious of secure, comfortable, anonymous government officials. He had been content with his rebellion, but now he wondered whether the whim of that child had been a correct recognition of his adult potential. For with little demand for hairdressing in Paradise, and without the power he had enjoyed of making mortals look divine for brief moments, he was deflated. His professional reputation no longer counted for anything. In an effort to salvage a remnant of his sense of achievement, he sought out the other famous hairdressers who had preceded him, in the way exiles look up their compatriots in their first bewildering days in a foreign country. Old boy, old girl reunions were frequently organised, but they were nearly always flops. The unsuccessful found the successful arrogant bores, who, worst of all, made them feel bores themselves. Saturnin was grieved to realise that he had nothing in common with men like Champagne, who had been the tyrant of hairdressers under Louis XIII, or with Legros, who was proud that he cut the hair of a dandy chief of police renowned for his brutality, or Constant, barber to Napoleon, whose skill was debatable and who had a pretty easy task in any case, or with the grandiloquent Croizat who called himself the Napoleon of coiffeurs, and argued that hairdressing should be acknowledged as one of the fine arts, capable of imagining a hundred thousand different fantasies; least of all with Leonard, the first hairdresser to be admitted into high society, who licked Marie Antoinette's boots when he was not arranging her hair. Saturnin glimpsed with more than a touch of panic the possibility that he was a total stranger to the ways of Paradise, unwelcome; likely to be stereotyped as one more Figaro, the barber, symbol of the dissatisfied man, who is convinced that he is valued at less than his abilities deserved. He did not want to hear any more jokes about his job, to be told yet again that a *chien coiffé*, a dog who had been to the barber's, was the French for an ugly man.

Saturnin was stricken with regret, on the one hand that he was not immediately offered the chance to groom all those famous heads he imagined would be awaiting him, and on the other that he could not think of anything else to do in the meantime, regret that he had too blithely assumed that life would somehow go on much as it did on earth, regret above all that he had this ineradicable capacity for regret. Regret was another of the disabilities that Plus Persons suffered from, which astonished them, for they regarded themselves as forward looking. The realisation that they were prisoners of memory, even more than those who lived by inherited rituals, was a great shock. Every incident of infancy, every punishment of childhood, every trauma of adolescence, they remember religiously, as having made them who they are; and they cling to these memories for fear of losing their sense of being themselves, like miserly dustmen who cannot bear to throw their garbage away, and who suffocate in the stinking pyramids they accumulate around them. Regret, forget, beget: these three torturing preoccupations of earthly life do not fit people to enjoy Paradise. Saturnin felt like a child who has not learnt to ride a bicycle: he did not know how to be happy, which he supposed, with some trepidation, was the main purpose of his new residence.

Happiness, however, he had to admit, was something he had never known on earth. Born into a respectable middle-class family, he had felt uncomfortable in it: "I could not

43

accept myself." So he had travelled to India in search of wisdom, to Australia in search of luck, to Italy in search of roots and faith, but he had never encountered the right sort to suit him. Nor did Paradise seem to him to contain what he had been groping for. "We are all on our own," he had concluded. "We are all on the fringe, marginals." He knew only how to anaesthetise the pain of his loneliness by saying "Appreciate that each has his own direction. Respect others. There are no superiors and no inferiors." That did not make him happy. "We must learn to love our sufferings," he said, quoting, or for all Sumdy knew, misquoting, Gurdjeev, Edgar Allan Poe, Rimbaud and Lao Tse.

Know yourself. That panacea becomes meaningless when the imagination is liberated in the way it is in Paradise, and when there is a prospect that it can even reshape the features of the face at will. The whole basis of Saturnin's skills collapsed. He did not know what to say to old women who in Paradise felt even more baffled than when they had seen their faces disintegrating a little more every day, and a strange scarecrow stare out of the glass at them; the terrifying threat of Paradise is that it may make the body unpredictable, and so everything else too. That is the opposite of what is expected. In the long days Saturnin spent at the new salon he set up in the Village of the Angels, a usually empty salon, he gazed into his mirrors and wondered whether he had gone blind. The eyes were the windows of the soul, but they could see everything except the soul. They could not see themselves; and they could not believe photographs, of which no two were ever the same. In the long nights, he would come down sleepless, naked, to resume his vigil; in the darkness, his mirrors, entwining themselves with the shadows, seemed more coy, grew more hesitant in their answers to his questioning, and that was when he began to have what he called his visions, but which could have been no more than his acclimatisation to his new world and its new laws. The souvenir of Errol Flynn that he wore on his upper lip, the Byronic look that he cultivated, the dandy lisp with which he tempered it, like the lump on his big toe which tight Italian shoes had bequeathed him, his shrivelled fingertips, charred almost like candle ends by long immersion in hair dyes, his bitten nails burned each into a different shade of ochre – all these, which his identity card might have listed as his distinguishing marks, now seemed no longer part of him but borrowed props, picked up second-hand from a junk heap. He despised himself for having shopped all his life in the same mental supermarket, always coming home with the same brand-name tins. Even in his search for originality, he had had at the back of his mind a memory of other people, models whom he endowed with desirable qualities, and whom he thought he could partly resemble.

These so-called visions made such a deep impression on him that for a time he turned away from all human company. The birds and the fish of Paradise became the new objects of his meditations: nature was his crystal ball. Digging a channel through the beach, he brought the sea to his swimming pool, and then from it, in large pipes to his aquarium. The octopus became his favourite companion: it represented for him the saddest failure of creation, and the same frustration that he felt himself. The octopus, he said, had been destined to be the master of the seas, as humans were supposed to be kings on dry land; it had the most amazing gifts, a wonderful brain, even brains in all eight arms, but it failed. It did not make it. And that happened even though each octopus, like a human individual, has its own peculiarities; each learns from its experiences in its own way because, neglected by its parents, it is self-taught. It is willing to eat almost anything, only

45

humans have such varied tastes. Ever restless, it moves its home as often as an ambitious executive; pleasure-loving, it is fond of dancing, curling and uncurling with grace; it is liable to get depressed, even suicidal; it may eat its own arms, but then change its mind and grow new arms. Above all, it refuses to be consistent. It changes its appearance all the time, more than any follower of fashion. When Sumdy saw it, Saturnin's favourite octopus stared at them, a hint of entreaty in its almost human eyes, a dark, glowering, pimpled brown; but in the course of the conversation it changed to a vermilion red, then a greenish grey, and as it went even paler, to become almost transparent, it seemed to be laughing at humans obsessed by their sense of identity, their need to recognise, label and judge. As though to prove that it was not beaten yet, it squirted, with perfect aim, a mouthful of water into Sumdy's face, followed by a cloud of purple ink into its aquarium, of exactly its own shape; then, like a naughty child, it ran away, leaving that empty purple shadow behind for its angry enemies to attack and for its admirers to puzzle over. And yet this ingenious creature was a failure, because it could not hold its act together; it had become too complicated for its brain, large though that was; it could not keep track of what its eight arms were up to, each involved in its own hunting and dancing, stroking and eating. That was why Saturnin found it so human: it could not cope. It had made wrong choices, in the body it had developed, and it had not proved versatile enough to correct its mistakes: its heart, its blood, its kidneys did not suit it. Perhaps in Paradise it would find new solutions. What kind of existence were the fish and the birds making or planning for themselves in Paradise? The Scriptures had said that they had been put on earth to be governed by humans, but that was over now, they were free. Saturnin was going to watch his octopus for at least a few years, watch

46

it grappling with its weaknesses. Paradise was there to encourage long, deep thoughts. Sumdy too, he said, must put more thought into what she wanted to look like. She would have to visit him many times before they could agree what kind of haircut she should or could have.

There was no option but to leave. Sumdy walked down to the beach, picked out a middle-aged woman sitting alone on a bench, staring at the sea, and sat down beside her. The woman's fingers were nervously twitching, her bare feet were scratching at the sand, there were sad pouches under her eyes. Pain was at home in Paradise, and, curiously, Sumdy felt comforted to be beside someone who was in pain, and showed it. Could souls share their troubles, lighten them by throwing them one to another, like a ball? The woman smiled feebly, neither rejecting nor welcoming Sumdy's questions, and only sighed, repeatedly, as though to say that there was no point in saying anything. Sumdy took her hand and squeezed it. The woman seemed grateful, but went on sighing. Her name, she eventually said, was Tamara. Why was she alone? Where was her family? Tamara had been avoiding them in Paradise, though she loved them: she could not continue to be a burden to them for all eternity, because she was not the sort of wife or mother she had hoped to be. No sensible person, unless it was from pity, or from habit, could find her good company, she said; all who pretended to like her must have something wrong with them; when she opened her mouth, no interesting sound ever came out of it. Her thoughts had long been no more than puffs of smoke that vanished the moment they were uttered; there was no substance in them; they were empty; she was empty. She had visited some of her ancestors, and they had told her to rest, calm

47

down, but that was the last thing she wanted to do. She felt as though she had not yet lived her life. What had happened on earth was a series of accidents, of surface cuts and bruises, which kept on postponing real events. She had never grown into the person she could have been. She had expected Paradise to give her another chance, but it was no easier knowing how to start a new life here than it was on earth. She had chosen to come to the Village of the Angels where everyone else was in the same turmoil as herself, helpless, good for nothing. Here at least no one expected anything from her. She could stare at the sea, remembering how events almost turned out otherwise, how once upon a time she had been as effervescent, as irrepressibly joyous as the spray of the waves, how people said she would become a poet, how her childish scribblings had been praised as the opening buds of genius. The effect of coming to Paradise had been to convince her that she was irredeemably stupid. Looking back, she could see that she had begun to change soon after she got married; not that she had a grudge against her husband, who continued to reassure her that she was wonderful (and she was sorry for him because he had his troubles too), but she now realised that people had gradually paid less and less attention to her, had increasingly introduced her only as his wife, no longer as the girl who would one day be a poet. Intellectually, she was as good as dead by her thirties, when she stopped dreaming about her future, when she existed only as the mother of her children. To be a burden to them in Paradise, after having been such a disappointment to them on earth, would be too awful a punishment. She preferred to spend eternity looking at the ocean, seated on her bench, where she was left alone. That was all she deserved. Would she ever cease despising herself? Paradise seemed to have no other furniture for those who did not like themselves.

Sumdy guessed that Angel Village was a retreat for those who were afraid to enter Paradise, who were used to saying that the world was mad, and who saw it as even madder when it moved into eternity and lost its cloak of hypocrisy. It was with more than a little nervousness that she accompanied Tamara to the palace with minarets that was her home. The lodgers, young and old, were all seemingly closed to hope, or cherished only hopes that were impossible. As soon as she stepped into the entrance hall, she was jumped on, and embraced, by a soul who looked at once ravaged and austerely beautiful, and who claimed to be expecting her. Had Sumdy not come to deliver a letter? This was Ulrika, who greeted every newcomer in the same way with the same words: she had been expecting a letter from her husband ever since he had run away with another woman, a long time ago; he had never been heard of again, but she was certain she would get a letter one day; the other woman was worthless and he would realise it. For, she said proudly, she was a goddess. Was Sumdy a goddess too?

Sumdy became frightened. Was this a village not just for the discouraged but for the demented? Her intense yet somehow charming questioner refused to be convinced that she was not a messenger. Sumdy repeated that she had come to Paradise to discover what happiness was, and as she did so she was ashamed of the inappropriateness of her quest. But Ulrika said she knew all there was to know about happiness. She did not say what. She changed the subject of the conversation. Each sentence seemed to be forgotten the moment it was spoken, or to suggest a new thought totally unconnected. Ulrika wandered off, as though she had something more important to do, but then forgot what; she returned to ask the same questions, with the same enthusiasm, treating Sumdy as a new arrival. It was only after many such encounters, that the

49

beginnings of a familiarity grew between them. Ulrika never did reveal her opinions about happiness, always losing her concentration before she could, but she did say, with great emphasis: "I have a nasty character. I am not worthy of the love even of a cat or a dog."

Another lodger, Grazia, introduced herself with the words: "I am timid." She walked as though every speck of dust in the air might be offended if she moved too brusquely, without due consideration for its habits, as though every tuft in the carpet might complain if her tread was not a caress. She opened doors as though trying not to wake them from sleep. Before she spoke, she smiled, waiting to be invited to speak. What was she frightened of, here in the safety of Paradise? Of everything. Her fear, she said, had no precise object. It was just a general feeling she had. She had been like that since she could remember. Nothing had changed since she had come here. Her first memory was of being afraid of the dark, and she still was. She used to be afraid of her shadow, imagining it to be a stranger following her, and she thought she was only a little more friendly with her shadow now. She was afraid of herself. She would have liked to have thought that a soul was impregnable in Paradise, safe at last, impossible to harm, but she was not convinced that it was.

Sumdy was puzzled. How could souls be so disturbed, so gloomy in Paradise? Had she missed something? Was there a happiness she failed to detect? She could not be sure whether these particular souls had always been so odd, or whether the shock of coming to Paradise had been too much for them, whether they had lost their minds when they had lost their bodies. But one unusual feature did strike her. There was a wonderfully peaceful atmosphere in this palace, indeed in the village. No one seemed to speak ill of anyone else. It may have been that they were all, without exception, so conscious of their own inadequacies, so certain that they were incapable of managing an existence in Paradise, that they could not criticise anybody else. When a soul heaved a great groan, or a belch, or, in the middle of a conversation, suddenly hid his face in his hands, or went off, hopping on one leg like an injured bird, the others showed no disapproval, no disgust. Every form of weird behaviour was accepted as natural, each soul seemed to be saying to himself, they all have a right to be as they are. And as Sumdy saw more and more signs of the distress of these villagers, she was increasingly moved by the gentleness with which, from time to time, when they awoke from their trances, they treated each other, even while they were obviously suffering themselves. There was no pride in that palace, no presumption. Perhaps that was what made it so unearthly. But there were also earth-like problems preoccupying them: who should share a room with whom, who should move to another room, who needed company, who should be left alone: they were for ever worrying, and changing their minds, as though constantly trying on clothes that never quite fitted, whose colours never seemed quite to suit them.

When they eventually got used to Sumdy's presence, some of them began to get a grim satisfaction from baring themselves to her and revealing their worries about being in Paradise. One couple, for example, had a rather extreme form of worry, about a lurking danger, which many others showed in various degrees: whom might they meet? They were scared that their past would catch up with them. This couple were only temporary visitors to the village, not permanent residents. Most of the time they spent in what they called the real Paradise, but they liked to come back to the village for holidays. The real Paradise, they said, was too tiring, and yet they somehow felt they must learn to like it. The strain of it was particularly severe for the wife, who worried about being seen in it, because she believed she may once have killed a pope; that may have been a delusion; she could not remember which pope it was; but the worry tormented her all the time. Perhaps it was because she had been educated at a rather peculiar convent and had nightmares about her experiences, or perhaps it was because her father had been a professor of child psychology, who started treating her for anxiety at the age of two, and she had irremediably learnt to imitate his own anxiety, which was so extreme that he could not bear to give his lectures unless someone accompanied him to the university and brought him home again; he could not bear to travel alone; neither could she. That was why the couple clung to each other. The husband found the real Paradise frightening too, for somewhere in it he might come across his first, divorced wife, and it would be too terrible to be reminded of the mess he had made of his life. But in the village they felt calmer, not just because of the atmosphere of tolerance, even respect, that they sensed, but every time they returned they thought they were recognised, greeted with the affection that habit creates, so that the place was attractive to them even if everybody was as miserable as themselves. They might not have that consolation if they stayed all the time; their happiness, in so far as they had any, was to keep moving.

One way the souls in Angel Village did keep moving was to alternate between the beach and the gardens. Sumdy went to the gardens in the evenings with them, when the air cooled and a soft mood of quiet reflection replaced the heat of the day. The gardens of Paradise have been frequently praised for their grandiose beauty, but there is no detailed botanical description or guide book to explain that visiting them entails more than taking a promenade in a neat municipal park. The plants are there to be talked to. Sumdy thought at first that they had to be talked to in German, because that seemed to be the language many souls were using. She had read that a quarter of Germans believe that plants have souls (as three-quarters of them believe that animals do also); she had assumed that was the reason why the Germans were the first nation to have a successful Green Party. But German was not the only language being used. When she listened more carefully, it became clear that each plant was being treated with politeness, even deference, with the sort of reverence that on earth is reserved only for the most extraordinary of them, like the living sky-scraper trees of the Sierra Nevada, which have grown three hundred feet tall and survived three thousand years of turmoil, the nearest known approximation to immortality. In Paradise, all plants live for ever; so they are no longer obsessed with imperialist ambitions, no longer deploy their seeds like armies, by sea, by air, attaching them to birds and beasts so that they can start new colonies in the most unsuspecting places, no longer parachute them into unoccupied territories. Having ceased to be food and fodder, they are watched with awe by human souls. But have these plants had a previous life on earth? Sumdy saw a monster of a walnut tree in one of the gardens, which some claimed might once have been the two thousand year-old Walnut Tree of Balaclava, which the soldiers of the Crimean War were amazed by, when it yielded a crop of a hundred thousand walnuts in a single summer, but no one could prove anything about its origins. Were individual plants individuals? Until 1694 the inhabitants of Paradise were quite sure they were not, but in that year the director of the Tübingen Botanic Garden, Camerarius, discovered that flowers were the sexual organs of plants. Virtually no one before that had guessed that sex plays a part in vegetable life. Attitudes in Paradise quickly changed. Human souls began to feel intimidated by flowers, as though creatures able to flaunt their sexual prowess with such abandon, such exhibitionism, such exquisite taste, must know something they did not; or was it some kind of provocation, a revenge for having been exploited by man on earth? When rumours spread that vast dark areas of Paradise contained forests, stretching without limits, where the trees which were once masters of the world were recovering their poise, plants were increasingly looked on as guarding some kind of mystery, as having some unknown power.

In Angel Village, the general opinion – and Sumdy was aware that the inhabitants of the village were somewhat peculiar – was that plants existed to stimulate thought, and that the rustle of their leaves and their dappled shade were like a gentle massage for the soul, designed to concentrate the mind. The gardens were a sanctuary for ideas. Ideas, they said, live in the gardens. Those were the very words used to Sumdy, but she could not quite understand what they meant. Ideas, they explained, were for the most part mere fluff, floating in the air like pollen and perfume, blown here and there, the puffs of smoke that Tamara complained about. But there were a few ideas which coagulated and settled down, profound beliefs held by a large number of people, guiding how they lived, and as much part of them as their bodies. These grew into plants in the gardens of Paradise. The best way to tell the character of any region of Paradise was to get to know its gardens.

Since the departure of the angels, many generations of discontented souls had successively squatted in the palaces, and each had left the memory of their particular disillusionments in the gardens. By the time of Sumdy's arrival, Angel Village included among its most remarkable sights "The Five

Disillusionments of Mankind". Each was a plant which was a sort of monument of defeat, growing out of hopes that had crumbled, decayed and then spawned something quite different to replace them. How should humans behave? Between them, these plants were believed to contain the essence of all the moral philosophies which had answered that question, and the disappointments which followed. The very notion that it was possible to be disappointed in Paradise is rejected by most immigrants, but Angel Village was where heretics and critics congregated, where new ideas became out of date the moment they were born, and where therefore the gardens grew particularly exotic fruits.

The first disillusionment of mankind which Sumdy was shown was a cabbage, a giant cabbage, larger than a house, taller than a church, which sprouted a new leaf every time reports of a new therapy, a new panacea, a new religious sect, a new plan for disarmament reached Paradise. The message of the cabbage, as Chinese souls put it, was that it is not enough in Paradise to *Follow the Way* (the *Way* being any miracle solution). More simply, others said, the Great Disillusionment was that it is not enough to *obey*. The philosopher Mo Ti (479–381 BC) is reputed to have planted the first wonder cabbage, after having spent many centuries listening patiently to all the remedies for mankind's problems being explained, in many languages, by sages who could never agree amongst themselves; it was impossible, he concluded, to know which to prefer, whom to obey. Sumdy found these words of his written on a label by the cabbage: "Men have different opinions. Therefore one person had one opinion, two persons had two and ten had ten. The greater number of people, the greater number of opinions expressed. And everyone considered his opinion correct and that of others false. Thus all people began to criticise each other." There is a legend that the first

55

cabbage was fertilised by the sweat of the gods, which perhaps explains its peculiar smell, but it was honoured in Angel Village despite its smell, and perhaps because of its smell.

The plum tree's message was that it is not enough to *pray.* This second symbol of disappointment was no ordinary plum tree. The Japanese sage Sugawara no Michizane (AD 845-903) is supposed to have brought it with him to Paradise, being so fond of it because it reminded him of the spring, that he taught it to fly. This sage, despite his wisdom, and despite having had twenty-three children, also became discontented in Paradise. He could find nowhere to hide in it, where he could not be reached by his importunate countrymen. He had once been an honoured adviser of the Emperor, Minister of the Right, advising that his country should borrow western learning (which at that time meant borrowing from China) but preserve its "Japanese spirit"; at the time of his death, he was disgraced and exiled, "carrying less weight than a mustard seed", as he wrote in a poem; a few decades later, he had been proclaimed a god, "Heaven-Filling Great Self-Sufficient Deity", and appointed (posthumously) Prime Minister of Japan, so worried were his enemies that he might take revenge on them for not having recognised his true worth. Students adopted him as their special god, praying to him to help them with their examinations, conscious that they too would not have their true worth recognised. He regretted that he could not help them, certainly not all of them; many failed despite him and he did not like to feel guilty, to be blamed, just as he had not liked the honours given to him, because they put obligations on him which he could not fulfil. "What use to cry in pain to the blue sky?" he had written in another of his poems. It is an ever-jarring disappointment to discover how difficult it is for a soul to respond from the blue sky to human prayer, how difficult, how impossible it is to get what one wants, to give others what they want.

The pumpkin's message was that, when one had grasped these truths, it was no solution simply to attempt to dismiss all thought from one's mind, and to *cultivate* one's garden. The pumpkin was like a giant bust of the head of Voltaire, who according to some witnesses, planted its seed on a brief visit, but that resemblance was obvious only to his own country-men; other nations see the likeness of other heroes in it. However, they all agree that a pumpkin has a tendency to consist mainly of water inside, to become uneatable if left to grow too old, which is taken to mean that not thinking is even more dangerous than thinking.

The great disappointment which the papyrus or water reed commemorated was that it was not enough to copy, to *dupli-cate*, to scribble, to accumulate knowledge and savour its beauty. It is claimed that two mythical heroes, Bouvard and Pecuchet, passed through Angel Village, searching for more paper on which to copy the knowledge they found in Para-dise, and that it was here that they realised they were getting tired of copying. So they planted a papyrus reed, whose roots can be used as firewood, or made into vases, whose leaves can be woven into light boats or clothes, or bandages for mummies, whose aromatic core can be eaten (grilled, boiled or raw), whose soft pith can be burned as a torch. There were so many other things one could do with paper, apart from covering it in ink.

Finally there was the carrot, the most recent plant to grow to monstrous size in the Village of the Angels. Its message was that it was not enough to *opinionate*, to say what one thought. This was the most bitter disappointment of all, and they had chosen the symbol of modern civilisation itself to be its monument. The sweet carrot was that symbol because it represented a goal always out of reach. Fashionable ladies had given that meaning a new force in the eighteenth century, when they took to wearing its fernlike leaves in their hats to show that they too were unattainable, unfathomable.

Sumdy went and stood in front of each of the Five Disillusionments of Mankind, overwhelmed at first by their grandeur, silenced by the air of finality they exuded, as though monuments of that size were too impressive to be contradicted. Then she found herself uttering exclamations, and little speeches; it was easy to get into the habit of talking to them, as others were doing. But one of the Great Disillusionments she could not understand. The monster carrot did not convince her. What could be wrong with talking, even if it was about one's problems? Surely that was the great discovery of modernity. She had been brought up to have faith in words, and to respect the need to utter them. A Paradise that told souls to keep quiet did not accord with her sense of how things should be. The right to say what one thought was the most precious of all rights and millions had not yet won it; hundreds of millions of children were waiting to enjoy it. It was absurd that Paradise should be disillusioned with talk before a fraction of souls had even opened their mouths; they might have very interesting things to say, beautiful things, which could well be the seed of the salvation of mankind. Sumdy felt very strongly. She asked for an explanation, but in vain.

Then one night, as she was wandering almost alone in the gardens, very late, as the murmurs were dying down and as the village withdrew into quiet, she saw an indefinable, indistinct fuzz moving before her. It could have been her imagination, or a dream. Or perhaps she was learning to have visions like the hairdresser, a sign that she was at last being initiated into the ways of Paradise. From the fuzz came a voice. It said it was a ghost. Sumdy did not believe in ghosts. But the fuzz insisted that in Paradise ghosts are different. Everything that existed on earth was capable of being imported into Paradise, and it was only natural that ghosts, or the ability to imagine that one has seen a ghost, should be too; the difference was that the ghosts here were of living people, memories that the dead could not leave behind. And indeed the fuzz talked in a voice that reminded Sumdy strongly of someone on earth, whom she had never met, some voice on the radio that distinguished itself by never being at a loss for a word, always having an opinion, like a saucepan of milk boiling over and never running dry. Could it be a mundane broadcast that was reaching her? It was not, for the fuzz answered her questions. She realised that when she walked in the gardens and heard souls mumbling in front of plants, they were talking not just to them, nor quite to themselves, but to a world they were no longer part of, and the ghosts were like relatives visiting a jail; their conversations were half memory and half foreboding, as her conversation with the radio voice was. Human souls, she thought, in the gardens of Paradise, were like cows chewing their cud. Every leaf could turn into a ghost, when a soul ruminated on past experience, trying to redigest it, or to search in it for meanings that got lost in the confusions of life. The sound of that radio voice made her think about talk. It was the kind of memory she liked, which stimulates new thoughts; it made her spend several days asking everyone why they talked, what it meant to talk in Paradise.

Souls talked to plants, she was told, partly because they were worried about the state of conversation in Paradise. The inhabitants of Angel Village believed that humanity having passed through the Ice Age, the Iron Age, the Romantic Age and all other Ages, had reached the Age of Talk. The amount of talk on earth was now greater than it had ever been. Never in all history had the air vibrated with so many conversations taking place at the same time, never had people been so busy trying to communicate, never before had gossip been accorded such respect, even ennobled into a science, nor technology devoted to recording and multiplying what was said, so that the future would never again be able to escape from the sound of the past. And people were talking in a new way, using another tone. Pomposity was discredited. The rich could no longer address the poor with their contemptuous bark. Haughty politeness was ousted, to be replaced by at least a pretence of caring. It was not only permissible to say what one thought but, for one's health's sake, one was urged to say also what one never knew one thought, what lurked in the musty bottom drawers of the mind. The world became a freer place thanks to talk. But the things that people now said, both about themselves and about others, were devastating, more terrifying than any bloody revolution. The right to talk became intolerable unless it was accompanied by the right not to believe oneself when one did talk. Self-doubt was ensconced as the new religion. Parody became the new litera- ture. How to avoid listening became the supreme art. Talk grew increasingly complicated and incomprehensible, out of self-defence. Words became biting gnats hovering around the face, and every morning talkers woke up with their hopes covered in sores and swellings.

So when the new talking generation came to Paradise, they looked forward to seeing what was scheduled to happen next, after the Age of Talk. They rejoiced that in Paradise they could say what they pleased, but in this ultimate refuge of free speech they were not sure whether all souls would be treated with absolute equality. Would fast and smooth talkers steal the most delicious fruits of Paradise too? Would Para- dise offer only equality of opportunity? They had had enough of that kind of equality, the equal right of babies to scream while a few are declared to be luckier, more gifted, more deserving. Was a ticket to Paradise a lottery, and the prizes still unequal? They were tired of being judged, graded, selected and rejected, and even more of the endless talk which justified and excused their never winning. The people in Angel Village were those who had placed most faith in talk, and were appalled that no amount of talk could save them from feeling ugly or lonely. They were exhausted by talk. But they did not know what to do instead. A few of them said that in the home of the Creator, they should try to learn to create. But they were not sure how they could do that, whether everybody could do that.

Sumdy found herself talking about how ugly she felt herself to be. She began to think that the inhabitants of Angel Village might not want her among them, even though she felt, in some ways, almost at home; but she was also saddened by their company. Slowly her worries expanded, as though sensing that they had room to grow, as though encouraged by having so many worrying souls all around. She became convinced that the Archduke Francis Ferdinand was on his way, to search for the cockroach, assuming that this was precisely the sort of retreat where a dangerous creature would go to hide. She felt panic coming. To endanger her stay by being associated with souls whom the authorities clearly regarded with suspicion – authorities, it is true, she could not see anywhere, but who must exist somewhere – was the last thing she wanted. Her urgent need was to find these authorities, not to play hide and seek with them. But she was also determined to get rid of her sense of ugliness if she was to enjoy her visit and achieve her aims. She decided she must leave this sad bit of

Paradise – how unusual it was she could not yet judge: surely it could not be all like this? If only she could find a guide. She begged everyone she met to reveal to her the whereabouts of the guardian angels.

Their absence was an old puzzle, she was told. Generation after generation had been complaining of being neglected by them. Indeed the last set of arrivals not to complain were the Babylonians, who alone had made previous arrangements to be met by the angels. On earth, every single Babylonian used to have his own personal god; he knew his name; he talked to him every day. At every meal, four times a day, he set aside a portion of food for him; and occasionally, in splendid banquets, he would feed his god to bursting point, with as many as fifty sheep and seventy birds of different sorts (though it was the priests who ate the food on the god's behalf). No Babylonian felt safe without his god beside him; the two went around together everywhere; if illness or misfortune struck, it was a sure sign that the god had left his side, was dissatisfied, inattentive, or disgusted by his dirtiness, and needed to be assuaged and won back. That is not the sort of comradeship that is abandoned or forgotten. In Paradise the Babylonians made sure they got the same personal attention. The golden age of this friendship of humans and angels lasted for seventeen centuries, for as long as the sad songs of Gilgamesh, their famous poet who yearned for the secret of eternal life, were recited on the banks of the Euphrates; and as long as the Babylonians remained a bilingual people, intellectually amphibious, able to talk in the idiom of foreigners and angels.

However, later waves of immigrants into Paradise did not, deep down in themselves, feel in the same way. A personal god on their back all day and every day was too much of a good thing. They decided there was only one God. The personal gods were relegated to subordinate duties, reclassified more humbly, not just as angels (which means messengers) but as the lowest kind of angels. Perhaps the guardian angels, for their part, got a little tired of humans too. Nobody she spoke to had ever met an angel himself, but a mediaeval monk called Denys, who was writing a book about angels, had visited the village a few months back, to look at their vacation homes, and he had confirmed that there was no point in seeking to meet them. Angels, said this monk, were pure intelligences, with no passions, no servitude to the senses, but with enormous willpower. That frightened the inhabitants of the village, who said they were not surprised that angels had difficulty in communicating with humans, or that wild rumours should circulate about them. Nevertheless, someone determined to meet an angel could doubtless find one in Babylon.

Sumdy did not know whether they were pulling her leg, but this was the only clue she had. So she set out for Babylon.

In her letter home, she admitted that she was beginning to worry about Forgetmenot; there was no sign of it. And Jolly seemed to look more worried as he searched for the cockroach, sniffing relentlessly. Perhaps both he and she were learning new ways of worrying. But Jolly had been fascinated by the plants in the gardens; he had watched them motionless, open-mouthed, as though he too was having visions, as though the rustling leaves appeared to him as fluttering eyelids and whispering lips, saying something he ought to be listening to; and he was listening very hard; he did seem to be developing a new kind of curiosity.

The letter ended with these words: There are many people arriving here who do not seem to be totally happy, and, what puzzles me more, would be unwilling to admit it even if they were. They regard it as old-fashioned to consider happiness possible. Previous generations were so hungry for the sweetmeat they called happiness, so quickly addicted by little licks of it, that they became ready to swallow any utopia that had the shallowest sprinkling of sugar on it. That has put off the recent arrivals, who are proud to be blasé. They have a taste for savoury dishes and bitter drinks. Gloom seems to be the glue that holds them together. But maybe it is different in other parts of Paradise.

CHAPTER THREE

The roads of Paradise were becoming crowded. In the past, there used to be few travellers on them, for most of the old residents had little taste for adventures whose end they could not foresee; but now there were more and more lost souls wandering about, searching for something to search for. Sumdy could not tell whether that would make it easier or harder to reach the angels, because she was still unclear as to what difference it would make to her, being situated in eternity, trying to get from one place to another. She set out for Babylon without any precautions, without any vaccinations, and indeed without any uncertainties. She assumed that she would get there safely. There could be no diseases in Paradise, and no possibility of failure either. Everybody had to succeed in such a place. But she could not quite understand how that could be, for success, as she had understood it on earth, meant the victory of some and the defeat of others.

To travel, neither she nor Jolly had need for wings. The sensation of being as light as air, of being totally free to go anywhere, is there to enjoy, for everybody who can forget his worries. The pleasures of touring in Paradise are unique, and it seemed strange they were not indulged in more. But then travel was no mere pastime. Certainly, it is possible to go on the kind of voyage which is familiar to humans, and progress through town and country heading for the horizon that is never reached. They call that horizontal travel. It was such a journey that Sumdy took to Angel Village. But the souls she encountered were from the twentieth century, sharing the same landscape. Beneath them, however, are innumerable other landscapes, inhabited by residents who arrived earlier, who are used to the ways of other centuries, or who prefer other sights. So the geography of the place has this singular quality, that it is also possible to travel vertically, up and down from level to level, to visit previous generations in their own surroundings. For example, there is a massive recreation of the city of London, but not just one London: each new set of arrivals, from the Ancient Britons onwards, bring with them the London they know, the memories of the homes and haunts and sordid smells they cherish. London in Paradise is built like a mine, each seam of which contains a different metal ore, rock or clay: the modern arrivals complain that it resembles a gigantic multi-storey car-park. The Babylonians and ancient Egyptians live on the lower floors; the Incas, Mongols and Elizabethans enjoy the splendour of the middle levels; towards the top, the landscapes become more confused, for each generation, or even each decade, thinks itself so special that it must have a slightly different level for itself, making it more bumpy and dangerous. But at any particular level, one can be quite unaware that any others exist. Most people tend to stay put at the level where they feel thay can revive and continue the best years of their lives. Angel Village was at the very top of Paradise, as though the discontented of all ages had come to the surface, gasping for air.

In the past, almost all souls used to join their families, as quickly as they could. But more recently, separated relatives have not been rushing to live together quite so automatically. For the best years of their lives are a nostalgic fantasy about having been a hero or an innocent, a knight in armour, a pirate who never got caught, a courtesan who kept pirates in their place. So increasingly each individual has been tempted to head for a level where he believes he truly belongs. Couples separate because they have different dream worlds. They can visit, often or occasionally, but they are on their own. It is not so different from how they lived on earth, where each inhabited a separate world of the imagination, while pretending to share in a common normality. The lower floors are therefore by no means as deserted as one might expect, nor do the top floors remain overpopulated. Many souls seem to like to go downwards into the past. The Dark Age floors, as far as one can see in the dim light, have several times more inhabitants than ever lived in that period. There is also movement upwards; the masses who flocked into Paradise at the time of the Black Death are becoming obsessed by medical progress and feel the urge to move up one storey every few years.

A soul in Paradise is not merely a survivor, the familiar pot-bellied clerk pickled to last for ever. A soul in good condition, undamaged, is a being that is essentially independent. On earth, it is difficult to spot that characteristic, for the frailties of the body, the hallucinations of the mind obscure it. Indeed, it takes a whole lifetime for the cutting of the umbilical cord to cease to be a physical symbol and become a genuine reality. Often, only in old age, when people grow more detached from the squabbles of their children and their neighbours, do they begin to see the possibility, usually with terror, that they must leave the womb of the community they have tried to adjust to, that they have less in common with it than they thought or pretended, that they have to go to

Paradise alone, utterly alone, as alone as they were when they were born, except that when they were babies, those around them did their best to conceal that loneliness. So what Paradise demands is a special sort of courage, the ability to start again from scratch. For most people, worn out by the trials of earthly existence, such courage has always seemed difficult to muster. All they can yearn for is sleep, and even in sleep they fear change. They want to relearn the sleep of the womb in which they had once bathed, the unbroken indifference to the world's noise, the right to yawn, stretch and turn, to please only themselves; they are keen to cast aside that ersatz slumber which they have to accept as adults, for lack of the real thing, that sighing, twitching, teeth-gnashing sleep during which the brain is brutally invaded by charwomen wielding buckets, supposedly to clean out the debris of the day, but never succeeding in doing more than make the eyes blink in amazement at the indecencies they uncover, and the heart jump its beats in fear that they might jumble their memories too much. However Paradise does provide an alternative for those who cannot sleep, who are too incorrigibly nervous; they can become students of the art of hibernation, which teaches them to remain cool, to stare unmoved at temptation, to wake only to brief pleasures and then to return to gentle, unremembered, vacant daydreams. The unsuspecting traveller may be disconcerted to pass by so many somnolent souls. They represent normality, as it has existed since the beginning, millions of reminders that most of the inhabitants have nothing to say to visitors like Sumdy, and no desire to find something to say. Their quiescence is understandable, for they have chosen the course of safety.

To travel vertically is more exciting and more dangerous. What a challenge to follow the scent of the history of the world in reverse, to sense the change in the lightness of the air as one moves from the subtle but confusing perfumes of modernity to the raw pungencies of the past, how exhilarating to tread paths, neither too hard nor too soft, that welcome the feet with a gentle obeisance, how delightfully distracting to pass through the playgrounds of insects that invite the passer-by to stop and watch their games, how soothing to hear so distinctly the flapping wings of the dragon-fly practising its ballet jumps or the determined shuffling of the black beetle, absorbed in its own mysterious pilgrimage. But it is a real art to know how to drop from one level down to another, or how to rise to a higher one, though occasionally this does happen by accident; one can suddenly, without warning, as though by quicksands or by a whirlwind, be grabbed and transported into completely different surroundings. Which undoubtedly has its fascinating side, for the jump across centuries can bring about the meeting of souls who would never have thought that they could be an inspiration to each other, and the juxtaposition of vistas can give new shape to the familiar or the forgotten; but there is also a bewildering side for those who do not have the strength to appreciate such delicate surprises, or who, as with Sumdy, are burdened by the feeling, which she could not shake off, that she was ugly and lonely, a feeling that worsened as she saw Jolly also beginning to exhibit a state of perplexity not dissimilar to her own. Vertical travel, some souls believe, is a solution for such moods, but only if it is pursued with care; when it happens by accident, which may be nature's way of shaking souls out of their depression, the experience can be liberating or shattering, depending on how quick and adaptable they are. To be able to juggle with time and break the shackles of strict chronology, to be able to unite in a single intuition what has happened in the past, what is happening at the moment and what may happen in the future, to turn the boring grey of eternity into a pattern of brightly contrasting fragments of colour, is one of the most important but least known and, for long, least used of the skills that can be learnt in Paradise. It is a skill indispensable for all who want to know how to cope with the shock of moving from a world of consumers, concerned with affluence, to one which seems to have a chance of reflecting the creativity of God, and which involves an attitude to time that does not come easily to humans, for whom the present is alone fully real.

It was very soon after she set off on the road to Babylon that Sumdy discovered one of the hazards of living in eternity. At first she thought she had had an accident, or perhaps it was Jolly who had the accident, trying to investigate what he took to be a molehill, which turned out to lead to so much larger a hole than he anticipated, that he was swallowed up. When Sumdy went to the rescue, she too vanished. Molehills are the discreet signs by which those who know recognise the tunnels that go from the top to the bottom of Paradise, tunnels that are eerily silent. As she passed each exit which led to a new level, and a different century, she could hear only snores; so she allowed herself to go deeper and deeper. Then cries of agitation in the distance made her pause. Peeping out of a molehill, she saw that she had reached the fifth century AD. She decided to emerge. No harm had come to her or to Jolly. They resumed their walk, in the direction of the noise. The landscape was more heavily wooded; the straight road was engulfed in shade; birds and animals of varieties she had never seen stared at her; but she was far from being the only modern person to arouse their curiosity. For at the end of the road stood the Hotel de la Decadence, built on a cliff, eager to welcome tourists. It was a series of Roman villas placed each above the other, a sort of monstrous pile of Californian versions of Roman gentlemen's retreats; and it was humming with activity. The whole top floor, she was told, was occupied by Henry Ford. Several coach-loads of women doing a tour of Literary Giants filled most of the hotel. There was only one guest who came from these parts, and he was indeed the reason why these women had come all this way: he was the local literary giant.

And he was the first lost soul whom Sumdy met, while taking a stroll in the fine gardens, waiting for a meal. He was a Greek-Egyptian, a man clearly of some importance, for he managed to look dignified even in the ridiculous position in which he was sitting. It was Jolly who found him hiding behind some bushes. At once she realised that she had been wrong to assume that illness was impossible in Paradise. This man was suffering from a disease that was beginning to sweep through it like an epidemic, an epidemic, according to him, introduced by modern settlers.

Nonnos was his name. How many people remember his fame? Nonnos of Panopolis. How many even know where Panopolis is? A splendid city, cooled by the Nile, famous as the home of the once great poets Horapollon, Kyros, Pampeprios, as well as of great stonemasons who sculpted grand tombs and of great weavers of intricate, sought-after textiles: it has vanished from the face of the earth, just as Nonnos' own reputation has. He had been the last bright star of the ancient world of Plato and Cicero, born just as decadence was disintegrating into rot; Nonnos was not merely the most popular poet of his time – that would be underestimating him: he was so ingenious and erudite a writer that he was called the Homer of his day. He wrote a poem longer than Homer's, forty-eight books in all, a poem to break all records, and to please everybody; and it did make his contemporaries laugh and cry and savour what they took to

71

be the true taste of ecstasy. His poem was crammed with contradictions that made them gasp, with digressions, anomalies, endless repetition, bombastic eloquence, and verbal ornamentation of unprecedented exorbitance. What genius! said his readers; and even his critics could mutter only that he expressed the taste of his time, every taste of his time, every reader could identify with him somewhere. Nonnos was so scrupulous, he would leave no possible admirer in the cold, he took no chances. Having in his poem sung the sensuous joys of the pagan world, he went on to write a book that was everything his poem was not: a theological commentary on the Gospel of St John. He persuaded the Christians that he was secretly converted; he flattered the pagans by showing that a good pagan could be a Christian at the same time: there was no pleasure, no wisdom that he did not appreciate. The decadent Romans admired him because in a world that is falling apart, the most admired people are those who find everything admirable, who can praise everything as being amazing, wonderful and great, when ordinary people can see only gloom.

Since his arrival in Paradise, in the fifth century AD, Nonnos had slept soundly, unperturbed by the news he received from time to time, that there was no news to report about him on earth, that his reputation down below had disappeared, that the manuscripts of his works had vanished from sight and memory, and that the few surviving ones were being mangled by plagiarising monks, recopied full of mistakes, with his name left off the title page. For the fame which Nonnos (and many like him) yearned for was of a different kind from the fame which has become the irritable bowel syndrome of modern persons. Fame can nowadays be accumulated in infinite quantities, and the more widely it is recognised, the more it is envied. But when all that mattered was to acquire a reputation which would get one into heaven, fame was no more than a measuring-rule with only one notch on it. When death was visible in every street and present in every home, life on earth was like an uncomfortable seat in a station waiting room, which stimulated only one thought: would one catch the right train, to the right destination? The great aim was to survive beyond death. Nonnos had sought glory on earth only as a foretaste of the eternity for which all humans used to hold out their hands, terrified of being engulfed by nothingness. And once the eternal life was achieved, once the threat of death was gone, Nonnos was content to bask in the pleasure of being a nonentity, nobody in particular. For another difference also separated him from the likes of Sumdy. The idea that he was a unique personality did not occur to him. He might have idiosyncrasies, but they had no value in themselves, and were not worthy of being cultivated. He never saw himself as a separate, autonomous being, which he would have in any case considered a sign of incompleteness or impoverishment, for, in his view, no man was wise or strong enough to be simply himself. That was why he was proud to model his poetry on great predecessors, who everyone agreed should be admired. By contrast, Sumdy was not just the child of a different civilisation, but also the expression of a different form of existence, created, over the centuries, by precisely the sort of people who had no place in Nonnos' traditional vision of humanity, but who had a rare gift, the strength to justify their eccentricities – inventors and artists who could perform wonders that no one else could, writers who proclaimed the most daring of all versions of the rights of man, the right of the individual to be ineffable, so complex that no outsider could do him justice, who had to work out, each for himself, the significance of his life, who saw in death not a longed-for permanence, a marble statue, but nature constantly innovating by discarding its past, and giving the individual an example to do the same.

Jolly found this great poet hiding behind a bush because his peace had been shattered, and he had become a lost, wandering soul. Nonnos was the first to whisper to Sumdy the news of the epidemic. Its terrible symptom was insomnia. Nonnos could no longer sleep. He had been woken up first by an obscure German professor, who, accompanied by a little army of earnest students, demanded to see him, saying that they had devoted their whole lives to exhuming his manuscripts, studying every word, finding meanings that no one had suspected (not even Nonnos), worrying themselves to death as to whether they had spotted the right symbolism behind each character in his poems; and they had concluded that Nonnos was a major precursor of the modern novel. He belonged to modern literature. They had come to salute him, to get him to preside over congresses they planned to hold in his honour, where he might explain his thought, his style, his motives and reveal any little detail about his personal habits that had escaped their research; they promised that never again would he be neglected, there would always be a scholar from one country or another knocking at his door for advice and enlightenment. Nonnos was appalled. That was the beginning of the vigil from which he had not been able to escape.

And then another breathless expert arrived to tell him that he had got his identity all wrong and that he must change his fascinating little habits; he must no longer think of himself as a decadent, nor indulge in the lazy heavy-lidded stupor he had always found a perfectly satisfying form of existence. The Age of Decadence, of which he had always thought he was the child, recent scholarship had proved, was not decadent after all, but a rebellion against the dull repetitiveness of classical rules, representing new insights, a new view of nature and of man, a refusal to have ideals that were impossible to attain; the Age of Decadence was not shameful, its art was not crude, its artisans not incompetent provincial hacks, but the mouth-pieces of popular feeling, of genuine rustic roots. At last that art was being appreciated. The Mona Lisa would no longer be the most admired of all portraits. The statue of Dioscurus in the Museum of the Bardo, Tunis, replaced it: for centuries it had been regarded as a third-rate failure, because the face, instead of being carefully sculpted to look like a real man, was a blank, except for one enormous eye that filled it entirely. That could now be seen as wonderful art, man triumphing over nature. The decadents were the fathers of the moderns. They must awake: new triumphs awaited them.

Nonnos would have been able just to turn over and go back to sleep if that had been all these modern persons had to tell him; he might have slept even more soundly. But they added something else, that frightened him and that explained why he was still shaking now, hidden behind the bushes. They insisted that he was like no other person. It had never occurred to him that might be so. It was nonsense, he replied, everybody acknowledged that he had followed in the foot-steps of a thousand poets before him, he had never had an original thought in his life, he was quite innocent of any such accusation, he belonged to a tradition that taught one how to be like everyone else, and to boast only that one was the favourite of the gods if one obeyed them, did one's duty in the ritual manner, as one's father had done before one. They said he might think that, but he had never done anything quite like anybody else, and no one had been quite able to imitate him; his life had been his very own; he was not inter-changeable. He did not believe them. The thought of being alone of one's kind was too terrifying even to contemplate.

He resented being got out of bed, dragged to parties to be

introduced to writers who, he was told, he simply had to meet, expected to give his opinions of their works, though he had never read them, never heard of them, and did not want to, forced to answer questions from aggressive lovers of literature purporting to admire him. At first, he let all this happen to him, unresisting, unable to believe it was real; he said as little as he could, smiled and shook hands politely and everybody was told he was very shy; no one seemed to mind that his mumbled comments were incomprehensible; on the contrary, this was hailed as a charming eccentricity. He could still remain half-asleep through all such ceremonies. The first suspicion that he was being infected by some disease that was new to him came to him when he began to find amusement in this game of celebrity, and consolation in seeing just how obscure and perverse he could be, how much complete nonsense he could speak and still keep the rapt attention of his audience. Then came a second symptom: he discovered that there were no limits to what he could say, which should have diminished his pleasure by making it predictable, but instead, he saw himself helplessly growing addicted to making pompous and empty pronouncements. He was certain something was seriously wrong when he felt the urge to compose poetry again, and to his surprise, was dissatisfied with what he did write. After that he could no longer go to sleep the way he used to. Old friends began to shun him as though he had some dreaded infection. Worst of all, the paradisical coma which had been his idea of bliss now seemed unworthy of him, a waste of his talents. Then his distress gradually gave birth to a new kind of desire, whose characteristic was that it had no clear object; instead of contentment, he was filled by a yearning for some other happiness which he could not define. That was the final calamity. And as more and more people felt as Nonnos did, Paradise began to rumble. As more of them woke

76

up, as the lights came on one by one, it became evident that the place was indeed no longer what it had been. That was the effect Plus Persons were having on the old residents, simply by asking inconvenient questions.

Nonnos had been hiding, shivering, in the bushes to escape for a while from the rapacity of his admirers, who were determined to possess him and to make sure that he stayed awake; he had been brought to the hotel – almost kidnapped – for the purpose of reading his poems, poems he had long forgotten, which sounded strange even to him. How pleased he was to be greeted by a dog who did not want him to explain his poetry, who did not bark at him, who licked his hand and fell asleep at his feet, miraculously concealing him from his pursuers. How relieved he was when Sumdy showed a sympathetic interest in his insomnia, took pity on him, gave him refuge in her room, sang to him, nursed him, cooled his fever, calmed his anger. They talked about his future: the prospect of having a future, all over again, was too much for him, and he wept. He wanted to escape, hide, and in Paradise there seemed nowhere where one could hide. He was no longer comfortable in a landscape he had always taken for granted, as being natural to him, but he could make no guess as to where he might be more at ease. He knew only that he was restless.

Nonnos was only one example, illustrious but not untypical, of the restlessness that was spreading in Paradise. If the lost souls had imitated the lost souls they knew on earth, they would have remained lost for all eternity. But some of them had grown impatient, and decided to do something about it.

Sumdy's great achievement was to put this lost soul in touch with another, with results that she never foresaw. It was the first indication she had that accident is the lifeblood of Paradise, cleansing it of boredom, bringing nourishment where there was famine of the mind. It was an accident that Henry Ford was also staying at the hotel. She seized the opportunity. Together with Nonnos, she went up to the penthouse, to see the great inventor of the Model T, in the hope that he might whisk the poet away from his tormentors. But Henry Ford had himself become a lost soul. He had taken up residence in the fifth century because he had discovered it was the best place to be if one wanted to communicate with God. He had no intention of moving till he heard the divine voice. He was quite comfortable in the hotel, even though Mrs Ford was not with him. He had long relied on her help; but when he had had the idea of standing for the Presidency of the USA she had said, "Mr Ford can go to Washington if he pleases, but in that case I shall go to England." And now indeed she was in eighteenth century London, from where she urged him to be patient: had it not taken him twelve years to perfect the Model T? Henry Ford did not need, had never needed, human company, so he was not specially pleased to receive the visit of Nonnos, Sumdy and Jolly, but he knew he would need assistance in receiving God's messages, and was keen to recruit suitable people for that purpose. It was not that he took a liking to them – on the contrary, that would have made him suspicious. "There is altogether too much reliance on good feeling in our organisation," he had once said. "People have too great a fondness for working with the people they like. I pity the poor fellow who is so soft and flabby that he must always have an atmosphere of good feeling around him before he can do his work." Henry Ford did not conceal that he would get rid of them when they had done what he needed them for. To escape the lovers of literature, and in the hope of being present when the Great Communication took place, they accepted these conditions and installed themselves in his villa-penthouse.

The hope that God might speak to Henry Ford was no more improbable than the hope of mass-manufacturing a motor car for two hundred and fifty dollars. Henry Ford had died in 1947, but he had arrived at the Hotel de la Decadence only recently. Why the long delay? It was his second coming to Paradise. The first time he had stayed only briefly, deciding he had got off at the wrong station. The very idea of a place devoted to happiness alarmed him: happiness was not something he knew about, he had written it off as a child's dream in his teens, when his mother died; he was convinced there was no possibility of happiness for him after that, the most terrible event of his life. He never changed his mind, for he did not like to admit that he was wrong. When he had the chance of seeing his mother in Paradise, he was upset: she was not what he remembered; he realised he had invented a fairy story around her, and that the person he really wanted to see was God. It did not occur to him that he might be refused an interview: a successful man in his position does not envisage refusal. He claims he asked for and got that interview, though what God said he would not reveal. It is most likely that God said nothing at all, that Henry Ford did not give Him a chance, because his purpose was to tell God what he, Henry Ford, had to say. All one can be certain of is that the next day Henry Ford cleared out of Paradise and went back to earth.

There are those who claim that God did speak, asking Henry Ford what his religion was. At first Henry Ford would say no more than that he was of the religion of all sensible men, and sensible men never said what religion they were. God is supposed to have replied that that was His own religion too, but His disciples would never believe Him. Fearing that God was trying to flatter him, Henry Ford then changed his

79

answer and confessed what he did not normally make public, that he believed in reincarnation, the only doctrine, he said, that could satisfy a person who considered the purpose of life to be not happiness but experience, of which he could never have enough. Whether Henry Ford did indeed persuade God to let him experience the pleasures of reincarnation, or whether he arranged his descent back to earth by some other means, can only be guessed. But he definitely was shuttled instantly back to Detroit, reborn as the child of a lorry driver and a laundry woman. His soul had the opportunity to live and suffer in the body of a being who had emotions that were new to Henry Ford. The child grew into a woman who had ten children, who lived on welfare, abandoned by her husband, devoted to her children, rating them more highly than anything else the world could offer, but raging eloquently, inexhaustibly and helplessly at the world, which, she said, treated her as a slut, because she could not earn enough to support her children, because having trained as a secretary she could never find any better job than as a charwoman, because she did not want her husband back, and was indeed not sure that she wanted any man, never having met a single one who could come up to her idea of perfection. And the soul of Henry Ford, which had once worked miracles producing fire and smoke out of thin air, and raising cities and chimneys out of empty fields, felt what he had never felt before – powerless. Henry Ford, who used to preach that willpower could achieve anything it wished, if it tried hard enough, was reduced to silence. Doubly so, for she died prematurely, run over by a drunken driver, and she and Henry Ford went to Paradise together.

For two souls to live in one body is common enough; such combinations are the making of every rich personality, as well as of every split one; but usually they are glad to forget the encounter and go each their own way as soon as they can. However, Henry Ford's sojourn inside another body transformed him, because never before had he been obliged to listen to the thoughts of someone other than himself, and he found that surprisingly interesting. This time he came to Paradise no longer blaming money lenders and arms dealers, tobacco smokers and alcoholics for the world's ills. The world, he told anybody who would listen to him, was even more mismanaged than he had ever dreamt possible; what appalling inefficiency, what useless suffering, what waste – and waste was always his bugbear, all could be cured by the elimination of waste. The need was for entirely new management at the top. If God had any decency He would resign and let someone more competent take over, though he did not say who he had in mind. In Paradise, souls are allowed to say what they please, and no offence is taken, because it is not customary for anyone to listen to what anybody else says. What was remarkable on this occasion was that Henry Ford really did want to hear what God had to say in reply; he had developed a taste, still in its infancy, for getting into the skin of someone else, though so far it was only what went on inside God's skin that interested him. That is why he had come to the Hotel de la Decadence.

The peculiarity of this hotel was that many minor gods had made a habit of dropping in at the hotel bar. For in the fifth century AD, a vast number of deities were declared redundant and pensioned off – that included most of the gods of Greece and Rome, and some from other continents associated with them, who found that they had nothing much left to do when Christianity was established. They remained settled in this region, which for long was a superior kind of spa resort. But it had more recently become much more than that. The hotel was not built just so that parties of women could come and do honour to Nonnos; it dates from a considerably earlier period, when rather different American tourists started coming here. For every new nation needs a new religion and if it cannot invent one, it resurrects and modifies one that has been forgotten about: that is the first stage of what is called modernisation. The United States of America, soon after its foundation, without being aware of it, became a dedicated worshipper of Roman paganism. The essence of this religion was that it was the religion of success. Its originality was that it eliminated worry about whether a person deserved success. You did not have to be a good or a moral person to get what you wanted, and you could get it on earth, immediately, without having to wait for another life. All you needed to do was to fix the price at which the gods would sell you success. At first, they were quite simple forms of success that these Roman gods sold, for the very idea that humans could succeed in anything on their own was a very bold one; humans generally accepted that they were mere instruments, pawns, ruled by the stars and by destiny: merely to get safely from one place to another was a great achievement, those who did that were the founding fathers of the achieving society. The Roman gods, who were not without a sense of humour, had developed many brands of success; they invented gods of fast-talking to preside over business, gods of craftiness, in charge of the craftiness by which women were supposed to enslave men in return for being enslaved themselves, gods of thieves, and they were not above being thieves themselves. So though you might strike a bargain with them, they did not always keep it. They began by offering good luck, but then just plain luck; success became a lottery. The Roman Empire decided that was not good enough and abandoned its gods. But then the Americans came on the scene, and luck came back into favour. The Roman gods woke up, surprised to find themselves the object of worship once more, secretly, but on a huge scale. The Americans liked these gods, because Roman paganism made a promise of immediate success to everybody for a clear price. You made a sacrifice to the gods, and they delivered the goods, even if the goods turned out to be phoney. The Americans were by no means the first or only modern people interested in success, but they were willing to pay a higher price than any other nation could afford. An ulcer, a broken marriage, a mind-destroying job, these seemed mere trivialities by comparison with the persecution and poverty they had escaped from; they were certain they had a good bargain if success could be obtained for no more than that. Besides, success was fully guaranteed. The Romans also bequeathed to the Americans a unique insurance system. The essence of the Roman cult of success was that failure must be avoided at all costs; its special method was that you backed both sides, all sides. So in addition to being pagans, worshipping success in this world, they also adopted Christianity as soon as it seemed to be fashionable, just in case there was another world they did not know about. Virtually all mankind has since then followed the Romans in having at least two religions, just to be on the safe side. Nonnos had indeed been a true precursor.

Now Henry Ford was even more interested in success than most Americans, because somehow, for all his genius, despite having built the largest factory in the world, he had spent much of his life being mocked as a failure. Cars, he said, should last a lifetime and be as cheap as possible, but that idea nearly drove him to bankruptcy. His rivals proved profits came easier with a new model each year, more expensive each year. Ford was not keen on in high profits ("We do not seem to be able to keep profits down," he complained), nor on inventive engineers ("We have found it unfortunately necessary to get rid of a man as soon as he thinks himself an expert"), nor on aggressive salesmen (they stimulate greed and "unspoken desires" instead of "satisfying needs"), nor on winning the affections of his workers (he employed thugs to beat them up). All the choices he made were unpopular. "The world," he concluded, "has been, is, and will be run by mediocre men." There was no place for a genius in it. "Birds," he finally decided "are the best companions," but nobody has remembered him for the five hundred bird hotels he built. His experience was the very opposite of Nonnos', he had discredited himself more and more.

There was some secret that had escaped Henry Ford, and it was through the intermediary of these Roman gods that he planned to have it revealed by the voice of the God of all gods. He could not hope to be welcomed as a popular visitor to Paradise, he knew that, for his most immortal saying was that History is Bunk, and Paradise was of course full of nothing but history. No one had understood what he meant (the universal complaint), which was that history as written by historians was bunk; not that he had read any historians, he did not even know the date of the American Revolution. But he had heard it said that historians wrote about kings and generals, whom he abhorred; he enjoyed history that he could touch with his hands, houses, old furniture, or history that he could see, face to face encounters. So he did not believe anything that he was told about how God was supposed to have created the world, or what His system of management was. He had come to find out for himself, and to ask the question: How could he succeed better in Paradise?

Sumdy thus became well placed to witness at close hand the great interview which Henry Ford was busy arranging. A whole succession of Roman gods was invited to the penthouse and offered soft drinks and soya bean biscuits (Ford was among the first to hail soya as the answer to the world's hunger). Nonnos acted as the interpreter. Sumdy wrote down what was said, for the gods promised that Henry Ford would get what he wanted, and he promised all the sacrifices they asked for. Sumdy took the place of Mrs Ford, putting the guests at ease, which was no light task, for even gods were made uncomfortable by Henry Ford. However, everything went according to plan, and in the atmosphere of the adventure, all forgot their private petty tribulations.

It happened, unfortunately, when both Sumdy and Jolly were temporarily absent. They returned one evening from a day's outing in the woods to find the Gospel according to Henry Ford all written out beautifully on parchment. Henry Ford was in raptures, because though the interview had unexpectedly taken place in what he took to be Hebrew, a language neither he nor Nonnos knew, yet miraculously they had understood. Sumdy was therefore never able to vouch for the authenticity of this document, on which experts are still disagreed; privately, she suspected that it was Nonnos who wrote it all, at last a successful poem, at last a new audience. Henry Ford could not have dictated it, for its ideas were too remote from his own, and its style too different; above all, he would never have admitted, what Nonnos confirmed, that the voice of God was distinctly peculiar, sounding female rather than male, not at all like thunder. Who exactly Ford spoke to must remain a matter of conjecture. The interview having been finally arranged by the Roman god Mercury, who is of Indian origin, there is a likelihood that it was to one of Mercury's Indian grandmothers that he was introduced, known, in different parts, as Uma, Parvati, Durga, Kali, Kumasi, Ambika or Candi: she is the mother goddess of the earth, of love and of death, long esteemed as the best guide to the mysteries of existence. But that is only a guess. Whatever its source, the Gospel according to Henry Ford seemed destined to become an influential document in Paradise, but, like all such documents, highly controversial, on whose exact meaning it is impossible to agree. It is best therefore to read the document for oneself:

Travellers in Paradise, it is for you that is written this true account of how Henry Ford climbed to the top floor of the Hotel de la Decadence, and took up watch, and waited, hoping to be admitted into the presence of his Creator. It happened that for long he received no answer to his prayers. Then one day he heard the raindrops knocking on his window. He opened the window, but there was no rain. Yet still the raindrops knocked. And Henry Ford was overjoyed, for he recognised that at last the messenger was calling him. Tears came into his eyes, which was not usual for him. He said out loud: Why am I sad? And through the window came a voice which said, Why am I sad? It was not an echo. For God too was sad. The voice chose Henry Ford to tell the inhabitants of Paradise why the glory of God was not complete.

The voice said: When the warmth of the sun grows too hot in Paradise, my sadness is the wind that blows from the sea and refreshes the soul. My sadness is a seed that grows into a tree, and without it there would be no greenery on the hills or flowers by the streams. I am sad only because I have not taught my creatures how to savour the joys of sadness and the rewards of failure, for only those who see the fault in their own work and do not weep are truly my children.

This is the first of the pillars on which happiness is built in Paradise. But do not expect that pillar to hold you always. Mine is not a paradise that is built on solid foundations. Therefore must you have a second pillar, which is the pillar of courage that sustains you when the first one yields. For no pillar can stand by itself. And so it is with all pillars on which happiness stands.

Henry Ford said: I hear you, O Creator, and I am confused and I am not comforted. You tell me to build a pillar and promise me that it will not hold. You order me to search for a second pillar, but do not tell me where I can find the courage of which it is made. No engineer can accept such a specification. Send me a sign, that shall be more clear and more exact.

To which the voice replied: My sign is a mistake. Many were the mistakes I made in the creation. Many have been the complaints from my creatures, who cry out that they suffer pain and evil. Why, they ask, each in his language, are so many people allowed to make such a mess of their lives? Their horror at their fate is nothing compared to the sorrow in my own heart. But it does not make me want to stop. For my creatures are weak and their minds are easily confused. It is their pleasure to worship me as the perfect, omnipotent being, and to shut their ears to what I have said to them, so clearly, so often.

I am in a mess myself. It took me no less than twenty-six tries before I succeeded in creating the world. There should be no surprise that my creation is not perfect, and that it does not work as well as it should. It is an experiment. In truth, if my creatures would but recognise that it has been a failed experiment, I would pull it all apart into pieces, and make another attempt; only out of consideration for the strange love that they have developed for their painful existence have I postponed starting all over again. I am touched by the admiration that they have for my work, but their applause does not please me. I often beat my breast when I hear how confused they are about me. They cannot make me out at all.

Let us put our cards on the table, said Henry Ford.

I am the Creator, said the voice. I am, above all else, a creator. That means I can never stop. Even before I complete a task, I am conceiving new ones, and new worlds into which to place them. It is inevitable that I should lose interest in my past works. I am sorry that should lead humans to feel neglected, but it need not be so. I hope that in future they might learn to appreciate me as I am.

I could never get people to appreciate me as I am, said Henry Ford. It is interesting you have the same trouble as myself.

Humans are only prototypes, the voice went on, much simpler than I hope to make them one day. They yearn for simple solutions to their troubles: I do not. Humans wobble emotionally, they want to be secure. I know I have not yet found a way to make their emotions work properly, to create fruits without bitterness. Like all humans, you, Henry Ford, dream of finding clear-cut goals; and if you can achieve such goals as well as find them, you rejoice and imagine you have found success. Your ideal is to know what you want and to obtain it. That is what you call a successful life. That is indeed, more and more, the real religion of all mankind.

But my universe is made of chaos, uncertainty and change, which is the way it has to be and also the way I like it. I would die of boredom if the chaos could be reduced to immobile perfection. I need invincible forces to wrestle with, not merely evil forces – which are too easy to condemn and too despicable to challenge. Only unpredictable ones are worthy of me, over which there can never be a final victory. It is not victory that I seek: victory is only for children. I have not yet made humans strong enough to live with such thoughts. Until I do, I must endure them worshipping the false god of success.

You will have to make us a better offer, said Henry Ford.

The mess of the world is not as bad as you think; it is just not easy to see the spot where the groove and the tongue will meet. I have my grand plan, even if I change it all the time. Just look at the burning of Desire. In each of my creatures I have placed this spark of a fire, that they call desire, one of my most ingenious inventions, though they blame me for the torment it causes them. I watch them, especially in the east, struggling to put it out, which I do not hold against them, on the contrary. What wisdom has emerged in that battle! I have learnt a lot from it. And I watch those who in the west struggle to fulfil all desires, which is of course even more impossible: what marvellous creations have been forged as a result, even new forms of living beings, not unworthy of being compared to my own. I grieve only that all this struggle makes humans prisoners, each of his own struggle, each of his own way of thinking. I did not make them versatile enough. They feel obliged to choose between opposites.

Paradise is where the circle is squared, where contradictions can live amicably together. It is where I carry out my boldest experiments, before launching them into the rest of the universe. But I find the souls up here too exhausted or frustrated, often dull, nearly always comatose. That is what I want to put right next. To understand what is going on below on earth, it is necessary to see how it fits with my present experiments up here.

Don't tell me, said Henry Ford, that you too are planning a new model.

It must have been a premonition that made me give humans a brain divided into two parts. I wanted each part to be independent, to be the monitor of the other, to take turns in piloting the body, each with its own awareness of the shoals, and its own taste for vantage points. Had I succeeded, I would have been really proud of my work. It would have been not just a two-engined aeroplane – I smiled when they invented that – but one where the engines are rivals, friends, teachers, spies, artists who never see a landscape alike. Alas, the brain fussed and fretted so much about the body, got so agitated by it, far more than I foresaw, so many signals were exchanged, so many false alarm bells rang all the time, that the two parts joined up to form a single whole; tougher perhaps, but less versatile than I had intended. In Paradise the soul and the body can understand each other better; and yet the soul still needs some help from me: I am ashamed that it falls apart so easily. I wish to have another try at creating the kind of soul that I have myself dreamt about, to be like a boat which will not capsize, to be capable of flights of imagination which are truly free, and yet which do not fall out of control. To do that, every soul must be a double soul.

When these words were spoken, silence reigned in the penthouse of Henry Ford, for he could not understand how one soul could become two souls; and though he begged for more guidance, he heard nothing more. His disciples could not agree what the divine words meant. The youngest, Sumdy, proposed that they should be interpreted to mean that every soul must find and join himself or herself to a mate in Paradise. The oldest, Nonnos, who was wise, said that God was condemning the folly and ignorance of souls, and that it was by acquiring knowledge of the truth that their vigour would be doubled. Henry Ford, for his part, feared that God wanted to make geniuses of all the inhabitants of Paradise, that geniuses were only mad people who happened by chance to hit a nail on the head, that mad people had split souls, and that therefore it was in some transformation of insanity that the key to the doubling of the soul was to be found.

It was decided to call a meeting of all the retired managers and administrators who were willing to come, and who were not pretending to be too busy, to debate how one or all of these objects could be achieved, but they could not agree. The only proposal they approved was that the Hotel de la Decadence should be closed down and turned into a research and development institute, and that the animals of Paradise should be invited to volunteer to have experiments carried out upon them, in the interests of the happiness of mankind. But the animals did not respond, and it was clear that they found Paradise very suited to their taste as it was.

So Henry Ford summoned a meeting of all the bankers in Paradise, to find inducements, in gold or in kind, to think up new sorts of perks or bonuses, to attract creatures who would consent to have their souls split, doubled or repaired, for he believed that souls needed inducements, though he was not sure of what nature, or for what purpose. A lavish banquet was ordered for the benefit of the bankers, since they would not meet without one, but not a single fish or fowl could be found to agree to be eaten by the bankers, even that the problems of Paradise should be solved. And the bankers refused to meet with a menu consisting only of unleavened bread.

So Henry Ford summoned a press conference of all the journalists of Paradise whom he could rouse from sleeping by their telephones, waiting for stories that never came. He invited them to spread the good news that a double or split soul, of the right kind, was indispensable to anyone who wished to show himself in public without shame, even though no one knew what a double soul was. The fashion writers were asked to explain how each half should be worn, to the best advantage. But though all the newspapers carried the message, none was able to find a photograph to show a soul both split and smiling; and without a picture, the message was not believed.

Henry Ford then met with the gods and goddesses of Greece and Rome, or those of them that regularly frequented the bar of the Hotel de la Decadence, and in the presence of Sumdy and Nonnos, declared that he was sure he was speaking for the whole of mankind when he said that he did not wish to be too demanding or unrealistic, but he could not be satisfied with what he had been told, for no one would come to Paradise if he knew that it was run to be a failure. Sumdy added that she was particularly sorry for the children of Paradise, who seemed to have neither toys, nor the hope of a successful future. Henry Ford said he was not a sentimental man (which was not true, he liked to have his wife sit on his lap even in extreme old age, and she always insisted he was the most sentimental man she had ever known), so he could not possibly feel sorry for anyone, children or adults; he did not complain that Paradise did not offer its inhabitants happiness on a plate

91

– he would despise such demagogy – nor even success, which was what most people settled for as a substitute for happiness; but he was deeply troubled that it provided no opportunities for work, which was the only thing that had ever given him satisfaction, or kept his employees out of mischief. The place was beginning to look to him like a grand doss-house for the unemployed. Paradise must provide incentives, and it must not shirk its responsibilities: it owed something to those who came such a long way to live in it. So he proposed that they make a contract, which he got Nonnos to write out: For whereas the Divine Word was difficult to understand, and it being necessary to make interim practical arrangements until it was understood, it is agreed between the inhabitants of Paradise on the one hand, and the gods and their associates, being specialists in the art of guiding mankind to success, on the other hand, that in future a fixed scale of charges should be negotiated at the beginning of each year, or other term to be agreed, payable in cash by every inhabitant for the successes that he, she or it was desirous of winning, so that the said inhabitants should always get what they wanted, that being the purpose for which they had come to Paradise; that the delivery of goods promised by the gods should be punctual and free of unexpected snags, and that if there was any complaint or disappointment, the price should be refunded, so that the inhabitants could never lose, whatever happened, for only thus could Paradise deserve its name. And Henry Ford put that contract on the table and said it was his final offer, for otherwise he would pack and leave, there would be no point in staying in Paradise.

There was loud laughter from the gods; they laughed so much that they could not answer; they drank up their glasses spluttering, holding their sides, and left the Hotel de la Decadence drunk with mirth. Only the boy god Pushan remained, who offered to carry Henry Ford back to earth in his goat cart, and Henry Ford would indeed have had to do as he had threatened and leave, had not Sumdy begged to have one question answered first. What was so funny about Henry Ford's proposal? Pushan, being only a boy, and so willing to talk of matters too obvious for adults to mention, explained that success was never sold in Paradise, it was only exported to earth, and was regarded in the same way that marbles and bangles were by those famous conquerors who sold them to "ignorant savages" in return for their freedom. Success was a toy suitable only for the living, even the children in Paradise had no use for it. The gods had invented success only to keep humans amused, for otherwise there were complaints that life had no point to it, humans having great difficulty in recognising the point of things. But Paradise had no need of a point or a purpose, for it lasted for ever, and so could never reach its purpose. Any child could see that, said the boy god Pushan.

Henry Ford was struck dumb, for a brief moment, by this news that there were matters which children could understand but adults could not, for he had such a respect for the process of becoming adult that he had come to the conclusion that there was no such thing as a gifted child; to be gifted could only mean to be old in experience; Jesus Christ, he liked to say, was an old person; he was not prepared to do business with a child.

His brief moment of dumbness allowed Sumdy to ask the boy god, very politely, whether he could take them to see a divided soul; they would promise to be very quiet, and neither gasp, nor giggle nor scream.

"There is nothing to see," said Pushan. "I have a double soul myself. All gods have double souls."

"Is it the secret of your immortality?" asked Nonnos.

93

"How does a double soul work?" asked Henry Ford.

"Does it mean you can never be unhappy?" asked Sumdy.

"I shall try and describe it", said Pushan, "in a way that an adult can understand. One of my souls is no different from the soul that humans write poems about: it aches and boils and coos and spits, and feels everything that humans call emotion. While my other soul looks down on it as the moon looks down on the inconsolable wind and the helpless waves, remaining beyond their reach, with a smile that never fades. My second soul is the spirit of creation, for which all that the first one does is only a story that fills it with wonder, material out of which it weaves its own endless, ever-changing tapestry of thoughts; it is the soul that resists, that never falls into the absurdity of being disconsolate; for it, failure is only a move on a chessboard. And there is no secret about how the second soul is born. Even the amoeba knows it, even the lowly sponge. Every soul can create a second soul inside itself; this is the first act of creation that it must make if it is to learn to live like a god, which means to be a creator."

"But where," said Sumdy, "do you get the courage to split yourself and even more to watch yourself?"

"No human," said Nonnos, "has ever learned to see himself, let alone see himself as others see him; it would be too discouraging."

"What is the price of courage?" asked Henry Ford.

"We Roman gods never were much good at giving humans courage, which is doubtless why the Roman Empire collapsed. The specialists in courage are the guardian angels. They know how to turn citizens into martyrs. But I have not seen them around for a long time. They alone knew how to whisper the right words into human ears."

"But I like to stand on my own feet," said Henry Ford. "What can I do myself? What kind of ambition can I have in Paradise? Where is ambition gone?"

"Ambition is a plant we could never get to grow properly on earth; it always went to seed. Humans got too excited by ambition, like lovers wanting to possess a loved one, and to love only that one: success in a single, obsessive ambition becomes the purpose of their life. But that is the equivalent of praying for death. The ambition of Paradise is too intense for mere humans."

Henry Ford was now certain that there was no place for him in Paradise, any more than there was place for him on earth. He thought humans were silly, and he did not like silliness; he thought nations were silly too, wasting their wealth on war and politics; he had hoped that once every family had a car there would be no more war, because they would be able to visit each other, and they could not be so silly as to fight people whom they knew; but he had to admit he was wrong; people were indeed very silly. And now it was the worst of disappointments to be told that in Paradise one half of the soul, at least, still remained silly; that there could be no happiness without silliness; what a silly idea happiness was, he had always known it. There was only one other place he could go: why had he not recognised it long ago? He was destined to ferry souls between earth and Paradise, so that he could avoid living in either. That was what he had invented the Model T for, if only he had known it. The trouble with inventions is that it is impossible to predict what use they will be put to. Just as he could not predict what Paradise would make of his Gospel, which he bequeathed to it, with his compliments, before getting into Pushan's goat cart and driving off to the gates of Paradise; and then disappearing into the thin air, where at last he felt comfortable.

Nonnos was sorry to see him go; he hated the idea that Paradise was not for everyone, that it could not please those who did not want to be pleased, a goal he had set himself on earth, and which he was surprised to see rejected here. But, now thoroughly awakened, forced to think about his future, he saw how he could escape the lovers of literature; there was no need for him to masquerade any longer as a literary giant; the message of the Gospel according to Henry Ford was that Paradise freed humans from the need to masquerade as successful beings at all; no need for them to dress like aging managing directors in the hope of winning the respect of managing directors, no need to surround themselves with the accoutrements of power to give themselves the illusion that they enjoyed it, no need to lick boots, for fear of being kicked in the face if they did not, and in order to join the ranks of those who were proud that they had the right to kick others in the face. Nonnos felt enormous relief that he might be appreciated as a literary failure instead of a literary giant, that Paradise was the place where all failures had the right of asylum, where the art of failure was understood and valued, where all those billions who had a novel inside them but never succeeded in writing it down, or having it published, all those millions who after painful labour had given birth to a humble entertainment, a modest act of compassion, an ingenious repair, a printed volume, and then seen their child misunderstood, insulted, neglected and could not understand why they had bothered, could celebrate their conviction that they could do better next time, without feeling any bitterness, without having any regrets. After the strain of being a success on earth, Nonnos was glad of the dignity to be won being a failure in Paradise, without pretence. He slipped silently out of the Hotel de la Decadence and vanished into the woods.

So Sumdy was left alone in Henry Ford's penthouse. From it she wrote her letter home, on the grand notepaper she found there, for the first thing he had done was to have some notepaper printed, as a sign that he meant business. Jolly was perplexed, she said, because when he had met other dogs, not one had come up to smell him, or to growl at him; they had only stared, as though he was different from them, which he undoubtedly was. She did not know whether this was one more sign that every creature had a different idea of what happiness was, what Paradise was. Every angel too? Was there something missing from Paradise? The angels were missing. Forgetmenot was missing. She had thought Paradise was where there was never anything missing. She was determined to find the angels, quickly.

CHAPTER FOUR

Several accidents happened to the Gospel of Henry Ford. Jolly did not tear and chew it up. Sumdy did not pack it away and take it home as a souvenir. These are the sorts of accident that the newspapers of Paradise like to report, not because they are short of news, but because they care as much about what does not happen as about what does. These are the sorts of accident that have resulted in Paradise having whole warehouses full of bright ideas that, for one trivial reason or another, got lost on earth and are waiting for some soul to find a use for them. Chance is treated with respect in Paradise. And it was pure chance that in the lobby of the Hotel de la Decadence Sumdy did not pass without noticing the posters advertising lecture courses, language classes, prayer meetings and art exhibitions, and that these posters put the thought in her head that it might be interesting to show the manuscript to an expert in gospels, who could assess it scientifically. That is how she came to take the gospel to the local university only a few molehills away. And it was there that she was burnt at the stake.

She had no reason to expect that anything so drastic should befall her. True, the university Sumdy found was no longer the peaceful university Paradise had once been proud of. The old professors could remember how only a few decades ago they had inhabited a veritable paradise within paradise, where students were perpetual students, with no ambition but to gratefully, unquestioningly, copy down whatever their teachers said to them, where sensual pleasure was the smooth feel of paper and the perfume of dusty tomes, where the only music that disturbed the silence of the libraries was the symphony of sniffing, throat-clearing and gasping by which each communicated his presence, each in his own inimitable way. Nor did students take their studies too seriously. They refreshed themselves with long periods of sleep, understanding that a university need be no more than a dormitory for optimists with the dream of waking up more intelligent every morning. All those who regretted not having had a university education on earth could here repair their loss, and were somehow never disappointed. And the professors themselves had no need to bother about preparing new courses, updating the syllabus or moving with the times, as they inevitably do in earthly universities constantly disrupted by their luminaries dying, and their ideas with them; for in Paradise professors survive for ever, and so the doctrines and the fallacies of every century and every sect go on being taught regardless and no one complains. There are no arguments about which textbooks need to be scrapped. It is possible for professors of medicine, for example, endlessly to find imaginary cures for imaginary diseases. It is possible to package and repackage experiments, so that what is a fact one day, is no longer a fact the next. In Paradise professors are no longer haunted by the fear that one lifetime is too short to fulfil their grand plans for solving the riddles of the universe, and that they will be forced to end every publication with the same sad lullaby: "Further research is needed"; they know that they are at last free to write long books so interminable that their pages cannot be counted, and that no one will mock them because they never finish; they can dip their pens in bottles of ink that are eternal fountains, and by this means consider themelves forever young. Clad in their gold and scarlet gowns, experts in all subjects can amuse themselves inventing wittier words for the celestial hymns, and good-naturedly allow tourists to walk around them on tiptoe, admiring their large heads, as though they are monuments.

Anybody in Paradise can be a professor if he chooses to, just as any professor can, if he chooses to, imagine himself to be a genius. The only problem is, how to be a genius, how should one behave if one is a genius, or a professor, or a student? That was Paradise's challenge to the imagination. Many were too timid to take it up.

So it might have gone on till the end of time, had a new kind of student not begun to arrive, protesting that the professors were attached to outmoded fashions (as though anything can go out of fashion in Paradise), accusing them of being afflicted with chronic intellectual constipation (as though rest was not the universal aim), demanding that the atmosphere of the university should be tonic not soporific (because they had not learned to savour the special taste of the paradisical coma). New kinds of professors arrived too, distraught, full of doubts, apparently permanently damaged by their experiences on earth, complaining that the mundane universities from which they came were no longer a refuge of laughter and hope, but conspiracies which upset, disturbed and discouraged people more than they inspired them, that they had even lost the knack of picking correctly in advance the winners in life, which was what had once given them their prestige, that they were bloated with arrogance even though it was said they could do nothing right. There was a danger that Paradise might go the same way. Indeed from Paradise the earthly universities looked like smoking volcanoes, rumbling with discontent; it seemed as though before long their fumes would suffocate Paradise itself.

If Sumdy (or Jolly) had smelt the air more keenly, and been able to interpret the peculiar heaviness in it, she would have perhaps guessed that reading and sleeping was not all that the professors and students now did. If she had listened harder to them mumbling to themselves, she might have made out the words of their favourite prayer, which they recited under their breath:

> God, who sings a secret song,
> What You say I have no clue,
> Help me keep my secret too.
>
> I am right and they are wrong,
> They tell lies, my words are true,
> None knows this but me and You.

Everybody is aware that universities may appear to be sleepy and contented when observed from outside, but that their silences and their slow tempo are deceptive. Behind the twinkling eyes, there is nearly always a hidden turbulence. Every new truth conceived by a scholar is the illegitimate child of doubt, and is invariably insulted and mocked. The pretence of immobility is there only to conceal that nearly every self-respecting academic wears a hair shirt under his smooth gown; for without the itch of permanent anxiety he feels naked, though there are of course academics who prefer more fancy underwear. Few would ever have agreed to go to Paradise if all it offered was truth served on a plate, for truth is the prize of a battle, and battle means slaughter. The hair shirt is only one of the items of equipment that the scholar

101

needs. He likes to bring his sharp quills out of his sleeve and stick them into his opponents' behinds; in Paradise he expects to fulfil his dream of at last getting the better of those who have argued with him, proving them wrong, being vindicated in the theory, the cure, the solution he has championed. One of the most eminent traditions of the academic life is the burning of heretics, the solemn condemnation of falsehoods, or what are declared to be so from time to time. The frown on the forehead of the learned person who comes to Paradise is a sure sign that he is worrying about his bête noire, the academic rival who contradicted or scorned him: he is dying to extirpate him. So the burning of heretic souls was established as a regular Saturday afternoon entertainment in this university, as in many others, which everybody looked forward to with pleasure. No historian has bothered to report this, because it is often regarded as a sport, and sporting results are seldom recorded in serious chronicles. And yet, it was more than a sport.

Sumdy was quite open about her purpose in visiting the university. She was perhaps too naively hopeful that she would find a learned professor to decode Henry Ford's gospel for her, show her how to split a soul, perhaps also tell her something about what happiness meant here: did the search for knowledge, or its possession, make professors happy? She might, she thought, perhaps even meet someone who was not totally absorbed in the perplexity of finding himself in Paradise; Jolly might be inspired to recover his sparkle, for his tail, to her great distress, was now almost permanently pointing downwards.

Certainly, the university of Paradise was interested in animals, and not in the way that Jolly feared. There seemed to be no scientists here gouging out the eyes of either dogs or rats in order to be able to write learned papers about the working of their eyesight or brain; in Paradise neither dogs nor rats agreed to undergo such experiments, they could not even be systematically bred here, to grow two tails or anything else, for each was free to choose his own destiny. And the founder of the university, whom Sumdy met briefly, with the same sense of shock that many new immigrants did, had a very personal reason for not treating animals as inferiors or mere tools. The wise Ganesa had a physical peculiarity, which perhaps explains why he is not known or appreciated in the west, with its rigidly conformist standards of beauty. Ganesa is the oldest of all the gods of learning and of intelligence, of students and of teachers. In the east he is known by many names, among others: Bestower of Perfection, The Incomprehensible, and He of the Full Belly. But he once lost his head – literally. No one is sure how this accident happened. His original head was replaced by that of an elephant. It is said that was an accident too, that an elephant's head just happened to be around, but that is not so. Ganesa chose to have an elephant's head because memory was what he valued most highly. He had other interests certainly: his statues, to be found all over Asia, always show him distinguished by a zest for good living, though he also has a cunning wit; it is a snake that he wears around his belly, to stop himself exploding after his very indulgent meals. In his four hands, he holds a water lily, a discus, an axe, and a sweetened rice ball, his favourite food: he is equipped with all the talents needed for success in the academic hurly burly, and in ancient times virtually every learned author acknowledged this, beginning their books with a dedication to him. But as the elephant-headed god, who never forgot anything, he rejoiced in the position of guaranteeing all creatures that everything they ever did would always be remembered. He was the symbol of ancient wisdom, which held that the most precious possession of the learned was their memory.

Ganesa was displaying either his cunning or else his habit of repeating himself, when he gave Sumdy a lecture of welcome, warning her not to expect to find answers too quickly: the moderns were always in far too great a hurry: there was so much to learn and to memorise before she could hope to understand anything, that she had better prepare for a very long stay. This warning showed that Ganesa was not in his habitual state of complete serenity when Sumdy called. He seemed more preoccupied with the memory of his meals; the only part of his message that he spoke with pleasure was his invitation for her to come to dinner. The reason may have been that he was still upset by the now celebrated letter he had received from George Stephenson, whom the university had asked to come and give them a lecture on steam engines. Stephenson had refused, saying he hated being remembered for the rest of eternity as their inventor; he would like for a change to be thought of, for example, as the inventor of the cucumber slicing machine. He wanted a new life in Paradise: the cucumber machine implied a wholly different set of memories, not smoke, not coal, but long drinks and cool sandwiches in summer gardens. Ganesa was worried that, more than an insulting refusal, this was a sign that souls were beginning to grow restless under the burden of their memories. Ganesa was proud of his neat pigeon-holes, into which he could fit everyone who came his way. He liked to register that Sumdy had two black marks against her, one for being different from everyone else, a temporary tourist, and secondly, for having caused a scandal on her very first day, bringing a cockroach into Paradise. He could not forget these facts, and he labelled her with the only memory he had of her.

That is one of the snags about memory, it is a fragment, it never tells the whole story, something can always be added to it, which is one of the reasons why it was an unsatisfactory basis for a perfect existence in Paradise. It was not satisfactory that Sumdy should for ever be associated with her pet cockroach.

What to do with their memories? That is one of the most difficult questions which every new arrival has to puzzle over. Common wisdom has it that it is best to keep one's memories in good order, carefully packaged and labelled, and to try to add to their stock as much as possible: the more the better. The elephant god was the model most people tried to copy. That explains why over so many centuries Paradise never invented anything or had any new thoughts, it was too occupied collecting old ones. And now new professors were arriving with memories more bulky than had ever been known. Never had Paradise contained so much knowledge. George Stephenson's gesture was a sign that some souls were beginning to feel that they were overweight with memory, that ways had to be found of jettisoning, or lightening it. But they did not know how. Memory seemed out of their control, a burden they could not avoid. No angels gave advice on how to use it in Paradise.

One of the obstacles that souls constantly encounter is that they have so much difficulty in talking to each other. They arrive with hopes of meeting their soul-mates, but they are mystified as to how they are supposed to contact these. Even the business of finding a professor who would answer a question was not simple. How could Sumdy spot the one who was likely to be helpful? All she was familiar with was the earthly system – a guess, an intuition that, by the look of him, by the sound of him, a professor might like her and she might like him. In Paradise she expected better than that. She determined to find professors whom she would test and examine properly, so that she should not be disappointed. She insisted she wanted to know them thoroughly, their private quirks mattered as much as their public pronouncements. Jolly must be free to lick and smell and make a mess as much as he pleased, so that together they could recognise the professor who would be right for both of them.

By chance, she met a likely-looking and recently arrived professor of psychology who she was assured was famous, or had been, for the fame of professors seldom lasts long. She did not quite catch his name, she could not ask a famous man his name, she would offend him, she had to pretend to know it. It is a constant difficulty, meeting people in Paradise, who assume one knows who they are. This particular professor's name sounded like Purda, which seemed unlikely; there is no record of any such psychologist. But whoever he was, he looked like a professor, he talked like a sweet and learned man, he was willing to speak to her, to submit to her tests, practical and theoretical, and she could understand what he said.

She encouraged him to talk, and her first test was to yawn as he did so. Each yawn, a true student's yawn, stopped him in mid-sentence, but each time he resumed his monologue with a barely perceptible loss of aplomb. So she pretended to fall asleep. He went on talking. Then she pretended to wake up, and said that she had dreamed that she saw him walking down Jermyn Street in London, in the days when it was full of hatters. He was trying to buy a hat, but his head was swollen to twice its normal size. He was explaining to the smart shop assistant with a carnation in his buttonhole that he needed a new hat because he had outgrown his old one: his head was

106

getting bigger every day, but he had nowhere else to store his books. The assistant suggested that what he needed was an expanding hat, but they did not make them any more. That annoyed the professor: surely they must make some sort of hat to fit him, he was not fussy about style so long as it was not too new-fangled. The assistant advised him to stop reading books, that would stop his head growing. But the advice came too late. His head expanded as he was talking, it upset the shelves round the shop and hats of all sorts cascaded around him as he continued to explain the importance of getting a hat that fitted properly. When he finally pushed his way out of the shop, his great dome of a head was covered, as though by pimples and boils, with berets and bowlers, boaters and top-pers, deerstalkers and pork pies, but large parts of it were unprotected. And he went from hatter to hatter, buying everything he could to cover his head, but never able to keep up with the expansion of his scalp. He grumbled loudly that a country which no longer made expanding hats was doomed, ossified, mean. Sumdy's test was: how did the professor inter-pret this dream?

It was simple, he replied. The most significant object in the dream was obviously the carnation in the assistant's button-hole. Carnations are so-called because they were once carnal, of the palest pink, flesh-coloured. The assistant represented carnal temptation. But the professor had rejected his advice, and the temptation he held out, and had refused to be dis-suaded from the quest for knowledge, despite the difficulties it caused him. It was true he could never acquire enough knowledge, or hats, but he had remained true to himself. Which showed, added the professor, that the key to his sur-vival was the ability to find an explanation that put him back in the saddle.

Rightly or wrongly, that impressed Sumdy, because Purda

gave the impression of not being overwhelmed by the incomprehensibility of Paradise.

So she went on to the second question in her examination: what was the professor's state of health? She had always thought it odd that students did not enquire into the tics and fears of their teachers, before entrusting a mind to their care; an unhappy student snuffs out only himself, a sick or depressed teacher is a specialist in mass asphyxiation. Her enquiry interested Professor Purda because his health was worrying him, had always worried him and did so even more now that residence in Paradise had not miraculously cured him. He told her that he had first begun to suffer from faintness, headaches and acute sensations of cold when he had, in early middle age, lost his most precious possession, his research notes, thrown away by an over-zealous cleaner. It was like a presage of death, a sudden revelation of the flimsiness of the foundations of his reputation. He felt threatened by academic annihilation. And then his memory, which was his pride, betrayed him, playing tricks on him, hinting to him that his ability to concentrate was faltering, that he was no longer as intelligent as he once had been, until that excruciating occasion, which made his faintness quite alarming, when he was accused of fraud, or as some kinder colleagues put it, of misreporting his experiments, misinterpreting or even inventing his evidence. Perhaps it was because his memory and his fantasy got confused. He had denied the charges with great vigour, and his reputation survived, for academics, like politicians, are used to being attacked, but he could not continue to fight in Paradise, where he imagined himself to be shunned as he had never been before. Soon after his arrival he changed his name, calling himself Purda, with bitter irony, a self-inflicted insult to obscure ones that hurt even more. Only later did Sumdy discover that this was the first psychologist ever to be knighted, the first foreigner to be honoured by the American Psychological Association with its highest award, loaded with distinctions by almost everybody that had distinctions to bestow. How could he exist peaceably in Paradise when his own biographer concluded that he had indeed been guilty of deception, and when envious colleagues wrote self-righteous articles entitled "Are Researchers Trustworthy?" and more directly "Cheating in Science". He felt cold in Paradise, even though the climate was beautiful. He could not stop clinging to the memory of his earthly self, unpleasant and confused though many aspects of it were to him. Though he tinkered with his name and his outward appearance, from habit, from timidity, he could not imagine himself completely different. Paradise does offer the option to a soul to imagine itself to be a butterfly and to fly away, released from the pins that stick it down and condemn it to be a mere specimen of a species, a tribe, a clique, a generation; but even someone with such good reasons as Professor Purda did not dare seize his opportunity. He blamed his helplessness on not finding enough reassurance in Paradise. Whenever he emerged from his protecting sleep, he had no alternative to clutch onto but his own memories, and he held onto every one of them, as though he feared that through some slip he might at any moment make a childish mistake, which would be, in so august a place, irreparable and disastrous.

He expected no indulgence, because he was oppressed by his anguish at not being understood by other souls. He persisted in regarding that as being their fault. Surely, he thought, he expressed himself elegantly and lucidly enough. And yet how ironical it was that he was misunderstood worst of all by his very closest colleagues. In particular, he could not get over the breach he had had with one of them, with whom

109

he thought he agreed on all matters of principle and on all technical details as well; he could detect between their respective positions no more than a few nuances of sympathy or technique. And yet, when they confronted each other in public in Paradise, misapprehensions were evident, giving the impression that they had standpoints in polar opposition. He could not forget a work published by this colleague, which, said Professor Purda, "was a frightful misinterpretation of my view. He did me the honour of quoting an article of mine directly in five places, and on every occasion he got me wrong. This strengthens my feeling that he regarded my work as unworthy of his detailed attention. One mistake in a direct quotation is a scholar's licence, but five out of five does suggest a certain disregard."

Paradise does not provide any guarantee of respect from others, or any assurance that what reputation one has will remain inviolate. That is why Purda had welcomed Sumdy. He was searching for props to his self-esteem. He needed disciples. His health demanded it. Playing the role of a master talking to devoted pupils greatly improved his digestion. But now such disciples were becoming rare. He was delighted to be charming to anyone who came to him meekly for information, and to behave like a wise, weatherworn gardener showing off his prize flowers and giving little cuttings of rare plants away, unruffled by pests or storms. It had been only those who claimed to be his equals who had made him freeze and hold himself aloof, to the point that he regarded a university as, by definition, a place of permanent cold war. He could not lose his habit of freezing. Such are the kinds of memory that float in Paradise like droplets, from which the all-pervading mist is constituted. To learn to navigate through the mist, to create a new landscape out of it, to see the droplets become jewels which one can juggle in one's hand, that is what some long to do. But it is not easy.

Purda surrounded himself with a fortification of mistrust, but not because he despised the souls around him. He feared they despised him. Even when he had become one of the grand old men of his native country, proudly exhibited to foreigners as proof of its scientific distinction, so irreplace-able that a special exemption was made to allow him to con-tinue after the retirement age, he had still always treated the slightest argument as a threat to his very existence, physically almost paralysing him, like a premonition of rigor mortis. Now he imagined he was attending committee meetings in Paradise too, and that same rigidity had returned. He gave the appearance of cool detachment, he never lost his temper, but he saw disagreement everywhere, and treated every gesture around him as an attack. He argued relentlessly, like an ever-barking dog, determined to get his way, devastating in his comments on the opinions of others, though any hint of a criticism of his own that he thought he heard filled him with a deep anguish, and he retaliated as though his fame was a balloon that could be deflated with a pin prick. Once he had woken up from the paradisical coma, all his old physical tor-ments had returned.

When a professor confesses so much to a pupil, the pupil cannot hold it against him. Sumdy felt a surge of warmth towards Purda; what teacher had ever been so honest with her? But was he open to new ideas? This was a delicate matter to raise, but her third question was direct: what was his opin-ion of the Gospel of Henry Ford? It was particularly difficult for him to answer that, because at the age of eighteen he had written in his diary that his aim in life was to become a perfect man. He had done his very best to attain that status, and yet

111

here he was in Paradise still not feeling perfect. His wish had not been a mere childish fantasy, nor a vague religious yearning. He had his formula for perfection all worked out. It was a well tried one, approved by innumerable scholars both on earth and in Paradise, and the god Ganesa, the Bestower of Perfection, confirmed that it was a sacred one. The formula stated that the path to perfection was the pursuit of knowledge. Purda had invested far too much in implementing that formula to abandon it lightly in favour of any other, let alone that of a mere mechanic like Henry Ford. He had read all his life, almost without pause, for fifteen hours a day. There was virtually no philosopher or theologian whose ideas he could not summarise either in a biting phrase or in a long, long paragraph, and whom he could not link in an ingenious way with his own ideas; he was master of the art of juggling erudite references to a dozen different subjects. So when Sumdy read out the Gospel of Henry Ford, Purda interrupted her repeatedly. The mention of Nonos led him into a long digression on the translation of Egyptian hieroglyphics. The difficulties of the Model T set him off on a discussion of the virtues of the different sorts of alloys suited to the internal combustion engine. The handwriting of the gospel suggested asides about ancient Hebrew calligraphy and the development of the typefaces used to print the Bible. Henry Ford's panoramic view from his penthouse reminded Purda that the heavens looked different from Paradise, which led him to attack the errors into which astronomers from Ptolemy to Hoyle had fallen. He speculated on whether the gospel could be set to music, and played some notes on his piano. Did he always digress in this way, Sumdy wondered: did he think of discussion as a battle to be won by drawing the enemy off his own ground? It is true he had always regarded life as a battlefield and now Paradise seemed one too. Was he trying to dazzle Sumdy by showing that he was a Renaissance man? But the Renaissance man is not a satisfactory model in Paradise, nor was he the ideal of perfection into which many scholars expected to mature. Total knowledge was only a half of what Renaissance men attained. The price they paid was an insatiable need to be always best in what they did, to be applauded and appreciated at all times, by those who had not reached their eminence. In the mists of Paradise it was futile to depend on the admiration of others, for it was too hard to know what they thought; there was much less mutual admiration floating around in Paradise than there was on earth.

The truth was that Purda had already, quite recently, given his allegiance to another sort of gospel, for gospels abounded in Paradise; there was no need to invent new ones; solid antique ones, usually better made, were more interesting, more subtle. There is a strong temptation for learned professors to transform themselves into hunters for antiques. Purda had seen that his formula for perfection had gone slightly wrong somewhere; it clearly needed amendment; he did not know the right dose to take. His fame as a psychologist on earth came from very spectacular experiments, designed to discover why some people are more intelligent than others. These experiments had, of course, not quite succeeded. He arrived in Paradise saying, as they all did, that a scholar needed at least half of eternity, and much more lavish laboratories, to solve so difficult a problem. But now he no longer had to search desperately for original solutions or new ideas, for all ideas, of whatever age, were regarded as being equal. Unlike an immigrant on earth who has to familiarise himself with current trends, and submit to adapting himself to prevailing ideologies, he found that in Paradise all trends are current. It is possible to bump into a murderer one minute and a public hangman the next, each with his own different view of what is going on, and they let each other be. That was not exactly tolerance, but rather the easygoing indifference of souls too sleepy to notice or care. On earth Purda would have tried to think of something no one had ever thought of before. In Paradise it was easier to shop around the debris of the past, and that is how he became a believer in the gospel of the Nose.

This was an example of one of the most disconcerting features of Paradise, which is full not only of unused modern inventions, but also of all the discarded old ideas: every belief man has ever had lives on there for ever. It is possible to modernise oneself in one's ideas, but also to do the opposite, because the souls who hold outdated and bizarre doctrines are frequently not bizarre at all to look at and can be very attractive if one succeeds in getting to know them. One can find new reasons for believing in discredited theories. Purda may have become interested in the nose because he wished to be more friendly with the elephant-headed Ganesa, whose splendid trunk, the most versatile of all noses, increasingly fascinated him; or because he made the acquaintance of a charming if eccentric Berlin physician, Dr Wilhelm Fleiss, whose book, *The Relation between the Nose and the Female Sexual Organs* (1897), had claimed that the origin of most mental troubles was to be traced to the nose, and that whatever remaining difficulties there might be to life could be remedied by understanding the male menstrual cycle of twenty-three days, hitherto unnoticed. Freud had apparently called Fleiss (his best friend) the Kepler of Biology; few agreed; but Purda thought it was perhaps only an accident that Freud became famous while Fleiss was forgotten. Purda may have been won over because he then came across no less a person than Professor John Noland Mackenzie, of Johns Hopkins University, sometime president of the American

114

Laryngological Association – could anyone be more respectable? – who had come to the same conclusions as Fleiss. Purda was not a silly man: why then did he suddenly become a believer of a silly doctrine? It was not as silly as it sounded; it had some genuinely appealing insights embedded in it; it was no sillier than the many thousands of other apparently silly theories in which over the course of history sensible people had believed. The only disconcerting result is that the ideological divisions into which mankind breaks itself up are multiplied many times in a place where ideas never die. This means that souls are even more isolated from each other; they have so many more choices, they can endlessly refine the nuances which separate them from everyone else.

Or maybe it was ambition that led Purda to believe in the nose; perhaps he was hoping to become a guru in the university, or an adviser to the archangels, an official pundit under whose influence smelling lessons would become compulsory for all souls, or under whose reign of terror parents would be given a new fear to worry about: Did their odour suit their child's? Conceivably Purda experienced a yearning for a little flippancy, his old sandpaper wit, that was usually so grating and so smooth, might have been reviving. But deep down there must have been the strain of being in Paradise, which was unquestionably proving too much for him. There was no general panacea to greet immigrants, no universal explanation or guidance that any soul had yet found, which is why souls spent so much time sleeping, it was the only panacea they could recognize. In recent times, every new resident in Paradise arrived hungry for a panacea, and it could be a bitter disappointment not to find one waiting, or at least nothing more exciting than sleep. Purda found consolation in the theory of the nose.

Even if he had not, he could spot that Henry Ford's

alternative was too horrific, for it revived the fear that he shared with all immigrants, of being lost in chaos. Henry Ford's vision that Paradise was chaos sounded terrible to Purda. That gospel, he finally exclaimed, needed to be torn up. It was dangerous. He was a tolerant man, but he could not tolerate chaos. There was enough of that on earth. Paradise had to be an escape from it. Much as he desired to acquire new pupils, he insisted that if Sumdy and Jolly wanted him for their professor, she would have to throw away the Gospel of Henry Ford; she could not be loyal to both. The principle, love me, love my dog, applied also to the realms of high intellect.

Purda, like every new arrival, wanted truth to be at last simple, to have a clear shape; he yearned for certainty about what his right course of action should be; to him the fluid uncertainties of Paradise could only appear as a dangerous quagmire. He had always worn spectacles, to make the world appear clearer, better defined, more stable, but now no spectacles, and indeed no amount of determination, could achieve that effect for him. Sumdy noticed that he had not expressed much interest in her personally; he was honest enough not to pretend to be interested. She did not understand how that absence of curiosity fitted in with his craving for knowledge, unless his idea of knowledge was no more than a blanket to put out the fires of doubt that terrorised him. She was not convinced by his rough dismissal of Henry Ford: most new students, also, now no longer believed their professors. She decided therefore not to decide about him; she would keep him in suspense. Telling him that she would write to him when she had counted up her marks, she went off to dinner.

She had no idea how much more touchy a bare soul becomes in Paradise, which is another reason why they keep out of each other's way; she never imagined that this conversation should have plunged Purda into a new sense of humiliation, and that she should have confirmed herself as a candidate for burning at the stake.

Nor did dinner at the Sacred High Table appear to be a dangerous activity. Here the professors, awakened from their slumber, seemed concerned only to exhibit their own merits. Dinner, for many of them, was their central preoccupation, where they showed how they could illuminate those who observed them; they talked, and they behaved, in a way ordinary folk could not; and though many of them were hard of hearing, they never allowed it to be seen that they had difficulty in understanding each other. Ganesa seemed to have invited Sumdy to witness how wonderful their powers of intellect were, and to sample the variety of talent on which she could draw in her search.

But Sumdy did not find it easy to get them to speak to her, let alone to answer her. Each seemed to be playing a game of his own. Some, she thought, behaved like birdwatchers, with an astonishing capacity for keeping silent, while appearing to be in a state of deep reflection, pregnant with emotion, but never judging the moment opportune, nor their thought quite ready for publication. They gave the impression of wanting to hear what others said first, and then take time to consider the implications of what they heard, if they did hear. They were never so foolish as to say anything that could possibly be thought foolish. When Sumdy asked them her questions about happiness and souls and chaos, she got no reply. Perhaps, for them, to be inexplicable was one way of being charming, leaving everything to the imagination. At any rate, everyone seemed to stand in awe of the birdwatchers, but what these thought or felt Sumdy could not fathom. But there was one among them to whom Sumdy instantly took a liking, she did not know why, a soul with an ancient Chinese face that was somehow as young as a girl's. They exchanged only glances.

Playing quite another sport, Sumdy puzzled over the professors who were like marathon runners, with a different kind of stamina. Their taste was for a relentless, steady, predictable jog of words. Firmly resisting all temptation to try any dangerous tricks, any conversational sprinting, any intellectual pole vaulting, each one regurgitated his own expertise over and over again; their ears were cocked, waiting for any subject remotely related to their speciality to be mentioned, so that they could burst into talk again; when it came to repeating themselves, they were tireless. But all topics that might be too personal they shunned: to intrude into the privacy of others broke their golden rule that intimate emotions must be excluded from civilised conversation; their preference was for those inoffensive subjects with which they had tried to kill time on earth, and meant to go on trying in Paradise, complaining about their colleagues' inadequacies and the difficulties of daily existence. To Sumdy, they appeared not quite sure whether they were alive or dead. And after Sumdy had questioned them about what interested her, she was not sure whether they had given an opinion or not: she could not remember what they said.

It was a tiny minority of boxers who made the Sacred High Table into a spectator sport, giving it the excitement of an event which could be experienced nowhere else. Among the heavyweight champion talkers of the university, Sumdy quickly saw that the up-and-coming one was a plump and rotund soul called Mausole; she guessed he was Latin American, but she was not sure, she never found out where he came from. He was very definitely awake. He was one of those who had never slept, whom even Paradise could not put to sleep, who had come with the firm intention of making his voice heard, the archetype of the modern immigrant, the negation of all scholarly reserve, whose booming voice it was impossible not to hear. If he had not been human, he would have been called a perfect filing system, in perfect working order. For every word uttered in his presence he could instantly turn up at least one joke, one historical anecdote, one reference to a great author, and a reflection on the implications for liberty or civilisation. It was impossible to catch him out without an opinion, on any subject, even if, very occasionally, he played for time by saying that a question was very interesting, important, complex, until he found a suitable rejoinder. Then he declaimed it in a voice which contained a whole symphony orchestra within it: drumbeats of anger, trumpet blasts of derisive laughter, teasing flute-like understatements, moans, groans and the barely audible whisper of secrets imparted in the strictest confidence. He seemed to be very much at home in Paradise, having brought with him his own standards, his own values, ready to judge it on its merits as he saw them. He had never been able to forget the habits he had learned from his schoolteachers: he gave marks, all the time, to every person, event or point of view that was mentioned; he poured out anecdotes to show how original, reliable, vulgar, difficult, solid, nice a person was, and there always had to be a winner; in referring to a place, he could not refrain from awarding points to every one of its hotels, monuments and streets, judging how difficult every art gallery was to visit, and how excellent, good or mediocre each painting in it was; there was always a prize when the right score was reached. However, he did not aim to reduce his audience to total silence, seldom administering a final knock-out; he knew how to give whoever did listen to him the impression that they were almost as quick-witted as he, and he did indeed sometimes stimulate them to repartee of a kind they rarely exhibited elsewhere. That was one reason why his opinions were coming to be so revered and his way of uttering opinions copied, the ultimate sign of influence. He delighted Sumdy, because he appeared willing to talk about any subject in heaven or earth. He had something to say about guardian angels, even if it was only for their singing that he gave them high marks, but he did promise Sumdy an introduction to a former pupil whose family had for many centuries made harps for them. He had (of course) met Henry Ford personally, whose ignorance in matters of food and wine he deplored but about whose collection of violins he was quite enthusiastic. A team of biblical scholars, of the first, or at least upper second rank, would be put to work on the Ford Gospel straight away, he promised. Of course Jolly would also be welcome as a student at the university, of course they welcomed animals, Jolly would get on very well with Pangor Ban, about whom the professor of theology, an Irish monk (and almost a first class man), had written the immortal poem:

> *I and Pangor Ban my cat*
> *It's a jolly game we're at . . .*

And Sumdy herself must stay as long as she liked: it was absurd that she should be travelling without any proper arrangements being made in advance for her; he would see to it personally.

How wonderful, Sumdy thought, at last to come across a soul that radiated so much good will and energy and wit. At last she could hope to find the road she was looking for. It had taken a long time.

Jolly raised his tail just a little, and looked up at her with pleading eyes. She stroked him. She was confident. What a wonderful boon education was, she thought. And at last every creature could benefit from it.

Jolly duly met the cat, and made no protest at the implication that dogs and cats were equal. Sumdy sent a photo home of him and the cat, with Forgetmenot's empty jam jar between them, both staring intently at it. On the back she wrote: "It is very moving the way Jolly is upset about not being able to find Forgetmenot. But what would happen, could the universe work, if animals stopped treating each other as enemies?"

CHAPTER FIVE

In the universities of Paradise, those who talk but hardly ever listen, and those who listen but hardly ever talk, have in common the desire to be noticed and appreciated, so strongly that when anyone is noticed, all ears instantly prick up. Why had Sumdy been chosen by Mausole for such special favours? Was it because she was new? But new visitors came all the time. Because she was good looking? Mausole did not care about that. Because she would soon be returning to earth? Obviously, thought the cunning ones, Mausole had plans to send a message back to his old worldly haunts, to extend his domain to both hemispheres, to get the living to listen to him, since the dead watched him with too much envy and too much pity. It was so rare to be noticed, that those who were immediately appeared to grow larger heads, like a cat raising its fur to look more formidable. Part of Mausole's strength was that he played dangerously with himself and his favourites.

Sumdy did not suspect anything more than the twittering of academic bickering when the hitherto silent, girl-like Chinese face smiled at her and drew her into a corner. She was Pan Chao, a poet as well as a scholar. Mausole ranked her as a seventh-rate poet, and told her so. She was rumoured, without much evidence, to have feminist inclinations, and Mausole gave very few women, let alone feminists, high marks for anything. But Sumdy, by that magic interaction that leads two people to imagine they have something in common, brought Pan Chao out of the silence with which she had for so long been content to confront her colleagues.

Pan Chao said to Sumdy: "I like the look of surprise in your eye. I like it that for you surprise is married with pleasure, surprise of any sort is sweet. I like it that you are not even dismayed that Paradise invites its newcomers to shed tears. Poor Professor Mausole, how sad to be his favourite. How helpless he must feel that he cannot fulfil any of the promises he made to you. He has no power to send souls here or there. Everyone loves to see him pretend that he can, but it is only pretend. No soul can boss another soul."

Sumdy said to Pan Chao: Why had Mausole put on such a show?

He was just clever enough, Pan Chao replied, to realise that he was not as clever as he made himself out to be, but not clever enough to know what to do about it. On earth, Mausole had been able to busy himself collecting honours to distract himself from the worry that he was no genius, that the books he wrote were boring – he knew they were – and that no useful purpose had been served by his criticism of the great masters of literature: he had only hashed them up to make bland and oily rissoles. All his brilliant talk was froth to give him the temporary illusion that he was taller than he really was, not even an illusion, for he was never taken in by it. It was only the appearance of success that he had ever thought it worth aiming for, for he had had no hope of attaining the ideal glory he considered outside his grasp. In his affections on earth, it had not even been the appearance of a person that

123

had attracted him, but his or her garments; love, for him, had never been more than a form of fetishism; he had never married; he had never known what happiness meant; he had been able to mesmerise only the initiated, those prepared to play the same game as himself. And now in Paradise all his bonhomie was a pure drama of self-torture, for all hope had vanished from him, he was no longer acting even to please himself; he was only repeating himself, parodying his earthly self, because he did not know what else to do. These professors did not know, when they woke up, what to do with themselves. There was no one to tell them how to be a genius. Mausole's effort to make Paradise as like earth as possible was a charade. In Paradise, one can no longer be judged, that is the great liberation that it represents. One can assume any title, honour or decoration one pleases, and none counts for anything, it is mere decoration, like a bow in the hair. Mausole's attempts to keep people in their place was no more than a game he played with himself.

Sumdy liked Pan Chao and her gentle and seductive way of speaking, but was also impressed by Mausole's ebullience. She did not know whom to believe. The last thing she wanted was to be dragged into an academic quarrel, into those so-carefully woven spiders' webs from which there is no escape.

"If you do hear anything in Paradise," Mausole said to Sumdy, "you must never trust your ears, you have to be quite certain you are not imagining it all." And in a very loud voice, he listed Pan Chao's misdeeds, like a court clerk reading a criminal indictment. Her students had lodged a formal complaint of dereliction of duty against her, which had never happened in the whole history of Paradise. She had neglected them, failed to appear at lectures she promised to give, refused to answer letters, never returned the books she borrowed from the library. The university was girding itself to expel her, which it had never done in the whole of its history either. Only a few friends defended her, claiming that she was in fact a genius, and that a few lines from her were worth more than all the heavy tomes of her critics put together.

Then Pan Chao on her side launched into her own indictment, and it was against the whole university. She said that she had never before made a criticism of anybody, but she had come to realise that this university, which had been her home for so many centuries, had become like a herd of husbands (or spouses), each trapped in a marriage that had gone wrong. The professors were in love with ideal goddesses, or gods, or genius, or Science, or Omniscience. They could never have enough; they always needed more to reach satiety. The awfulness of Paradise was that they would never know as much as they wanted to know. It might be possible to settle for second best on earth, but in Paradise it was a humiliating disappointment, to have to be content with something so mundane as mere expertise in one small branch of knowledge. They could fool themselves that they were masters of a speciality, but it only made them intolerably, obstinately attached to their own opinions. Time and time again, that killed their conversation. In days long past, said Pan Chao, a person could reasonably hope to know more or less what was known, so to be a learned person, to be a wise person and to be a happy person all meant the same thing; and since only a few people were learned and the rest were illiterate peasants, to possess knowledge was to enjoy something that everybody envied. But recently knowledge had become a fattening, over-rich food. To love it came to mean something quite different. For now the more knowledgeable you became, the more you saw your own ignorance. The more learned people there were, the more books you had to read to keep up with what was known, and the less time you had to think for yourself. Now, therefore, learned persons could seldom be wise also. The scholar had become a greyhound on a track chasing after a bait he or she could never catch; he, or she, always raced hopelessly against time; he, or she, could never cram enough into a single head, nor shovel it out fast enough, as it went stale or out of date. There was less agreement than ever, not just as to what the truth or knowledge were, but how even to approach anywhere near them. To remain sane, scholars had to become willing prisoners in a tiny cell, because here at least they could lay down the law about some tiny fragment of truth, like the habits of the earwig or the foreign policy of mediaeval Zanzibar. A few ambitious ones might grow dissatisfied with being master, or mistress, of only a small domain, and they might build up, on the basis of what little they knew, grand theories which they pretended were applicable to other domains; and their imperialism kept the academic world simmering in permanent nervous conflict. The less ambitious ones survived in this turmoil because they treated scholarship as a pastime like fox-hunting, a way of killing time and minor so-called pests, taking care not to ask awkward questions, feeding morsels of compliments to each other for mutual protection. They idealised into a hero the humble perpetual student, devoted to the pure joy of discovery, who, however, knew that the only safe way to keep the esteem of colleagues was to be no more than a glorified clerk, classifying information in different ways, sticking new labels on old ideas, and above all copying. Most scholars were copyists, with or without quotation marks. A quotation showed erudition, respect for authority, talent for ornamentation; it opened up opportunities for comment, using yet other quotations for better effect. To find an old document that no human had set eyes on since it was first written was thus raised

126

into the greatest of all triumphs, to copy it was hailed as proof of original research. By these methods universities escaped having to put government warnings over their gates: Study can damage your health.

Why, asked Sumdy, were the professors so reluctant to answer the questions she had come to have answered, to interest themselves in what she cared about; why was conversation always in some kind of code, a ritual to avoid an issue? Pan Chao replied: Because Paradise did not automatically give souls either courage, or imagination, or sympathy. That is why animals had been so slow to accept the invitation to enrol in the university: they could sense that the bird-watchers, for example, were dominated by the fear of making themselves ridiculous, which was something animals never worried about; they could see that the marathon runners had turned conversation from a game into a routine and so had nothing to teach them about play, which was their special joy; while the boxers made it clear that they had not discovered the precious secret that the animals were seeking, which was how to escape from their most serious limitation, that each species could communicate only with its own species, for professors suffered from the very same trouble.

Mausole was not one to argue; he was skilful at winning his scholarly disputes by the most traditional of all tactics, a special form of intimidation which involved showing that he had the esteem of eminent figures, however irrelevant their eminence was to the dispute. To flatter the president of his university, he had gathered an apparently devoted following of elephants around him, which enabled him to hold court in an undoubtedly impressive way. He took Sumdy to see them. They were no ordinary elephants; he was convinced that if he could charm what he called the important elephants, all the rest, and indeed all animals, would follow them. That was always his method. Here was the elephant who in the year of the birth of the Prophet Muhammad had single handed, so to speak, saved Mecca from the attacking armies of the Negus of Ethiopia. Here was one who had fought Kublai Khan, and been among the first to capture Delhi in 1299. Here was Surus (he supposedly came from Syria), the famous elephant who had carried Hannibal from Spain to the Alps, to wage the first anti-imperialist war in history, against the Romans. All these elephants wore many medals round their necks, and seemed to listen politely – in the way that statesmen listen to speeches in foreign languages – to the flattery of Mausole, and they eyed with awe the medals he wore round his neck. Pan Chao whispered that it was disgusting that military elephants should be honoured in a university devoted to the arts of peace; why had they not invited much more interesting elephants, who had achieved something artistic, like those who had built Tamerlane's beautiful and immense mosque at Samarkand: they were not just the bulldozers and cranes of their day, but true creators.

If Pan Chao had been a twentieth-century revolutionary, her protest would not have been more than one further incident that showed the discomfort of the new immigrants. But she was a very different sort of soul, who had come to Paradise almost two thousand years before, and had held her tongue for all that time. That she should suddenly speak out now, when she had a reputation as a true believer in keeping everything as it was and always had been (though no reputation is ever justified) suggested that something was churning very deep down in the bowels of Paradise, and that for some, at any rate, the mists were if not dissipating themselves, at least taking on a meaning. It was assumed that the old Chinese professors who had been among the earliest residents, would be irrevocably attached to the tradition they used to call "filling the earth with peaches and plums", which meant sending out well-taught pupils reared to respect their masters and to repeat after them: All occupations are lowly, only the study of books is supreme. The university had many such professors who on earth had achieved just that, to the envy and wonder of their western colleagues. So it was significant that such a normally subdued scholar as Pan Chao should suddenly appear in the guise of a dissenter, and that she should proclaim the opinion that the holy relationship of master and student, raised to its highest expression – at least in theory – in Imperial China, was, in Paradise, flawed, doomed, a menace. The very idea of a university, as monks and cranks and kings had conceived it, was impossible in Paradise, and a university existed there only as a harmless, sleepy, ineffectual parody. It was a terrible revelation, to realise one was living not in a truer world, but in a parody of one. Pan Chao had an insight of something which should have been obvious long ago, that souls could not be taught in Paradise. They were too independent by nature; they were not receptacles waiting to have yet more information slotted into them; rather each, like a caterpillar, constructed its own cocoon around itself, but each in its own irregular and peculiar style.

Her colleagues were puzzled that it should be Pan Chao who should abruptly have this flash of understanding. They tried to find explanations of why her ancestral assumptions should melt away. They made guesses about why she started thinking honestly about the meek language she had been in the habit of using for so long. Pan Chao was probably the first person ever to write a book on paper, whose invention was announced by the eunuch Tshai Lun in AD 105, just as she was completing the chronicles of the Han Dynasty, which she modestly allowed to be published under her brother's name, though she had done a good half of the work. She was one of the first women ever to publish a treatise on how women should behave, a treatise inspired by her own married life, filled with the fear of disgracing her parents and her husband, fear of not fulfilling her wifely duties properly, "bitter apprehension" that her sons would bring disgrace on her in turn. She had good cause to be tired of fear. She had urged her daughters and women in general to obey their husbands, never to complain, and to wash their hair frequently, as frequently at least as government officials who were given a holiday every fifth day to enable them to wash their hair. But now reading that book, which begins by saying "I the writer am a lowly person with but a monkey's wit," she realised that she, who had been poet laureate to the Emperor, and whom hundreds of generations had honoured as one of the greatest of writers, did not honestly think that she was a monkey, nor, as she also called herself, a worm; nor that she had given good advice when she told women, "Do not think of opposing. Do not struggle to divide the crooked from the straight." That was precisely what she wanted to do now. And out of the mist she thought she heard wailing from the shamanesses who had been prophets in old China and Japan before women had fallen subject to men, a wailing of joy, encouraging her to speak out, to silence the condescensions of Mausole and his likes, to question the very notion that in Paradise there could be souls condemned to be subordinates, or even modest pupils, than whom everyone knew better. In Pan Chao's great book, the scholars say, what she wrote was at times so complicated that only those whom she had personally instructed could understand it. She would no longer pretend that she could wholly understand what her own book said, for poetry is a well that must yield a different taste to each, according to

130

his thirst; she would no longer pretend that she knew the answers, crystal clear, for in Paradise there are no answers.

It might once have been true that nothing ever changed in Paradise, and that souls went on for all eternity exactly as they had always been. There are many old theologians who think it cannot be otherwise, influenced no doubt by their being unable to imagine themselves as anything but old theologians, fearing change, which is another name for fearing death. And certainly Sumdy could not quite understand how change takes place in Paradise. Pan Chao had metamorphosed from a humble, quiet soul into a bold and restless one. Humans have much difficulty in believing in sudden change, because on earth their efforts are absorbed in trying to slow time down: important changes, they insist, are really slow revolutions, barely perceptible, usually invisible, not something to be met in the daily lives of ordinary people. Indeed for two millennia Pan Chao's soul had been held firmly together by her memories. A soul of course has no shape, but if it did, it would look like an egg. A soul's yolk is surrounded by its memories, more or less soggy, more or less hardboiled, and the shell is the hypocritical facade that every soul presents to the world, easily painted, easily cracked, impossible to guess what is inside. Since most souls are terrified of breaking, of falling apart, of being unable to recognise themselves in a mirror, jabbering on about the need to preserve their identity, they mainly sit tight in their shells. But a shell can break. How? By accident. Accidents happen more easily in Paradise. The freer a place is, the more accidents there are. Pan Chao was the victim, or victor, of an accident. It needs only a small crack, a minute mutation, inexplicable, unpredictable, to bring about a change. Then the memory that holds the soul together can harden or soften; if it gets very hard, it may never budge again, or it may split. Careful and moderate souls try never to

131

change in Paradise, but they cannot be sure of succeeding. A yolk is after all made to metamorphose. It can eat up the memories around it until nothing is left of them, at least not in the form they once had. But of course accidents do not happen when one wants them to. Burning a soul at the stake is an alternative way of making an accident happen.

For that, however, a soul needs another soul willing to act as the executioner. Sumdy was still hankering to be advised on the merits of the Gospel of Henry Ford, and Pan Chao, all smiles, was refusing to give an opinion, even one of her incomprehensible, oracular ones. Presumably she was implying that each must make up his own mind; and that professors do not exist to give answers. Sumdy could not believe that the roads to happiness were not clearly mapped out, somewhere in so erudite a place as this university; amid all these professors struggling with themselves, trying to adapt to the odd ways of Paradise, she must surely be able to find one who could at least set her in the right direction. But there was no map, there were no signposts, there was no expert in happiness; no university teaches that subject.

So it was by accident that she stumbled on a solution, the accident being Professor A. A. Smirnoff. A few readers may perhaps still remember this name: those who happen to know Russian, and happen to be interested in the organisation of the Aztec armies, may recall his giant book on the subject; those who do not may have come across him in some other capacity, for he was a sociable person and a constant traveller. There is no reason to think that he was descended from the vodka manufacturer, but he liked to say he was, and used to do all he could to prove it, by showing that he could drink any quantity of that liquor with impunity. However, only those who knew him more than superficially were aware that vodka was more than a joke for him, it was his magic potion into the past. He was, above all else, a nostalgic man. He abhorred modernity: stupid, ugly, boring, everything new he damned – buildings, music, fashions – without a hearing, without hesitation, instinctively. How could one who prided himself on being a good teacher so openly express his contempt for the ideas of the young? Dullards, conformists, humourless twits, he screamed at them. Were the young any better when he was young? Arkady Arkadevich (he liked to be friendly with his students, and insisted they should address him without formality) said that was irrelevant. The nostalgia addict is not concerned to explain the past, but to transform it. As actually experienced, the past is a muddle of ignorance and uncertainty. Nostalgia is a way to purge it of the pain it contains, to see it in a different light, to improve it and so to improve one's own image of oneself. The trouble is that nostalgia does not work in Paradise. It is (ironically) a modern invention, still unknown in the eighteenth century, when the word meant homesickness, particularly among soldiers, and it was believed to be a kind of nervous disease. Then it was discovered that if carefully cultivated and allowed to ferment, it could bring about a pleasing haze of fellow feeling, and so it came to be valued as a way of bringing together people of the same generation who until middle age never knew that they had ever had anything in common. The depressed found that it could produce hallucinations about their adolescence, which they were able to remember in warm and rosy colours. It enabled the desperate to shut out despair, and the timid to eliminate all thought of the future. Nostalgia was transformed from a disease into a pleasure.

But in Paradise the past is alive and well all around one; it is much harder to fool oneself about it. Nostalgia's spell does not last, and one's imagination needs to work in a new way.

Arkady Arkadevich had been what scholars call "a mine of information". In Paradise, however, his relentless scavenging of facts ceased to have a purpose, since anyone could, by taking a short walk, visit the Aztecs. Immediately on his arrival therefore, he had a serious problem. Even as a mature and respected adult, he had never enjoyed a sense of security except in memories of the little town of Viatka, hidden in the forests, where he had spent his childhood, one place that seemed to stand for ever still in his memory. When he got to Paradise, he went to see its copy of Viatka, and it did not seem authentic or pleasing. The reason was that he loved his memories; his purpose had been to escape from life and to avoid having to think about himself as he was. He did not know how to enjoy being himself. Introspection terrified him, to such an extent that anyone who engaged in it roused him to fury, as the most dangerous subverter of the peace of mankind. To discover yet more weaknesses in himself than he already knew about was pure self-torture; to search for explanations of those weaknesses only made matters worse: social scientists were, to him, representatives of the devil.

Someone who did not understand the workings of Paradise might assume that a scholar like Arkady Arkadevich had precisely the tastes that Paradise could satisfy. On earth, he had loved history passionately. He had devoted himself to a safely extinct civilisation. Paradise had as one of its major peculiarities that it allowed immigrants to go and live in their preferred century and their preferred country. But the whole purpose of Arkady's love of history had been to escape his surroundings, and to live in an imaginary world of which he was master. He liked to hide his head in old documents and in archives, which he called "the secure refuge from fear", to imitate the dead, to avoid his own identity – how he hated the word. So the last thing he wanted was to go and live among the Aztecs in Paradise, who could contradict him, who might not appreciate his mimicry of what he guessed had been their peculiar accent and gait, mimicry on which he had for years dined out so successfully; nor would the Aztec slaves find amusing his romantic vision of them, his idealisation of their century of drunkenness, which he found so congenial, boasting that theirs was the first nation to decimate itself by alcohol, a tragedy which they preferred to forget. Arkady's problem – which was the problem of all nostalgics – was that he could not just continue in his habitual ways; he needed to learn to create a new kind of imaginary world. That was not easy for one who loved routine, whose first preoccupation in every city he visited had always been to establish a safe, regular round of duties, to take the same routes always, in the way that rabbits regularly leave their droppings in the same place. It was not easy either for one who, for all his hatred of modernity, suffered severely from the modern disease of loneliness. He had a hole in his soul; he had tried to plug it with all the facts his learning could accumulate, but in vain. Coming to Paradise had made no difference, for the impression that no one is listening grows very strong. He knew a lot about the great men of the past, but he meant nothing to them.

A. A. Smirnoff set up in Paradise as an organiser of Aztec-style human sacrifices, a kind of specialist funeral parlour, which proved very successful. He had his office in the university, because that was where most of his clients came from, interested as they were by public executions, for the main function of many of their lives had been the shooting down of falsehood. Arkady frequently said that professors are particularly qualified to be executioners, in the sense that, on regular occasions, they are executioners of sorts, every examination being an execution for those who fail it, and who leave it for ever mutilated. And he wanted to find an occupation that had no trace of modernity in it, above all without any nonsense about being constructive, or positive; he did not want anything to happen in Paradise, he looked forward to no pleasure in it, because he could not possibly enjoy the place or the time of his own existence, anywhere. He had chosen to become an Aztec specialist with good reason. The gloomiest of all civilisations appealed to him, ruled over as it was, for him at any rate, by the Four Hundred Rabbits, who were the gods of drunkenness, a sad repressed drunkenness, punished in vain on the first offence by the public shaving of the head and on relapse by strangulation, a drunkenness that had no humour in it; even children's games among the Aztecs were cruel and violent, pillow fighting being their highest idea of mild amusement; even the adults' favourite ball game, in which the ball could be touched only with the hips and the knees, was so dangerous that many died in it, while the survivors regularly had incisions made in their buttocks to let out the blood from their bruises; gambling, their supreme passion, played with dice made of beans, was the only relief from their terrifying religion, which preached that every day there was no certainty that the sun would rise next morning, and that only a bloody sacrifice could persuade it to continue to shine. The Aztecs lived to supply "the precious water" – chalchivatl, which was human blood – for the gods. Arkady chose to live from day to day in the same way, with no hope, fighting his own gloom with his own kinds of precious waters, his vodka, his Aztec archives, and not least his incessant talk.

Being a scholar is not only a matter of accumulating learning, it is also a social activity, it gives one the right to participate in an endless series of international jamborees, at which one can meet other scholars who have the same obsessions as oneself. That had always mattered a lot to Arkady. So his complaints that the world was going to the dogs were redoubled when he reached Paradise, for there he found it very much harder to get people even to pretend to listen to him. Arkady used to talk to anyone he met, in a bar, on a train, in a shop queue, in a library, anyone who would notice him. Women were important to him because they often seemed gratified that merely by listening to him they could have an instant if temporary healing effect on him; he convinced them that he would be even more miserable without them, they often hesitated to desert him even when his monologues grew tedious. But in Paradise women students are not automatically flattered by the attentions of male professors. For all Arkady Arkadevich had to offer was his memories, his anecdotes. He had a prodigious collection of them; he could resurrect every minute detail of his own life too, and of that of everyone he had met, the exact shape of the shoes and hat, for example, that his grandmother was wearing when she came to the funeral of his uncle, the colonel with the finger missing, who had once had tea with the Tsar's former governess; he liked to pass on this information; he liked to repeat verbatim the speeches of both prosecution and defence counsel at scandalous trials he had attended; he treasured his hoard of anecdotes, but he did not know what else to do with it except to let them pour out, like a disc jockey who must keep talking at all costs, and who did so irrespective of how his audience was reacting. Arkady Arkadevich talked to relieve himself, not to get a response. In this it pleased him to think that he resembled the Aztecs, who were famous for their love of talk, and for the long and turgid speeches they made at the slightest provocation, without gestures, without looking at those they spoke to, their eyes always lowered, as though vomiting something uncontrollable, which in their case was a moralistic, philosophical banality. They admired those who

137

said the obvious at great length. But they were not prepared to talk to a blank wall, and neither was Arkady.

One of the first decisions he had to make was what kind of circle of friends, or what he called friends, he should try to build around him, to provide him with an audience. He did not see that friends are not made in Paradise as they can be on earth. His idea of friendship was inherited from his childhood; his ideal was to be a kind of teenage gang leader, not too proud to share with his admirers his tales of disaster as a woman chaser, but able to charm them, like a colourful dragoman to forbidden pleasures, with guidance as to what they ought to despise and what to value, how they ought to discriminate between the sordid, the disreputable, the hopeless and the macabre. When Arkady was a professor on earth, with his select band of pupils, they valued his judgements because they were electrified by his constantly changing infatuations and indignations; when they talked and drank together long into the night, they were convinced that they were mastering the world with their epigrams. But when Arkady sought out these old pupils in Paradise, he was dismayed to find them distinctly cool about resuming relations with him. Mere comradeship in the battle against boredom is not enough to create bonds between souls in Paradise. It was the same with the several dozen women to whom Arkady had proposed marriage in the course of his life, usually after only a brief acquaintance. There must have been at least a thousand women also to whom he had poured out his heart, and who had then acted like dismissed publicity agents, telling all those who imagined themselves to be his friends what he had said about them in his bouts of drunkenness and his fits of rage. For him, it had never seemed necessary to like one's friends, who could quite easily be turned into enemies. Far from fearing, as Purda did, that he was surrounded by enemies, Arkady needed enemies. He was attracted by the Aztecs not least because they had built a whole civilisation on the creed that they needed enemies, in order to sacrifice them to their gods. Their religion required them to be always at war, and when they could not find enemies and were not at war, they had to invent their version of a cold war, called the war of flowers, which allowed them to capture victims for sacrifice all the same. For them, friends and enemies were interchangeable. Aztec warriors called their captives their beloved sons until the moment of sacrifice.

"He is my friend and I despise him." There was no contradiction for Arkady when he said that. There was nothing surprising in his having spent long hours on earth in the company of a female professor, with whom he appeared to be friends, until she died, and he wrote a resentful attack on her, accusing her of being a feeble and trivial scholar, with no real talent for the subject she was supposed to be an expert in, lacking in judgement and burdened with silly anxieties. His version of the academic stab-in-the-back echoed the double standard of cruelty that the Aztecs held, who were horrified by Spanish methods of torture, but could see nothing wrong in their own practices. Arkady had not waited for his friends to be safely dead before wielding his knife and spitting his scorn into the wounds he made. His smiles and his insults alternated. He wanted to matter in people's lives, in one way or another. And anybody who did notice him and drink with him and help bring him solace was assured of gratitude so long as he continued. He wrote testimonials for his pupils which were almost poems of passion, overflowing with lyrical and unrestrained praise, but the phrase "the best pupil I have ever had" was used in every one of them.

139

In Paradise, souls did not move about in gangs, even if they occasionally met to sing together. The only gang Arkady Arkadevich was able to find was that of the Seven Sages of the Bamboo Grove, philosophers much esteemed in third century China. Hsi K'ang, the most famous of them, had been executed at the age of thirty-nine on the ground that he had preached that the ideal man was the sage who always held a bottle of wine in his hand and seemed permanently drunk, the ideal disciple was not a holy man but a lazy disorganised official, who worshipped the bottle, and perhaps also wit and art. These sages had met again in Paradise and set up a little principality, known as Tsui-Chih Kuo, which means Land of the Drunk, whose citizens had the title of Chiu-hsien, "Immortals of wine". Arkady was at first attracted by the prospect of being a member of a select and exotic literary group. But they did not suit him as well as he had hoped, for though one of their main activities was to engage in public confession of their sins, with them that was designed to show their indifference to the world, to Paradise, to everything and to everybody. Indifference did not suit Arkady, if it meant that the gang would be indifferent to him. He was not made to be a hermit, even in the company of hermits.

So here he was holding office hours in his funeral parlour, waiting for victims to execute, victims to whom he could be both friend and enemy, and whose sacrifice would be spectacular enough to attract an audience for him. Outside, he had a doorplate, on which were engraved pictures of an eye, a tin can, a bee, a horse, a hole in the ground and a table. This is the Aztec way of writing, "I can be hospitable". When Sumdy arrived, Arkady was talking volubly. But there was no one in the room. Had he learnt to listen to himself? It was Jolly who found the answer. He gave a great yelp of joy and performed his favourite dance, running as fast as he could in small circles, as though chasing his tail. Then Sumdy saw that the room was not empty. In the corner stood the cockroach Forgetmenot, peering cautiously from under a chair, waving its antennae very slowly, up and down, almost as though it was listening to Arkady and nodding. Arkady was lecturing it on the place of cockroaches in the sacrificial rituals of the Aztecs – a subject to which sub-specialists have devoted more study and thought than many laymen may imagine.

This happy reunion was a triumph for Jolly, who had finally smelt Forgetmenot out. Forgetmenot, however, did not respond. Jolly might have been upset, had he not noticed in the air more than the usual rancid body odour of the cockroach. From time to time, Forgetmenot had with great deliberation turned its back on Arkady and ejected at him the spray it carried with it to frighten off the hedgehogs, frogs and spiders which were its enemies on earth; it may have discovered a new defence against boredom; there is a limit to the attention span of any cockroach, which spends at least three-quarters of its life at rest. But Forgetmenot had not walked away from the lecture, because it was irresistibly attracted by the stench of alcohol, which the professor exuded even here; cockroaches are very partial to beer, and overwhelmed by vodka. Forgetmenot had become drowsy, almost numb. Sumdy could hardly believe it, but she was thrilled, when she saw Jolly pushing Forgetmenot with his whiskers, very gently, in the direction of the jam jar. Forgetmenot hobbled in like an invalid retiring to bed. Jolly sat by the jar as though on guard. The atmosphere of Paradise seemed capable of giving birth to a new kind of friendship. But did it affect only animals?

Forgetmenot was by no means Arkady's only client. He had quickly found that there was a plentiful supply of souls who could not get rid of their taste for suffering, and who

141

longed to be pilloried or crucified or burned, each for private reasons into which he did not care to enquire. But more interesting were those who felt uncomfortable in Paradise, because they realised that it did not suit them, who not only wanted to move on, but were willing to take some risks to do so. Sumdy herself recognised that the souls she was meeting here were not quite her sort. To Arkady, for example, she was no different from a cockroach, or from any other human, simply an enemy and a useful tool, an ingredient for the ancient Aztec magic recipes for spells and charms, on which he had published a so-called important contribution to knowledge. A public Aztec burning proved to be exactly what Sumdy was looking for. She had not yet met anyone who had conversed with the angels or seen them, and it was becoming clear that she never would reach them if she went on treading the same ground as people like Mausole and Purda; with them, she would be a witness only of a pantomime Paradise, playing a parody of earthly confusions. She could not believe that in Paradise all souls were expected to behave like cocks who had had their heads chopped off and still staggered on as before. Paradise was pedestrian because most of its residents were twitching with the same fear they had felt on earth. That was not the way, she was sure, to discover its charms in their fullness. Sumdy knew she must learn to fly, to walk was not enough; she must throw off the ballast of her past; she must allow her old self to go up in smoke. If she seriously wanted to visit the angels, she must get herself ready; she needed more than directions or a map; she must change herself. She was realising that there were two quite distinct ways of existing in Paradise, keeping oneself firmly on the ground, or reaching for the clouds, where the angels felt at home.

But voluntarily to be set alight . . . She did not think of herself as being brave. Suffering did not appeal to her.

142

Neither was she fond of contemplating horrors or disasters of any kind: her imagination did not work that way. She did not stop to wonder how appalling burning at the stake might be. Brave soldiers do not stop to wonder either when they rush blindly at enemy guns. To be brave, you do not have to be a brave person. Bravery is a matter of focus. Brave soldiers focus with such mad concentration on reaching a hill, or helping a wounded man, or finding food, that they forget about being frightened, because they do not focus on danger. It is not bravery that defeats fear, but curiosity, desire, single-mindedness, which do not notice fear. Sumdy did not worry about burning at the stake, because she was determined to see all there was to see in Paradise, to try out every shape under which a human could fit. To be transformed into thin air, to go up in smoke, aroused only her curiosity.

So Arkady arranged an Aztec burning for her, because to be at once useful and destructive was his pleasure. The Aztec idea of civilisation was that you do your victims a favour by sacrificing them; you do not need to hate them, on the contrary, you treat them with respect, feed them with the best food, clothe them royally, until they positively look forward to their fate, which is to be admitted into the presence of the gods. Sumdy, he said, should come to the university theatre on Saturday night and all would be ready.

The ceremony takes place there, because the theatre is used by the professors as a place where they can talk to each other in an indirect way, pretending they are not who they are, pretending they are not really talking. The burning is preceded by a theatrical ballet or operatic performance, whose style and content varies, though its purpose is always the same. For Sumdy, Arkady put on a play called The Missing Agenda. It superficially gave the impression of being a highbrow play about the difficulty of knowing what a play is about. It had thirty-four scenes without a break, each with a title that had no obvious bearing on what was said. All that was clear was that the actors, who were professors dressed as Aztec priests, danced around a green baize table, making gestures to suggest that they were deep in thought. They may possibly have looked very vaguely like A. A. Smirnoff's idea of Aztec priests, but for the audience they were parodying an Academic Senate, fantasising about the halcyon days when professors could still believe that they determined what the world believed. The benign old man who was the leading character wore the mask of a cuckoo on his head, jumping out of his torpor at unexpected moments, but keeping everyone mystified with a mumbling sound endlessly repeated, to show that he was thinking, but not what he was thinking about. Sumdy listened carefully, and detected three different sounds. Most often, it was a low warble – um, um, um – with varying pauses in between. He uttered it with such deliberation and conviction that the gowned dons were held in rapt attention. Sumdy thought that perhaps these Ums were the Yoga's Om, spoken in an Oxford accent. The cuckoo chairman skilfully kept everyone guessing to the end, as to what precise plot his thinking concealed. Sometimes he raised his warble into a screech, accompanied by a dramatic gesture: cupping his hand over his ear, he gasped: "I can't hear what you're saying." Sometimes the dons got excited and all talked at the same time, dancing in a frenzy of emotional abandon. The cuckoo would then silence them with desperate and pathetic chirps, which sounded like: We must get on with the Agenda. It was only at the very end of the play that it was revealed why they wanted to do that.

For scene after scene the professors danced around,

illustrating the themes of ambivalence, indecision and uncertainty. Each scene began with a question being posed and ended with nothing being decided, or rather with the same decision being reached, which was to decide nothing. Like a deliberately soporific tennis game, arguing on the one hand and on the other hand, back and forth, they seemed intent on wearing each other out in tedium, until the umpire called a halt, and the debate was adjourned for further study. It gradually began to emerge that the players were demonstrating that they all possessed an academic mind, which never gives a straight answer, because there are no straight answers. Thirty-three examples eventually made that point clear. One remarkable scene consisted of a pas de deux by the cuckoo and a female don wearing the mask of a dragon's head: they showed how it was impossible to decide whether a professor should appear to be modest or haughty to carry conviction. He danced the role of a British aristocrat, with a permanent look of total stupidity, protesting his ignorance, and explaining that this pretence had saved the privileges of the upper classes by making them appear harmless. She portrayed a French marquise, trying to look as haughty and impressive as she could, even if it led her to the guillotine. Once again, there was no conclusion. In another scene, the dons debated, miming even more grossly, where, if they ever did build a lavatory in the university, it should be sited. Paradise of course had no need of lavatories; but they discussed how water shortages might affect them, if they ever did occur, and whether it was possible to commit suicide in Paradise by hanging from lavatory chains, if such things existed. That was their delicate introduction to the question of how objects could vanish, in preparation for the vanishing trick the sacrificial victim was expected to perform.

One by one the dons gave signs of exhaustion with all this

argument, and in turn dropped their heads on the table as though asleep. Only then did the cuckoo raise the topic of the day, under Any Other Business. This was the high moment: the Missing Agenda was found. Of course they did not mention Sumdy. It was the case of Forgetmenot that was put to them: should a cockroach be accepted as a student, or be eligible to become a professor? There was no one awake to answer, so the cuckoo performed a solo dance, in which the dramatic gesture, repeated again and again, was the pointed finger. As he danced, he paid Forgetmenot barbed academic compliments, damned it with faint praise, suggested that perhaps theses should be written, books consulted, bibliographies compiled to clarify the issue. But then finally he stopped and announced: Nem. Con. It is agreed that the cockroach be burned at the stake. The dons raised their heads in delight. A decision had been taken. They had condemned the cockroach, but that was not what they meant: Sumdy was being given the option to interpret their decision as she wished. Everything depended on how decisions were interpreted. But by this rigmarole, the professors got as near as they could to saying what they were loath to say, that there was a soul whom they could not teach, for whom their university could do nothing. They needed the charade of exhaustion to admit it, to sign a deed of abdication. Sumdy was now free to go elsewhere.

Being burnt at the stake was a wonderful experience for Sumdy, the most exhilarating party she had ever attended. It was unforgettable first of all for the large number of souls whom she met at the ceremony that followed, and who had a few words to say to her, often very curious words, souls she might otherwise never have got to know. There was a Spaniard, who had once been an Aztec sacrificial victim, and who chanted a version of their weird hymn:

146

Intonam Intota
Tlatecuhtli tonotiuh,
(To Father and Mother,
The Earth and the Sun)

apologising that no other Aztec victims were present: there
had been no less than twenty thousand of them sacrificed with
him, by the learned men of the day, at the dedication of the
Great Temple of Mexico. She was impressed by the martyrs
of the early Christian church who took the trouble to emerge
from their hermits' hovels to give her advice. They told her of
their pride in having been through the same thing themselves,
or something similar. They spoke of their never-failing satisfaction at having been able to defy all those bumptious
inquisitors, those boring pedants, those brutal soldiers; their
pain, they said, had come not from the flesh but from the
heart; they were torn apart not by the spears or stones or
animals' claws, but by the pleading of their families to make
them relent, by pity for their children and aged parents, who
saw them as deserting their responsibilities, as being obstinate, ungrateful, callous; and it was above all sadness that
overwhelmed them when they saw such vast crowds of fellow
humans getting so much pleasure from the sound of bones
being broken or of the body tearing, from the sight of blood
flowing, shouting for the agony to be prolonged, and protesting that they were being cheated if the victim remained calm,
if in the very last moments the body, for all its self-control,
did not instinctively try to defend itself.

Of course a soul cannot be burned or destroyed. The stake
on fire may destroy the body, but for the soul it is only a kind
of baptismal font, and a fumigation of the mind. In Paradise,
where they do not have to bother about messy, smelly bodies,
that is rather clearer. A martyr here is not someone who

147

suffers death. The word "martyr" originally meant a witness. A martyr is a person who has a vision of something important, and has an opinion about it, and knows that he has the right to believe what he pleases, that nothing can make him think otherwise, as supposedly wiser persons might say he should. He is a Roman who refuses to live in the manner of the Romans. Perhaps that is precisely what a soul, if he wants to be more than a shadow of his former self, has got to learn to do in Paradise, where he is all alone and where pretending that he is still a Roman does nothing to assuage his loneliness.

The ceremony of burning provides an enjoyable opportunity for souls to say what they think of each other, publicly. They can pour out the hatred that is bottled up inside them and which, in their normal serene surroundings, they find it difficult to express. Hell has become so distant a target for their anger, so abstract, that it no longer suffices. They need at least a weekly event at which they can bring out their old scores and unload their scorn, just as they used to go out on Saturday night to break the rules of decorum they observed the rest of the week. For academics, this is particularly important, since their whole existence is bound up with criticising each other, and it is not easy for them to contain themselves. It was a pleasure for Sumdy to see them put aside their hypocrisy and freely utter all the nasty thoughts they had about her. Ganesa, ever tactful, did it by singing an incantation in praise of memory, damning all who did not pay due respect to the supreme masters of it: Sumdy surely had not bowed low enough when she had met him, nor been impressed enough by the great elephants she had been allowed to meet. Yes, Sumdy admitted, she was not respectful enough, of anybody. Professor Purda mounted the stage shyly, his face covered by a veil, through which he warned the audience that Sumdy was an incorrigibly subversive person, attracted by novel ideas, simply because they were novel, easily bored. Yes, Sumdy confessed, with a certain degree of pride, she was easily bored. Professor Mausole shouted aggressively that he was disappointed with her, she listened too much to idle gossip. Yes, Sumdy replied, she was interested by gossip, or at least by the other side of every story, because she could not believe what she was told. Pan Chao came onto the stage and simply embraced her, not saying a word; and half the crowd booed, for they suspected there was some plot between them, and half the crowd cheered, thrilled to see affection unite two souls. Arkady said that though he normally enjoyed being an executioner, he felt less pleasure than usual, for Sumdy was not the sort of person he cared to sully himself with. Then row upon row of souls got up to testify that they disapproved of Sumdy for all sorts of reasons, though they had never spoken to her, and indeed did not know her. Prejudice had a comfortable home in Paradise.

All this confirmed to Sumdy that she had not reached the Paradise she was looking for; and that this university at any rate was not interested in finding any other; no university she knew, indeed, had ever dared teach a course in happiness, how it could be otherwise here? So when Arkady lit the fires, their warmth comforted her. Her isolation on the stake ceased to be eerie; she was glad to be alone, and to be saying so publicly. The smoke seemed to penetrate into every pore, split, fissure of her soul, and all sorts of memories, whole colonies of worries, came scurrying out, like ants frightened from their nests. The crackling sparks formed themselves into changing shapes, a succession of mirages and broken rainbows filled the sky. She sensed her feet lifting off the ground. She understood that she had conquered the right to walk among the clouds in Paradise, because she had ignored fear, and shown her willingness to step into the unknown, beyond

149

the boring safety of the crowds. When Sumdy pulled herself out of the embers, when the last spectator had gone home, and there was none left but the sandwich-board man who always attended with his notice saying Keep Your Bowels Moving, she felt as light as air. She had discovered that it is not terrible to be alone or to be different; and that only pleasure in being so allows one to walk with a spring in one's step.

Did the sandwich-board man know the way to the angels? Not quite. He had been a Harley Street doctor in the middle of the nineteenth century, until struck off the medical register for believing that bran should be included in bread, and for selling wholemeal loaves to his patients. Now he was distressed that souls in Paradise were still in trouble. "Everyone here is so blocked up with memories", he said. "Constipation of the mind. Constipation of the soul. If only they knew how to keep their bowels moving, their memories moving; if only they would learn to forget sometimes, just occasionally." If Sumdy wanted to find the angels, perhaps she needed to forget her old ideas about them first.

Sumdy took one of the leaflets he was distributing to post home as a souvenir. She did not want to worry her parents with a letter describing her burning. If she told them that Jolly had watched the ceremony from a distance, looking sad, as though feeling sorry that in Paradise humans still needed to growl and bark at one another, that might only reinforce their disapproval of her travels. If she said that Forgetmenot was back in its jar recovering from exposure to a professor who smelt of alcohol, while Jolly watched over it like a nurse, keeping well clear of anyone who threatened to lecture him, they would not know whether that concealed good or bad news. She was reluctant to admit that she had not found a science of happiness, all neatly worked out, proved and guaranteed, or that wisdom did not appear to grow any better on this mountain of knowledge than it did anywhere else. She wrote several letters, but tore them all up. It was impossible for her to express the peculiar quality of her excitement, because so far she had met only dissatisfied souls, and yet she still believed that somewhere in Paradise they knew how to forget their disappointment, how to make disappointment a beginning, not an end.

CHAPTER SIX

Thunder and lightning are the sign of God's anger: many knowledgeable experts have said that and believed it. When they arrive in Paradise, they rush to the scene of the explosions in the hope of catching a glimpse of the Invisible. They find that the noise comes only from the kitchens: the lids of pots sometimes blow off, pans occasionally catch fire, even here. The kitchens prepare the different diets and potions for which souls become hungry when they realise that they do not reach perfection automatically, that to enjoy Paradise does not come easily. It was to one of these thundering kitchens that Sumdy went in search of the energy that would sustain her on her flight to the angels. According to the sandwich-board man, the most interesting and exotic restaurants in Paradise were situated inside the Pyramids of Egypt. So Sumdy travelled eight levels down to them.

However, as she made her way through one molehole after another, her elation gradually dissipated. She asked herself why she was, apparently, the only soul keen to get to the angels; was her search leading her into some kind of ambush? She began to suspect that Paradise did not really please or suit her. Its novelty and its surprises excited her too briefly; pleasure did not satiate her as luxuriantly as she had expected;

Paradise appeared to magnify the disagreeable aspects of earthly life, making them more prickly still, revealing how difficult they were to change, how deeply attached humans were to their weaknesses, their petty pride, their treasured vices. Moreover, she was becoming convinced that she was not being shown everything there was to see. Perhaps they were carefully concealing their most cherished private enjoyments from her. It worried her that her visit might only make her disgruntled with life, strip her of her appetite for it. Perhaps dead souls needed to be consoled in precisely this way. Perhaps that was why the clerks at the consulate had told her there was no point in taking a return ticket. How silly of her never to have guessed that it would not be the attractions of Paradise that would retain her, but nausea from seeing human folly so carefully perpetuated, embalmed. Or her disappointment, she said to herself, might be a sign of something even worse, her incompetence as a traveller, who does not have the patience or sympathy to discover the real, quiet pleasures of a foreign country: would she ever acquire that skill, who felt herself so very much a child of the twentieth century, taught, overtaught, to be always critical? Everybody in Paradise seemed to arrive loaded with a rucksack of guilt, of original sin, of regret, and, above all, of fear. Yes, that was what troubled her most deeply. Paradise was full of fear. And fear might possibly be a constituent part of the soul, impossible to wash out; all this sleeping might be a way of temporarily silencing it, but she could see the fear was there. There seemed no hint that Paradise offered any help, beyond sleep, in fighting fear. How terrifying to be faced with the certainty of having to fight fear for ever. Surely that could not be the prospect that Paradise held out. There had to be some secret she had failed to uncover.

The sight of the Pyramids added awe to her dismay. Why

153

had they dragged these giant funeral monuments all this way, could they not forget death? It was only slowly that she perceived how their majestic, dim-lit, sculptured chambers, no longer used as tombs for kings and queens, had been given a new purpose. Souls of every country came to eat in them, and not just out of ordinary hunger. When the Pyramids were the highest buildings in the universe, they were "the staircase to Heaven"; could there be any better taking-off point for a flight to the angels? Between the third century BC, when the art of deciphering hieroglyphics was lost, and 1822, when it was rediscovered, the Pyramids were regarded as a great depository of magic, in which had been put for safekeeping all the secret knowledge that the ancient world possessed, to protect it against future cataclysms – a sort of holy precursor of a nuclear shelter. And since most humans have believed in magic, they have come to Paradise agog to learn these secrets, with high expectations of what magic could achieve here. Every civilisation is illuminated by its own magic sun, that keeps it alive and hopeful: the magic end to suffering in an after-life, the magic chance to become rich and famous . . . but what kind of sun shone over Paradise? The inhabitants of Paradise had for long tried never to worry about that, they asked no questions, they lived in the present as though it embraced all the past and all the future. But now modern immigrants, though they never used the word "magic", made it increasingly clear that they were much more demanding, they were on the prowl for miracles even more wonderful than those of science or magic. They were impatient, for example, to get rid of their doubts. They wanted to be able to make precise forecasts of the future; they assumed that they would be able to manipulate the future with the same ease that a rabbit can be pulled out of a hat; and of course what interested them most about the future was their own fate, to what extent they could start a new life, become renewed while somehow still remaining themselves, and find the strength to do what they always thought beyond them. So they came to the restaurants of the Pyramids for what they hoped would be their most memorable, decisive meal, confused as to where it would lead them, but attracted, like inquisitive insects, by the pungent, steamy, awesome interiors, the bubbling sound of witch's brew, lit by great roasting fires which Sumdy thought only Hell possessed.

What is cooked in the kitchens of Paradise is not the food that humans know. The thought of food is another obsession that grips the soul the moment one recovers from the shock of arrival; eating is not a habit one wishes to abandon; even waiting for the next meal, where there is so little else to do, seems to be a pleasure worth cultivating. Those who have grown their own food, working themselves to exhaustion, are at once attracted by the idea of food that falls down from heaven. They eat manna, and with abandon. Some authorities claim this is the unique sustenance of the angels; and those living humans who have been privileged to try it are said to "have no need of relieving themselves, for it is full of goodness and nothing else, and so is absorbed in its entirety; only when they sin by complaining about its taste do they excrete like ordinary mortals." According to other authorities, the taste of manna contains the flavour of every conceivable dish: to the child it tastes of milk, to the hungry of bread, to the sick of "barley steeped in oil and honey", and women have used it successfully as a cosmetic. So it should be a food about which it is impossible to complain, and of which it is impossible to eat too much or too little, for the quantity gathered is always proportionate to the appetite. And yet it no longer pleases everybody. A good man is a man with a full stomach, the sorcerers used to say in tribes where hunger ruled; but

155

increasingly, modern souls are heard to moan that manna looks boring, a white powder, liable to get sticky, that it is too like a meal in a plastic sachet, that nothing much can be done with it to vary the appeal of the watery stew it makes. In vain have several (otherwise illustrious) civilisations trained their offspring to enjoy just that sort of dish. There are numerous kitchens which produce manna, and which, on occasion, manage to burn it or spoil it. But that is not what one comes to the Pyramids for.

A different menu appeals to women who have slaved over hot stoves all their lives, in drudgery, in poverty, without ever having produced the perfect meal. They are tempted to feast as a queen might do. Elaborate dishes appear before them, on giant banquet tables, at just the right moment, perfectly cooked, for ever replenished, always delicious, enormous roasted boars, rare delicacies, sheep's eyes and tongue of quail, puddings to spoil the sweetest tooth, wine in profusion. The boar and sheep and quail are of course impossible foods, but there is no way souls can be stopped from imagining that is what they are eating, and from refusing to accept that royal food palls with time. These grand dishes are sometimes so elaborate they explode with a terrible thunder. However, it is not for them that one comes to the Pyramids.

It is the third menu which is responsible for the worst of the clatter of flying pot lids and the occasional lightning. The Pyramid restaurants specialise in what they call individual cooking. Each soul is offered a dish peculiar to himself, which is supposed to match his character and his mood, in the same way that an architect might build a house with turrets and alcoves and oddly placed windows to meet the requirements of his client's hobbies and habits, or lay out a garden on which paths, arbours, hedges and pergolas are so arranged as to allow him to converse with nature in the different languages he knows. Those who want something more out of Paradise than a good doze, who yearn for adventure, and the energy to keep them going for all eternity, crave for some special, completely new food, even though the idea that the soul is unique is disconcerting, and though the creation of an original dish at every meal is an appalling challenge. Sumdy decided it was an individual meal that she wanted: she was here trying to solve the riddles of Paradise and it would be as well to solve the riddle of her own capacities too.

Walking from Pyramid to Pyramid, she searched for the one that would suit her best. Amid the crowds of loitering tourists, self-styled guides offered to make up her mind for her, and tell her what they thought she liked or needed, though they had never seen her before. She took them at first to be no more than the sort of salesmen, impossible to shake off, who hover around the carpet stalls in Oriental bazaars and whisper tall stories about fabulous bargains to be had, as a special, personal favour; but the one who attached himself most persistently to her had been no less a personage than a scribe in the service of the Pharaohs. "Be a scribe," they used to say in Ancient Egypt, "you will avoid all fatigue and you will be spared all painful labour. The scribe directs the work of all the people. Everything depends on him, even the army." This soul of a scribe was touting at the foot of a Pyramid, not considering it beneath his dignity, because he wanted to go on influencing the destinies of other souls. These restaurants have a hidden purpose, to determine the fate of others, the hardest, most elusive of tasks in Paradise. On earth, a mother often fixes her child's tastes from birth, mother's food aways retains a certain magic, but in Paradise taste becomes open to renegotiation, reconsideration, and food can be seen as the symbol of the new choices that a soul can make. A soul which is able to persuade another as to what it wants and what it is like is half way to being its master. The scribe inveigled souls into his restaurant because, like so many who had once wielded authority, he was disturbed that souls should dine where they pleased, eat one food or another, on mere whim: his self-appointed mission was to arrange reasoned marriages between a diner and his meal, to regularise procedures in the cultivation of appetite, to create formalities in satisfying it. And such are the intimidating powers of an authoritarian voice in a strange place, that simply by the manner of his questioning of Sumdy, interrogating her on why she was taking so long to reach the angels, he got her to say, and perhaps to believe, that she was trying to do too much, that she may have reached her limit, that she needed help: how could she take Jolly with her, who was terrified, shaking at the very thought of flying; she could see no way of carrying him with her: could he ride on her back? Both she and Jolly were sorely in need of more energy, more strength than they had, a new dose of courage.

The scribe said that nobody fully believed they were in Paradise until they knew where they could replenish their stock of energy freely and easily. On earth one had to accept that energy was a gift at birth, some had more than others; one might try to increase it by various tricks, by diet, by training, by fasts or therapy, but it always remained unpredictable, slippery, like a fish that can suddenly escape the grasp. The restaurants of the Pyramids existed to reveal the source of energy, of will power, or at any rate to help in the search for them. The scribe's pompous self-assurance made Sumdy's strength shrivel up completely: she felt incompetent, unworthy, drained. At which point he guided her into the semi-darkness of the restaurant inside the Great Pyramid; and Jolly followed meekly.

A whole succession of souls have passed through the Pyramids, each with a new bright idea of what use such a marvellous monument could be put to in Paradise. For a long time it was popular among souls who came to lie in the empty sarcophagi, because they wanted to know what it felt like to be a king whom everyone genuinely believes to be a god. Kings came too, who had been insulted or assassinated by their subjects, and who longed to be respected unquestioningly, even if it involved shutting themselves up in the pitch darkness of an airless tomb. But it ceased to be a sad and silent resort when the Chinese King Tang of Shang came to visit it. The effect of lying in a sarcophagus on him was to make him feel hungry. It was thanks to King Tang that souls began to realise that eating was not, as most believed, an animal act, but that it could be as important an activity in Paradise as hymn-singing. Till then, the history of food had consisted simply in changing menus and recipes, finding new ways of cooking and new ingredients, inventing laws of hygiene or nutrition, and diets that usually do not quite work. But henceforth food could be almost an instrument of salvation for discontented souls. It took a long time to become so; King Tang only pointed the way. It was he who set the fashion for eating in the Pyramids. On earth, he used to employ two thousand four hundred servants in his palace to ensure that he was properly fed, including sixty-two pickle and sauce specialists, sixty-two salt men, and so on for every expertise; and he so valued culinary skill as a sign of general intelligence, that he appointed I Yin, whose cooking particularly impressed him, as his prime minister – the only cook ever to reach that dignity on earth. King Tang began filling the Pyramids up with stocks of the spices and rare foods of his country; and as other diners followed his example, the Pyramids became a unique emporium of ingredients, in which could be found everything that had ever been eaten, like a library housing everything that had ever been written. Visitors soon poured in, at first only to marvel, and to utter exclamations of wonder and horror at the strangeness of taste; but gradually this collection was put to more practical use.

The next important event in the history of food in Paradise is the arrival of the Holy Roman Emperor, Rudolf II (1552–1612). He had been a reforming monarch, convinced that the best way of solving the financial problems of governments was not to raise taxes but to manufacture gold out of thin air, or scrap metal, or anything at all, by alchemy, the science, as he believed, of the future, a science on which many of the best minds of his time placed all their hopes. Under his rule, Prague had become the most cosmopolitan city in Europe, to which he attracted all the best alchemists from every country, and in addition musicians and poets to create the right atmosphere for their research. Now in Paradise he did not have to concern himself with money or taxes any more, nor with other elusive goals like perpetual motion, since everything is perpetual in Paradise. So he had pondered the question of what, in Paradise, was as precious as gold on earth, what was most rare, most desired, what there was for alchemists to do where everything existed in abundance. He had decided, rather to his own surprise, that what was hardest to get in Paradise was a good meal. This may seem odd, given that souls could eat anything they wanted or imagined. But their problem was that they did not know what they wanted. Or else they wanted a great deal more than they ever had from their food: they expected their diets to be truly miraculous. In Paradise they assume that they can have everything. And yet that is not enough. Inceasingly, new arrivals have been wondering whether what they have is right for them. The interest in individual cooking has grown accordingly, among all those who cannot be easily satisfied, and whose hopes extend even beyond the need to discover, at every meal, new truths about themselves, on the principle of "Tell me what you eat and I shall tell you who you are." They want the meal to reform them, to make new persons of them. The result has been that more and more souls are demanding impossible meals, which no cook, however skilled, can produce.

But alchemists specialise in achieving the impossible, and cooking is indeed very close to alchemy, in that it is concerned with transforming one substance into another, with making sweet what is bitter. So when Rudolf visited the Pyramids he knew he had found his niche and his mission: to win eternal glory by making the food in Paradise truly worthy of it, capable of fulfilling all the promise that it never quite attained on earth, where a meal simply assuages hunger, and is then only a memory; no-one has become a better person by eating. Paradise had to achieve more than that; eating must become an art that transformed character, temperament, outlook. The Emperor succeeded in gathering round him an even more dazzling team of alchemists than he had drawn to Prague, enticing them with the prospect that at last, by some as yet undreamt-of potion, they would make it possible to systematically convert human fantasies into realities, and in particular the most elusive fantasy of all, inexhaustible energy and will power. He was certain that was the key that opened the door to perfect happiness, a key that has exceptional importance in Paradise, where virtually everyone arrives tired. Indeed, the more recently a soul has arrived, the more is fatigue the overwhelming, deeply frustrating problem. The Emperor is said to have been much impressed by the opinion of Dr George Miller Beard of New York (1839–83), who identified fatigue (and the nervousness from which it arose) as the peculiarly American disease, and who explained to him

161

that everything in Paradise confirmed his view that it was not decadent nations that got tired, but young and vibrant ones, where stress knocked out all those who were not competitive enough, and they were the vast majority. Fatigue was called by many different names, partly from fashion, partly to make it deserving of sympathy, to suggest it was a matter of bad luck, not a fault; some wrapped it up in obscure terminology, in words like "neurasthenia"; some said they had the Da Costa syndrome, which was discovered in the American Civil War, when energetic soldiers suddenly got headaches and became breathless and were pronounced to have developed weak hearts; survivors of World War I came with the effort syndrome; those of World War II with battle fatigue; exhausted refugees from prosperity said they had chronic mononucleosis or the Epstein-Barr virus; victims of airplane crashes were incredulous that even lifeless objects had been affected and suffered from metal fatigue. Some souls had simply been traumatised by work and the thought of having to get up in the morning brought too many awful memories; it made them tired even to be reminded of work. Fatigue was definitely what souls were increasingly complaining about.

Each of the alchemists in the Pyramid had a different attitude to the tragedy of disappointment they all saw ever looming in Paradise. The Emperor Rudolf was proud that he had recruited one of the very first woman scientists, who had various names, among them Mary the Jewess and Mary the Prophetess. She had been the inventor of the most basic items of equipment used by alchemists since the third century AD, which is when she is supposed to have lived – the alembic still, and the *bain marie*, named after her, which is to be found in every canteen where soggy food is kept warm in a pan of simmering water; and now she was busy experimenting for a formula that would bring soggy food back to life, in the hope

162

that it could make soggy souls somehow crisper too. Rudolf had also attracted the great Arab alchemist Jabir ibn Hayyan (AD 730–804), no mean feat, since he is believed not to have been a person at all, but a committee, an accusation levelled against all who write long books, and his are so long and so difficult to make sense of that he is remembered only in the word *gibberish*; now he was devoting his efforts to writing the menus of the Pyramids in riddles, and he was renowned for making them incomprehensible. His function, as he saw it, was to ensure that all progress in Paradise – if Paradise did achieve any – should retain an aura of mystery, remaining for ever an object of wonder, and not become a matter of course as is the fate of mundane progress. In place of a maître d'hôtel, there was Theophrastus Bombastus von Hohenheim (1493–1541), one of Switzerland's long line of unorthodox but seductive doctors, charming and disputatious, who obstinately maintained that every disease must have a cure, even what in his day was known as the French disease, "the worst disease in the world" as he called it (meaning syphilis), and of course he had, more or less, been proved right; if anyone could heal the anguish in Paradise, it was he, who had so ingeniously married medicine and alchemy. In the deeper recesses behind him, hordes more of alchemists prepared to light up their fires as they were needed. The Great Pyramid glowed with excitement, and the ancient inscriptions on its walls shone like constellations of stars to inspire all who entered it. As they arrive, every diner is given, instead of an aperitif, a copy of Al-Ghazzali's *The Alchemy of Happiness* (*c.* AD 1100), with this wise saying underlined: "The Arabs have their own customs and the Persians have theirs and God knoweth which is best."

Under the Emperor Rudolf's guidance, the Pyramids acquired a reputation as a rendezvous where amazing menus

163

could be found, from which one could expect meals astonishing even for Paradise. The rumour spread that Paradise was about to enter an era of feasting and banqueting that would go beyond anything previously experienced. But Sumdy did not witness it.

There is never any need to be in a hurry once death ceases to be a worry. Sumdy's habit of gobbling her food as fast as she could was quite inappropriate. It was a long time before a waiter came to serve her. And then she puzzled, for even longer, over the menu he brought:

Cream of Pundit soup, with clockwork croutons

*

Roast Patina of Brazilian Mahogany, with brass sauce
Sauteed Niagara Rocks
Hooligan Peas

*

Savoury Sandal
String and Candle Sorbet

This was supposed to be a meal designed to suit her person-ally. But these dishes, she protested, were uneatable, un-cookable, inconceivable. Theophrastus Bombastus answered her: Paradise exists to bring about the inconceivable and the impossible. Alchemists spend all their time doing just that. She might have to wait a little while, or perhaps for ever, while they worked on the details of the recipes by which these dishes might be prepared, but anticipation was one of the pleasures that Paradise must take care to preserve. If every soul got what it wanted straight away, there would be no point in having a future. Alchemists, it is true, had never succeeded in achieving their aim of making gold, but people had continued to have faith in them, for several millennia, regardless, because everyone needs to have impossible dreams. If this restaurant was able to help Sumdy dream about the myriad forms that food could take, and the new kinds of happiness this could bring, it would have succeeded enough. Clockwork croutons, brass sauce . . . Sumdy did not like the implication that she was a person who wanted the impossible. She was not one of those who merely dreamed or talked of visiting exotic places: had she not come to Paradise by sheer determination? And she was going to meet the angels, however difficult that might be.

Immigrants often have the sad failing, said the doctor, of taking what they see in Paradise too literally. If only they allowed their imagination a little play, if only they understood that behind the obvious there is nearly always hidden poetry, Paradise would surprise them a little more. Surprises need to be prepared for. Only some people know how to be surprised.

Did that mean that they never intended to serve her a meal at all?

The important things in heaven and earth, said the doctor, are invisible. And they are impossible to describe. Imagination is the sovereign virtue. God Himself created the world with imagination and nothing else. A menu should be read as an encouragement to each diner's imagination, a stimulus to the realisation that searching is more full of pleasure than discovering, an invitation to savour the processes of initiation and reverie, a chance to fathom the meaning of apparently meaningless symbols. Alchemists are dealers in dreams, the last thing they want to do is to wake up their clients. And every soul is an alchemist without knowing it, having throughout life transformed food into flesh; souls come to

165

Paradise, though they do not always realise it, because they want to be alchemists in the fullest sense, in everything they do, transforming all they touch, alchemising the whole of reality, if only they had the courage. They had to start with food, that was fundamental, the most revealing, influential of habits. But the great danger for souls was that they might turn too many of their fantasies into realities. There must always be some that remained impossible. The skill of menu writing – and Jabir had much skill – was to ensure that at least one course would absolutely defy all efforts to cook it. Could Sumdy spot it in hers? They were world-famous alchemists in the Pyramids, and when the pots in which they tried out new recipes blew up, far from that signifying failure or causing anger, they were pleased and they came into the dining rooms to take a bow. The way to enjoy this restaurant, concluded the doctor, was to remember that the private world which every soul carried around with him – memories, dreams, a sense of inadequacy, the after-effects of disease – need no longer be a burden in Paradise.

Sumdy began to understand why nothing ever seemed to happen in Paradise, and why the alchemists had come to be so popular, so esteemed there. Most of the inhabitants had spent their lives on earth preparing for another life, or sacrificing themselves so that their children might not suffer as they did; when they arrive in Paradise they are so accustomed to wait-ing, expecting, postponing, that they cannot conceive of doing otherwise than they have always done, indeed they cease to be aware that they are waiting; waiting and existing are for them one and the same thing. And they bring with them their ancestral beliefs about will power: if you have interesting things to do you will always find the energy to do them, you will forget to rest if you are totally absorbed by a passion; energy is fuelled by hope; which means that they

166

take it for granted that Paradise will constantly invent new interests for those who used to say that they have no energy because they have no interests. And those who assume that energy needs to be accumulated like money before it can be spent are willing to wait until they have enough; those who say that it is the first step that counts, accept that only when they eventually learn how the world was created, will they discover how all sorts of virtues are suddenly going to appear in themselves, springing out of nothing, like flowers that were never buds. Humans have a lot of practice in waiting. Alchemists are the specialists in waiting; they never made gold, and their meals here are never quite ready, but they confidently expect to be successful, it is only a matter of waiting. The Emperor Rudolf found that his restaurant was most appreciated when it did not actually serve meals, but confined itself to announcing ever more succulent and bizarre menus. The one thing his guests did not want was to be disappointed. The alchemists knew how to transmute disappointment into hope, how to keep the mouth for ever watering, how to make the thrill of preparing for a ball so intense that there was no need to dance. So humans for whom life had been a matter of watching the clock ticking away, with a sound like the chop, chop, chop of an executioner, are fascinated by alchemists who know how to tell time to mind its own business and who refuse to be its supine victims.

But Sumdy was much too impatient even to understand any of that. She kept on repeating that she did not consider the meal they had offered her to be suitable. She had come to be cheered up, to revive her energy; she really intended to go on with her search for the angels. They appeared puzzled by her obstinacy. But eventually they said she had better speak to Mary. Mary dealt with complaints.

Diners who are dissatisfied with the menus they are being

167

offered are usually quietened by being tempted with dreams of ever-more succulent delicacies. But Mary is let loose on those whose complaints become unbearable, like inconsolable howling babies. Mary was the final resort. She alone was brave enough to reveal the brutal facts of Paradise, to bring difficult souls to their senses. Sumdy's protests won her the right to learn the really bad news about Paradise.

In ancient times, magicians frequently used pseudonyms, for safety's sake, and erudite writers published under the name of some deity or celebrity. Mary the Alchemist deliberately confused her identity with that of Mary the sister of Moses, to give the impression that her research had some kind of prophetic inspiration, and perhaps also to hint that her books were written by a woman who did not regard herself as a passive mouthpiece of men. For the sister of Moses had been a truly formidable person, who is said to have lived to the age of a hundred and thirty-two: she was the embodiment of fearlessness and outspokenness, obtaining fame for having openly rebuked the mighty Pharaoh to his face, and for leading a rebellion against Moses, on the ground that God had wished to speak not to Moses alone, but to her as well. Moses is remembered as a prophet; it is forgotten that in, as it were, private life, he and his wife Zipporah had both studied medecine at Heliopolis and his sister probably had too. They were a family of intellectuals and professionals, and that included their womenfolk, for women doctors were common in Ancient Egypt. So when Mary the Alchemist pretended to be speaking through the mouth of Mary the sister of Moses, she was revealing her own pretensions, and her own rebelliousness. What was more, she was a member of an Egyptian sect that held it to be a divine truth that men and women are equal; she had done her studies at the temple of Memphis under the aegis of the shaven-headed god Ptah, the most intellectual of gods, who claimed to have created the universe with words alone, through sheer literary power. Mary's theory of alchemy – the first to be elaborated in the western world – argued that metals were male and female, that the art of making gold was to find the right pair of metals and get them to agree to mate. "Unite the male with the female and you will find what you seek." But that perfect union had always eluded her.

Only a soul of her strength could bear the full burden of knowing Paradise's limitations. She decided to risk revealing them to Sumdy. In as gentle a whisper as she could manage, she said that there was, perhaps, an almost insuperable obstacle to Sumdy's going to the angels, though she hated to have to say so. It was sad to have to admit it, but though everything is possible in Paradise, some things were harder, very much harder to achieve, even by alchemists. Sumdy was not the first person to want to fly to the angels. They had had diners come to them in the past who were keen on flying and who had asked for a meal that would make them lighter. To be lighter in heart was a noble ambition, but more difficult than they realised. They believed all they needed was to eat food that would make them laugh. Was that not what Sumdy wanted too? Sumdy was amazed that Mary should have so perceptively hit on something that really did worry her. Though Sumdy had seen the gods laughing at Henry Ford, she had so far met very few ordinary human souls laughing in Paradise, seldom openly or uncontrollably, not even in derision against one another, let alone in pure joy. There had been nothing comic in the roar of Mausole. She had not laughed aloud herself either. Jolly was not wagging his tail as he usually did. It was almost as though souls were frightened of laughing in Paradise; yet another fear, always fear. . .

169

It was typical of Sumdy that she refused to believe what she was told, that laughter could be rare, rationed, or dangerous in Paradise. Mary was forced to bring out the whole truth. The last explorer of Paradise to have found anything funny in Paradise, she revealed, was the Celtic hero, Bran son of Fulda, who claims to have visited Paradise in the seventh century, and who, being Irish, described it as a series of islands, each with its own attractions; he says that he came across what he named the Island of Joy, from which emerged continuous gusts of laughter; but he only saw it from a distance, and not considering laughter to be worthy of his interest, he did not converse with the inhabitants, but sailed on to the Island of Women; these were not worthy of his interest either; and had the women not lassooed him out of his boat, and dragged him ashore, he would not have spent a whole year there, apparently enjoyably. This incident confirms that humour was always something of an aberration in Paradise, and those who wanted to laugh had to take refuge in an island, like smokers in a smoking room. St John Chrisostom ("the golden-mouthed", AD 347–407), who carried out an investigation of the plight of such souls, came to the conclusion that laughter is the work of the devil, and that a good Christian must remain serious at all times.

The decree of the Roman Catholic Church in Council (1418) which lays it down that "any priest who speaks jocular words such as provoke laughter, let him be anathema", seems to have been obeyed religiously in Paradise. A large proportion of souls did not consider it proper to laugh here, any more than in a church. There are no precedents for any important business being successfully accomplished laughing, anywhere on earth, even among the most eccentric tribes: war, examinations, visits to police stations, consultations with doctors, all have to be done with a straight face: could it be

170

otherwise in Paradise? When immigrants arrive at the gates of Paradise and hear the laughter of Ismail, quite often they refuse to believe their ears. Mark Twain himself, far from responding, as an American humorist might, to Ismail's welcoming joviality, voluntarily assured him that he would not disturb the solemnity of the place and would not be tempted to: "There is no humor in heaven," he affirmed, with deep conviction, even before he had been admitted or had a chance to look. "Everything human is pathetic. The secret source of humor itself is not joy but sorrow." And, by definition, for him, Paradise could not contain sorrow, and therefore could have no humour either. Most of the inhabitants of Paradise seemed to agree with him. Were they so afraid of sorrow that they were willing to sacrifice laughter?

But Sumdy continued to protest that Paradise without laughter was impossible: they were only trying to frighten her; she was sure that if they really tried, they could find some, somewhere. She was so determined and so stubborn, that Mary summoned the Emperor Rudolf, who was the last recourse for the most difficult customers of all.

That was how the Pyramid restaurant came to organise a gala night, just for Sumdy's benefit. The Emperor agreed to invite all the ancient comics he knew, all the jesters, wits, lampoonists, cartoonists, gagmen and wags of all sorts whom he could trace, to come and put on a show, to demonstrate what had become of laughter in Paradise. One by one, they came, but they brought with them neither funny hats, nor whistles, nor false moustaches. They arrived in cumbersome furniture vans, loaded with lecterns and soapboxes, which they laboriously set up, and from which they proceeded to harangue Sumdy and the diners in the restaurant with moralising speeches.

No professional entertainer had tried to smuggle laughter

171

into Paradise because the last thing they wanted to do in it was to laugh.

My allotted span of life has passed.
Oh give me peace and rest at last.

This was the refrain chanted by Jippensha Ikku (1765–1831), the first Japanese fiction writer to be able to earn his living solely by the sale of his books, and he spoke for all those who came to the Pyramid restaurant. The author of the hilarious adventures of Yaji and Kita came with a soapbox which was a copy of the monument in his honour in the precincts of the Chomei Temple in Mukojima, on which this thought is inscribed: "However novel and interesting things [in general, and jokes in particular] appear at first, when they become common they lose their interest, but things of which people never tire are a bright moonlit night and dinner, a book and sake." Ikku, twice divorced, his home twice burned down, an incorrigible alcoholic, had led a life full of disasters, in which, unlike his heroes, he had found nothing funny, and he was not keen to spend eternity sacrificing himself for the amusement of his readers.

The actor whom Shakespeare employed to play the Fool in *Lear* and the gravedigger in *Hamlet* came not with a soapbox but carrying a tray of jewellery from which he silently invited the diners to choose what pleased them. Robert Arnim used to be voluble, he had published a book of jokes entitled *Quips* and another, containing biographies of the comedians of his day, called *Foole upon Foole or a Nest of Ninnies*, but he preferred to forget all that. It was difficult to get him to speak: the most he would do for those who questioned him was to sing:

Many men descant on another's wit
When they have less themselves in doing it.

172

For all his glory in Shakespeare's company, he preferred to be a goldsmith in Paradise, which was how he started life, and how he described himself at the end of it in his will. "Is it then a profit to be foolish?" "Yea," he once replied, "for under show of simplicity, some gain love, while the wise, with all they can do, can scarce obtain love." But he did not get enough love as a clown; his appeal for more respect for clowns was not successful. He had lost faith in laughter.

One of the entertainers came into the restaurant and then went out, several times, constantly changing his mind as to whether he was right to accept the invitation. Jaroslav Hašek, who had created that ever-contented imbecile the good soldier Svejk, in order to show that "the only way to be free in the world is to be an idiot", could not himself decide what sort of idiocy was best suited to him personally, whether he had been more of an idiot as a drunken journalist writing a masterpiece he could not finish (a journalist for whom everyone was sorry, but with whom everyone was also angry for being irresponsible and unreliable) or as the efficient, unsmiling secretary of a Communist Party cell, which is what he also was (and in that guise everyone had been frightened of him). He could not decide which of his two bigamous wives he had been more idiotic to marry. It was not so easy to be an idiot, particularly when one was, as he considered himself to be, "one of life's enigmas . . . who has never found anyone who understood him." It was impossible quite to hear what he was mumbling to himself; he seemed dissatisfied with Paradise because he did not want to decide between all the alternative forms of idiocy available; surely Paradise was the one place where no decisions had to be made.

The clergyman next to him was not the stupid army chaplain to whom Svejk had been such an understanding batman, but the great Gogol, dressed as a clergyman; that is how he liked to disguise himself. Gogol had become a humorist because at school his playmates laughed at his long nose, and he could defend himself only by shooting their ammunition of ridicule back at them. Now he was puzzled that all the targets he thought he had blown up for good were here in Paradise unscathed; the same civil servants who had bored him to tears and to laughter in St Petersburg by talking about nothing except the gossip of their government offices, were still doing just that; each one of the absurd characters he had spotted, "crushed under a great weight, drowned by the trivial meaningless labours at which he spends his useless life", was content to go on as before in Paradise, doing his best to turn it also into a "graveyard of dreams". Gogol was bemused by what he regarded as the great riddle of existence, that each generation laughed at the mistakes of its predecessors, and then followed them straight into the same abyss. He had wanted not to make his readers laugh, but to help them become good and wise; in despair of achieving that, he had taken to his bed, refused all food and moved to Paradise. But here too the solution to his riddle, how to turn silly people into sensible people, still eluded him.

Even the ghost of Monty Python, who came uninvited to haunt the restaurant, uttered groans of lament that it had been so foolish as to go into a rage as a child because all its friends at school had been made prefects and it was not, that something should have snapped in it then, and driven it to spend twenty years trying to win recognition by making the public laugh, wasted years, because these antics never gave it a sense of achievement, always left it feeling it was cheating, and getting away with another trick. There was no entertainer who did not agree that the profession's war against solemnity had been a failure, and who did not long for Paradise to offer some other means of escape.

Laughter is rare in Paradise because it has been so inextricably linked with sadness on earth; and souls cannot imagine how else to laugh without an accompaniment of pain or pathos or cruelty or imbecility. Yet, though humorists are keen to stop laughing, many souls are on the look-out for entertainers to bring some new kind of laughter into their endless existence, which, everybody agrees, can often be dull, solitary, or drained of hope. Souls start with the idea that in Paradise one is entitled to live like a king, and every king must have his court jester. There are however no old court jesters willing to continue in their former profession, which they had practised only because they had something seriously wrong with them. This was so from the time of the very first court jester, Knumhoptu, the superintendent of the Pharaoh's royal linen, who was promoted to be jester as much because he was a dwarf as because he was witty, right down to the reign of Peter the Great, who kept ninety-nine fools to entertain him, and who used to breed dwarves, as misshapen as possible, to serve as clowns, so that while he laughed, his subjects would thank God that they were not dwarves, and would appreciate the wisdom of being content with their lot.

The one or two court jesters who did briefly try to repeat their success as laughter-makers quickly found that it was just impossible. Though everything lasts for all eternity in Paradise, and vegetables remain fresh and never wilt, jokes do grow mouldy and shrivel; they are the one thing that can die. Friar Mariano Felti, the most famous buffoon of the sixteenth century, so famous that Raphael painted him, court jester to Pope Julius II, was foolish enough to think that his antics might be an exception, because he used to be considered so uproariously funny when he chased live poultry over the papal dining table, catching and killing it with much wit, when he smeared his face with gravy, or organised battles

175

with terra cotta pots, making so much noise that the Holy Father, for all his gravity, was forced to smile; but, apart from the difficulty of finding chickens willing to have their necks wrung for the fun of it, even he finally said sadly, like an old man, that people no longer had the sense of humour they once did.

Sumdy, for her part, imagined that at the very least Paradise must contain a music hall, or there must be some dramatists writing in it who specialised in poking harmless, gentle fun at souls, so that they could laugh at their neighbours, and give the impression that they were not above laughing at themselves; surely that had to enjoy some popularity in Paradise, if only because it enabled one to sleep more soundly, comforted, exorcised. But no, even that kind of humour is regarded as devilish also, as is the humour of the parasites, employed by the ancients to insult their guests at dinner parties, as a way of averting the evil eye from the well-to-do. Buhlul al Madjnun, the mad clown of Bagdad, who reduced the Caliph Haroun al Rachid to tears from time to time, was the most skilful of this sort of brutal humorist, but he too was out of work in Paradise, and so despondent that he refused the Emperor Rudolf's invitation to make a come-back. Humour which produces only episodic laughter, a smile of a few seconds, a laugh of a few minutes, a sense of well-being of a few hours, is seen as helpless against the great yawn of eternity, a mere flicker of a candle on a dark night. Even humour at the expense of scapegoats is absent; goats, of every kind, have as much right to be in Paradise as anyone else. Souls give up eternally repeating their old jokes, because eventually they lose confidence in them, realising they are mere pea-shooters, irrelevant and powerless in the great war against cosmic gloom. They are more easily intimidated in Paradise by the memory of the wise men who say that

176

laughter is silly, or an evasion of manly duty, or childish. Nobody claims to have heard God laughing, and so long as they could not hear Him, souls considered it wrong to laugh either. Nobody whispers that laughter might be creative, because no one has thought that God could have a sense of humour.

If they organised cabaret shows in Hell, Sumdy thought, they could hardly devise one which contained more painful torture than what she had just witnessed. She had not expected to see souls for whom she had much affection parading around Paradise like captured prisoners stripped of all hope. These stories about laughter were too absurd. Were they playing a joke on her, or on themselves? But when she tried to laugh out loud, the sound was hollow and hesitant. Was this some aberration of the children's game, where you are forbidden to laugh and everyone does their best to make you? Was it indeed all a game? Even the fear that she sensed everywhere?

This was the lowest point in Sumdy's visit to Paradise. It was only from then that she began to enjoy the place. She suddenly had a sensation of understanding. She was in the home of the imagination. The imagination is free in Paradise. It is freer than it is in childhood, when one can talk to imaginary friends, and invent a world of one's own, until one is told to stop and grow up. Ordinary adult humans are not used to having free imaginations. Life on earth is sewn together with regulations and restrictions; souls assume that in Paradise it is their business to discover what the regulations are. Why should she believe them, these bogus tourist guides, who claimed to know what Paradise was like, when all they were doing was perpetuating their own expectations? She herself was probably spying fear in every corner of Paradise because she was used to bumping against it everywhere on earth. Paradise doubtless seemed to be a lattice work of problems because that was how a modern person is taught that the universe is constructed: if you cannot recognise a problem in every situation, you are taken for a simpleton, just as a mediaeval person was considered blind if he could not spot demons walking along every dark alley and goblins peering from behind every stone. But poverty and oppression did not exist in Paradise. The imagination had only itself to worry it.

The pitiful performance of the humorists touched Sumdy in a way that none of her other encounters, however frustrating, had done. She would never have guessed that laughter mattered so much to her. She began saying to herself that laughter was more than a relaxation, and did not come second to grander ambitions. For without laughter the world would be brought to a standstill. Nothing need change if nothing is laughed at. Perhaps that was the most important reason why they did not laugh in Paradise, for fear that they might shatter its peace and bring down the sky. A smile is a green light, which indicates that the imagination is simmering its fantasies. Progress often begins with a fantasy, and fantasy often begins as a joke; a good part of the art of life consists in preventing fantasy from deteriorating into hallucination. The psychiatrists protest: Happy people do not need to have fantasies. But how many happy people did psychiatrists know well enough to be sure of that? Without laughter, the precious pearl inside many souls would never be revealed, the potential of Paradise would never be realised. The strongest bonds between humans are shared fantasies. The surest sign of old age is the replacing of fantasy by reminiscence. Sumdy did not accept that laughter was only for blotting out worry.

The turning point came when she decided she would no longer listen passively to old souls telling her what Paradise was like, what she could or could not do in it. She was going to construct Paradise for herself. She would not be intimidated by the pseudo-facts that everyone repeated, nor be buried under a mountain of second-hand opinions. Much better to create her own experiences and be able to say: This is what I was able to do in Paradise. This is the place it is capable of being. One only truly existed in Paradise so long as one was constantly re-inventing it. One might as well remain asleep if one was content to observe and obey the example of others, imagining only obstacles, asking others to settle one's doubts. If she wanted to know what happiness in Paradise was, she had better find it for herself, taste it with her own tongue, in all its varieties, rather than ask sleepy souls what their view on the subject was, as though they would tell her what they really thought, even if they knew what they thought, even if they could remember, even if they had tried all the options open to them. She would have to paint her own painting of Paradise and it would look like nobody else's; that was the way it had to be: she would not go home having seen only touched-up photographs of it. At last, she felt, she had found something real to do. On earth, the air is for breathing, and the sea is for swimming. Paradise is for imagining. One could imagine everywhere, at all times, even while singing hymns. Even prayer was an act of imagination, not (as many souls continued to regard it) a ritual for begging, or flattering, or promising or apologising.

If they wanted Paradise to live up to their expectations, the residents themselves must reshape it. They must not be too polite, too timid to suspect that there might be flaws in it as they saw it. To put right the absence of laughter would be as difficult as giving a sense of humour to a person who does not have one. But Sumdy was certain God did not intend His creatures to grow more pompous as the centuries passed, to take themselves more and more seriously; the elimination of all sense of humour could not be His ultimate purpose. Humans had simply failed to find the true Paradise, Paradise as it could be.

Sumdy asked Mary whether it had perhaps occurred to her that laughter might be the missing link which she had been searching for in her alchemy: was it not conceivable that a thorough immersion in self-ridicule might be what was needed to make male and female unite successfully at last? Was she sure that God intended the two sexes to take their differences so seriously? Might there be a divine joke concealed in the absurdities which those differences produced? Perhaps Mary's research had got nowhere because it had been carried out in the wrong spirit, too seriously. But Mary replied that she could not see how research could be carried out in any other spirit.

Sumdy was obliged to prove that it could be. She let Jolly loose in the kitchen. If she could not get a meal that would make her fly, perhaps Jolly had a better chance. And indeed Jolly found the kitchen the most exciting place he had ever known. All those weird foods collected over centuries amazed him: he poked into the jars and barrels, opened every box, bowl and bag he could, from each of which escaped aromas that were like revelations to him. Scented oils, roots, crystals, resins, barks and leaves soon covered him entirely, and as from time to time he shook himself dry, the guests in the restaurant were increasingly spattered. Jars fell off the shelves, which exploded with a din that might have sounded like thunder far away. The symphony of smells seemed to inspire a sort of ecstasy in Jolly, as though it announced that he had at last reached his true home, where the battle against boredom could be finally won, a Paradise conceived to suit the inquisitive mind, or dog, for whom gluttony is the need always to have something new to sniff at and to meditate on. The warm haze in the restaurant grew electric from the rubbing of perfume against perfume. The guests began to cough, splutter, grow pale, in fear that souls could perhaps, despite assurances to the contrary, suffocate. Soon they must have become quite drunk with the smells released in the air, for they began to stare at Jolly as though bewitched, as though he was performing an extremely serious ritual. It did not occur to them that he might just be playing. They were soon certain that Jolly's arrival in their midst was a divine sign. Souls, it should be explained, are always on the lookout for divine signs; and many of the souls dining in the restaurant had a special reason for doing so, because they included a large number who had won some fame on earth for predicting the end of the world; this restaurant was naturally their favourite haunt, it was where one went if one was waiting for something to happen that never did happen.

People who prophesy the end of the world are of several sorts. St Andrew the Fool, a Byzantine who wrote a best-seller on the subject in the eighth century, described exactly how many floods and fires would sweep mankind away, and seemed to look forward to them almost with glee, while others, who are often far from being saints, have only used the prophecy as a threat to frighten the world into better behaviour. There were a particularly large sample of these in the Pyramid restaurant on this night, former government cen-sors most of them, ever optimistic in their search for things to censor, ever pessimistic about the folly of mankind, and they kept a particularly keen watch for any traces of laughter, to which, they claimed, Paradise had an incurable allergy. On earth they had worked hard, and they were proud of it, to stop humans from laughing; they had tried to kill laughter, though they could not explain why it never did die, why it should be immortal on earth; they sincerely hoped it had finally passed out in Paradise. Other diners, hidden neither behind dark glasses nor under large hats, and looking just like any person one might meet in the street, were the amateurs, prophets of catastrophe, censors in their little worlds, whose lives had been made miserable by the thought that people were always laughing at them, and who had got to hate laughter with passion; all their religious beliefs would collapse if Paradise should prove not to be free of laughter, which they knew only as an instrument of torture directed against themselves. The heralds of the end of the world had many other worries in Paradise: would Paradise disappear too when that happened? They never thought so previously, but that was something to worry about; they were not sure that they wanted the cataclysm to come until they knew to what even more exclusive refuge they would escape. Meanwhile, they warned all those who would listen that people would then regret that there had not been more censors to save the world; people would lament, for example, that a king of France should have been so foolish as to establish a Royal Corps of Censors in 1742 with a mere seventy-nine members, ludicrously inadequate (if that adverb could be permitted them); it was now obvious that to have only eight worthies to censor mathematics, only ten to censor medicine, natural history and chemistry between them, a mere thirty-five for belles lettres (what horrors slipped in under that epithet!), only one for painting, and only one for architecture (enough perhaps in those days of classical columns, but thousands more were needed now), showed a criminal incompetence in dealing with the true enemies of society. People would regret having laughed at censors for silencing authors – however worthy of pity these might with hindsight be – once they realised all the disorder that laughter caused. Paradise had to be protected from being contaminated by laughter, or it too would go. What else might happen if souls began to laugh at each other?

However, none thought Jolly was laughing. This was Ancient Egypt. Every Ancient Egyptian who had entered Paradise had been specially welcomed by the god Anubis, who has a dog's head. Ancient Egyptian dogs were very special, and they used to have a city of their own (Cynopolis) which humans treated with great respect. A visit from a dog to the Pyramids was almost the equivalent of a visit from an angel. Mary the Alchemist, to show her own appreciation of dogs, pointed out that whereas humans found nine out of ten smells unpleasant, dogs could cope with the four hundred thousand different odours in the universe, and the latest news was that the number of odours was growing all the time; it used to be thought that whisky had thirty smells in it, but recent discoveries suggested that it had at least three hundred, most of them still without a name. Jolly certainly knew something they did not.

There was an old Chinese gentleman in the restaurant who had done a lot of brutal censoring in his time, but who had as his gentle hobby the alchemy of his country. He had been discreet so far, because the alchemy of his country specialised particularly in making humans immortal, or at least very long lived, and there seemed little scope for his knowledge in Paradise; but he came out with the information that his ancestors had always believed that dogs were the best cure for "diseases caused by sorrow" and he himself had often eaten dog's heart to get rid of gloom; dog's spit, he added, was accepted as the most certain remedy for haemorrhoids; the appearance of Jolly was obviously a sign. A witch brewing a foul-smelling potion in the corner of the kitchen added that "dog" was "god" spelt backwards, which might mean he was the devil, but one could never be sure.

183

To find the Paradise that suited her, Sumdy knew she had to make a choice. She could fall asleep like most souls, and let her imagination live only in her dreams; that way she caused no trouble to anyone, nor to herself. But what happens when you wake up? To concoct fantasies all on your own is to flirt perilously with madness, even if no one realises that you are mad, or even if a touch of madness is regarded as normal. That was not her idea of Paradise. The other choice was to find a way of communicating with at least a few other souls. She had made an effort to do that, but she thought she had been miserably unsuccessful. There had been no communion of souls so far. It was no use waiting for a miraculous meeting to take place. Her only course was to infiltrate a myth into Paradise, almost like a germ.

A new Paradise must rest on new myths. A new world of the imagination needed to be created, which could shake itself free from the clutch of earthly fears. The restaurant gave her the opportunity. There is an insatiable shortage of myths and fairy tales in Paradise, because the boundaries of the possible are always being enlarged, and there is always a demand for new scare stories. Old tales became too ordinary for Paradise. But myths do not come from nowhere. Someone has to think them up. Censors have a lot of experience in creating myths. They know how to change history, turning truth into falsehood and back again, with a mere flourish of their pens; the invention of imaginary news, with their help, has been one of the main functions of civilisation. Sumdy appreciated not only that Paradise could not be different until it had a new set of myths, but also that if she introduced too outlandish or revolutionary a myth, it would take many times longer to get established than those spread by the powers that be. Most humans, she was convinced, and more than ever so after her travels in Paradise, are innately conservative; in Paradise that was quite clear. On earth what are called revolutions are often only superficial alterations brought about by those who have something to lose, who change a little to protect themselves from too much change. What Sumdy wanted was for Paradise to change its mind about the impossibility of flying and laughing and communicating. The only way was to get the censors to invent a myth, which might make that possible. Only a myth could induce people to rebel against themselves. Unintentionally of course: the most drastic revolutions are accidental, unplanned. Jolly was exciting them. Let them invent a myth about him. Sumdy was persuasive. They were soon dictating their myth to the scribe, who wrote it down for eternity in hieroglyphics. His papyrus, one of the earliest works of literature composed in Paradise, can be summarised thus:

The history books written by humans do not mention the achievements of the dog in the rise of civilisation. They say it is man who civilised the dog. Yet it is the dog who discovered laughter, one of the most dangerous of the flowers of civilisation. It happened like this. Dogs used to be wolves, as everyone knows, and in those times their tail pointed downwards. When wolves became dogs, their tail at once pointed upwards. The ancients believed the reason was that dogs felt honoured by being admitted to friendship with man. For long no one realised what really explained it. Dogs were laughing, and could not stop laughing, though silently of course, at the two-legged creature who believed that in this relationship man was master. They kept quiet because they had a comfortable life on earth playing man's little charade. They even became quite fond of man, so long as he served them their meals regularly; as a gesture of affection they agreed to bark – which they never did in their natural state – when man persisted in wanting them to be more like himself, easily angered. But otherwise dogs thought it prudent not to speak, which is why authority can look upon them with a tolerant eye. If they had

185

spoken, they might have said that there was one characteristic of man's that they found particularly deplorable. They refused to laugh the way man did, with a guffaw or a spasm. The laughter of man, to them, was clearly dangerous, inflammable tinder, allowing a light to be struck, that may cheer for a few moments, but then blows out, to reveal a darkness that is sadder than before, sometimes even leaving a scar; they noticed that the very laughter of supposedly innocent children is frequently a variation on the theme of cruelty. Dogs thought it wiser to develop two different kinds of laughter of their own – the wagging of their tails, but also that enigmatic smile that so worries humans, because it is difficult to draw a clear meaning from it – does it hide contempt or politeness? Does it mean yes or no? Or is it saying that the world is so incomprehensible, paradoxical and incoherent that it cannot be taken seriously? Dogs were the first to discover that a sensible being does not reveal what he is laughing about. Man was never able to understand how dogs managed to do this, until modern science found the explanation. It discovered that dogs have more chromosomes (seventy-eight) than most other animals, far more than man, who has only forty-six, and who in the real hierarchy of creation comes only just above the rabbit (forty-four) and the rat (forty-two), and a long way behind even the goat (sixty) and the sheep (fifty-four). Dogs have therefore been able to assume a far wider range of shapes than any animal, the largest breed among them is forty times heavier than the smallest, and there are more breeds of them than of any other creature. Which is why the dog can cope with complexity in a way man cannot, and why man is jealous of the dog, and treats him harshly even while claiming to love him. The moral is that the dog has learnt how to laugh properly, but man is not yet fit to do so.

Paradise was altered by the creation of this myth, at least for Sumdy, like a country that is transformed when its archaeologists dig up an unknown ancient civilisation under its ugly buildings. To prove that laughter was a seed in Paradise, waiting to germinate, gave her an immense joy to look forward to. And for their part the censors felt very pleased because they thought they had created a myth that reinforced the reasons for not laughing, bolstering their prejudices. It was a myth which might have a chance of surviving, because it was ambiguous; the more ambiguous a myth, the more likely is it to be believed, as more people can find something in it to suit them. The power of myths comes from their being open to contradictory interpretations. A Greek philosopher explained how it worked. He had spent many centuries in Paradise walking around with a lighted lantern in broad daylight, saying he was searching for an honest soul; he called himself a Cynic (which comes from the Greek word for dog, that may have had something to do with his role in the proceedings). He observed that once a myth is born, reasons for believing it sprout up on all sides. Fiction gathers moss until it fits into the landscape and becomes indistinguishable from the truth: who was to say whether the landscape had not once all been fiction?

That was real progress, thought Sumdy. Laughter thrives on ambiguity, which is not necessarily a weakness. The way to discover the potential of Paradise was to probe its ambiguities. Laughter revealed where the ambiguities lay, like hidden crevices.

She did not have to wait long for the myth to have its unexpected consequences. Mary suddenly said that she at last understood what humour was. She had not been able to make any sense of what Sumdy had told her about sex. But now she thought she might have some drops of a sense of humour in

187

her after all, for she had always enjoyed interweaving fact and fiction, in the same way as she had delighted in mixing her wax and pigments on her artist's palette, in order to paint her colourful and mysterious symbols, in the same way as she ground bizarre ingredients for her cosmetics, or as she mismatched her eccentric garments. Had she been laughing without knowing it, when she tried to transform and recombine elements? Was there a sense of humour hidden in far more places than people realised, if only they knew how to find them?

Jolly now became not just an important guest, but a sort of beacon, an inspiration. Mary said he must be given the best table in the restaurant, which meant at the very top of the Pyramid. With him permanently there to protect, to ward off the danger of laughter spreading indiscriminately to the masses in Paradise, they might perhaps experiment secretly in laughing themselves. Mary took Jolly in her arms, and, accompanied by the Emperor and all the cooks, carried Jolly up to what had once been the roof of the world. The censors, sensing danger everywhere, rushed ahead to clean the top of its graffiti. Everything was done in silence, as though all were agreed that they were doing the right thing. Jabir ibn Hayyan arrived with five empty plates, to prepare for the moment when a meal might be ready for these visitors from earth. He said he had calculated that gold could be made out of base metals in about five thousand years' time, but he could not promise when the meal would be ready. The later the better, because it was always enjoyable to wait, particularly in such splendid surroundings. He was no more a dreamer, he said, than were the utopians and believers in ideologies who say that one day humans will solve their problems and organise themselves in a rational way. The menu he had thought up for Sumdy was no more fanciful than the promises of politicians.

One day, he was sure, it would be possible to extract a pundit's wisdom and serve it in a soup, and one day croutons would surely not only taste nice, but also record the time at which they are consumed. One day, when trees are made fit to be eaten raw, as they already are by termites, once the problems of processing their protein and cellulose are solved, then it is more than likely that mahogany patina will be as prized a delicacy as caviar. The time would come when those who are anaemic intellectually will dose themselves with minute quantities of metals, served in a sauce. If one waits long enough, then even stones suitably treated will melt in the mouth, and new, more liberal varieties of peas will be bred, that will refuse to sit regimented in straight rows in their pods. In a perfect world, nothing would be wasted and old leather sandals, instead of being thrown away, would be fermented into delicious, yoghurt-like savouries. The only unlikely dish he had imagined was string and candle sorbet. He thought that was too far-fetched, since string had suffered too much serving as a wick ever to be reconciled with candles. Sumdy, said Jabir, must learn to be patient. It might take several thousand years, but ultimately Jolly would get his meal, and would wag his tail once more, and then he would surely take off and fly. On the top of the Pyramid, at any rate, he had the best chance of experiencing something truly wonderful.

Jolly smelt each empty plate in turn, walking round them in a continuous circle, but on three legs. There was general consternation. Why had he suddenly developed a limp? Dr von Hohenheim examined him and could find nothing wrong with the leg. It was a divine sign, everybody said, but of course they did not know what the sign meant. They withdrew to the restaurant to argue. As soon as Jolly and Sumdy were left alone, Jolly's tail began to wag, and his eyes lit up with his mischievous look. He performed a pirouette. There

189

was nothing wrong with his leg. He was just having fun. They could not stop him from laughing, however hard they tried. Sumdy was so pleased, she burst out laughing, and this time her laugh was loud and full hearted, so loud that it echoed all over Paradise. Down in the restaurant, the sound was terrifying, but they thought, or pretended, that it was Jolly laughing. The gods are allowed to break their own rules, to laugh, even to get drunk, in private. So long as they do it in private. And Mary went off to her little laboratory, and began practising how to laugh, in the same tones, when she thought no one could see her.

Sumdy spent a long time admiring the view and trying to decide which of these experiences in·the Pyramid she should write home about. They were not disconnected anecdotes. She felt they added up to something more. That was her real news.

She wrote a letter saying that her parents doubtless believed the old tales that Paradise was for ever immobile. But it can be whatever souls imagine it to be. So there had to be freedom in it. It had to be capable of changing. If freedom had a shape, she thought, it would surely be a spring of crystalline water, ever renewed. She felt excited because freedom no longer appeared to her as a treasure that asks only to be protected against its enemies, eternal, frightened enemies. A soul could feel safe in Paradise, but if it always thinks the same thoughts, it soon ceases to be free. Freedom was like life; it could not stand still. The point of freedom was the creation of new freedoms. Change was an essential ingredient of freedom.

But she had come to Paradise with little experience of changing things; that was true of all immigrants. It was so difficult to change on earth, because though new ideas are born every day, humans instinctively twist them so that they confirm old ideas. It is never enough for change to occur there; it needs to be recognised, or it fades away. The inhabitants of Paradise have all witnessed innumerable governments come and go, leaving life pretty well unchanged; they have seen laws passed, then disobeyed and forgotten; if the powerful could achieve so little, what could ordinary individuals hope to change on their own? No wonder they looked on change as a mystery, or a delusion.

Her news was that she thought she was beginning to get an inkling of how freedom travelled, where the water was percolating. The more complex the world became, the easier it was for freedom to find a place in it. The more confusing details there were, the more gaps into which freedom could infiltrate. The possible combinations and permutations of civilisation were increasing all the time. Paradise too was becoming more complicated. Here she could see how the gaps were kept plugged. The most common obstacle to freedom was myth. It was myth which explained why things could not, should not budge. Souls liked to repeat that they must accept their destiny: that was the oldest myth of all. A myth appears solid only until it is found to be absurd, soluble in water and laughter. Once it is dissolved, the facts it used to hold together are released; what once passed for truth falls apart, and can be reconstructed afresh.

What she had not discovered, however, was why humans did not unmake myths more often, since they made them in the first place. Perhaps the answer was that they did not know what else to put in their place. Could one live without myth? Here, too, souls seemed to like myth, because it gave their existence much of its cosiness, a feeling that everything was explained.

Did Paradise have an alternative hidden away somewhere?

CHAPTER SEVEN

The souls who were awake enough to hear Sumdy's laughter cringed, fidgeted, tried to plunge back into sleep. But not the soul of Sir Isaac Newton. For him, it sounded like the erupting of a new volcano, the most important thing that had happened to Paradise, or to him, for centuries. Newton had never previously been known to show any interest in women, or in laughter. The only love he had felt had been for the one person, twenty-five years his junior, whom he considered his soul-mate, Fatio, the mathematical prodigy of his age who never fulfilled his promise, who won Newton's heart by the effusiveness of his admiration, affection and curiosity, but who then broke it by revealing himself to be too wild, too unstable, and their hopes of living together collapsed. Newton had not tried to see Fatio again in Paradise. And he was not spellbound by Sumdy's youth, or bloom; he did not think she was as clever as he was. But she had the one gift that he did not possess in Paradise, the one quality he missed there: she was alive. It is very easy to lose touch with life in Paradise, to imagine that Paradise is the only place that exists in the universe, to forget what life is. When Newton had been alive, he had been too close to life to be able to regard it impartially, as a scientist might wish to do; life can be studied coolly only in Paradise, but by then it is too late. Sumdy's visit was an opportunity he was determined not to miss: he had an intuition that Sumdy's laugh might be the beginning of a new age in Paradise, where immortality and gravity had reigned supreme since the beginning of time.

The Egyptian desert might not seem the place one would head for if one was searching in Paradise for an eminence like the discoverer of the law of gravity, and indeed it was not where he normally resided. For several centuries he had sat under a favourite apple tree (Fatio had written a book about apple trees), battling against the temptation to fall asleep, and trying to master the art of half-dozing, which would allow him to think while appearing to sleep, turning dreams into tools of reason. He had no wish to rest. The prospect that eternity had to be spent in idleness horrified him; he was aghast that Paradise had never achieved anything, had never managed to invent anything, no gadgets, no medicines, not even a philosophy. However, it was not easy to think here, or even to sleep, for a person like Newton; though he had all eternity before him, he insisted he had no time to waste, and yet he was constantly being disturbed. Every soul who had been touched by the passions of science considered a visit to Newton an attractive afternoon outing. The trees in Newton's orchard had to bear their fruit all the year round to enable him to offer an apple to each guest as a souvenir, his way of indicating that the interview was over; the speed with which he distributed the apples told scientists who came to boast of their discoveries how puny their efforts appeared in the light of eternity. Newton accepted this burden of fame, because he got something in return: a complete, first-hand history of all science, but different from that which he could find written in books, for his visitors only pretended to come to him with success stories, as pioneers in the march towards truth. What they left with him was a sense of an omnipresent ignorance, error and guesswork, of a fumbling to reconcile old and new constantly changing visions of the universe. That comforted him, for he had lived in doubt and fear himself, more than his admirers ever knew. He liked to feel he was being useful in Paradise, listening to the scientists' confessions. Every soul needs someone to boast to, and inexplicably there seemed no appointed place, no special person to go to if one wanted to boast in Paradise. Newton experienced a strange fascination observing how much difficulty these visitors had in talking to him and to each other, how they picked up only signals telling them what they already knew, or that they could easily fit into familiar ideas, how they puzzled over Paradise being full of misunderstandings. This isolation of the soul in Paradise, magnifying human loneliness to the point that each appears to the other to be a distant star, and each feels to himself that he is a desolate planet, pitted with craters of boredom, suggested to Newton that there was an astronomy of the soul that still waited to be explored. He was expecting that he would soon witness some kind of explosion of the souls around him. The more his modern visitors talked to him about the amazing opportunities opened up by their Age of Communication, the more he noticed how much trouble they had in communicating. He became increasingly interested in the source of the energy that kept them revolving, each on his own axis; and he began to form a theory suggesting that beyond gravity laughter might be the force that mathematicians should study next; even more, that beyond laughter there was a third force in the universe, which would at last give the immigrants of Paradise what they had really come for, but never dared to expect.

One day, Newton slipped quietly out of his overcrowded

orchard, and made his way towards the Pyramids, setting up his new warmer residence on the soft sands by the Sphinx. A famous person like him cannot move without the gossip writers getting wind of it. They advanced different explanations, for it is very hard to guess what motivates souls. Some were convinced that, realising the extraordinary prestige he enjoyed, he had developed political ambitions. Other newspapers claimed that Newton simply wanted to escape from the science-lovers who were besieging him, and whose mathematics were getting beyond him. The third explanation was that he was finding the food of Paradise unsatisfactory; his hospitality having been returned by endless invitations to meals of every kind, and souls being such poor conversationalists, he often ate in silence, which gave him an opportunity to develop a Theory of Food: the Pyramids were the place he had chosen to publicise and expound it. At first sight, this last suggestion is the least believable, because Newton had been notorious for being so careless about his meals, that he often used to forget to eat them, so busy was he thinking his thoughts. But in Paradise he was having new kinds of thoughts. He had decided it was time that science studied the soul, described its shape, measured it, weighed it, and indeed at the Pyramids, he was to make his discovery of how eating influenced and moulded the soul. He went there with the feeling that he was near to completing his research, but that there were still riddles he could not solve. The sound of Sumdy's laughter now proved as decisive for him as the fall of the apple had been in enabling him to understand gravity.

As soon as he heard that peal of laughter, he set about organising an experiment. That meant, first, enticing about a hundred souls, of a special kind, to the Sphinx; and then getting Sumdy to join them. He went to her and said: What is the time?

Sumdy was alarmed. It is very far from normal for a soul who wants to start a conversation with another soul to begin by asking the time. No soul had probably ever asked the question before, because the sense of time among the dead becomes too peculiar for a plain answer to be possible. Sumdy remained silent, not knowing what deep implications she was supposed to recognise. What day, what year was it? Did she continue to be aware of such trivialities? Did she find it disturbing that people who had lived in different centuries should be mixing together in Paradise as though time did not exist?

No, Sumdy was not disturbed by that. The date of a person's birth had never mattered to her much. What she cared about was what epoch the people she met lived in mentally, whether they picked up their ideas in childhood or in youth, and then went on living with them as though their private clocks had stopped the day they decided they knew how to behave like adults. While not sharing the tastes of fogeys who kept putting their watches back to an imaginary summer time, she had some sympathy for visionaries who made theirs work at twice the normal speed, or romantics who got theirs to dance to the time of a waltz. Freedom from time seemed to her one of the forgotten rights of man. She could see nothing abnormal about people from different centuries being able to meet in Paradise. They did so constantly on earth.

Time, said Sumdy, was only a bubble of stale air, that humans swallowed and have different ways of burping out. Then they quarrel about the art of burping. Politics is a quarrel about what time it is, between people who would prefer to live in the past and others who wish it was tomorrow: there could be no politics in Paradise; there is no point in arguing in a place without clocks, where there was always time for anything to happen. And yet she had seen souls rushing about

196

Paradise, snatching glances at their watches, with the all too familiar look of desperation, so common on earth, sighing deeply: it was a habit, using up one's energy battling against time; no wonder they did not have the energy to do what they really wanted to.

Newton was pleased that Sumdy's attitude was compatible with his, that she felt more comfortable with what is timeless than with what is fashionable; only such people are capable of making use of the opportunities of Paradise; and only such people know that what is timeless has to be more real than ordinary reality, it has to be invented. Sumdy was flattered. She was curious to know what he was planning to invent. She wanted very much to believe that she had at last met someone who recognised her as special, with an opinion worth enquiring about. Perhaps the great Newton was great enough not to be totally absorbed in himself.

This could not be taken for granted, for Newton had never been a sociable person, and was well prepared for the loneliness of Paradise. That indeed was probably why he was so interested by loneliness, as something that appeared strange to him. However, he had his reasons for making an exception of Sumdy; he was willing, even keen, to explain his interest in her. He said he had lived more or less as a recluse while making the discoveries for which he had won fame; he liked just to sit in a chair and think. A person who does that inevitably gets a reputation for being odd, and he knew that he was considered to be austere, abstracted, cold, with seldom a good word to say about anybody. It was suspected that he thought the world was a fool. He gave the appearance of being self-sufficient, which the world hates more than anything. They jeered when, at one stage, his room was decorated entirely with drawings by himself. He seldom sought out the company of others, even if in later years he occasionally gave splendid entertainments; he always ended by withdrawing into himself. His scientific discoveries were like solitary games he played with himself, which he had no wish to publish for the world. Nothing displeased him more than having to dispute with fellow scientists; the obligation to talk to them about his work seemed to him to be a form of slavery, particularly since they were so obstinate and slow about understanding him; originality was a private satisfaction; he resented wasting time defending himself against scientists whose idea of scholarship was like a dog's idea of urine, a sign by which each one can mark the boundaries of his personal empire. He had not discussed the thoughts he had had in Paradise with anyone. But now he could make no further progress without Sumdy's help. The weakness in his budding new theory was that it was based on the study of dead souls. He needed to examine a living soul to be certain that he had discovered something fundamental about the permanent properties of souls in general, and not simply about what happened when they decayed after death. So he was very pleased by what Sumdy had said, because it encouraged him in his belief that the trouble immigrants gave themselves on their arrival in Paradise, deciding where they should reside, whether they would feel more at home in this or that vanished civilisation, among the Incas, among the ancient Hellenes or in a modern Greek tourist resort, all that was superficial and unnecessary, it showed a misunderstanding of what a soul was. What the calendar said did not matter, it was only a decoration on the wall. What did matter was what one wrote on the calendar, and he thought that Sumdy had come to put her mark on Paradise in just that way.

She replied that she had indeed not come to Paradise to relive

198

the faded pleasures of the past. For her, Paradise was not the past but the future. She knew enough about the brutality of the good old days to have no illusions about them; otherwise, if they had been an object of worship for her, she would have stayed at home, and read historical novels about knights killing each other, while she sipped cocoa in bed. No, she had come to see what had never been seen before, which was why, before they went any further, she wanted to make sure that Newton in Paradise was more than Newton on earth. Could Newton understand what a modern soul was searching for? Should she be seeking out Einstein rather than him?

Though Newton may once have been a physicist, that was never all he had been. Another of his passions on earth had been hunting the green lion – a code phrase, designed to keep secret the meaning of the long hours he spent at his steaming cauldrons. Lion means gold. Green means life. Throughout his career, he had been searching for the life that lay hidden in objects (gold was only one of them) which people took to be dead; and in Paradise he made no effort to deny that he was tired of those branches of science in which he had become famous, as he had often protested in his lifetime; he found them too limiting; to prove that the world worked like a machine, always symmetrically, was not entirely satisfactory; machines, and matter, were interesting in their way, but what really excited him was life: that was a mystery offering a challenge worthy of him. He wanted to understand more clearly how God created life, and how he, Newton, a bachelor who disdained mere reproduction, could become a creator truly in the image of God. He had appreciated alchemy as the nearest thing to a science of creation, taking chemistry beyond its limits, and not just for the sake of knowledge; to explain was not enough; he wished to achieve what no one else had done. On earth alchemy was interesting to him because it had seemed to hold out the hope of multiplying not just objects but virtue itself; he deplored its decay into esoteric mysticism. Now he yearned to discover whether there were any limitations to the ambitions that could be fulfilled in Paradise. What gave him the greatest thrill was the hunch that creativity was not just a divine property, not a rare gift, but an inevitable stage in human development, an inescapable fate for every person, the very essence of a soul. So he was planning to set up the most difficult experiment he had ever attempted: to bring life to Paradise. In Sumdy he saw an instrument quite unprecedented for discovering what life was, what a soul, which supposedly contained the germ of life, but which no one had ever seen or touched alive, was really like. He was now fully into the astronomy, the physics, the chemistry, the biology . . . of the soul.

Sumdy said she was interested, because she had gained the impression that souls in Paradise were only hibernating, hardly existing: when would summer come? Was there any point in waiting for it?

Something had indeed gone wrong with Paradise, said Newton. He thought it had to do with humans getting confused when they were told God created them in His image. They behaved like mass-produced reproductions, pale travesties of the original. But there was one quality that God had which humans clearly did not. He was never lonely. Why, by contrast, did humans so often feel like deprived orphans, desperately in need of a perfect father? Had He deliberately not passed on His immunity to loneliness? Or was it there, unnoticed, hidden in an appendix that they were not using? Or maybe He had made a mistake in the way He had installed it in humans. A creator inevitably makes mistakes. Man was quite likely one of His mistakes.

Sumdy was astonished to hear Newton almost quoting out

200

of the Gospel of Henry Ford, which he had not even heard of. Everybody had his own opinion in Paradise: it was very strange that two souls should agree.

Newton admitted that he had left mountains of manuscripts on earth on the problems of alchemy, that he had even copied out five whole treatises about the philosopher's stone. These papers, he knew, were examined, for the first time, only in the twentieth century, by a scholar who concluded in amazement that Newton was the last of the magicians, the last of the Babylonians and the Sumerians. Newton was not pleased to hear that, sad to be misunderstood, but then almost half of the Nobel prizewinners who had been to see him had told him that they were sad also because they had not been given their honour for what they considered their most important work. Only spineless people, indeed, agree with the opinions that others have of them; those who do are certainly not modern persons. Newton felt himself much more of a modern person than a lot of those who queued up to tell him about their bright ideas. A modern person is one who, without denying his past, sees no reason why he should be a slave to it; he is the opposite of a peasant who accepts his place and his fate. By the age of forty, Newton said, his hair had turned grey. His great discoveries and the passion he had put into them haunted him only like a youthful love affair, from which it is impossible ever to disentangle oneself completely; but in maturity, he was more interested in matters of the spirit, in prophecy, on which subject he scribbled endlessly and at length. His interests were expanding; he felt he was about to flower at last. New theories bubbled inside him, as though here the sun shone brighter, with a more nurturing warmth. Perhaps he was wrong to think they were good theories, but they made him purr within himself. His search for the green lion had taken on a richer meaning.

He was relieved that the great Age of Science of which he had been a pioneer was over. Those who followed in his footsteps, invoking his name, often appalled him, because they took his principles too literally, or too partially, as disciples do. Between the eighteenth and early twentieth centuries, the scientists who came to see him were very peculiar, he thought, quite different from those who came earlier, or later. They believed they could describe the rainbow in prose and matter in mere numbers, that reality was waiting to be observed and measured by man, compartmentalised into little specialities, until finally, one day, everything that could be known would be known. For all that time, Newton had heard their confessions with a respect that was tinged with sadness. But his excitement had returned. Recently the scientists seemed to be less conceited, more imaginative, to have once more a touch of the alchemist about them. They gave him the impression that they were relearning ancient skills, when they juggled with anti-matter as he had once with "philosophical matter", when they talked of particles without mass, just as he had of "aetherial spirit"; they became more congenial to him when they proved what he had only guessed, that the world was not stable, and that an element could spontaneously transmute into a different one. He had always said that only one seventh of any object was actually solid, the rest of it was empty space, and they had more or less confirmed that. It made him feel like a grandfather welcoming delightfully mischievous new additions to his family, when he heard about the birth of quarks with scientific properties called "charm", "naked charm" and "strangeness", capricious bosons, elusive leptons, wayward neutrinos, all so skilled at playing hide and seek. When, for the first time, he saw protons dancing, a hundred thousand times smaller than an atom, with a mad wit he could not quite fathom, he thought that science had at last proved that it was the little things that mattered in life, and that space was an open invitation to the imagination to join in the dance.

How could it matter when a soul had lived, if it spoke as Newton did? Sumdy felt ashamed that she was suspicious of Newton simply because he was a Grand Old Man. Was he out of date? Was he out of fashion? Those questions were absurd. The calm in his eyes, his way of looking in the distance as though there was always something interesting about to come into view, was deeply attractive to her, and reassuring. She could not take her own eyes off him as they walked back together to the Sphinx.

About a hundred souls were waiting for them, clustered round it. On their brows the furrow of anger or suffering was clearly visible, as though they had been branded for all eternity. Newton had collected a sample of former slaves. His aim was to confront Sumdy not just with dead souls, but with souls from whom the life had been beaten out even when they were alive, and who came to Paradise with the hardest of tasks, to reconstitute their damaged souls. Newton wanted to know whether the experience of life was so draining and destructive, that souls had no warmth left for anyone but themselves, whether the climate of Paradise induced such languor in them, that they could not restore their energy, whether the fire in Paradise's kitchens was pure theatre, and the agitation of immigrants a mere sham, whether in short it was possible to do something drastically new in this environment which everyone thought was made for tranquil repose, and only he, apparently, believed was capable of amazing new creations. He did not want to fool himself or cheat: he had chosen the most extreme victims of life for his experiment.

Historians have never succeeded in counting how many slaves there have been since the world began; their guess is that at least one third of all humans have been slaves, legally declared so by judges admired for their gravity. (At times, nine tenths were slaves in some of the colonies of Britain, Spain and Portugal, as many as half in some parts of North America and Russia, much less in the Islamic world.) But many former slaves were too tired to accept an invitation even from Newton; some excused themselves saying they needed more time before they felt like going to social gatherings again, they were still not sure whether souls, in Paradise as on earth, were not invented to make each other miserable, to draw tears from each other, perhaps that was how the universe avoided drying up. Some were so totally absorbed in forgetting the world, playing the music of the heavens, composing new tunes and rehearsing old rhythms, that they had no wish to break the spell with bitter conversation. Some were too shy, still humiliated by their experiences, uncertain whether they had indeed ever lived at all, for the judges said slaves were not quite persons, and in the eyes of the law they were the living dead. Others resented his invitation, still being thought of as slaves; even worse, slave in many languages means foreigner. They sent him letters saying that every civilisation has justified itself by its ability to protect its members against foreigners and their dirty habits, was Paradise not going to be different? One particularly angry letter said: Why did he not realise that Paradise is full of nothing but foreigners, trying to forget the lessons of their teachers who taught them to admire generals who destroyed foreigners, generals like Julius Caesar, who put about a million foreigners onto the slave market, for the greater comfort of senators who spoke Latin prose? What Newton had to do with Julius Caesar he could not guess, unless that he too was a

204

famous name of the past. Newton had not realised what sensitivities he was offending. How could a former slave foregather with other souls, said one of them, where he might meet one of those highly respected moralists who proved that slaves were part of the natural order of things, and that war was too, because war was necessary to acquire slaves? He might be in danger of bumping into one of those rich patrons of the arts, immortalised in museums, who had made his money buying and selling slaves. How could he exchange politenesses with the likes of Dr Samuel W. Cartwright of Louisiana, if he met him, who won his fame diagnosing scientifically the two appalling diseases that separated slaves from the rest of mankind: *dysaesthesia aethiopica*, whose symptom was "the aptitude to do mischief and be careless due to stupidness of mind and insensiblity of nerves" and *drapetomania*, "the habit of running away", an illness however, that "with proper medical care" could be cured by "whipping the devil out of them"? These replies made Newton aware that he had got a very limited view of what was going on in Paradise by talking only to scientists. Some souls appearing to be asleep were bubbling inside.

And there were others who demanded to be invited when they heard about his experiment: the vast numbers who had been treated so nearly like slaves, that they had boiled with similar resentments, children who had been turned into machines, set to work as soon as they could walk, women who had promised to obey, and did, the grey-faced products of the Industrial Revolution, alive only as creatures of the night, who had by day been meek prisoners in their offices and factories, earning no remission. It might seem that there were very few souls who, in one way or another, had not been slaves in some part of their lives. On the other hand, many were wary of becoming victims of a trick, they did not want to be looked at too closely, analysed, perhaps even persuaded to fill in questionnaires. Newton was lucky to get enough souls for his purpose without causing more upsets than he did.

The experiment began with Newton placing Sumdy on one of the giant paws of the Sphinx. He called out to the hundred slaves to come forward, and seat themselves one by one on the other paw, so that their weight could be compared to that of a living soul. As each one filed past, Newton questioned them and made careful notes. They then all watched expectantly while he calculated. For a very long time, the silence was broken only by the sound of his pen, and by the distant music of the heavens, playing an accompaniment to the rising and declining heat of the day. The sun fell and came up again, and still Newton was calculating. But finally he scratched his head and announced in some confusion that the difference between the dead and the living was not as simple as he had assumed. Many souls appeared to have arrived in Paradise already dead, to have been dead for most of their natural lives, and many of the inhabitants of Paradise had clearly not known how to make a new life for themselves. To be truly alive, he thought, is the hardest thing in the universe, harder than to be rich, or famous, loved or feared. And to be dead is not a negative state, it takes a lot of energy to remain dead in Paradise, despite all the pleasures it offers. He could no longer accept that energy came and went with birth and death.

Now Newton turned to Sumdy and said: "I want to touch your soul. I want to feel it."

Was Newton trying to made advances to her, so quickly, and in public? A soul cannot be touched. It has no shape. She told him so.

Newton did not agree. He had not spent three centuries interviewing scientists without having learnt something about the soul. People might say that a soul was just a breath of air, but that was because they had not looked at it hard enough. He had spotted both dust and dew in that air. At first he had assumed that was an illusion, caused by the fact that in the light of Paradise everything is liable to turn into a sort of Impressionist painting, a mass of dots and of lights, simply because one can, if one likes, see detail more clearly, as though magnified many times. Dust to dust . . . had that phrase been misunderstood? He had as open a mind about souls as he did about tables and chairs, which were said to be made of tiny electric shooting stars. Unfortunately he had inspected only dead souls so far, and it was possible that they, like rotten nuts, became empty shells, disintegrating inside into debris and dirt. That is why he wanted to see a living soul, Sumdy's soul, to discover what the effect of life was.

Sumdy agreed to lie down on the great paw of the Sphinx and let Newton examine her soul, which he did for a long time. But when he had finished he would say nothing. The slaves who watched him did not ask him what he had discovered, for they all had their own opinions as to what a soul was. Many came up to Sumdy and poked their fingers into her ribs, or pulled at different parts of her, as though trying to borrow bits of her soul for themselves. They saw what they expected to see, as people always do. One, for example, who had been a witch doctor in better days, said that Sumdy was not one soul but a colony of souls: his tribe had always believed that thirty souls lived in every body, in the hands, in the feet, in the eyes, in the mouth. Other enslaved medicine men, from various tribes, each gave a different number for the souls they claimed they could see in Sumdy. But Newton kept his opinion to himself. He too had known what he expected to see. All he would say was that his observations had confirmed his hypotheses. He asked Sumdy to pass on to the next stage of the experiment, in which he hoped her soul would give new life to the damaged souls he had collected around her.

Sumdy had fallen under Newton's charm. She was overwhelmed by the sense that she was in the presence of a genuine adventurer, with the courage to climb up a rope which was not dangled by anybody, not suspended from anywhere, and that led no one could guess where. And she accepted that Newton did not like publicising his theories. However, to be a mere tool, to be used as a sort of bicycle pump for deflated souls, did not appeal to her, at least not unless in the process she was herself inspired, by learning the secret of how a modern soul could become happy in Paradise. If Newton found it impossible to talk in plain language about the soul, if that was too much like prying into nakedness, then, she said flippantly, let him wrap his message to her in music and song.

She should have known that Newton had no ear for music at all. On earth he had not concealed that he had "no skill and no experience" in that direction, to the extent that he could not even get his calculations about the velocity of sound right. But Newton now was not the Newton who had once been. Sumdy seemed to reinforce his desire to be a Newton who was more different still, who could do what he had never done before. He did not think Sumdy's suggestion was silly. To find a new way of announcing new ideas, so that the announcement was itself a work of art or at least a spectacle, and not merely a repetition of a thought, appealed to him: an envelope deserved to be as sweetly perfumed as the letter inside. He had been meditating on why even science was asleep in Paradise, and he had been thinking that perhaps if it could be made to speak in a more attractive way, dead souls might creep back into the silent laboratories and light up the bunsen burners once more. He would be prepared to abandon his notorious reticence if he could think how his unique discovery could be expressed in a unique form, as dramatic as his message. It was Sumdy who improvised the scenario that enticed him from his silence. She invited each of the hundred souls to dig a shallow grave in the sand, the size their own coffin might have been, and then to lie down in them; only a few refused. She went round shovelling the sand over those who agreed, until only their faces were above the ground. Suddenly, a cemetery had sprung up in front of Newton, with noses for tombstones and questioning eyes as the indecipherable inscriptions. Newton was moved by the sight, because the souls seemed both alive and dead, no longer certain whether they were one or the other, the most impartial kind of audience, almost calling out for him to put on a performance for them, to settle their doubts. He felt as though a theatre had been raised in front of the Sphinx, and that perhaps scientists needed to use the theatre in Paradise, where there was no point in concealing that everybody is always playing a theatrical role.

So Newton agreed to explain his opinions on the biology of the soul. To do so, he needed to do a vanishing trick. For to understand the soul, it was necessary to understand gravity, and to understand that, one needed to feel it. It was not enough to make calculations here about apples flying down from their tree branches to the ground like pigeons. Humans on earth have never thought to taste gravity, or to watch its effect on the soul. Neither had he, till he reached Paradise. He asked Sumdy to dig a hole for him too, but much deeper, and he would go into it gradually, feet first: he needed to experience the sensation of gravity sucking up the soul, and to suffer the agony that gravity induced, as he spoke. The scientists who had visited him had not noticed that as they made

209

their confessions to him, he had imagined that he was a worm crawling into their souls, boring his way through the husk that was supposed to keep strangers out, hardly able to see anything in the pitch dark, bumping into all sorts of bric-a-brac, smashing his face against stone walls, getting swept away into bogs or streams, losing himself in cold and empty caverns, becoming bolder nonetheless as he learnt the art of burrowing in what at first seemed like a messy garbage dump. In this way he had learnt that what mattered most in a soul was its consistency. Many were as dry as dust, hard, or parched, or pulverized, or brittle or crumbling: he wormed his way through dryness in all its forms. Other souls gave the impression of being made of slime or grime, to be fizzy drinks, or sweet lemonade, variously murky, oily, slobbering . . . he had never imagined there were so many ways of being damp. Other souls still, less frequently blew at him like miniature hurricanes, or appeared to be just bubbles of air, or a heavy atmosphere thick with nothing but thought, made of invisible gases that somehow had unmistakable though invisible faces.

It had taken him hundreds of years to make sense of this. Finally he hit upon his great discovery. The force of gravity had even more influence on the soul than it did on the body. The dryness showed it. The mention of the word "gravity" seemed to shake him: he stepped into the hole in the sand down to his waist, as though to steady himself. It had been a surprise to him, that though the souls in Paradise were supposedly free from their bodies, so many were heavily weighed down by gravity. Gravity took on a different meaning in Paradise. On earth, gravity may be the force that attracts bodies to each other, but it appeared to have a contrary effect on souls, to keep them apart, to encourage them to sleep, or to stare at each other with indifference, to grow into bores rather than poets, and doubtless to put aside all hope of flying to the angels, or searching for the rarer joys of Paradise.

Sumdy noted that Newton had said that he had only imagined he was a worm. The question was whether, when death released the imagination, it let it go wild, perhaps back to the wild state of infancy, or whether there was a release of lucidity, perhaps the sort of lucidity that came after deep sleep, at the very moment of waking. Newton had been practising for centuries the art of culling the thoughts that came at that precious moment. One of the things that attracted Sumdy to him was that he was a day-dreamer: but she wanted to know why Newton continued to be so obsessed in his day-dreaming by gravity. Was it a sort of nightmare to him: did it haunt him because he was so full of gravity himself, a dignitary loaded with honours? "No man understands me," he had written in his diary; it was still true; no woman either. "I do not know what I may appear to the world, but to myself I seem to have been only a little boy, playing on the seashore, and diverting myself, in now and then finding a smoother pebble or a prettier shell than ordinary, while the great ocean of truth lay all undiscovered before me." While he had listened to the lectures of his endless stream of visitors, he had a clear feeling that in Paradise he was still a boy, that he had lived only partially, that his visitors were in much the same state, of longing to complete their lives, if they only knew how. Most of them had been stunted by despair as he himself had. He had not forgotten how in his fiftieth year he had collapsed in what Sumdy would call a nervous breakdown; his skies had suddenly turned stormy and angry, all those around him seemed to scowl at him, his achievements vanished from sight, to leave only a great black hole of his failures and his vain hopes. He had not searched for the philosopher's stone with the intention of turning base metal into gold, that was too old-fashioned for him; he was not interested in being rich; it was a more sublime illumination that he had sought, the cure for all human suffering, and to him the worst kind of suffering was gloom, the great fog that hid life from itself. On earth he had supposed, like most other people, that the answer to gloom was security. All his physics was designed to make the world appear more secure, safe, solid, immovable, to show that space was always the same; he had done his best to extend the range of what was predictable. Gravity had been his anchor. In Paradise, most souls still felt the need for gravity, because it promised peace, and gave them a sense of certainty – they knew where they were, who they were; gathered all their contradictions into a solid ball so that at least they appeared to be in one piece, enabling them to cherish their habits and be proud of their achievements. It was reassuring to regard oneself as consistent.

Was it then the force of gravity that made souls happy? And if so, why were modern immigrants having trouble in being happy?

There are many forms of bliss in Paradise. That is the first truth that unfortunately new arrivals are never told; bliss is a subject seemingly too intimate to mention. Happiness is only the mildest form of bliss. It is the best-known form, having been invented on earth and imported into Paradise. It is not realised just how mild it is, this mild, mild shampoo that washes away gloom but needs to be used at least twice a week. Most souls never dare to ask for anything stronger; gravity keeps them prudent; they prefer to get used to what they know; in Paradise, they go on revering happiness; and continue still to regard it as the ultimate miracle of the place. A small dose, souls say, is all that is needed to make one feel satisfied, and sleep soundly. Its simplicity is one of its main attractions. On earth, people pick up folk wisdom: are you

212

married with beautiful children, do you enjoy your work, do you have interesting hobbies? Then you have a good chance of winning the lottery. But of course many do not win. That is bad luck. Happiness is always as much a matter of luck as a reward for following the rules. But humans are fatalistic, what they call realistic. They have not demanded that happiness be improved, even in Paradise.

Did Newton think it was worth coming all this way to Paradise, just to be happy, on these terms? Sumdy said she had some sympathy for the modern immigrants who sneered at happiness, complaining that there was never enough of it to go round and satiate all appetites. The more populous Paradise became, the more diluted happiness seemed to be. In crowded conditions it was less effective; Paradise had been ruined as a haven for happiness, once it became like a get-away-from-it-all beach swarming with bathers unable to move. Modern people needed something more reliable, efficient, and up to modern expectations. The great inconvenience about happiness is the fact that it is only possible to be happy if everybody else is happy. Though invented on earth, it could work properly only in Paradise. On earth, one has to blindfold oneself to be happy: opening one's eyes and seeing the suffering around one makes one choke with pain and shame. Paradise had obviously been happy when no one did anything at all except listen to the music, but as soon as the distraught modern hordes started arriving and moaning, the calm vanished. As soon as souls began worrying about their future, it was all over. Perhaps it was still possible to be happy in Paradise if one slept, but sleep was constantly being disturbed. Or are some souls specially suited to happiness? How can they know if they are?

Sumdy had invented a test, without realising it. Newton told her to bury herself in the sand, as she had buried the others. The sand would be warm; she would feel its embrace as protective, and she would know that she could rest like that for ever if she pleased; she could sleep the calm sleep of eternity, her face would alternately glow in the rays of the sun and cool off in the shadow of the Sphinx; she could find peace in that sand. Let her look at the expressions in the eyes of the slaves she had buried, and judge what their answer was. All those who are searching for an ultimate miraculous solution to their problems are made for happiness, as are all those who believe there can be a solution to a human problem. Happiness is for souls who want to live in a universe that is predictable. Sumdy could see that happiness bore all the marks of an import from earth.

Some of the slaves, as Sumdy walked round her imaginary cemetery, had indeed fallen asleep; some were licking their lips as though in satisfaction, or moving them as though repeating what they had heard Newton say, memorising his words, comforting themselves with them; to do and to think as wise men did was for them an assurance of respect and of self-respect. The world has been largely full of people who believed that to challenge authority was a crime and that obedience was a virtue, that other people are more likely to know best. But there were also some modern victims of slavery in that cemetery, and among them Sumdy saw faces grimacing, gasping for breath, eyes pleading for release. Newton's own face wore an increasingly pained look of nausea and boredom, as it slid almost to the level of the ground. His return visit to gravity had been like a journey to a childhood haunt, once full of magic, but indescribably ordinary, even ugly, when looked at in maturity. Sumdy did not want even to try a burial in the sand. The mere thought of it set off a panic of claustrophobia. She knew she was too impatient to sit in one place even for a fraction of eternity, there was always, for her, something more hopeful elsewhere. What a terrible piece of news to receive from Paradise, that she was not made for happiness. She was, whether she liked it or not, modern. It looked as though wanting to be happy was a legacy modern people inherited from their forefathers, but had always regarded as somewhat puzzling, and had never got round to unwrapping from its tissue paper. She was not in tune with the majority of the inhabitants of Paradise. Newton, without saying as much, seemed to have shown that happiness in Paradise was a sort of helplessness, and gravity a sort of hypnosis. The symptom of dust in the soul was tiredness.

By now Newton had sunk so far in the sand that he was almost completely buried and his face was twisted in anguish. The tombstones meditated in silence on the peace and the pain that gravity could cause. Sumdy stood alone among them for a long time. It grew dark. She waited till the following morning before resuming her questioning.

Meanwhile Jolly and Forgetmenot had been exploring the Sphinx together. For a time it seemed as though they had set up a partnership, sniffing side by side, combining to solve insoluble puzzles. They examined the warm sand and the tombstones, moving in a slow procession. However, Jolly would interrupt the search from time to time, and lie on his back with his legs in the air; Forgetmenot would then walk about on his stomach, tickling it with its antennae, while Jolly uttered snorts and sighs of pleasure. Occasionally, Forgetmenot would climb onto Jolly's back, who would then run round the tombstones shaking himself violently, as though they had invented a game in which Jolly had to keep running until Forgetmenot was unseated. Or suddenly Forgetmenot would disappear, and Jolly would hunt for it, beaming in triumph when he spotted its antennae peeping out of some impossibly minute hiding place.

Watching them now, Sumdy cheered. They had learned to play together. What a carnival Paradise could put on if all its animals and insects and fish did the same! But Forgetmenot was still a creature of regular habits; it had always been so even in dark recesses where day and night were indistinguishable. Suddenly it would stop playing, and retire to its jar. Jolly too would abruptly forget Forgetmenot, curl up and fall asleep, as though he could not exist for long without dreaming. It was clear, Sumdy thought, that two beings could be more profoundly separated by boredom than by enmity.

CHAPTER EIGHT

What other bliss could humans hope for in Paradise, apart from the happiness they had been told about on earth?

Newton wanted to set up some new scenery before he would reply. He brought a hose and sprinkler and got it to spray cold water over the whole audience, and the Sphinx, in a fine drizzle. Was this designed to make them feel cool, or exhilarated, or damp? The answer came in the form of a song. The rain had an instant effect on one of the tombstones, which, like a plant limp with thirst, suddenly revived.

> *Come and be my friend*
> *Frivolity*
> *Please don't be so shy*
> *Come and show your face*
> *No need to know your place*
> *You matter more to me*
> *Than dignity or gravity*
> *Than common sense, than pounds and pence*
> *Come make a mockery*
> *Of all this misery, this cemetery*
> *Don't sigh, don't die*

Guide me, side with me
Frivolity.

But there was no frivolity in Paradise. Sumdy knew it. Everybody knew it. That was exactly what Newton was trying to show with the cold shower. The song was a cry in the wilderness. Why does one so seldom come across a soul that is not as dry as dust, why did the drizzle splash off the tombstones – all but one – without either softening or nourishing them? Newton told Sumdy the story of the tombstone that had burst into song.

There is a place called Gedara, by the Sea of Galilee, not so far from Bethlehem, where on a day that has, alas, never become a feast, a child was born called Menippos, in the third century BC. He is the forgotten one among the many strange and wonderful prophets who have sprung from that part of the world.

It was Menippos, buried in the sand, who had sung that song. He had once been a slave. Newton believed it was he to whom God had entrusted a divine mission: to pour cold water on grave and pompous people. Menippos spent his life preaching that nothing was quite worth its reputation or its price. Whether or not he was the first man to have said that the world was a silly world, not to be taken seriously, and that humans incorrigibly pretend to be what they are not, he was certainly the first to write forty books to prove it. He wrote with a bogus earnestness which made all earnestness absurd. He was the prophet of Irony, and Sarcasm, and Frivolity. Forty prophets in one. That is how frivolity came into the world, where previously gravity reigned supreme. There was room for frivolity in every soul, but till then it had been vacant, souls had been dry as dust. Frivolity was doubtless destined to become as powerful a force on earth as gravity itself. But, as usual, the divine plan did not go quite as

218

expected. First, all Menippos' books were lost. He is known only from what some of his disciples have reported. They mocked each other too much to be able to start a religion of irony, and succeeded only in sowing confusion and doubt about what exactly the word means. By their jolly singing about the sham and dissonance in the world they made despair almost a pleasure; but they sniped at everything, with the result that far from making the world more amusing, they gradually shrouded it in gloom, perhaps so that they could illuminate it with their wit. And then Menippos himself did not turn out to be quite worthy of the trust imposed in him. He had been a slave, who bought his freedom, and he became very rich as an insurer of ships and as a money lender. He lived a full life, both as a witty philosopher, and as a miserable and insecure businessman, like so many others, except that he could play the silly world at its own game and come out on top. Then one day he was robbed of all his gold, and he committed suicide. It was assumed that he could not find enough humour to bear his loss, and that discredited both him and everything he stood for. The truth was even sadder. Menippos had revealed to Newton that he had committed suicide not because of the money, but because he decided that he was a prophet sent to the world too soon, a prophet of a cause that would have to wait a long time to win respect. Humanity looked upon him as the leader of a heresy. It was committed to treating gravity as its firstborn child, and to scorning frivolity as the bastard. He was confident that secretly it really preferred the bastard, but he would have to wait. Would they ever be disillusioned with gravity? Only then would they see that frivolity had a new kind of hope to offer. And meanwhile frivolity would have to break its ties with gloom. Menippos had come to bide his time; he was still being scorned, even though he noticed that the number of

219

souls who were tired of being happy in the old way, no longer happy to be searching for happiness, was increasing; they were looking for something else; but they could not find a name for it.

Newton had examined Menippos' soul. It should have been moist, as frivolous souls are, absorbent, thirsty for variety and distraction; but the sleepy atmosphere of Paradise seemed to dry it up quickly every time it got wet, so that it was like a river that was victimised by the seasons, doomed to recurrent droughts, ever frustrated. Newton understood that frivolous souls in Paradise were clients for a bliss that was different from happiness. They are too sophisticated to want to be happy, so sophisticated that they do not like to say what other hope they have, because they know they can shoot down any hope as being ridiculous, any ideal as being naive. But Newton, an outsider to their mutual denigration, was able to identify the bliss that they were seeking. They wanted to be in a state of levitation: not actually to exist floating in mid-air, but to have that feeling, of being detached from the cares of the world, and from its hopes too. That was the second kind of bliss that Paradise could offer. But of course frivolous souls could not resign themselves to having an ambition, even the ambition not to have an ambition. That was the cause of all the trouble that the modern immigrants were causing. To be frivolous, to levitate, is to have no purpose. They could find no purpose in Paradise. And Menippos knew he had no right to be disappointed that those souls who might have been his disciples floated aimlessly past him, refusing even to recognise him.

Newton decided that Menippos was a very important person, one of the really great figures of history, who had brought to the world a seed from which there would one day grow an attitude to life that would change life. What began as little more than a verbal game might one day give birth to something as revolutionary as science, becoming the most versatile tool humans had after logic itself. Because while logic enabled them to seek out truth, frivolity could be their instrument for coping with truth when it turned out to be unbearable, for balancing conflicting truths, for cultivating a flowering garden around truth, where they could relax and feel they had some freedom, where their sense of individual dignity could blossom. That had not happened yet, because frivolity by itself could achieve nothing positive or constructive. That was why there was no laughter in Paradise. There were traces of frivolity in many souls, traces of damp, but Newton had seen no movement in them. To hear Sumdy's laugh had been a great thrill.

Menippos did not know what to do in Paradise. He spent a lot of his time chanting bizarre lamentations that were not quite a song, as though for a religion without a doctrine.

Is there a home in Paradise for me?
Will jailers, judges, juries, janitors let me be?
I am expert at tying experts in knots;
I can blow up thrones with explosive jokes,
Reshape a sweet dream into a cruel hoax.
But no one in Paradise wants to join in my plots.

Is there a job in Paradise for me?
Will aesthetes, gourmets, critics and prudes scorn my plea?
I can cook raw nerves in garlic and spice;
I can comfort consumer societies;
My hunger gobbles up all pieties.
But I cannot accept that a sense of humour is a vice.

Is there a friend in Paradise for me?
Will hecklers, objectors and protestors show charity?

221

Out of prickly words I can make a soft down bed;
I need no temples, have no priests;
I use chloroform as incense at my feasts.
But for all the fun I get, I may as well be dead.

Or is then Paradise my enemy?
Will fanatics, dogmatics, pedantics always scowl at me?
I who can never say yes, never whisper no,
Whose joy is to be ambivalent,
Who think I am too intelligent for argument,
Who am my own, my only impresario.

Is Paradise a place where I can be free?
Will medical hacks, therapist quacks, give me the energy?
I can't take the dot from my question mark,
I can't straighten out its squiggle,
Nor cease to tease, to worry, to wince, to wiggle.
Will they amputate my chuckle from my bark?

No, perhaps in Paradise there is no room for me.
Mavericks, lunatics, heretics are not made for tranquillity.
I don't hear the same with each of my ears.
No celestial music sounds quite in tune to me.
Staying here is going to be agony.
But what refuge is there from my own sneers?

While Menippos chanted, Newton explained how to test a soul for its frivolous content. It was not people who laughed a lot and loudly who were frivolous. The fact that there was no laughter in Paradise did not mean that all humour had been purged from it. He had found plenty of traces of frivolity in it, and not least among modern immigrants. Frivolity was a special kind of humility. Frivolous souls know that they are only slime or grime or lemonade inside, chaos of one kind or another. Grave souls may suspect that is true of them too, but they conceal it from themselves, they congeal, thinking that they would fall apart, dissolve, if the chaos were allowed to reveal itself, that the whole world would fall apart if everyone allowed the truth to be revealed: that was what gravity was for, to hold pretence together. The test for frivolity had been demonstrated by the shower of cold water on the tombstones. Only Menippos had responded. The rest were unaffected because gravity protected them, keeping them impervious to new ideas, to ridicule, even to hope; they put all their efforts into shedding frivolity as oil sheds water.

The water was turned off. There was a pause while the sun dried the sand. Then Newton was ready to explain the most mysterious of all the elements in the soul, thin air. For that, he set up new scenery again. Collecting a pile of sticks, brambles and old newspapers, he set them alight so that smoke swallowed up the Sphinx and everyone around it, turning all into a dark grey nothingness. He wanted to demonstrate how, when the soul was creative and truly ethereal, it could see into even that kind of invisibility, where the possible has no limits. Every soul was capable of being inventive, imaginative and creative in Paradise; he was convinced of it. His purpose was to show why, so far, the infinite wonders that lay beyond gravity and frivolity remained a dream.

Many amateur scientists had been to see him, who enjoyed battling their cunning against the ingenuities of nature. They told him that they felt deeply that every individual had potential talents which were not given an opportunity to blossom in life on earth. How, they asked him, does Paradise put that right? Many who had shown originality in their infancy, had been schooled to abandon it; the fear of being regarded as

223

abnormal was too strong; many learnt to accept second best, transferring their higher hopes to the world of their dreams. Those who as children thought they were clever, until the world persuaded them they were not as clever as they believed, would have liked, on arriving in Paradise, to have said, if anybody would listen to them, that they were now ready to become the geniuses they should have been.

The world is full of gifted children, said Newton, but of very few gifted adults. Where does all that promise vanish? Was the accolade of genius reserved in Paradise for the same tiny minority who enjoyed it on earth? Were geniuses distinguishable here too by their eighty-four peculiar characteristics, combined in the most secret of formulae? Surely Paradise must be more than an asylum where those who had not fulfilled their hopes could ponder the story of their sad decay? He did not believe the rumours that humans could not change, that intelligence was fixed once and for all at birth; those rumours sounded to him as no more than propaganda for a feudalism of the conceited, who pretend to have a monopoly of intelligence, and a right to exact tribute from the gullible for ever, as once landowners were kept fat by starving serfs; it was because of those rumours that most intelligence went down the drain of timidity. In Paradise, it was, or could be, different. There was no need to listen to what others said, indeed it was difficult to hear. That produced a terrifying loneliness in many, for which sleep seemed the only remedy. But in Paradise loneliness could be recognised as a sign of freedom, of the ability to do what one pleased and to see for oneself. Genius had never flourished except in solitude. On earth, loneliness might be distracting, but in Paradise it could be the opposite. It was not a disease, but a gift, to stimulate souls to a new kind of existence, in which the imagination took flight. Far from being a sign that God was abandoning them, because He did not spoonfeed them with His love every hour of the day and night, loneliness was a certificate of uniqueness, which also contained a divine invitation. Humans have always had difficulty in deciphering divine invitations; they receive so many, and many more than they realise, they ignore them, postpone answering, even get bored with them. Boredom is the yeast that ferments their gloom; it and not loneliness is the source of the misery in Paradise. Boredom is the inability to recognise an invitation. Newton admitted that he himself was not always immune; he had got bored sometimes with his stream of visitors, not because he did not find them interesting, but because they sometimes made him feel that their meeting was a fancy dress ball, in which he was expected to dress in a question mark and a pair of inverted commas, playing the part of one who conceals that he does not know the answers. Paradise was an invitation to invent answers. Sumdy's laugh had sounded to him like the detonation of dynamite, to blow up boredom, to end complacency, a willingness to invent another answer. They still had to learn to laugh in Paradise, for every creative act, he was discovering, had to contain a touch of laughter inside it.

When the smoke cleared, the Sphinx came back into view, but there was something indistinct about its head, under the royal bonnet; its face looked different. The more Sumdy looked at it, the more she thought it had come to resemble Newton's. Newton himself was nowhere to be seen. But his voice was still here, and it spoke from out of the Sphinx. The test to discover how much thin air, or creativity, there was in a soul was the most difficult. He was trying to show how it worked. The indispensable condition for a creative existence in Paradise was the ability to feel what it is like to be someone else, to get into another's skin. He was practising on the

Sphinx. It might seem a paradox, for to be original meant to be unique. But to have an originality that could be valuable, that was not mere eccentricity, one needed to have inside one a whiff of as many others as possible: original, creative souls were multiple. Grave people refused to be creative every time they said "It's not me". Actors were the heroes and heroines of modern times precisely because they pointed the path to originality, which was the conquest of the right to be more than themselves. Paradise was a stage, for those bold enough to turn it into one. All that was missing was the applause.

One of the world's great experts on applause was Einstein. When modern souls arrived in Paradise saying they wanted to be geniuses, they usually added "like Einstein", because he was the first scientist to have been lionised by the media, while remaining incomprehensible to them – even the most expert scientists took many months of hard work to understand his theories – and yet he won universal reverence for having thought something that no-one had ever thought before. The Einstein story became one of the fairy tales of Paradise. The child in every adult said: "If only I had been appreciated like that, when I had my fantasies, when I said things that only I could understand!"

So Newton threw more old newspapers onto the fire, which billowed up in smoke again, and when that smoke cleared, it was the face of Einstein that seemed to sit on the shoulders of the Sphinx, with the familiar half-smile beneath the moustache, the familiar abstracted look in the twinkling eyes, the ruffled mane in the shape of a halo, so lifelike that Sumdy could almost hear the echo of drawling, backwoods voices clinging to it like dandruff, muttering, "Why don't you get your hair cut?" Newton was imagining himself to be Einstein. Perhaps he realised he was saying something that few would believe; it always took ages for what geniuses said to be believed; he could not forget that his own colleagues at Cambridge University had long refused to teach his discoveries, preferring old ideas they were more used to. Perhaps he felt that if he spoke with the voice of Einstein, two geniuses would be more likely to be believed than one. Perhaps he wanted to prove that he was not jealous that immigrants should want to be geniuses like Einstein rather than like himself: it was not his idea of joy to have Einstein's sort of fame, to be like a prize animal in a zoo, whom heads of state and archbishops came to feed with the peanuts of their platitudes. Or perhaps he had no choice: if everybody could be creative in Paradise, then the great Einstein had to be creative too, but it was common knowledge that that was not the case. Newton needed to explain how the cards were reshuffled in Paradise (as they were on earth too, though people did not realise it), how all the effort humans spent grading their fellow creatures in order of merit, sorting the failures from the successes, was self-deception, and certainly not a pastime that made any sense in Paradise; having been creative in the past was no guarantee that one would continue to be so in Paradise. Newton put on the face of Einstein so that it would be clear that getting into another person's skin did not mean trying to imitate them.

Einstein was having more trouble than Newton getting away from the Einstein who had existed on earth. A creative soul needs to become as light as air. But Einstein's was nothing like that. Large parts of his soul had petrified. He had more or less stopped being creative in middle age; even scientists of his eminence are affected by that occupational hazard, just as miners are threatened by lung disease. In Paradise, he had not

227

found a way of escaping from middle age. There were two reasons. The first was that, for all his intellectual courage, he was scared. He did not feel strong enough to put aside his long-held conviction that "everything is determined by forces over which we have no control". He kept on repeating "We all dance to a mysterious tune, intoned in the distance by an invisible piper." On earth, like Newton, he had wanted the "security", as he called it, of "a universe existing independently of us", and "liberation" from "the chains of the merely personal", from "an existence which is dominated by wishes, hopes and primitive feelings". He was bewildered by the fluidity of Paradise: it looked as though the laws of the universe, or at any rate those of Paradise, were not fixed for ever, as though God changed His mind from time to time, as though there was room for random changes which even He did not predict. It shocked him to find he still could not understand God, that maybe God did not intend that He should be understood. Would he have to accept that no soul could have the pretension of understanding any other soul, that all that could be hoped for was occasional moments of illumination, when a flash of sympathy shot between two beings: is that what was meant by getting inside someone else's skin? He could not be creative again until he acclimatised himself to the freedoms of Paradise, which does not offer answers, where one has to invent one's own answers and even one's own vision of the place, constantly, where nobody knows what the rules are, where nothing is certain.

There lay the second reason for his troubles: he could not give up wanting to be proved right. He had spent so much effort, he had exhausted himself, inventing his Unified Theory. But nobody had come to him in Paradise to tell him, conclusively, that the theory was correct. If anyone knew how creative people work it was Einstein; he had always worked on his own; originality is lost if it has to depend on the opinion of other people. Einstein used to say: "I am happy because I want nothing from anyone. I do not crave praise." All was well so long as that was true. But one day he let slip this phrase: "The only thing that gives me pleasure, apart from my work, my violin and my sailing boat, is the appreciation of my fellow workers." In Paradise no such appreciation is forthcoming. When God created the world, He saw that it was good: no-one told Him so, no-one praised Him, He went on regardless. The notion that God wants to be praised all the time is the invention of weak humans, desperate for praise themselves. Einstein was not totally independent: perhaps he could not get used to the idea that he would have to last for ever without praise of any sort. But there was a deeply combative streak in him: he needed at least to prove his rivals wrong. And that definitely seemed to be impossible in Paradise. It was unsettling. It stopped him going on to other things. He was wondering whether the guardian angels were somehow neglecting their duties, deliberately causing chaos.

The first public statement Einstein had issued in Paradise was to announce that he did not agree with it. Agree with what? He did not feel at home in Paradise. That was the remnant of the breath of air that was his creativity. Only the weight of gravity made souls settle down, but Einstein had never settled down, never quite felt at ease in any place. His very first adult act had been to deny that he was a German, though he was born in Germany of German parents; in old age, living in America, he could not accept many so-called American values – commercialism, religiosity, even family life – and he never bothered to learn to speak English properly. He believed very strongly in the uniqueness of the individual. But he had never actually got to know many individuals; he had almost no intimate friends; the

229

brotherhood of man was a notion dear to him, but his warmth towards all the peoples of the world went with a distinct aloofness towards its individual members. In Paradise that attitude presented a problem: all souls are aloof towards each other. So for the first time Einstein saw that he was surrounded by an infinite number of mysteries, perhaps the place was full of nothing but abstracted geniuses, how could he tell? There was no-one to disagree with. His motto on earth had been: "Never lose holy curiosity", but his curiosity had been concentrated on a single problem: "I want to know God's thoughts, the rest are details." Creativity in Paradise seemed to involve a universal curiosity, in which no detail is irrelevant. He had never been interested in food, clothes, languages any more than in people. How was he going to catch up? "I know little about nature and hardly anything about men," he complained.

However, he had thought hard about his handicap, and what he wanted to say now was that his conclusion was that the purpose of being in Paradise is not to be happy. A creative soul seeks not happiness but ecstasy. Mortals weighed down by gravity did not bother themselves with ecstasy, which they assumed was the private concern of religious mystics, on the borders of madness. When poets touched the fringes of ecstasy, they were, in common opinion, odd; when they tried to probe it, while remaining sober, they could not hold onto it for more than a few seconds. Ecstasy on earth resembled an experiment with the nuclei of atoms, which could be raised to an exploding temperature for only a tiny fraction of time; but on earth they had not yet discovered how to produce a chain reaction of ecstasy. According to Proust, the illumination of ecstasy happened by accident, sparked by a trivial memory; for many, it has been like a heightened form of drunkenness, followed by regret, depression, disgust with the world.

Einstein, and Newton, were ambitious enough to think that the art of experiencing and savouring ecstasy was the reward of Paradise; they could think of no higher goal. They were convinced that Paradise would not be complete without it, for ecstasy alone abolishes the abyss that separates humans from each other, and from God, and from the angels. It had to be the true, universal language of Paradise, through which souls could communicate with the universe, or at least feel that they could understand it. Perhaps the guardian angels were the compilers of the dictionary of Paradise. Einstein was optimistic. Certainly, he expected that there had to be a variety of bliss that did not pall, that was not sullied by guilt or shame, or any of the other feelings that on earth he had had to push out of his mind.

Whereas happiness is a private emotion, which tells one nothing about the world, ecstasy is the feeling that the world makes sense, that every part of it has a meaning, and that it is possible to exist in it in peace. On earth ecstasy has been the privilege of saints and eccentrics. Paradise had to offer it to every man and woman. Einstein still had to get used to the idea that each illumination would be different, that there was no longer any single truth to satisfy everyone. He did not know what kind of chaos that would produce. To prepare for chaos seemed to be the first step towards creativity. But perhaps it was not as terrifying as he might have thought on earth, where people get tired so easily, cannot concentrate (or on only one thing at a time, like him). In Paradise, they had the chance to get a good sleep first. Paradise would be more wonderful than anyone ever imagined when they awoke really refreshed.

Once again the smoke billowed, and Einstein disappeared.

231

When the air cleared, Sumdy and Newton were sitting each on a paw of the Sphinx. That was the story of the soul, as much of it as Newton knew. Slowly the slaves came out of their coffins in the sand, rubbing their eyes, so sleepy that Sumdy wondered whether they would ever waken enough to be aware that ecstasy awaited them. They gave no hint of any longing for it.

When Sumdy looked more carefully at the most comatose of the souls gathered around the Sphinx, she saw that some were donkeys. Looking more closely still, she saw that each of these donkeys had, hanging round its neck, a bottle containing the private parts of a human male. It is an ancient belief among the Chinese that a eunuch will arrive in heaven in the shape of a female donkey, unless he takes his private parts with him. The clinics in Peking which performed castrations used to keep the flesh they cut off safely bottled until the customer's death, and then placed it in his grave. These donkeys were not proof that occasionally some little fault in the procedure could prevent the trick of salvation from working. It was just that some eunuchs worried so much that they might be doomed to become donkeys, the idea so haunted them, that they became convinced they could be nothing else. Theirs is the kind of helplessness that is found quite commonly in Paradise, not just among eunuchs, but among all who feel they are somehow not masters of their destiny, that it is not possible to escape from one's lot, that there have, inexorably, to be unlucky ones. And yet, in their past lives, these particular eunuch-donkeys had shown exceptional gifts. One, from the Tang Dynasty, had been an eminence behind the throne, who had made and unmade emperors, and was far from unique in that, for the Byzantine and Ottoman empires, as well as the Chinese, were, at some periods, covertly run by eunuchs, just as other empires have been run by celibate priests. Another of the donkeys, from the Ming Dynasty, had been responsible for selecting eunuchs for service in the imperial palace, no easy task at a time when there were twenty thousand applicants for only three thousand vacancies, and when ambitious boys knew that, competition for government jobs being so severe, the way to get on in life was to have oneself castrated; the operation had opened the door to many wonderful careers and to much disputation as to whether this sacrifice was lesser or greater than that of other ambitious careerists in other nations, who castrated themselves in less obvious ways. One donkey had been in charge of manufacturing the imperial toilet paper; another officiated in the imperial water closet, where much important official business was done, while two maidens held bags of incense to perfume the air; it was no mean honour to be part of the origins of cabinet government. Some had been commanders of the Red Horsemen of the Western Esplanade, the secret police on which the eunuchs' power rested. Many eunuchs had made illicit fortunes in property speculation, thanks to their friendship with the imperial concubines. One was a famous cook, whose masterly recipes are still parodied in take-aways all over the world. And yet, for all their importance and their power, they thought of themselves as slaves, prisoners of their own bodies, obliged to accept that they were monsters, smelly, incontinent, forbidden the pleasures of vanity.

Sumdy felt daunted by the task Newton expected her to perform: to rescue these donkeys from their despair, to rekindle their vitality with hers, to prove that creativity was everyone's right in Paradise. Worse, Newton was relying on her because he had reached the limits of his own inventiveness. How change occurred in Paradise was still something he understood only in broad outline. He explained that the scientists he had talked with said sex ruled the

233

universe, and so sex produced change. Sex was what humans cared about most; indeed many modern scientists seemed incapable of talking about anything except sex, and wondered what had become of sex in Paradise. The donkeys, on this view, were stuck because they had a sex problem. But Newton, who had little personal experience of sexual matters, obstinately maintained that humans had got sex quite wrong. Sex did not create change, but on the contrary made the world go on as it had always done, in pairs, triangles, and circles, introducing only minor variations on a repetitive theme. In his opinion, the decisive force in human affairs was not sex but frivolity. It held the balance in mankind's future, and it made change either possible or impossible. By itself, as he had said, frivolity was powerless, but it was the catalyst which determined whether the soul was capable of change or not. If frivolity allied itself to gravity, change was effectively thwarted. Gravity was the enemy of change. Its weak point was that it stimulated boredom. If frivolity was used to mitigate boredom, gravity could rule for ever; and indeed most ruling classes cultivated a mild sense of humour to divert attention from the asperity of their domination; a pinch of frivolity was enough to create an atmosphere of bonhomie, more or less hypocritical, which guaranteed that the essentials were never made fun of. Frivolity was one of the secret pillars of every established order. On the other hand, if frivolity joined the side of creativity, it exploded conventions and it made inventiveness and experiment possible. Frivolity was either a consolation or a stimulus, either a mustard dressing for the wounds of society, or dynamite. Now in Paradise, most souls were behaving as though they were dead, not realising that they had the choice of being either dead or alive here. The interesting observation he had made in examining Sumdy's soul was that it was stuffed neither with dust nor dew

234

nor air but was in continual flow, changing from one to the other even as he watched. For him, who was used to the stagnant quiet of Paradise, that mobility had been amazing to observe, an amalgam of hard obstinacy, squelchy doubt and wisps of hope, transmuting into each other. To be alive, Newton concluded, meant the very opposite of what he had assumed. A soul that was truly alive did not have a firm and recognisable shape but changed, melted, evaporated all the time, with that quality of unpredictability which had terrified him on earth, but which was increasingly fascinating him here. He had lost faith in gravity. Unpredictability now seemed to him to be the essence of life.

Sumdy was indeed melting and evaporating with desire to please Newton, and above all, not to disappoint him. Having got to Paradise by her own efforts, she tried to convince herself that it was not beyond her ingenuity to persuade these donkeys to do something more than marvel endlessly at the beauty of empty space. She went straight to the Warehouse of Discarded Ideas, and asked for a gadget that would make plain to them what they seemed incapable of seeing, that they were not prisoners. The storekeeper said that of course they kept such a gadget: what Sumdy needed was a mirror, not an ordinary mirror, obviously, but a mirror of the soul, which Edison had invented without realising it. She came back to the Sphinx carrying a beautiful antique gramophone, with an elegant horn. She wound it up ceremoniously. The donkeys stared at the shiny record on the turntable and saw their long faces reflected, but that told them nothing about their souls. Sumdy too saw nothing but her own face. Jolly sat with his ear in the horn, seemingly unable to guess what message he was supposed to be receiving. But Newton understood. The gramophone was a mirror because once it had played its tune and got stuck in its groove, revolving endlessly and uselessly, it became the exact reflection of the soul, full of energy, but unable to do anything with it. It was like dust rotating in a whirlwind. The record, capable only of obsessively repeating itself, mirrored the most common kind of thinking: the donkeys were stuck in a groove, as most humans were. The gloom, a large part of all gloom, was just energy going round in circles.

Explaining to the donkeys that they were in a mess did not get them out of it. Sumdy went again to the Warehouse of Discarded Ideas and searched for some other gadget – she loved gadgets, even if they did not quite work – which would entice them out of their lethargy, by revealing to them the romance and wonder that surrounded them, for they were behaving as though they were blind. Again the storekeeper had no trouble in meeting her request: he gave her a kaleidoscope, invented in 1814 by the Scottish optician Sir David Brewster, who was probably the first modern scientist to complain about the decay of science, just when everyone else was beginning to worship it; he spotted that scientists were losing the ability to explain what they were doing, or to understand what was happening outside their specialty, already in the 1820s. His invention had been dismissed as a mere toy, but at the Warehouse they thought it was much more, because it could bring beauty to whatever it was pointed at. Sumdy cajoled the donkeys into looking through the kaleidoscope, which made everything twist into new and often beautiful shapes, forming strange patterns, splitting every trivial object into a whole ballet corps of leaping dancers, always in step. This, she thought, must be the gadget that Paradise was waiting for, to shake up its deathly stillness, in the way that infants with rattles could chase boredom, routine, peace and quiet, from their parents' house. But though the donkeys seemed to find it interesting to see their

236

surroundings assume new shapes, these did not fill them with passion or hope. Sumdy regretfully concluded that the kaleidoscope could only reorganise the world into symmetrical, triangular patterns, in the same way as theories redistribute the facts into differently shaped pigeon-holes. The donkeys could see no reason to change their habits, to swap one shape for another.

Sumdy's faith in gadgets was only faith. She always had a feeling that they would not quite work, that they would never do all she hoped from them, but she could not help having that hope, she could not resist trying out gadgets. It would have been foolish to visit Paradise and not see how marvellous its gadgets were; she always had, and always would have, a weakness for mad inventions; and she liked Paradise for giving them shelter in that warehouse; there was a place for everyone and everything here. But she herself was back where she started, when she came to the Pyramids in search of the energy that would propel her to the angels; she had to accept there was no short cut to breaking the long chain of timidities that imprisoned energy.

Soon the donkeys, Jolly, Forgetmenot and Newton were installed at a table in the Pyramid restaurant, as her guests, for a meal that she would choose. She would do for the donkeys what she should have done for herself when she had first arrived, but had been too polite. Jolly's appetite and hers, the donkeys' lack of it, the desire for adventure, Newton's wish to bring life to Paradise, were at last all tied up together. Paradise can indeed sometimes have this effect, of giving an inhabitant a momentary impression that he can understand everything all at once. The journalists who had reported that Newton had a Theory of Food had only reported a rumour,

237

but, as sometimes happens, they predicted what was to come true, though it was Sumdy who thought much of the theory up for Newton. She knew only a little more about cooking than he, it was only an occasional pleasure for her, and she had never linked that minor compartment of her life with her other beliefs. But now she thought she saw how food could change the way a soul functioned, how it was as important for the soul as for the body.

They still ate in Paradise as though they were frightened of Foreign Bodies. There is no danger, so why do they do it? The foreign body is not only the fly in the soup, but everything that is unusual, forbidden, unhealthy, unfashionable, un-economical. It was in the process of learning to eat, she decided, that humans first make out of their fear of foreign bodies a virtue, and call it taste; and gradually they see the good life itself as a fight against foreign bodies. History is about how foreign bodies are conquered, about how nations win independence from foreign bodies, about how the oppressed win their rights against aristocrats who live like a distinct species of foreign bodies. And now in Paradise every soul looked on every other as a foreign body, too. While nourishing the body, food slowly strangled the soul, giving it habits, encouraging it to be comfortable only when those habits were a regular routine. Newton and Einstein had not cared what they ate; on earth they were geniuses abstracted from mundane pursuits, thinking about just one or two subjects all their lives, each concentrating everything into a single ray of searing light. In eternity, however, there is more time, a genius can diffuse his light more broadly, into places he had never thought he could illuminate.

Newton had not mentioned it, doubtless because he was not interested in food, but it seemed to Sumdy that she, and all the inhabitants of Paradise, had tragically misunderstood

238

what was going on in its kitchens. They served many different kinds of food, and she imagined she was choosing what she liked. But what she ate had no effect on her. How she ate did. There were three ways of eating, just as the soul had three modes of being. That was no accident. At last Newton's theatrical lecture made sense to her.

To eat until one is full up is one way of eating. It is a sign of a peculiar kind of hunger, which expresses a whole attitude to life and dominates one's whole enjoyment of Paradise; it reveals a soul under the influence of gravity, unable to tolerate a vacuum, believing that there is a right answer to every problem as food is the answer to hunger; a soul may search for satiety by eating manna, or royal food, or a special diet, but all with the same purpose; it chooses well proven, traditional foods, because it wants to be certain of the consequences, with no surprises, to exclude foreign bodies from every aspect of existence. That is how it proves it exists.

The frivolous way of eating is quite different. If life is a game, so is eating. Cooks are not seen as doctors but as eccentric leaders of a jazz band, trying to extract all possible harmonies from their instruments, improvising playful flourishes. The purpose is to excite sensuality and wit, and to maintain a relationship of flirtation with foreign bodies. That is what the great cuisines do, for whom eating is a form of permissiveness. Frivolous eaters aim to forget the big problems, like starvation and stupidity, which seem insoluble.

By contrast, souls trying to be creative attempt what appears to be impossible, to make eating primarily an exercise of the imagination: they treat all ingredients as honoured guests, nothing, nobody is a stranger, they refuse to reject anything as a foreign body, every meal becomes an adventure into the unknown, as is every moment of life, and every step in Paradise; a meal is a poem, from which one derives

239

inspiration and ideas about the world at large.

Sumdy believed she now had the answer to the donkeys' plight. It was possible to develop an imagination in Paradise, that was what growing meant here. The donkeys must systematically taste everything in the Pyramid larder. They must purify themselves of their distrust of the unfamiliar. That was the necessary condition for anyone with the ambition to embark on an adventure in Paradise. Unfamiliar combinations are the essence of the creative act. To be creative, it is indispensable to like what is strange. Only by relearning the art of eating could they escape from their bondage, an escape that would prepare them to be creative in Paradise. There was a diet for the soul too.

Newton listened to Sumdy – who was not used to talking so much – with that rare astonishment which occurs when a disciple almost understands a master and adds to his insights with an independent originality. He smiled. Sumdy was bold enough to think they were becoming friends. He said her words reminded him of his experiments on earth, when he was preoccupied with the fact that different kinds of matter, like stones and metals, were what he called "unsociable", reluctant to mix; one of the aims of science was to make them sociable, by the mediation of a third party. "Water," he had written, "which will not dissolve copper, will do it if the copper be melted with sulphur." He was enchanted by what Sumdy said, because she was suggesting a way of carrying his idea further to the living world, and to Paradise, which might well, as a result, become a place where there was not only something to do, but where there was also the desire to do it. The breaking of old habits was certainly the only way to ignite fireworks in the heavens, and to search for a joy more intense than lukewarm happiness. The peaks of civilisation, as he could see them from Paradise, occurred at those moments

240

when people moved from fearing foreign bodies to becoming connoisseurs of them, when instead of battling against strangers, they imported and exported strange goods and ideas, for pleasure and profit, when they bravely went in search of extraordinary sights that made them sprout new antennae, when they opened doors to new classes, new minorities which previously had been outside the pale, when education began to excite curiosity about the unfamiliar, when artists did not hesitate to talk and paint as no-one had ever before. But in Paradise many souls fought against foreign bodies in the most traditional of ways, by keeping to themselves. They did their best to pretend that Paradise was just life on earth without the snags, denying that it was a country full of foreigners and refusing to accept that every new day is a foreign day. The battle in Paradise was not between good and evil but between timidity and curiosity, and timidity was what sleeping souls would always feel so long as they only pretended to be awake.

It was not the solution Newton had expected, but he was willing to try: they would taste their way through all the foods and smells and memories stored in the Pyramid, in alphabetical order, leaving out none. They started with aa. A small piece was placed on each of their plates, where it sat like a prickly, overripe blackberry. Aa is a form of volcanic lava. There was nothing appetising about it. But Sumdy was determined to show that taste could be a totally different experience in Paradise, in which acceptance or rejection, praise or condemnation were not the alternatives. Aa appeared to be a dead stone. But nothing deserves to be condemned as completely dead, least of all a stone. Stones just happen to be slow, the slowest tortoises in the universe, moving so imperceptibly as to demand an eternal patience to watch them, warming up and cooling down too gradually for ordinary humans to notice; but in Paradise there was time to see them melt and recombine with other rocks, to realise that they are not all that different from caterpillars who become butterflies, to appreciate them as artists of the landscape, to value them even in decay, when they dramatically turn into fire, to admire their constant metamorphoses as examples of procrastination elevated into a science. It was a mistake to dismiss them as mere things; and it was inappropriate to ask where exactly in Hawaii they came from, or what other lava they resembled, because nothing in Paradise is irretrievably what it appears to be, nothing likes to be permanently categorised. They should observe each piece of aa until it had a meaning for them, until it had ceased to be a foreign body.

The staff of the restaurant gathered round to watch the diners. It may not have been the first time that a herd of donkeys, a cockroach, a dog and two human souls shared a table on equal terms, each on a stool appropriate to its height, each confident that it would not be shooed away, but it was a historic dinner for Paradise, because modern immigrants remember it as the event that first gave them new hope. Dr Bombastus Theophrastus von Hohenheim offered the comment that aa was also the pharmaceutical sign for mixing two medicines prescribed in equal amounts. Mary said that Aa was a goddess of the Dawn in Mesopotamia. The Emperor Rudolf, aware that one of the donkeys, the Master of the Toilet Paper, had a special interest in water closets, asked whether they knew that aa meant "water" in Old German, and that several rivers, flushing out of Flanders, Germany and even Russia, were called the Aa. Sumdy added: aa was the exclamation she made when faced by a large number of facts with which she did not come into contact every day. The donkeys echoed the aa in a long bray, and everyone repeated after them: Aa! Newton said they might think it odd that Paradise did not have more words to make confusions of this kind impossible, but any word that was worth anything had to have a window – or several, the more the better – to stop it suffocating, to save it from being too dry, or too grave. That was why the ambiguities of words survived in Paradise. Conversations from window to window were one way that creativity began.

Sumdy concluded that this first dish had been a success, because everyone had been surprised by it in some way, made curious about it, so that they could not dismiss it out of hand as a foreign body. To her, the blackness ceased to be a uniform nothingness; the holes seemed to fill with memories; the sulphurous smell whispered thwarted, soured emotions, the spiky texture commanded attention, suggesting a stubbornness that was not ashamed to avow itself. This was the kind of exercise she thought eating should be in Paradise. There were no right answers, only the answers of the day, like the dish of the day. She preferred this kind of meditation to waiting forever, for the perfect solution, which would never be as perfect as promised. It would suit her to add new bits of evidence later, about aa, to reconsider, revise, change her mind. Only the dead do not change their minds.

For a long time, as they continued in this way to examine every object in the kitchen of the Great Pyramid, the donkeys showed no sign of changing their minds, or of being stimulated to being anything else but donkeys. Sumdy's optimism began to weaken. She remained convinced that she had the right answer, even if it did not work, but she was growing impatient. Then the service from the kitchen became less prompt. She and Newton went into the entrails of the Pyramids to persuade them that this was an experiment worth persevering in. They got back to find Jolly and Forgetmenot behaving as if the Master of the Toilet Paper had turned into thin air, for they were staring at his empty stool with great interest, just as though he was sitting on it, which, as far as Sumdy could see, he was not. Had the donkey been inspired to turn into a pure and ethereal soul? Newton did not think there was a totally invisible soul. But then Sumdy noticed that Jolly was looking at a particular spot on the stool, and there indeed was a small creamy white moth. Newton identified it as *Bombyx mori*, the white silkworm moth. It was impossible to be certain whether the donkey had turned into a moth, or had gone away and been replaced by a moth which happened to be passing. Silkworms are the most abject slaves mankind has ever got to toil for it, victims of the most prolonged of all holocausts, carried out in gas chambers specially designed to asphyxiate silkworms as soon as they have spun their half-mile of silk thread; and it is no consolation to them that most humans do not know that this holocaust still regularly takes place, or that at one time many believed the fairy tale that silk is made from the petals of flowers. Sumdy thought that if it was the donkey, it was significant that it had chosen to become a silkmoth rather than a silkworm; the moth is of course the adult form of the worm, remarkable for seeming to hate being an adult; having no mouth to eat with, it always hurries to lay eggs and to die, as though unconvinced that life is worth living. She felt there was some kind of protest in the transformation, if that is what had happened. It was not quite the kind of creativity she had tried to inspire in the donkey, but then creativity is never predictable, and not necessarily always admirable.

Newton thought Sumdy was onto something. He grew quite friendly, even talkative, and began telling her about his boyhood, and saying that he too felt he had been prevented from becoming an adult – by less violent means, it was true.

He had been obliged to remain an ignorant boy by the absurd complexity of nature. Perhaps it was an illusion that living creatures ever did become adults; perhaps the earth was only a children's playground in God's scheme of things; perhaps God never intended that any being should turn into an adult – that to Him it was an unfortunate weakness that they overgrew and went to seed. It could be that the moth with four lives, the egg, the larva and the worm, represented a divine experiment to get even ordinary creatures to see the world from several different points of view.

Sumdy was interested to hear Newton talk about divine experiments. She was emboldened to tell him about the Gospel of Henry Ford. He thought there was a lot of sense in it. Paradise, at any rate, he was sure, was made for experiment. Souls were free to try being anything they could imagine. It was sad that in practice they were so obstinately attached to their past, and went on thinking of themselves as worms, or dogs, or lame men, or sad women, or Chinese donkeys. God's enemy was History, which glorified His mistakes. Newton agreed with Henry Ford about history. No wonder human souls had so much trouble learning to fly.

It was possible that the donkey, in turning itself into a silk moth, had performed the very same trick that Newton had when he substituted himself for the Sphinx; the donkey could be getting into a silk moth's skin precisely because he had been touched by the desire to see the world with fresh eyes, and this was the first stage in the growth of his desire to create a world of his own. But Sumdy could not be certain. This was a good example, said Newton, of the way Paradise refuses to provide certainty, or to answer questions, it simply invites the imagination to find its own. But Sumdy concluded that she was making progress. The imagination did indeed hold the key to the art of escaping from loneliness.

Hitherto Sumdy had always been restless, anxious to reach her destination, but for the first time she felt differently. She was sad that her meal with Newton would inevitably, sooner or later, come to an end. Watching him think was giving her a delightful sensation of being invigorated. His confidence was infecting her. He did seem not to despise her ignorance. Perhaps he actually appreciated her. Why go on searching for angels, who might not exist? Would Newton's wisdom not suffice for her? She had at last found a corner of Paradise in which she felt both cosy and inspired. Her mind was very soon made up. There was no need to hesitate. She asked him if he would let her stay with him. This was the kind of existence that gave her a thrill. She wanted no other. What she had come for, she now realised, was not to hurry back to earth with news to astonish the living, like a fisherman with a prize catch, but to construct new forms of happiness. Only with Newton could she see herself embarking on such an adventure.

No, Newton wanted no assistant, no admirer, no acolyte: to exist in his shadow was against everything he understood by Paradise. He valued her company. He liked her, indeed admired her, but it would impoverish her if she stopped her wanderings now. She must see everything there was to be seen; that was the unprecedented task she had set herself, and she was a long way from having fulfilled it. How could she know, till then, where her favourite home in Paradise would be? It was wonderful that they had been able to exchange more than words, more than information. She had made him think thoughts, say things, he would never have, but for her; it would please him to be compelled to have to go on answering her questions, the more naive the better, they were always the hardest; but there was something she could do, which no-one else in Paradise could. Everybody was waiting to meet the angels, waiting for them to say something. Only Sumdy seemed to have the determination to search them out, the courage not to give up hope. She must find them. She could come back after that, if she felt she wanted to. But she must achieve something no-one else had, before she became, in his view, a true citizen of Paradise. In Paradise, one was either asleep or awake. But to remain awake without knowing what to do with oneself was pure agony.

Sumdy was so confident that finding the angels would solve all problems that she was not too upset by his rejection. The full meaning of his words did not penetrate. She would return very soon, and Newton would be astonished by what other things she could do, once she had a guardian angel by her side. Her meeting with him had put her in far too optimistic a mood to worry about the difficulty of getting to Babylon and back.

Sumdy wrote in her letter home that her parents might be worrying that she was too young to be visiting Paradise alone. She could reassure them: all the souls here were really children. Even great souls like Sir Isaac Newton. She could not restrain herself from dropping his name. She had to tell them that he was much more wonderful than his theories would ever lead them to suppose; but she hoped they would not spoil things by asking too many questions about him. They probably did not realise, any more than she had, that a soul's life on earth was only a period of infancy, in which there was not even time to complete its potty training. Arriving in Paradise, a soul is still as mystified by its emotions as a baby unable to control its motions. When a soul gets angry, gloomy, jealous, or frightened, those feelings seemed to be, in the light of Paradise, like an infant's dribblings. Ecstasy was the fashionable word, though most souls did not understand what it meant. It took a long time

247

to achieve. That was what eternity was for.

The consoling news was that those who were not happy on earth need not worry about whether they would be any happier in Paradise, or whether they were suited to being happy. Souls could have more exciting ambitions.

You could tell they were all children in Paradise, because even when they were asleep, they liked playing Pretend. No-one paid any attention to souls who pretended they were great generals, dictators or millionaires; you could be them if you wished, but it was not the same as on earth; that pretence did not make you one of the heroes of Paradise. The souls who have the best time here are actors. That may sound unhelpful, since everyone on earth tries to be an actor, to learn politeness, to do the right things, to play their part, though they forget they are actors. In fact, they are just beginners, playing the same parts always. Having a small repertory of parts was not enough here; imitating was of no use; the challenge was to get under the skin of everyone in Paradise, however briefly, however long it takes. That, too, was what eternity was for.

There was no need to feel lonely, unless you chose to, nor bored either. She was looking forward to seeing what would happen to the friendship of Jolly and Forgetmenot when they tried to do more than play.

CHAPTER NINE

As soon as Sumdy reached Babylon, she consulted the many-volumed directory which is kept there, from which souls can discover to which guardian angel they have been assigned. She found the books in tatters; many parts were missing; her name was not in them; they were no longer kept up to date. The angels had stopped giving advice or protection, long before Sumdy was born.

The last time the angels in the sky were counted was in the fourteenth century. The total came to 301,655,722. The human population of the world was then about 370,000,000, which meant that almost but not quite everyone who felt the need for a guardian angel could still have one. Never had there been so many angels. The discovery of angels whose existence had not been suspected (or who perhaps came into existence to meet the growing demand for them) is one of the forgotten achievements of the middle ages, an imaginative adventure comparable to the discovery of new continents and new technologies. However, the few humans who had no guardian angel, or chose not to have one, and succeeded in life nonetheless, boasted that they possessed miraculous powers of their own. Slowly, people began doubting whether

249

angels were real, or as helpful, as was claimed. In Amsterdam in 1656, it was still possible for a philosophical polisher of optical lenses, aged twenty-four, Spinoza, to be excommunicated for saying that angels are a hallucination. But as the landscape changed colour, as humans took the place of trees, as the air echoed more loudly with curses and groans, less and less was heard of angels; fewer and fewer were sighted. When the world's population reached one billion, in the nineteenth century, the angels suffered a shock from which they never recovered. They became aware that they could no longer go on in the same way as they had in the past. It was impossible for them to give individual attention to three people at the same time, while still continuing to perform their many other duties. For they were not just guardians of souls or messengers of God, nor only musicians who sang in massed choirs; they assisted humans in numerous painful tasks; some are reported to have worked as farmers in the Third World, or as cooks, to have been both lifesavers and gravediggers, and soldiers too; whole armies of them appeared from nowhere in the course of many famous battles to wreak terrible havoc: a single angel is recorded as having slaughtered five thousand and eighty of King Sennacherib's troops in one night. Some of them were occupied, with never a moment of respite, pulling the planets round their orbits, ox-like (Kepler made allowances for this in his explanation of how the universe worked); others held the sky up on the palm of their hand. Were they happy in these tasks? Humans have never bothered to ask that question. No history has ever been written from their point of view.

There was much in the world that caused them distress. A number of them had objected to the creation of mankind. They were silenced. Their warning that the human species was still too imperfect to be let loose on earth was ignored,

250

but in some corners of Paradise they continued to twitter, secretly, their carping, heretic substitute for hymns.

We told you so. We said
Don't do it. We knew it
Would spoil the status quo.

For something new, we said,
Let fish talk, let plants walk,
And keep men in a zoo.

On the other hand, there were angels who were fascinated by humans, and intermarried with mortal women, but their offspring were much criticised, called giants and devils, and felt misunderstood. Other angels grew embittered because they believed their peculiar skills aroused jealousy even in the prophets, like Job, who called them foolish, even in St Paul, who warned against placing too much faith in them. So the angels were by no means at ease. They were not satisfied with their role in the universe. Their many failures with the human race rankled; they felt resentment invading them as though a tapeworm was slowly eating up their energy. Like most healers, they were interested in healing because they were suffering themselves; they went on working long after they had any real hope of making a difference to the world.

Eventually, they all retired. Most sank into the exhausted sleep that Paradise can prolong for ever, and the only relaxation of their waking hours was singing hymns. Some angels, however, on withdrawing from mundane affairs, preferred to take a vacation by the sea, being curious about the pleasures of relaxation; they did not know what leisure meant and thought they would find out why humans had suddenly become so enamoured of it. At Angel Village, where Sumdy had spent her first days in Paradise, they quickly tired of lying

251

immobile in the sun reading light novels, and they got bored with gossip. Instead, they started discussing their future amongst themselves, quietly, discreetly, because it is not done to talk about the future in Paradise. They were agreed that they had had enough of rushing around on futile missions, mending disasters which they knew would be repeated the moment their backs were turned, that as the fire brigade of the universe, never allowed to rest, they had lost some of their legendary dash; the call out to a catastrophe no longer excited them, quite apart from their seldom getting the credit for their rescues any more. But the real change was that they decided that they were too imperfect themselves to go around any more giving advice to others. They spent much of the twentieth century worrying about that. There is no way of measuring whether they were more or less gloomy than humans at the same period.

By the peacock-blue ocean, they reread their Bible in search of guidance. In the book of Genesis, one particular passage held their attention: "And it repented the Lord that he had made man . . . And the Lord said, I will destroy man whom I have created." They were much struck by God giving as His reason that He found "the imaginations" of His creatures too narrow. He had, they now agreed, made man insufficiently imaginative, and too obsessed with evil. When, eventually, He did destroy His creation in the deluge, sparing only one family whom He happened to have taken a liking to, together with examples of different species of animals, these were clearly the only souvenirs He considered worth preserving of His first attempt to have creatures He could be proud of. It was galling to the angels to realise that they had been put to work among these inadequate humans precisely because they were so inadequate: they should have realised long ago that their task was hopeless. Only now did they understand

252

that meanwhile God had set about imagining the improvements He could make if He created a second world, a world that they began looking forward to as the next world. The history of the descendants of Adam and Noah would not be the total history of mankind. God's exasperation with those descendants, how He felt sorry for them, even a little guilty for them, under His wrath, how He tried to help them and love them, without too much success, all that had been so well chronicled, fully and unforgettably, that the rest of the story had been ignored. He had given His attention to many other subjects since then. The creation was not a single event which happened long ago; there have been many creations, some successful, some not. There is another history, the angels exclaimed to each other, still unwritten, of God's other existence, of His preparations for His next world, of a series of historical events that have not yet occurred. Once the angels ceased to feel sorry for themselves, they saw that there were more interesting opportunities in Paradise than they had suspected, where time is flexible, and where they could, if they wished, participate in what had not yet happened. They wanted to experience the feeling of an imagination that was not obsessed by evil. Though their beach resort was seductive, they left it, without regrets, and went to Babylon.

Babylon was the place of which they had the fondest memories, or the least painful ones. Not only had their relations with the ancient Babylonians been wonderfully close, but it had been exhilarating to be present at the most spectacular of all dawns, the dawn of invention, where the wheel first turned, where humans first learned to move the immovable, where two-wheeled chariots, drawn by four wild asses, first raced, and the triumphant cry of the pitiless victor first made the angels shudder, where humans first chose to huddle together in a city, and put glass in the windows of their homes, so that they could both hide from and keep watch on their neighbours. Above all, the Babylonians built the Tower of Babel. It was designed to reach right up to the sky, because they wanted to establish direct communication between heaven and earth. Even though they had excellent relations with the angels, they worried that they did not always fully understand the divine laws, and they yearned to hear God's word from His own mouth, to plead their case directly with Him. But however high they built, the distance to the sky remained the same; however many little ladders they added to scale the gap, they could not reach their goal. In their frustration they blamed God, saying He feared they would discover His secrets. Their conceit was perhaps another reason why He wanted to start His creation all over again. When the Tower turned out to be a disaster, it never occurred to them that God might have looked down on the first city and decided that cities were too liable to go wrong, to grow too big.

In Paradise, the Babylonians hoped that their close relations with the angels would continue for ever, but the angels said: Times change; after death, humans could look beyond the struggle for survival, beyond feeding themselves and reproducing themselves. They had something quite different to worry about now: boredom. The angels could no longer comfort them in the old way; they had to have more interesting things to say to human souls, if they were not to bore them too. The Babylonians insisted the angels were worrying unnecessarily. But they could not deny that it was not easy to go on just as they always had done. Since their arrival in Paradise they had been trying to rebuild the Tower of Babel, in its original form, with everyone in it speaking the same language; they longed for a Paradise in which there would be no possibility of misunderstanding, mistranslations, disagreements; but their tower kept falling down. They seemed to be asking for something impossible even in Paradise. The angels watched these efforts with interest. They were of the opinion that it was not in the Garden of Eden that the world had started to become a dangerous and difficult place, but in the Tower of Babel. In Paradise, where no one is expected to obey anyone else, the disobedience of Adam appears less serious than the inability of humans to understand why they did not understand each other in Babel. That, the angels thought – and they had spent all their existence trying to make themselves understood – was the origin of all later disasters. Incomprehension, in their view, was the most misunderstood of all mysteries. It was a terrible illusion that humans had ever understood each other; even worse was the belief that to speak the same language was all that was needed to know what was going on around one. From those illusions came all wars, all quarrels, all the hatreds of mankind. Language was a guessing game. Some perhaps guessed better than others, but even they were never more than translators of doubtful accuracy, inescapably interpreting according to their own personal needs. The tragedy of the world was that people could not bring themselves to accept that words did not necessarily mean what they seemed to say. From the cacophony of sounds around him, each human picked a few morsels, which he thought made sense to him, or were relevant to his own purpose, and those morsels were for him the whole world. The noisy complaints of the recent arrivals, protesting against the inefficiency of Paradise, demanding that the rules governing it be clearly spelt out and advertised, filled the angels with dismay, who could not believe that there would ever be agreement on what the rules were supposed to be.

When the earth's population approached five billion, the angels became quite sure that any lurking idea they might still have of ever influencing it was foolish, as impossible as the hope they had once entertained of taming the gnats or saving the worms from the massacre of the birds. The earth now appeared to them as a blown-up caricature of Babel: the more they looked at it, the more they saw how confused it was, and they marvelled that it should still be preaching mutual understanding, when not one of its inhabitants could even say, honestly, that he fully understood himself. The angels had no silly illusions about being able to change the world; they had tried long enough in vain. But they wondered whether they could change themselves. They felt sore about what God had said on the subject of imagination; perhaps theirs had been as narrow as man's. They were very tempted to try to stretch it. What if they found a way of coping with misunderstanding, which seemed to be inevitable, accepting it, turning it into a virtue? Just for themselves. If they were to be eternal insomniacs, they must make their wakeful hours more bearable by putting right at least some of their own defects. They were more and more conscious of having faults, despite the rumours spread about them. What they disliked more than anything was telling humans to perform miracles they could not do themselves, giving advice that they did not follow themselves, criticising when they could not do better; they still shuddered every time they remembered sad, anguished philosophers to whom they had been guardian angels: how could they have allowed them to pontificate to humans about how not to be anguished and sad?

So they decided to build their own Tower of Babel, that would not be destroyed by confusion. They could not conceal from themselves that Paradise, as it was, bored them; the human imagination, being so cautious, had turned the place into a dull imitation of earth. It was time for them to enjoy themselves, to expel the terrible gloom which had infected them, to find new occupations, to prepare for unknown, divine adventures. Their own imagination must no longer be a slave of their experience.

This was a momentous decision. For the first time, Paradise would go its own way, ceasing to be a depository for the broken remains of earthly folly. A new sort of ambition blew through it, its own. The angels did not copy the Ziggurat Temple of Marduk at Easgila, built of heavy brick and bitumen, stepped like a pyramid, which was the original Babel. They had a look at the tower which Brueghel the Elder had a vision of, a cross between a theatre, a palace and a castle, but though they admired it, they thought it too defensive, likely to discourage souls on the outside from wanting to visit. They decided to build their own tower in the shape of a huge egg whisk. It was round and bulbous at the bottom, and then rose up high into the sky, ever slimmer, ending up as though suspended from a cloud by its handle. From a distance it looked like a monument made of pure light, for it was nearly all windows, held together by pillars that were gently curved needles, sewing empty space together. This was the first large building in Paradise that was not a copy, so it expressed hope by its very existence.

Why did the angels have to spoil the skyline with this monstrosity? asked the Babylonians, who moaned that it would take them several centuries at least to get used to it; the whole point of Paradise, for them, was that it contained only antiques. They liked their old customs, and they did not want to be told that their way of doing things was wrong; surely it was the job of angels to help them, not to embark on wild escapades? The tourists who came to Babylon were also displeased to see the angels neglecting their duties. Why did

257

they put on this new-fangled cinema show for them, offering the old, sad, unfinished film of the Tower of Babel, cutting and re-editing it in the vain hope that a happy ending might be dragged out of it? They said to the angels: Is our past not good enough? It lives for ever here: why insult it? To put the past into black and white is to make the shadows darker than they ever were. The angels replied: We do not wish to copy the past, but to discover how it could have been otherwise. The arrogance of the past dissolves away with the years; history ceases to be an unbreakable chain of events and falls apart, like the metal and the stones in your gaudy jewellery; and all humans who wear jewellery are saying, though they might not know it: these stones could have been arranged in a different way; what is there in the world that could not have been arranged in a different way? So the rumour spread that the Tower of Babel was designed to work miracles, and the onlookers occupied themselves with wondering whether only angels could work miracles, whether humans had to reconcile themselves to being only humans, or whether the tower might give them, too, the confidence to work miracles. But they were too used to relying on the angels for guidance, too respectful of them, to dare to go into the new tower. Humans and angels were different, they kept saying to themselves, reluctantly, waiting to be convinced it was not going to be true for ever.

The architect of the new tower was Colopatiron, who used to be an obscure, minor angel, in charge of releasing people from prisons, so unpretentious in the performance of her modest duties, that her name is rarely familiar even to those whom she has helped. Angels are usually thought of as male, but they can be whatever sex they please, and to Sumdy, at any rate, Colopatiron appeared as female. Colopatiron had not gone to sleep, because she had not quite despaired of humans. She liked them. Not all of them, but she felt there was something wrong in her when she failed to find something likable in a human. She had compassion. All angels begin like that, all are idealists, sometimes even revolutionaries, who cherish the hope that the world will one day be put to rights. However, most of them had gone to bed because after so many centuries they had finally lost faith. Colopatiron was one of the few who was not completely defeated, so far. The established archangels did not obstruct her building, for they recognised that she had gradually become the busiest of all angels, the most active. The reason was not that more and more people were sent to prison – though they were – but that more and more suffered from the feeling that they were imprisoned, even though not locked up in a cell. Colopatiron discovered that modernity is as much a prison as a release. Modern persons think of themselves as imprisoned by the daily grind of a job, by habits and prejudice, by their own incompetence or cowardice; their ancestors could resign themselves to their lot and call drudgery destiny, but they could not. Colopatiron, who began as an expert at prising open the prison bars, became a connoisseur of helplessness, impotence, fear, and the tangled knot of feelings which restrains people from escaping out of the dungeon of their narrow imagination; increasingly, she found that she spent far less time opening prisons, than persuading the inmates that they were not prisoners, who refused to believe it.

The idea which inspired her architecture was that the yearning to be free was at the root of all desire, which is why desire is insatiable. She proposed to the angels who were awake that they should build a tower that would be Paradise's monument of freedom: not a commemoration of past victories, but a machine for creating freedom. If they themselves wanted to be free, from their worry about being misunderstood, from their feeling of guilt that they really should still be struggling with their traditional, hopeless chores, and that there was no escape for them, ever, from the tasks that had been given to them, many thousands of years ago, then they needed a new morality, of their own. It would have to be a morality which they built themselves; they could no longer continue to borrow bits and pieces of the moral codes of the civilisations they had worked in, now decaying or extinct; they would have to stop paying lip-service to principles which they could not live up to; they needed more than principles, more than an ideology, there were enough of those already. A new morality, said Colopatiron, one that suited angels, would be like no morality on earth: it would not be a book of unbreakable rules, neither prophecy nor threat, nor etiquette, nor timid conformity to convention, nor worship of old customs that had only old age to recommend them. They needed a morality that did not moralise, an attitude rather than a dogma, an immunity rather than an orthodoxy, a vaccination against the sclerosis that invariably sets in when ideologies are accepted as obvious and get established in power, an attitude that expressed a desire not for guidance but for stimulation, not for certainty but for growth, rejecting, above all, cowardice and the feeling that there was no point in even bothering to try because destiny always has its own ideas. Colopatiron was only a minor angel, and most of the angels in Paradise, if they had not been so sleepy, would have condemned her as an upstart, disturbed by ideas above her station; they would have smelt Satanic rebellion in her words, and perhaps shamed her into silence. But they were sleepy. The angels who were awake were the discontented ones. They had never heard an angel talk like that before. They listened to her, and agreed she had charisma. They believed that a new Tower of Babel might give them not just the gift of tongues, but the inspiration to look at existence with new eyes. So when Sumdy, after her long trek through seemingly endless mole-tunnels, eventually got to Babylon, she found no angels who gave private consultations. Indeed she thought at first that this meant there was no one in Paradise who cared about her. Had it all been a wasted journey? And yet, perhaps it had been worth while, just to see this extraordinary building shaped like a flask. It was an elongated moon; it was a balloon; it was a holy mushroom standing on its head: each soul who came to look at it had his own way of expressing his wonder at it. Some idlers stood outside, waiting patiently, as only inhabitants of eternity can be patient, for something to happen inside it. They were frightened to approach too closely, and they assured Sumdy that the angels would not want to be interrupted by her, they were far too busy. The rumour was that the Tower was not even fully furnished yet; the angels were having trouble deciding, they could not make up their minds about anything.

It would be a shame not to see an angel, Sumdy thought, even if angels no longer had anything to say to humans. She could understand that they might not welcome visitors complaining about their building, but clamouring for assistance with their problems all the same. She went up the short flight of steps leading to the entrance, and peeped cautiously in through a window. What she saw reminded her immediately of Saturnin's hairdressing salon by the sea. The ground floor could have been a giant beauty parlour, except that instead of mirrors, there were artists' easels. Hundreds of angels were sitting in a variety of poses, having their portrait painted. Were angels also worried by their ugliness, by vanity, by loneliness? Only some of them had wings; many looked like

261

ordinary humans. Angels enjoy assuming strange shapes. Did that explain their interest in their faces?

It was upsetting, a disappointment. Perhaps the angels looked so ordinary because that was what Sumdy was expecting them to be like. Then she caught sight of an angel who somehow stood out of the crowd. Later Sumdy used to say that she had at once picked out the most beautiful angel anybody could see; but when asked to describe that angel's appearance, she was imprecise, she could not explain what was so special about any of the features, all she could say was that there was something electric, magnetic, supersonic, in that angel's manner. In fact it was only after Sumdy had met Colopatiron that she began applying such adjectives to her. Perhaps something about Colopatiron's bearing made Sumdy aware that here was the architect of this extraordinary structure, who was surprisingly approachable, indeed invited, attracted others to approach her. In her moments of greatest enthusiasm, Sumdy used to say that no one has been able to describe Jesus Christ, there is not a word about his appearance in the Bible; she did not mean to compare the two, but it did show that anyone who is extraordinary is indescribable and suffers from being described. At any rate, it was the sight of Colopatiron that determined Sumdy to go into the Tower. There was nothing to stop anyone from entering, except fear of the consequences. Jolly poked his nose in with no ill effects. Sumdy followed. The idlers outside groaned, as though witnessing a voluntary immolation.

No one challenged Sumdy. She thought that perhaps they mistook her for a fallen angel, or perhaps they were too absorbed with themselves. She slipped into a vacant chair quickly, sat motionless, wiping all expression from her face, as though to make herself invisible, focussing on empty space, thinking of eternity. Slowly she became aware that her portrait was being painted. The painter looked like a painter. His painting, however, did not look like her. Decidedly modernistic, sparsely though powerfully drawn, it could have been the work of Modigliani. Eventually she summoned the courage to speak to the painter, and asked what he was doing. He said he was painting her "expression of silent acceptance of life". She was appalled: he had misunderstood her as completely as anyone could. There were very few things she accepted, least of all life, which she thought was cruel, hard, unforgiving. He did not seem impressed. She grew increasingly agitated by what he had drawn, and by what he had said. She went on looking at the painting for a very long time, searching for its reasons. But eventually she capitulated: she told him perhaps she agreed: yes, she did accept life; if the choice was between life and death, she knew which she would choose; she preferred the suffering of life to perpetual sleep. He replied mysteriously: Do angels who keep awake in Paradise need to suffer too?

She moved to another chair, and her portrait was painted again. The artist made her look very beautiful, or, more exactly, he drew a picture of a very beautiful woman, and then began introducing little touches, until Sumdy said: I see a likeness coming. That meant that his painting was finished, he replied, and he stopped. What he painted was an ideal, how she would like to be, her own vision of herself in a perfect world. How had he guessed her vision? The canvas showed her as an aristocratic lady of the seventeenth or eighteenth century, all health and purity, very English. Had she stumbled on an English angel? But she remembered that they were foreign artists who invented the stereotyped aristocratic English face, aloof, wearing a polite and urbane mask, all traces of rusticity polished away, and finished off with an air of confidence for men, and for women a varnish of modesty.

263

Would she meet Van Dyck, Hoppner, Kneller here, turning all comers into English lords and ladies?

A third chair, a third painting, and she was undeniably ugly: every coarseness was accentuated, every irregularity was emphasised, as though in Paradise the scars of her sins and her weaknesses became inflamed, as though the artist wanted her to know the worst about herself, and to suggest that she could escape from herself only by her own efforts. Somehow, she preferred this painting to the last; without the glamour she felt less of a fraud; ugliness had its compensations; it was like wearing old clothes; she had been made unpretentious and real.

But no, the reality was an illusion. She was next turned into an elongated, spindly Giacometti-like statue, all legs and arms, thin as matchsticks, a stranger, impossible to get to know, barely a blob of life in a funereal shroud. Be patient, said the artist, a work of art is never finished, least of all in Paradise.

Nearby an African artist was transforming his sitters into miniature sculptures, fly-whisk handles, verandah-posts, awesome masks. Soon she was sitting in front of him and he was carving a branch of a scented eucalyptus tree into an image of her, or perhaps of a spirit, her eyes egg-shaped, cartwheels hanging from her triangular ears, a gaping mouth full of teeth filed to a point. She felt as though her body was being taken away from her; she became alarmed, cried out to him to stop. He said: I have made beauty. Sumdy mumbled that in her poor judgement she was being revealed as more and more hideous. Beauty, he replied, is a messenger who can melt the heart. He had melted hers. That was not easy to do in Paradise, where indifference reigned. He was once a specialist in sending messages to the gods, to dead ancestors, to invisible forces; now, his task was much harder; in the Tower of Babel,

264

the angels were only beginning to send messages to each other.

Other artists showed Sumdy as a graceful, round-faced Han figurine, with long flowing sleeves, pouring out generosity, as a pious icon with eye lashes that did not blink, because surprises succeeded each other too quickly, as a nude with long legs, as a head cut off on a coin, as a Zen splash of ink, as a calligraphic squiggle, as a caveman's arrow. It was exhausting to have the feeling of being moved from one body to another, and to be shown each was a fantasy. Confused, she sat in front of the artists in almost a daze, whimpering; she begged them to pause, but they seemed to find it even more rewarding to paint her as a coward, a malingerer, a collapsed wreck. Finally she did collapse. She carried herself away, to recover in an alcove. She had done very well, she thought to herself; surely few angels (who were not used to being stared at) could last as long as she had done.

She placed her portraits around the alcove walls, to meditate on them. There was only one which she could almost accept as being herself, where, perhaps because the artist saw something of himself in her, he had picked out that hint of a smile that brought her so much trouble, but which she cherished nonetheless, that piercing look of curiosity, never satisfied, but which gave her inexhaustible satisfaction. Anger, however, surged up in her at the sight of the portrait beside it, which seemed to her to be nothing less than a prosecutor's indictment: I put it to you that this face is the smug mask of one so suffused with pride, that you are justified in convicting her without even listening to the evidence. A painting in hues of blue made her out to be exactly the sort of person she took an instant dislike to; were they trying to show qualities she refused to see in herself? Some of the artists appeared intent on refuting her conviction that she had

265

nothing in common with faces she instinctively mistrusted. One showed her prickly and touchy. Another had captured fright in her features, and had drained all warmth, all trace of generosity out of them. Some were aggressively contradicting the obvious answers to the questions: what nationality, what age, what sex? She was dressed in costumes she would never wear; they changed a feature here and there, as though searching for a stranger in her, and yet it still was, vaguely, her.

Were the artists angels? Or humans who had become angels, like the prophet Enoch, who had never died, but had been raised to heaven to be an angel? Did that still happen, was that the ultimate kind of immortality, not just to survive death, but to escape it? It seemed that some artists, or would-be artists, had been bold enough to enter, and the angels were treating them as though they were angels. It was difficult to tell who was an angel and who was not. Perhaps in Paradise there was less difference than humans assumed.

From where she was, she could see Colopatiron, even more handsome and striking than before, being painted, wearing a smile with an irresistible complicity in it, surrounded by a group of angels. Colopatiron did not appear to be frightened by the artists, and yet she was speaking with hesitation: there was fragility and vulnerability in her voice, a peculiar kind of modesty, without shame. Sumdy listened, at a distance, unnoticed. Colopatiron was saying that some angels were complaining that the artists were depriving them of their sense of identity; humans might, perhaps, from habit, feel that they needed identities, but angels were better off without them; they needed to transcend their past as caricatures of humans, to be free to stop always asking themselves, Who am I? She preferred the question: What can I become, how many lives can an angel live? It was inappropriate to speak of an angel in the present tense; angels changed all the time; only the future tense made sense. They had no need to pretend that they were simple folk, for they were unfathomable: every being had to admit, sooner or later, to being unfathomable. Acceptance of that had to be the basis of a Tower of Babel that did not collapse from confusion. Humans used to pester angels to state precisely what their duties and properties were, what exactly they believed, what heavy past they carried around with them, but those were human worries, not theirs. She herself was categorised as being of minor importance, a lightweight in the hierarchy, which suited her; she was glad to appear light to some, to be different weights at different times. And she was sure humans would not continue, for ever, to be satisfied with having only a single identity. It was understandable that they should have put up with that when they lived short lives, and were the property of lords, or husbands, or the rich, not of themselves, but now that they could blossom for as many as a hundred springs, and now that their fruits need never be the same from year to year, it was not even convenience that made them keep the same name all their lives, only fear, always fear. Sumdy was not clear whether the implication was that a human who surrendered his fears, and abandoned having only a single identity, could become an angel.

Saturnin the hairdresser suddenly came to mind. She wished she could telephone him to enquire about his search for his identity. Did he still cling to his French identity card? Was there any news of his unfathomable octopus, growing new arms? It would have been pleasing to hear that he had grown new identities too, so that she could see how it worked. Then perhaps she need never decide what the right hairstyle for herself was.

Colopatiron was saying that it was hard to get rid of the temptation to have a fixed identity. That was what artists were for, to free the world from the prison of their identities. On earth, of course, artists were weird, incomprehensible, and their works were riddles: the most that could be done to understand them was to group them into misleading Movements and Schools. But what they had been doing, silently through the centuries, was creating beauty where there had been none before. There was a time when mountains were terrifying obstacles, barren and dangerous: it was artists who turned them into objects of delight. They were brave pioneers who went out not to spy on the hostile world beyond the frontier, but to mix part of their souls with what they saw, and bring back an image of it that was beautiful, cleansed of fear. Beauty is the reward that comes from the rejection of fear. Though they appeared to work haphazardly, at cross purposes, each in his own bizarre way, they were all busy on the same eternal task, of transforming the ugly and the strange into something that inspired respect. They were expelling hatred and suspicion from the world, ever so gradually, which was the only way possible, by finding beauty in minute details, a mere glance, or a ray of light, by showing that beauty had a thousand faces. There was a time when it worried people that they could not agree on what was beautiful; they huddled together, for security, around what they called good taste, which meant stopping the expansion of beauty. But new artists regularly came along to show that bad taste could contain beauty too. Artists were not armies, their purpose was not to give security or defend prejudice; on the contrary, they were guerrilla fighters, impossible to restrain, always on the move; and they showed how to acquire the strength to live with insecurity, to derive joy from its challenge. So Colopatiron had not placed artists at the foundations of her Tower in order that angels would have pictures to hang up on their walls as decoration, still less to buy and sell, but because art was an expression of optimism in its purest form, never giving birth to perfect beauty, but producing proof that beauty could be sought and found even amid ugliness, that when beauty lost its charm, another could be invented to replace it, that even tragedy was not all gloom. If the angels were to recover their courage, and attempt to play a role in the next world, when it came, they needed to find beauty in themselves, even in their incomprehensible gestures, even in features which no one had admired, till a mad artist painted them. The artists did not say anything while Colopatiron talked, but one did whisper to Sumdy that this was the first time they felt that they were being heard.

Eventually Colopatiron came to see Sumdy. Sumdy said: Do you like the pictures? and she thought: Do you like me? She was terrified that Colopatiron would question her, ask exactly who she was, what she was doing there. Her absurd idea of passing for an angel appealed to her more and more; but she was upset that the artists had revealed her to be such a bundle of defects, so inconsistent, so illegible. Colopatiron seemed to sense her anxiety. Would Sumdy prefer, said Colopatiron, to be one of those worthies who are commemorated by a single portrait that glues them to a canvas for all eternity, unchangeable, immovable, dead? Was she not free behind so many alternative faces, invisible? Was the inability of each artist, in painting his vision of her, to agree with any other, not the best guarantee of her autonomy? They were saying things about themselves, as much as about her; each portrait was a hand held out, a cry for help, a cry of hope.

Colopatiron seemed to make no distinction between angels and humans. She suddenly became impatient to show Sumdy the rest of the Tower, as though worried that she was not getting a good impression of it. Sumdy was overjoyed, but also suspicious. Was it simply that Colopatiron saw in every new visitor a new opportunity to win approval; was she attractive because she had an unquenchable thirst for the good opinion of others, and worked ceaselessly to win that good opinion?

Sumdy would have liked to have discovered whether the artists could be persuaded to talk more clearly and freely about themselves. Or did artists always have to hide behind their riddles, because what they said would otherwise be too startling? Could anyone become an artist? Was it only a matter of courage, to accept that everyone began as a bad artist? Was courage no more than a willingness to imagine new possibilities, to sketch out a reality other than as it appeared to be? Was an artist a prophet? One of them put at the bottom of all his paintings, in the place of a signature, this inscription: "The Prophet Moses said: 'Would that all the Lord's people were prophets.' " Was that what the hand held out led to, was that what friendship grew into in Paradise, the ability to see hidden qualities in others, and to inspire souls with courage? Would the skill to detect beauty where it did not appear to exist be the condition of admission to the next world? Could humans become angels and work miracles too? Was that what escaping from the prison of a single personal identity meant? But all the answer she got from Colopatiron was that Sumdy must first look at the Tower, see how high she could climb, how it made her feel. It seemed as though Colopatiron was giving her a chance to show whether she could stand the strain of being among angels, perhaps of being an angel.

Sumdy remembered the Five Disappointments of Mankind, and wondered whether Colopatiron was engaged in replacing them with Five Hopes instead, or Five Escape

Routes. But Colopatiron was very firm that she did not like to proclaim grand principles, or even little ones, let alone lay down rules for others to follow: time and again, she had witnessed how principles became far less attractive in practice than they had been in theory, and how opposite principles somehow led to the same result. No, the new morality that did not moralise included a mistrust of all promises, and of all panaceas. The Tower was built only to investigate whether angels could make out of the confusion of tongues something different from what humans had been able to.

Sumdy went on to the first floor of the Tower, which was where the angels invited their enemies. In Paradise, souls who had been enemies on earth passed each other by every day; it was impossible to avoid; but they ignored each other, or even did not notice that they were surrounded by enemies. The worst enemies of Paradise remained outside its gates. The angels never spoke to the fallen angels. But here Sumdy was confronted by devils with sharp horns and big fangs, demons with goats' hooves and forked tails, their eyes blazing fire. Some had left their pitchforks in the umbrella stands outside; some had taken off their shoes, unashamedly revealing spiky, bloodstained, smelly claws, and sat in deep leather armchairs (false leather, she assumed, but she was not sure), like bores in a gentleman's club, pretending to be at ease, picking their noses as though they had no other care in the world, but their eyes flickered this way and that: they were keeping alert, uncertain as to what might happen next in these unaccustomed surroundings. On the top of the bookcases, spirits masquerading as black cocks sat perched, belching smoke and sudden alarming exclamations; on the thick carpet, black cats scratched themselves, sensuously, lazily; black rats scurried around, looking curiously, lasciviously, up the trousers and skirts of passers-by, though they did not bite, nor did they bare their teeth.

When the devils first arrived, there was a lot of whispering among the angels as to what this invitation boded; and the general belief was that Colopatiron's purpose was to rid the universe once and for all of all evil. Paradise could not be perfect till it was no longer threatened. Quite a few angels, gentle though they normally seemed to be, were surprisingly revealed to be secretly boiling with the spirit of revenge, and delighted by the prospect of crushing, liquidating, turning into thin air enemies who had caused them so much trouble. But Colopatiron believed that nothing would ever change profoundly until the angels altered their attitude to their enemies.

There are of course plenty of cinemas in Paradise which show films about the wickedness of devils, of every sort, played by actors, inevitably; it is easy to get hold of books about violence in all its forms; Paradise has everything to satisfy the fascination with evil, and when souls have had their fill, there are even petitions available for them to sign, protesting against such filth being allowed in. So long as the inhabitants could hate devils without having any direct dealings with them, they drew satisfaction from feeling sorry for them, and a cosy feeling from the certainty that the devils could do them no harm any more. However, now that the devils were suddenly before them, powerful feelings of violence and anger swelled up. But Colopatiron said to the angels that they had got it all wrong. The devils were not just enemies in the distance. They dominated the way of thinking of the whole world, even of Paradise. Satan might be in exile, but his power reached over them all, because it was Satan who

272

made them think that there were such things as enemies, that even if all was made perfect, there were always enemies lurking somewhere, who had to be guarded against. Evil was always the enemy, and the enemy was always evil. So long as that was believed, Satan could glory in the joy that he was indispensable.

"Satan" is the Hebrew word for adversary. Life on earth had always been essentially a struggle against adversaries. History was an endless series of confrontations with adversaries, the devil in ever changing disguises. Religion after religion had been established to extirpate Satan, but none had, so far, succeeded; on the contrary, each had uncovered more devils, more sins, more evil than the last one; and every government that wanted to be thought civilised passed laws creating new crimes, offences and misdemeanours. Whereas there had once been only seven deadly sins, there were more varieties of evil in the modern world than anyone had ever imagined possible. Even when conscientious people were doing nothing wrong, they thought it right to feel guilty that they were wicked nonetheless. Satan's business was flourishing. The calculations of the numbers of devils in existence are less precise than those for angels, but the experts in these matters state that devils multiply like flies, and never die, so there are many billions of them. On the first floor of the Tower, the receptions for them showed no signs of ever coming to an end.

Colopatiron was not trying to convert these devils, nor to make mild angels admire ferocious devils; misunderstandings between them would never cease. She had made that clear to her very first guest, who was the oldest, original Evil One, Ahriman. Born long before Satan, in the prehistoric Persia of Zarathustra and the Magi, he was the first being to have the idea of incarnating evil, and evil alone, to put evil on the map

273

as a separate kingdom, to unite the disorganised petty evils that till then had wandered about without a clear purpose. She accepted that he had no wish to change his ways. "It is not that I cannot create anything good", Ahriman had boasted to her, "but that I will not." He came accompanied by a magnificent peacock, whom he had created to prove that claim. He was evil, he said, and intended to remain so, because he enjoyed being evil. He had no personal quarrel with the angels, or anyone else, and he resented their attributing mean motives to him or finding excuses for him. He just had a different idea of what pleasure was: for him cruelty was power, and power was pleasure: for how many humans was it so as well? He was proud that every new truth was an advertisement for him, for there was always the opposite of the truth to denounce, *The Lie*, which was his other name. It was obvious that humans needed devils. All the prophets have publicly proclaimed the power of the devil in their preaching, immediately they met with opposition, for they could not imagine resistance coming from anywhere but sheer wickedness. Every new theory and ism needed an enemy to destroy, hate, or ridicule. He was the Irreplaceable, the Invincible, the Insoluble Problem.

There were thoughtful souls who believed that the only way to deal with him was to keep alive the memory of his horrible deeds, so that those who suffered at his hands should at least be honoured. To be defeated by him might be inevitable, but his victims should be spared a second defeat, of having their sufferings forgotten. The story of how the unendurable agonies he had inflicted were heroically endured should be eternally retold, as a tribute of justice, and as a warning against complacency. However, the souls who thought this way did so because they were ultimately baffled by him: they could not understand how he could induce

274

whole nations to commit massacres, or turn decent people suddenly into murderers. They did not know how to ensure, finally and definitively, that past horrors did not happen again, and again; nor could they forget their scars.

Colopatiron argued that the angels should go further, beyond a vigil of protest. Out of every evil deed, some good must be made to rise. That is what the first floor was designed to bring about. Here, Colopatiron probed the disagreement among devils about how evil a devil should be. Until Ahriman and Satan, entirely devoted to evil, came along, evil did not have their brash confidence. In religions without prophets, evil never expected to defeat good, but only to balance it. The ancient Indian god of destruction, Siva, the inventor of punishment, was quite obviously not evil, or at least evil was only one of his specialities; he was also the god of dance and of love; he used his third eye to save the world from darkness; he knew how to destroy, but only as a preliminary to regeneration; his five faces, four arms and one thousand and eight names brought hope as well as fear, and every evil he created contained the seed of something better. Since he lived in the Himalayan mountain of Kailasa, the horned western devils had never heard of him; they were surprised to learn that they had such an interesting, complicated cousin, and questioned him with curiosity. They were also quite taken aback by their meetings with the Seven Sitala Sisters, who conversed with them sitting decorously arranged on the branches of a nim tree, in a striking sculptural pose. Sitala dispensed smallpox, her sister Maraki spread cholera, Matangi controlled elephantiasis. . . These sisters had long been honoured, and worshipped as goddesses, because they also brought immunity to disease after each of their visits. In the Tower of Babel, they were discussing what should be done when old diseases were finally cured, when new ailments of the mind replaced

275

those of the body; the goddesses were willing to agree on the rules of battle with the angels, to talk about disarmament and antidotes. Colopatiron was trying to discover what other interests they had, what hobbies, but it seemed it would need a longer acquaintance before they would digress onto subjects outside their professional duties.

Sumdy found herself being made to converse with another of these half-wicked powers, half-god, half devil. She had no idea who he was, and was embarrassed when he asked whether she itched a lot: did people itch a lot where she came from, did they itch more in France than in England, how many times a day did she scratch, and where; which did she consider to be most evil, fleas or flies, or lice, or mites, or maggots; did they worship the nettle where she came from; and did she know why, though they had found cures for so many ailments, they still had not eliminated itching, why they put the blame for it on stress and senility? Because he was Ghantiku, the god of Itches, from Bengal; they paid him due respect there; he was horrified by the crudeness and ignorance of the horned devils he was meeting. Sumdy instantly began to itch, in every part of her; she scratched; and the itch was like a mouse running around inside her, impossible to catch; she scratched so much, the god smiled, thinking she was performing a dance of the itch in his honour. He suddenly became solicitous, and talked to her about the art of scratching, and its delights, with poetical enthusiasm. Was he a god or a devil, she asked? She noticed all around her, the horned devils' tails were curling from puzzlement; they were asking the same questions of every new creature they met.

When Colopatiron issued the first invitations to her parties, there was consternation and surprise, because she had a reputation as a vigorous fighter against Satan's machinations; no one seemed to hate him more. Why was she

276

suddenly supping with the devil? She told the angels that they were still listening to the devil in their sleep without knowing it; the world was made that way; neither good nor evil ever won; their wars against evil had made barely a dent in its armour. She accepted that the devil would always dominate automatic reactions, like anger, greed, fear, thoughtless cruelty; everybody had to live with at least some of the foul stench of the devil inside them; everybody was a bit of a devil too. Devils grew nasty when they were treated as though they did not exist; every time they were given just a little respect, they moderated their ambitions; every time it was accepted that they had their pride too, they became almost concilia-tory. These conversations with the devils were, of course, not working out quite as planned; some devils were too proud, too obstinate, too profoundly hurt. Colopatiron distin-guished between horned devils, whose horns warn the world that they choose not to belong to it, and devils with twisted tongues, who spoke as if they had no choice, who wanted to make themselves heard and could not. The angels and the fallen angels used to be on speaking terms once. With some of the latter a dialogue was possible; both sides seemed to long for it in moments of distress, but did not dare say so. Colopatiron agreed that the wicked corrupted the innocent, but not the half-wicked, who had a much more interesting existence than them. Pure evil was an absence of imagination. Imagination could be infectious. She insisted that the good and the half-wicked and the wicked should not shun each other's company and be ignorant of each other's ways. In her prison work, she had always thought it absurd that convicts should be shut away from any sight of good, of hope, of gen-erosity, and be expected to develop such qualities out of nowhere; she lamented that judges so rarely visited those whom they sent to prison, to observe the effect of their sentences, and even more, that decent law-abiding folk refused to admit that they had anything in common with the decent law-abiding folk who suddenly, inexplicably, committed crimes. There had been some disasters at these parties, some devils had expressed interest in the healing activities of those half-devils who did not just aim to terrify and punish. There were more surprises in store, she was certain. In the next world, the relations of angels and devils were bound to be different.

The other half of the first floor was used as an exhibition hall, in which the instruments enemies used to torment each other were laid out, with labels explaining how they worked. Colopatiron was soon overwhelmed by their variety. The exhibition had to be changed frequently to show them all off. When Sumdy was there, it was Explosives Week. The two thirteenth-century monks who had introduced gunpowder into Europe were invited. One of them, Bernard Schwartz, explained that gunpowder was designed to save Christendom from the Turks, and he had never guessed that Christians might use it against Christians, even children against their fathers. Then Friar Roger Bacon, a much-imprisoned heretic, who if he had been a saint would have been the patron saint of technocrats, confessed that he had regarded explosives as something of a joke, an advertising stunt for his controversial views: "You can make thunder and lightning occur if you know the trick," he had written; he was sorry that his joke misfired. For Colopatiron, it was like watching an absurd horror film, seeing what good intentions could do, how wickedness was not always capable of producing the worst evils.

The exhibit Sumdy spent longest at was that of Alfred Nobel. The angels were not quite clear whether he was there

278

as an enemy or a friend; while many souls complained of having been blown up, most painfully, by his dynamite, others praised his inventions as having been valuable to them in peaceful pursuits. Colopatiron had invited him because he had become a writer in Paradise (he was a secret one in his lifetime), whose novels, plays and poems dealt, in one way or another, with the theme of enmity. There were some protests, on the ground that he was a prophet of doubtful reliability: he had predicted, before the World War I, that there was no need to worry about the growing supplies of explosives, because once it became possible to blow up two battalions in a single second, armies would be abolished and war abandoned. But other angels had met him and liked him, because he spent much of his time wandering around Paradise, at home everywhere and nowhere, sleepless, searching for lost talent among the dead of every origin, and even among angels, a cosmopolitan determined to preserve his idealism. He had even tried to establish a Peace Prize for Paradise, which had made many a soul open an eye and many an angel smile. The great need here, he said, was to make peace between individual souls; perhaps that was more practical than seeking peace between nations; perhaps it was the indispensable first step. Whoever, each year (or at whatever time-scale Paradise adopted) succeeded in bringing about peace between the two souls who originally had stood farthest apart from each other, should, he proposed, be honoured, because in the vastness of limitless space, souls were moving more and more away from each other, like stars hurrying to unknown destinations; Paradise seemed to expand the distances between people which, even on earth, were hardly bearable. This was a subject he never tired of talking about to all who would listen; and Sumdy wanted to talk about it too, for it was what was baffling her more than anything.

279

In some way, she may have reminded Nobel of the poor Viennese girl who had perplexed him for much of his life, who passed herself off as Madame Nobel (though he never married), whose extravagances he supported with a mixture of generosity and resentment. He wanted to talk about her still. He had never found a sympathetic audience on earth; that was what he wanted to find in Paradise, souls to whom he could unburden himself. Sumdy's visit to Nobel's stall lasted many hours. Sophie had said to Nobel, he still vividly remembered it, that he was incapable of love. He could love even her, he had replied, if her ignorance, conceit and stupidity were not a continual torment to him. Why had he had those contradictory feelings, that attraction and repulsion? Why was the object of his love his enemy? Why did an uneducated woman, as she was, curdle his pleasure? Why did he like living in Paris but find the Parisian women he met dreary, and prefer Russian women, even though these "unfortunately have an aversion to soap"; why did that worry him; why did he succeed in resigning himself to it? Why were there so many reasons which made him complain that he was "completely alone in the world" and ponder "how sad it is to be without a friend", why was his mother the only person who cared for him, of whom he could be certain that she was not interested only in his money? Was money meant to separate people, to make them enemies of each other? Then why in Paradise did they grow even more separate? Since there was no money in Paradise, what prize could he award to the soul who established peace between the intelligent and the stupid, between the vain and the timid? There were so many problems to solve here. He was thinking that he ought to set about inventing an explosive which would destroy the empty space which divided souls from each other. But would he like that? As with dynamite, there seemed to be no solution which did not have both good and evil in it.

Nobel took Sumdy to meet several other exhibitors. She was interested by Hiram Maxim, who was there with his "Killing Machine", an automatic gun used in the Russo-Japanese War of 1905 with devastating effect, but also with his "Life-Saving Machine", which cured bronchitis. Maxim was a chronic inventor, who could not help seeing ways of doing things differently or faster; he had his amazing mousetraps, curling irons and coffee-makers with him too; he was not sure whether on balance he had done more harm than good. His brother, Hudson Maxim, the inventor of a deadly torpedo, wanted to talk to Sumdy about the "Science of Poetry" instead, which he claimed to have established, making it possible to judge literary merit without argument; what conflicts he would have prevented if anyone had read his book. The explosives exhibition was full of people who had never foreseen what their inventions would lead to, who wondered what substitute there could be for good intentions, which so easily lead to disaster.

Sumdy's thoughts kept going back to Colopatiron, of whose presence she was always conscious. Was she an angel who could not bear to be alone, and who saw every new face as an opportunity to exert her charm, to share her warmth, to try and establish that contact that was so elusive in Paradise? Sumdy noticed that Colopatiron was nervous before she met any unfamiliar figure, not because she worried about their past, but because she was uncertain as to how her welcome would be received; despite her charm, she never fully believed the charm would work, and that was part of her charm, for only the vulnerable are charming. Colopatiron made her mind up quickly about those she met, but she regretted it: one of the main purposes of the first floor seemed to be to counteract that tendency.

Sumdy wished she could spend more time with the devils,

as she had wanted to with the artists, but again Colopatiron was in a hurry to move on. Quickly, quickly, she kept repeating, incapable of waiting, even though she had all the time in the world; that haste went with her passion for something always more amazing; perhaps she was so energetic because she got bored so easily. And Sumdy kept answering that she had to pause to consider, that she hated branding anyone with a judgement, that she had enormous difficulty deciding about anyone. Indeed, whenever she was tempted to, she repeated the definition of a sinner that Aisha, the youngest wife of the Prophet Muhammad, used to give: "The sinner is he who thinks he is righteous." Clearly, there could be sinners in Paradise too. She asked whether it was impossible to be an angel if one had such hesitations: did angels always have to know their own minds, were they never sinners, was that what separated humans and angels? Colopatiron said Sumdy obviously had no idea just how much doubt and worry an angel could feel. Sumdy found it a very odd experience being treated as an equal by an angel. She felt enormous sympathy for Colopatiron's repugnance for the business of exposing the evil in devils, in souls, or in people. She agreed there were surely enough lawyers in the universe to attend to that. The thrill of a conspiratorial pleasure passed through her. She was so proud that she had not disgraced herself, yet.

When the party ended, she asked Colopatiron how it had come about that an angel like her, who everyone said had once been so combative, was now being so apparently conciliatory to the devils. Colopatiron replied that she still was combative, she still reacted with fury every time she saw callousness and cruelty, and she still found it impossible to love a devil with horns. But there were some enmities in the universe, very old ones, which made no sense any more; there were oppositions of principle which meant very little in

282

practice; there were personal animosities maintained by sheer habit and ignorance. Most devils enjoyed a fight, but some were tired of fighting. She was willing to talk to these. Occasionally, a devil needed a shoulder to cry on. She would not refuse her compassion. In the next world, at any rate, souls would not be the prisoners of their enemies.

However, the effect of this tour of the devils on Sumdy's pets was disastrous. They were extremely frightened. Jolly not only lost his smile, but was soon shaking, even more than when thunder made him think the world was falling to pieces. He had no time for Forgetmenot, which rushed back into its jam jar and became immobile, as though thrown by terror into the state of coma that it adopted in extreme cold. They were strangers to each other again. Fear put an end to their interest in each other. Sumdy thought there would be many people on earth who would feel as they did, disapproving of devils in all their forms, running away from danger.

Colopatiron noticed, and said she was not surprised. To be able to confront one's enemies without fear, it was not enough to decide to do so.

CHAPTER TEN

S o Sumdy was invited to climb higher. On the next thirty floors of the Tower of Babel, in the great bulge of the egg whisk, Colopatiron had her library. The saints have never mentioned libraries as one of the attractions of Paradise, probably because they know by heart all the books they want to read and do not wish to be bothered with any more; besides, most of the inhabitants of Paradise, until very recently, could not read; modern immigrants mutter that they have no leisure to read; while some angels insist that most books are either bad books or dirty books. So Colopatiron did not call her library by that name. Sumdy was told that they were going up to visit Chaos. Over the entrance door, she read this inscription: Chaos United with Spirit and Gave Birth to Desire.

Sumdy had always assumed that chaos was the yawn of nothingness out of which the world was created, emptiness and disorder. The angel at the front desk explained that the yawn is still there, but it is far from being nothingness; on the contrary, chaos is everything, it is the amalgam of all possible thoughts, words, deeds, memories, for which no one has an adequate explanation, or which everyone explains in a different way. To the inhabitants of the earth, chaos appears to be a curse, an encumbrance, a relic of the past, over which it is essential, and seemingly impossible, to win a final victory. Somehow, each day, a new chaos is born again, as perplexing as ever, and though it may almost look like the chaos of yesterday, it never quite repeats itself, which is why it is too slippery to grasp.

However, Colopatiron's idea was that chaos had been unjustly maligned. It need not be a nuisance. In Paradise, there is time and room to appreciate what chaos does, and can do. So in her Tower, she had brought together a collection of chaos, in the form of books.

Sumdy was not sure how chaos should be treated, but to be on the safe side, she bowed low as she entered, because chaos was once thought to be a god, and because in Paradise libraries (whatever kind of books they contained) might be recognised as holy shrines. In any case, she always approached libraries with a special emotion, half way between reverence and delight. However humble, however small, however poor, they were the abode of faith, of the only faith she had, faith in the future. As a tourist, she always tried to visit the library of every town she passed through, because that was where, she liked to think, the spirit of the town lived, even if the town did not know it, even if for the majority of the citizens "book" was a four letter word, even if the library was a bus and came only once a week. She was keen to know how Paradise could improve on what she regarded as the perfect haven of peace. But a library was where she went to reduce the chaos in her mind; she was puzzled to find one that prided itself on reducing life to chaos.

Colopatiron had chosen books for her collection of chaos because, when brought together, they produced chaos in its most concentrated form. As the angel of prisons, she had often dreamt that prisons should be turned into libraries, when she was not dreaming that there should be a library in every shopping centre, in every park, just like a bench, to rest the mind, just like a waste-paper basket, to throw foul thoughts into, just like a telephone kiosk, to prompt a conversation with neglected friends. She had become so enthusiastic about the virtues of libraries that she had come to think that a library could be made into the very heart, the motor of her machine for making freedom. For a library was one of the very few things that always had to be free; it incarnated freedom; it was where the mind was most free, where time ceases to be oppressive, where no book is penalised for being young or old, for the colour of its paper or its ink, where each has an equal voice, undisturbed by examinations about its precise beliefs, where no reader is accused of poking his nose into matters which do not concern him, where there are no secrets, where no promises are exacted, except to respect the right of everyone else, and of the books, to be there, though one may think what one pleases of their faded spines and glaring jackets.

In such an exceptional atmosphere, the angels could enjoy the conditions most conducive for loosening their ideas, for loosening their vision of the universe, for escaping from the appearance of finality that objects give. They knew, as everybody does, that appearances are deceptive, but they had found only two methods on earth for dealing with that inconvenience. One was to be cynical. The other was to doubt everything, accept nothing as true for which they could not find perfect proof, laboriously collect proofs, in the hope of ending up by being certain about everything they could be certain about. But Colopatiron wanted to start with a clean slate for a quite different reason: her aim was to pull the universe of knowledge apart so as to see what every bit of it

286

was made of, how it had come to be what it was, how chaos and accident had gone into making it what it was. In that way, she could reach the frontier between the possible and the impossible, and find out how the impossible could be made possible.

A library was a place that suggested the most perfect order, with every book allotted its exact place, and a record kept of its every movement, in and out, and yet a library eventually converts its readers to the view that the world is not in perfect order at all, that most things are increasingly difficult to understand, that no two books ever quite agree; it seemed designed to be a polite hint that the god Chaos is still very present in the universe, unveiling new forms of chaos all the time. Colopatiron was fascinated by misunderstanding, and in her library, she could gloat for all eternity on all possible varieties of incomprehension. She liked to show off her collection of old books whose purpose was misunderstood differently in each century, in each country, her equally large collection of new books whose significance, she believed, had escaped contemporary readers and would have to wait decades, perhaps centuries, to be appreciated; she was proud, most of all, of the piles of books still unwritten – the books all modern souls carried inside them – which were not sure what their meaning was. On the covers, she inscribed the many different titles their authors had thought of but not used. Every tome was impressively thick, for she bound into them corrections and changes, all they might have been; sometimes they had to be put on the shelf in boxes or trunks, to contain the hundred drafts in the course of which they had become unrecognisable. Visitors who spent long enough in her library would become connoisseurs of misunderstanding, not just of authors and readers misunderstanding each other, but of the universal dither, of how people changed their minds about what they meant, of how words were used in ways no one could make sense of. They might find it disconcerting at first, but eventually they would be proud to put "chaosologist" on their visiting cards.

Chaos was the one god who had never established a religion to worship him and yet his influence was enormous: he had his temple in every human mind. Colopatiron seemed to be wanting to liberate the angels from the belief that chaos was an outsider, the exception, obsolescent, and to be suggesting that it was not chaos they should be trying to escape from, but the outward appearances which gave the impression that order ruled in the universe. Every time they thought they understood something, they could be sure that if they applied the Upside Down Rule, which was perhaps the only rule to be found in chaos, and turned their wisdom up side down, or inside out, or back to front, it would reveal a meaning that might have some truth in it too. For example, laws, which are the the most august embodiment of order, very frequently replace one form of chaos by another. Motorways eliminate bottlenecks and become bottlenecks themselves. Taxes solemnly voted, solemnly collected, solemnly given to farmers to encourage them to grow crops which are then solemnly destroyed, are signs that chaos has a sense of humour: solemnity is the funny hat it wears. Chaos likes to play games too: the Unconscious is where it hides, nobody has ever been able to prove anything about the Unconscious, but nobody dares deny it is there. Anger is a different kind of chaos still: Colopatiron had debated endlessly whether there would be anger in the next world, until she saw it as a form of chaos: anger was frightening, but the chaos behind it, the fear and frustration, were, rather, worthy of pity; people got angry with anger, because they did not acknowledge chaos. There was no point in being angry with chaos.

Browsing through the library, Sumdy suddenly felt dizzy. She had the sensation that it was rocking like a boat, that it was revolving as though on a spindle, slowly at first, then faster. She then began having hallucinations. She was certain that she saw books flying off their shelves, leaves fall out of them, chasing each other like courting butterflies, or cascading like blossom from cherry trees, scampering through the hedges searching for a ditch to rest in, and the ditch was a new shelf. Then her sickness changed into a delicious sensation of being wafted through the library by this spinning whirlwind, swept into sections she would never dream of going near, astronomy, theology, bumping into books which seemed suddenly interesting, and indeed perhaps no longer mere objects. She thought she could recognise when a book was growing restless on its shelf and ready to fall off. She imagined books calling out to her as she glided past, complaining that readers never came to them, that they were lost, mislaid, wrongly shelved, or that they were being plagiarised; she saw them playing leapfrog over the cards in the catalogue, while a choir of them declaimed rhetorically: Spades should be called spades, books are not things, they should not be classified under Paper Industry and Allied Trades. And when she held up books close to her ear, like a sea shell, she heard a murmur inside them, not of waves, but of all the noises that they had themselves heard, the hiccup of the distracted printing press making misprints, the euphoric screams and nightmare groans of the publisher hesitating about his gambles, the jaunty whistling of the travelling salesman, smiling because people read his books for unexpected reasons, the unmistakable rattle of a bookseller's head saying no, it was an insoluble puzzle why one book sold and another did not. Sumdy wondered whether she was listening to the true hum of the universe, its infinitely complex sounds, the true babel of voices that normally never get noticed. If books had voices, did that mean they had souls? Or was the library designed to make fools of those who entered it?

Colopatiron had indeed designed the library to rotate, and books did indeed fall off shelves, and end up in sections they would never normally be put in, because a book with pretentions could not pontificate so complacently if it suddenly found itself among neighbours who could not understand what it was saying. Books are so reluctant to take exercise, to go on walks in inaccustomed fields. Readers are scared to penetrate into parts of libraries where all the words seem longer than they ought to be. The result is that chaos has time to become respectable, to grow solid, and to masquerade as order. A library was very far from being a place where nothing happened, for in it the world was rearranged in a million ways; rigidities dissolved, and reformed and dissolved again; a library was a great mountain of lies as well as of truth, and there was no better place to watch how the world told and believed lies, carelessly or wilfully. Colopatiron had tried to create a library which pulverised dogmatism – that was her arch enemy, perhaps the only enemy she would always refuse to be reconciled with.

Since she was searching for a new morality, she asked herself how the old moralities had come to be accepted as so immovable and obvious, even though they required such large amounts of hypocrisy to maintain them. She thought she got a possible answer when her books on physics strayed into the section on ethics, and miscellaneous works of literature got muddled up with both. It seemed to her that there was a link between the way humans believed the universe was constructed and how they thought they themselves should behave. The accumulation of property was the foundation of the good life when the world was believed to be composed of solid, indestructible matter. Ladies danced with decorum and obeyed etiquette as though it was a religion when the planets seemed to rotate according to fixed rules, leaving no room for anything unexpected, except the dire interventions of the hand of God. But they quickly took to dancing boogie-woogie and rock-and-roll when the micro-world was discovered to be full of chaos. The distinctions between the sexes became less harsh when electrons were found to be sometimes particles and sometimes waves. The consumer society became discredited as soon as the universe was revealed to be a giant factory of energy, and the sun and the wind and the earth freely and constantly produced infinite horsepower; consuming ceased to be the most exciting way of killing boredom when new kinds of excitement were discovered among the atoms, when it was seen that the greatest amount of energy is released by the tiniest fragment of matter transforming itself into something that it was not; then self-transformation became the new ideal and creativity seemed attainable by ordinary people. The principle that small was beautiful arrived when the ancient belief that strength comes from little groups joining to form larger groups was challenged by invisibly small electrons moving whole mountains. The worry about the dangers of narcissism blossomed with the discovery that the most powerful of all forces is the strong nuclear force which makes each atom hold itself together and refuse to have anything to do with any other. Romantic love flourished most luxuriantly at the same time as the theory of electro-magnetism was evolved. Colopatiron's conclusion was that, as the importance of chaos as a source of energy was recognised, it would affect the view that humans had of their own personal energy. The shaking up of fossilised opinions would be less of a terror. In the next world, the proportion of souls who chose to remain awake might be greater; but of course it would only be a proportion, because sleep would always have its attractions. That was what Colopatiron meant by chaos uniting with spirit to give birth to desire.

Sumdy remembered Henry Ford and the boy god Pushan saying that the only way to live comfortably was to have a double soul, one of which felt anger and envy, while the other did not, and just watched, and it seemed that Colopatiron had a vision of the world which was double as well, an ordinary world people could be angry with, but also another of chaos, full of accidents for which no one could be blamed, and in which envy was pointless. She was pleased that Colopatiron was not expecting the apoplectic emotions to be banished from the next world, when so many humans would feel lost without them, when so many gods were proud that their terrifying anger was like a consuming fire, when Homer had sung the praises of wrath, sweeter by far than the honeycomb, when many of the good things in life were the by-products of vicious greed. Sumdy was impressed that Colopatiron had nothing of the traditional utopian about her; it was most encouraging that the world was outgrowing that kind of dreaming. And yet, Colopatiron insisted, there was hope in her vision, because it saw everything as being in constant transformation, people need not be imprisoned by outward appearances, chaos was the natural state to which every system reverted, sooner or later, but it also promised the chance of new combinations.

Sumdy thought that she could make her peace with chaos, if that was the price of living among the angels. Indeed, she already imagined that the books in the library smelt no longer of dust, nor of leather, nor of old potatoes, but of something even sweeter than jasmine or musk: was it the smell of hope? She said to Colopatiron that she was tempted to spend eternity in this library. Colopatiron said, in that case, they must climb higher still.

292

Have you become any younger today? Those were the words that greeted Sumdy on the next level. She had climbed the stairs into the part of the Tower of Babel which narrows to become the handle of the egg whisk, and suddenly everyone she saw seemed very young. As she went up from floor to floor, she was met by the same question, in different languages. Es-tu devenu plus jeune aujourd'hui? . . . They asked the question casually, as though they were saying "How do you do?" Sumdy realised that all the souls she had so far encountered were fully grown souls, or at least souls pretending to be the mature fruit of earthly experience. If she had looked into the millions of little houses with curtained windows, in which the inhabitants of Paradise did their best to sleep, she might have seen children safely tucked up in bed; if she had stopped at the kindergartens of Paradise, she might have observed souls who had decided to spend eternity reliving their classroom days. She had taken it for granted that Paradise would be overflowing with youth, for a good third of humanity used to arrive here under the age of ten, in centuries when it was normal to die in the very process of growing, long before the bones grew brittle; and yet this was the first occasion on which she had come face to face with souls who did not claim to be adults, who did not think that they had yet lived their lives. It seemed that many of the young did not like Paradise, at least the Paradise of their elders, but there were only rumours about where they had gone instead. Some said that most wandered off to their own Paradise, amid the immense primeval forests on the fringes of timelessness, where they could amuse themselves in their own way, make as much noise as they liked and sing their incomprehensible hymns undisturbed. It was inevitable that they should become even less controllable, even less programmable than they were on earth, said disillusioned

293

parents, no longer needed to feed them, no longer able to do them favours. Pretending to be adult is one of the snobberies of Paradise, pretending that one has had a full life, as one might pretend to have had famous ancestors. Suddenly, Sumdy was appalled that she had missed what might be the most interesting part of Paradise, just like an ordinary tourist, who promises himself that he will return one day to see the real heart of the country he has been wandering through, protected by his dark glasses.

The inhabitants of these upper floors of the Tower of Babel were not human young, but cherubim and seraphim. They looked like children, but that was quite a recent disguise they had chosen to adopt. In the ancient world, cherubim were huge monsters, with four faces, of a lion, an ox, an eagle and a man, whose frowns were meant to intensify the terror of all who approached the throne of God and every holy place. But in early modern times, they began assuming the shape of human babies instead. That is one of the most important turning points in angelic history. The cherubim were the first angels to be converted to modernity. The earliest paintings showing a cherub as a child date from the fourteenth century. It must have been around then that they had their extraordinary inspiration, that immortality did not satisfy them, that to be forever young is the ultimate ideal, that youth is the only certain answer to the boredom of being wise and awesome. For them modernity meant eternal youth. They gradually watched that ideal spread, and saw youth worshipped in an unprecedented way, being given more and more privileges, working less and less, or not at all, until family life was designed to please it alone. The cherubim were right to recognise this as one of the greatest of all revolutions in history. But revolutions go astray. The young had trouble developing an art of remaining young. Looking young was not enough. Children came to be valued by adults as toys to play with; as a result, adults remained toys too, played with by what they called destiny.

In the new Tower of Babel, Colopatiron brought together some insomniac cherubim to try to discover the art of remaining young. These cherubim were determined not to grow up into aging beaux and dyed belles in tennis shoes, with no better goals than to "feel good", to keep fit and to wear casual clothes. The cherubim were all in favour of feeling good, but they did not consider this was the essence of youth. The cherubim's greeting to Sumdy was not an insult, merely a reminder of their predicament, that when time stands still, the soul constantly has to choose more deliberately, whether to grow old or young.

It seemed odd to Sumdy that the cherubim should speak to her in so many different languages. So far, almost everyone in Paradise had used only her own language. Every Holy Book states that the language of Paradise is its own. That had been confirmed. Every visitor hears what he expects to hear. Colopatiron had built a new Tower of Babel in part because she was convinced that the original one would have had a very different fate if it had been populated by children instead of adults. The worst prison, she said, was the one into which so many of the children in the world are put, the prison of knowing only one language. Children, in her view, are born to learn languages, joyously, naturally, just as they are born to eat and laugh; it is one of the few things they can do better than their elders; to be sentenced to express themselves in the same clichés, the same constructions, the same vocabulary for ever, is to muzzle them. To remain young, Colopatiron argued, is first of all to remain for ever delighted by the adventure of words, to fall in love with words over and over again, to flirt with words, to tease them, to find them exasperating but marvellous nonetheless. It was not just that languages grew lugubrious if they were not embraced and danced with and pinched and made to smile. Words do not just enable people to say what they want to say; they are indispensable in the flowering of the imagination; they are ambiguous; they make intense friendships, they have memories, they have ideas that beget ideas. It was a disaster that the Babylonians had been frightened by the confusion of tongues in the old Tower of Babel, and had failed to recognise it as a challenge to their capacity to remain young, had not seen that misunderstanding was inevitable. Manipulating the ambiguities of language was a way of manipulating chaos. The cherubim were children who accepted that there is always more or less make-believe in imagining the world. Juggling languages kept them fit, but it was also a way of putting the world together again after having dismembered it to see what it was made of.

In these upper floors, the playrooms of the Tower, the angels searched for games to help them remain young. They tried all the games that have ever been invented, but ruled most out on the ground that there was an element of violence or callousness or greed or pride in them, that some games would tame them, that others would infect them with unmentionable adult vices. They were not impressed by the advice of old workaholics, who assured them that work was really play, nor by pensioners from big corporations, still recovering from their ordeal, who said that office battles could be enjoyed as a game, nor by experts on games, who diagnosed that the best games were those one enjoyed losing. They did not want simply to be distracted from worry, or from the dull pauses, the dispiriting compromises, the interminable negotiations of the ordinary working world, and least of all to play like adults pretending to be children. All these kinds of games might give them pleasant sensations, but being pleased was not a sign of being young.

They decided that the only game that met their requirements was to pretend to be God, just as human children instinctively played at being father and mother. They called their game marbles, but it was not glass or bone or stone or nuts that they used. When Sumdy arrived, she could not see the marbles at all; they are indeed very difficult to see, they are barely visible specks, not even quite objects, more hints of punctuation marks, almost pauses or gaps in space. Sumdy had by now become accustomed to the atmosphere of Paradise, with its mixture of sun and mist that turned everything into an Impressionist painting made up of little dots. Eventually, she realised that the marbles were the smallest dots to be found inside these dots, the atoms and particles out of which the world is made. The cherubim were playing at creating new worlds with them. It was not an easy game. The dots came into sight, perhaps into existence, for only brief moments, like the twinkle of a star, and then disappeared, leaving only the feeling that there was something which might twinkle again, there or somewhere else, and it was impossible to be sure whether the dots which replaced each other were the same dots. The dots or marbles often refused to roll in a straight line, and wandered about, as though constantly changing their mind, suggesting by their vacillation that they too might have minds. Some had the habit of going straight through pieces of furniture, coming out unharmed on the other side, so indifferent were they to their surroundings; some on the contrary seemed obsessed by their surroundings, by every rumour that floated past, and behaved like distraught stockbrokers rushing from client to client, passing on bits of news, trying to set up deals; some were slimy toadies, coated with glue, who clung piteously to every passer-by.

The cherubim were playing their game to see what new shapes they could create out of these dots, which would be more wonderful together than they were separately. They said this was the only game that could keep them young, and save them from losing their sense of wonder, their taste for surprise, their delight in adventure. Creating new worlds and creating new words went together. Forming new groups of words which sparkled more brightly when they met, was no different from making new objects. Of course, it was a game in which it was impossible to win, in which there was no right answer, there always could be a better one, for the ultimate aim was to explore the unexpected. When all the players held up their hands at the sight of a new sandcastle of marbles, which they all agreed was remarkable, and exclaimed: This is beauty, they had to continue, the game only became harder; if the experience was repeated it was a foul. There were some angels who refused to play, on the ground that the cherubim were being not young, but childish, and were ignoring the fact that the world could not be changed: brick walls would always be hard and painful. But the cherubim insisted that they loved the delicate dance of dots inside brick walls, the delicate emotions inside souls. They agreed that massive walls were painful, and masses of most things were too; but to them detail was precious, sacred. To be young means to care about detail, to be curious about each piece of feeling in every soul. It was not for nothing that cherubim had wings, which were the symbols of poetry and of the imagination that took flight; they saw themselves as putting back the poetry into brick walls. And poetry was not mere decoration. Most truths are too elusive to grasp directly, they need to be approached in roundabout ways, by stealth, by poetry. It is often poetry that discovers or creates new truths, because it stretches truth to the utmost limits of its implications, to the very frontiers of plausibility, and when it comes on an abyss, a gap in knowledge, it has the courage to jump over it with a half-truth, or a metaphor; it appreciates how indispensable half-truths are because truths frequently begin as half-truths, or as tenths-of-truths, as inspired guesses, as poetic phrases. Whole truths are too rare, too magnificent to play games with, but bits of truth offer all the excitement of gambling, they may not lead anywhere, but sometimes they do. The dice the cherubim used in their game was metaphor. When they wanted to get two strange pieces of chaos to sit on a sofa side by side, and tentatively hold hands, when they played at being marriage brokers, they could not rely just on accident.

They invited Sumdy to join them. She asked whether the game allowed them to construct some object that she could take home with her: could they make a happy marble? Of course, they said. A cherub put down a dot of a marble, so tiny that it was invisible. She must not take a marble, he said, that might give the wrong impression. But they should not suggest, said another cherub, that happiness had a central, essential core, and he hurled his marble straight through the middle of the first one. A seraph was of the opinion that they should construct a mount, on which the marble could be stood, even if it was invisible, for no happiness can exist without a prop, without friends, without godparents, consolers, confidants. They went off to fetch every kind of marble, and spent a long time trying to fit them together, this way and that. Sumdy was astonished at their patience: if this was how chaos had to be handled to take on a shape, no wonder people preferred to buy it in ready-made lumps. Eventually the cherubim said they could not get quite what they had hoped, but they could make their marbles into a painkiller: would that do? No, Sumdy thought it might kill pleasure at the same time as pain. They tried again, and made what they said was a love potion, which could suppress the distaste that people had for each other, momentarily, and might fill the emptiness around them with fantasies: what more was needed for happiness? Sumdy replied that humans had enough potions that befuddled and deceived the mind. Then was happiness not immunity from the sorrows of existence, they asked? They could try to produce a vaccine made from all the disagreeable moments of life. No, getting used to misery did not make it pleasure.

Finally they thought they had the answer: let Sumdy take any marble at all back to earth, and clasp it in her hand. When people asked what happiness was, she could unclench her fist and show them the marble, which would be too small for anyone to see. Happiness, she could say, is what you hold in your hand: you all hold your happiness in your hands. But Sumdy protested: why did the cherubim offer humans a happiness which they did not use themselves, which was not good enough for themselves? She could understand what they were doing, even if she had only just arrived: they got their happiness by rubbing two truths together, and making a third one arise, by getting bits of chaos to lie side by side and inventing new kinds of ribbon to hold them together. At the very least, let them make her a matchbox, so that she could rub two strangers together and cause a spark, by which they would see each other as they had never done before. They admitted that she was quite right. They had been trying to invent one of those for a very long time, but had never succeeded: there seemed no way of mass-producing that sort of matchbox, and perhaps that sort of happiness. However, they were working on it, and they had invented many strange gadgets in the process. The trouble about inventing, when one had only chaos out of which to make things, was that one could never be sure what result one got. They had heard that God too had never been satisfied with what He had made.

Taking a marble away as a souvenir, Sumdy went to find Colopatiron, and asked how she persuaded the cherubim to keep on trying, when their efforts never quite succeeded, when in their game nobody ever scored a perfect goal. Colopatiron was surprised by her question. Of course it did not matter that the result was never the right one. The goal of truth is beauty, which can never be reached. The joy was in the conception, in the ingenuity of the execution. That was enough to ensure that there need be no sorrow when the outcome was less than had been hoped for. An enjoyable game was one which, even before it was completed, generated a new thought for a new adventure; it did not just give satisfaction, but also created hope.

And now Sumdy realised why the angels said Colopatiron had charisma. The first sign that a person possesses charisma is that he is repeatedly forgiven his mistakes; even if he is dangerous, even if his admirers know his weaknesses, they do not care, because he knows how to give them hope; a charismatic person is one who is a skilful player of the cherubim's game; he is master of the art of remaining young. There was no need to be anybody special to acquire that art. The distance between angels and humans, even ordinary humans, Sumdy said, was not unbridgeable. Colopatiron thought that was obvious. This time, she did not even ask whether Sumdy was ready to climb higher.

At the top of the Tower of Babel there was silence. Colopatiron now spoke in a whisper. Here were the thinking

301

rooms. The Tower became a slim spire, on each floor of which a single angel sat like a cobbler, mending invisible shoes, hammering at prejudices and contradictions, sewing brainwaves together, stretching them so that they did not pinch. Mortal souls come to Paradise thinking that they can at last stop thinking, but that is what it is most ideally suited for; in life, there is never enough time to think, usually the more important people become, the less often they can squeeze in an appointment to think, the older they grow, the more they are convinced that they know what they think and so have no need to think any more, have no surprises in store, have heard all they have to say before. The angels were here trying to learn to think – the one subject no one could teach them.

There was a little bonheur du jour desk in the room Sumdy was led to, the sort at which aristocratic ladies filled their diaries with thoughts they could not share with their husbands: can angels not think without writing? asked Sumdy. The chair looked Italian, sixteenth century, the "clucking hen" type: did angels need to sit to lay their thoughts? A Persian rug on the floor was covered with a labyrinth of paths, flower beds, trees and water channels: did they have to eliminate the contours from a landscsape before they built their dreams on it? A row of Chinese blue and white ginger jars with inscrutable decorations, their lids like round hats on oval heads, stood on a shelf: were these waiting to be filled miraculously with thoughts? Sumdy began thinking about thinking, she saw thoughts everywhere, hidden in every object, thoughts pretending to be speechless, though she could sense theirs was only a surface silence. Every object around her stimulated thought; even angels needed to be stimulated to think.

But what was Sumdy supposed to do with all these thoughts? Through the window, infinity stretched out before her, a magnificent view which immediately infused her with an infinite sadness. To see no end to anything suddenly seemed as terrible as to think that everything must come to an end. Paradise was so still. The birds which glided past now appeared to her to do so aimlessly, no longer able to find any reason to hunt, to chase, to start a fight: what new hunger could they feel, what new desires? Though there was so much to admire from this height, wherever she turned, Sumdy got only the impression that the whole universe was filled with a great emptiness. It was indeed as Newton had described it, full of empty space. And its hum seemed to be repeating only one thought, over and over again, as though to shut out all others: let me rest from my thoughts, let me have peace.

The thinking room was doubly sad for Sumdy, because it showed that the angels themselves had trouble knowing what to think: the business of existence could not be taken for granted even by them. Just being was still the most elusive of the arts. What could she tell people back home? That even in Paradise they had not found the secret of peace, which blew in the wind but could not be grasped? That the struggle will never end? That they must wait for the next world, and doubtless another one further still in the future, before things could be organised as they ought to be? That hopes were never fulfilled, that they might as well believe in their childhood's fairy tales, as expect final solutions to their sordid problems? It was so quiet here: she feared she would soon be listening to the splash of her own tears and trying to find comfort in them.

She saw that Forgetmenot the cockroach had spotted a spider in a corner, and the two were looking at each other: were they thinking? She was a long way from learning how to exchange thoughts with the likes of spiders, even though in every peaceful acre of green English field there were at least two million spiders, ignored, and in the whole of England there were no less than two million million spiders, two with a dozen noughts, constantly busy keeping nature in order like a secret police force, saving the human race from extinction, doing their duty, liquidating between them, every day, at the rate of ten insects each, a mountain of beings weighing as much as all the humans in the country put together; if it were not for spiders, there would be nothing for humans to eat, no gastronomy, no dinner parties with witty conversation; they were the foundation of civilisation; and Sumdy had trouble not screaming at the sight of one. How could she ever hope to know what thoughts went on in a spider's mind, if it had one, or how its oily feet felt as they trod the sticky web on the way to kill its prey? What could a spider think in Paradise, if it was not hunting, trapping, paralysing, sucking the juices out of its fellow creatures? Could the female Aranea be reconciled with the puny mate it had devoured when he had done his work of love? Was this the love that Sumdy missed? Who was there here to stroke and tickle the spider, and playfully bind it up, as it delighted to be on earth? Did spiders learn to answer questions like these, when they could finally rest from their quest for food? What would happen in the world if everyone stopped eating everyone else? These were the thoughts which Sumdy had in the thinking room. She was not impressed by her ability to think. Was she suited to Paradise, or was she simply not ready for a place where they sat and thought?

Colopatiron told her to listen more carefully to the silence. She thought she heard groans and sighs coming from below. Did it not comfort her that thinking was a labour to the angels also? No, she knew that thinking was a labour, which nearly always aborted. How often had she given birth to a thought that was not stillborn, or that was worth listening to, or that brought new life and hope into the world? Humans, she said, had lost faith in thought. What modern soul came to Paradise in order to think? Modern people put their trust in the senses and the emotions, because they had been betrayed by their thinking too often. They had been plunged into abyss after abyss by their logic, they were tired of being too stupid or too clever, they preferred to bask safely in sensual pleasure, where each had his own measure. She herself had a passion for equality, so she had to have a passion for sensuality, which is the birthright of every human being.

Colopatiron told Sumdy to listen again to the silence. Half of thinking was listening. Did she hear no music in the thoughts around her? Sumdy said her thinking had always made a spluttering sound, grinding, screeching. When it produced a thought, this was no more than a drip, a leak, a bleed, a sweat. Her thoughts distracted and alarmed her; and they were so painstaking, so much slower than the machine-gun quickness of others. Her thinking made too much noise for her to be able to hear any music, if there was any.

That was what the thinking room was for, to learn to hear the music of thought, to find it in one's own thought, for otherwise one could not hear it in anyone else. Of course this did not come easily. On earth there was too much distracting noise, the murmur of the guilty conscience, the hiss of those who know better, poised to find fault with everything one does; it was indeed difficult to hear oneself think, let alone take delight in the delicate movement of thought, still less to compose a symphony or a song out of thought; but here one did not always have to think the same thoughts, or express them in the same monotonous voice. Let Sumdy listen more attentively.

Was it the wind? Sumdy imagined she could just detect a sort of mournful dirge. She said that the thoughts of Paradise seemed to her to be sad ones, expressing regret that there

305

were no sensuous bodies any more. What human souls wanted was to be able to enchant and seduce each other, occasionally to do each other harm, sometimes to caress, most of all to be caressed.

That was one of the subjects the angels thought about in the thinking rooms. Angels could have bodies or not, as they pleased. Sometimes, they used to envy humans, and put on bodies, and parade them as miraculous, divinely designed machines capable of producing instant, delicious pleasure. That a body could fill up empty space amazed them; that they could touch one another thrilled them. But at other times their faith in bodies was shaken: strangely, that happened when they seemed to be taking most delight in their physical sensations, and when they gave the impression of being enslaved or obsessed by them. In such moments of enthusiasm, they expected more and more from bodies, and asked for what they could not give. First they would be enthralled by the idea of love between two bodies, and then they would be dismayed to find themselves concluding that love was not enough: they wanted above all, they decided, to be understood; they had to be liked for the right reasons. The more they touched each other, the more they complained they were not close enough: bodies gave an insufficient intimacy; instead of embraces, they began demanding companionship, a meeting of minds, relationships that would make them grow. When they called each other beautiful, an indefinable worry clouded their flirtations: they became frightened of being dependent on the good opinion of others, of being cast into stereotypes, or appreciated for the superficial aspect of themselves. In the end, they always took off their bodies half in joy and half in sadness. The pleasure of bodies, they said, was all in the imagination. The nose did not smell, it was only a jungle of follicles that vibrated; it was not the mouth that decided which fruit was fresh and which was rotten; there was no organ of the body capable of having an opinion. That explained why angels quite often lived without bodies. But even then they were not content. What they needed - they had to go through these experiences to become urgently aware of it - was not just more sensitive bodies, but also more active imaginations. Now that in Paradise they were no longer busy being travel agents directing humans to heaven, or therapists assuring them that, yes, they were normal, the angels had a chance at last to do something about their imaginations.

Colopatiron said she could only tell her own story, for even to her the thoughts of other angels were inscrutable. When she had first come to the bare thinking rooms, she had found them uncomfortable. At every excuse, she used to run down to the library, pretending to herself that she must look up, once again, what great minds had written about subjects she thought she ought to be thinking about. But every time she returned, she had to decide what she thought herself; she realised just how little such deciding she had done, just how much she had been content to repeat what others said, flaunting herself in borrowed clothes, which she supposed were safer. Then she said to herself that, after all, her thoughts were the only possession which she could truly call her own, which she had full control of, and which no one else could reach; and the thoughts of others, for all their glitter and charm, she could only guess at and parody. She made a resolution to bring no books back to the room from the library. Henceforth, she went down to it only for mental exercise, when she needed help to shake her prejudices. Simultaneously reading and thinking had been like coffee and milk, one of her favourite joys; mentally conversing with authors as she read them would always remain an indispensable hobby, but she decided that at times she needed to escape from them also, and to think by herself undisturbed, hidden away from their insistent voices. So she went through her old opinions as she might have gone through old clothes: why had she not looked at them every year, to see whether they still fitted, whether she still liked them? She had collected so many, pell mell. It frightened her to throw the old ones right out, and yet she often no longer agreed with herself, with the self that she used to be at various periods in the past. She did not want to be left naked, with no opinions at all. When she told other angels what she was doing, they asked her where she got the courage to carry out this spring clean, this clear-out of all the thoughts which nagged her uselessly, which distracted her from what she really wished to think about: they all said they had terrible trouble keeping away nagging thoughts and being host only to the thoughts they wanted to have.

She could not reply for a long time. Then she realised that she had always had the courage. So did everybody. It was as natural as having the delicious sensations of the body. But she had never noticed it because she had never esteemed having her own thoughts, assuming those of others were better because they were expressed with more elegance or wit. It had never been suggested to her that she could cultivate the pleasure of having thoughts. That became the new form of sybaritic delight which she proposed to the angels in the tower, one suited to angels who wore bodies only some of the time and who acknowledged the imagination as the sovereign arbiter of pleasure. The Tower was indeed the result of the increasing excitement she got from moving images around in her mind, reconstructing them, and finally creating new patterns out of them. More and more, she found that there was as much aesthetic satisfaction to be derived from the process of thinking as from the thoughts themselves, and quite as much as could be had from the sound of a beautiful voice or the feel of a smooth skin. Why had thinking never been included among the sensual joys? Beyond the sixth sense, there was a seventh sense, which when it was acting freely, when it was not merely marching about like a soldier on parade, had the same thrill of a chase, the same uncertainty of outcome, the same crowning ecstasy. It was imaginative thinking that created all pleasure.

Some angels protested that thinking had to be cold, or that it was dry, or that it gave headaches. Of course, she occasionally lost her nerve, worried that her mind worked like a grasshopper's, darting almost randomly from idea to idea. There was only short-lived reward in having ideas, if nothing could be done with them. Frequently when she was proud of having an idea which she believed no one else had had before, it was an illusion. However, what invariably consoled her was the satisfaction, which could only be her own, of kneading and pummelling an idea, blending it with another, continuing to knead, often for a long, long time, putting it aside and coming back to it, thinking about it, as it often seemed, endlessly, despairing of getting it to form a shape, suddenly finding a way, but then having to work on that slowly and painfully: a solution was always only a beginning, a pointer. Eventually the idea swelled up, rose and acquired a consistency of its own, and she could see that she had brought into being something that had not existed before and that was now quite separate from her. Half the courage to have her own thoughts was in the courage to persevere with thinking when there seemed no prospect of a solution, the courage to be patient, to try out every kind of seasoning, to go off on explorations in search of them in different directions, to risk getting lost, to find her way back again, to be able to recognise that she had found what she was looking for, even

309

though this was almost invariably different from what she had expected. There was always the joy of surprise at the end of thinking, doubled by the discovery that she had escaped from the prison of her old thoughts.

In the thinking room, Colopatiron came to treat ideas as though they were persons, as though the Rights of Man needed to be completed by a declaration of the Rights of Ideas. Thoughts might be foolish or even poisonous, but they had a right to exist. As with unknown mushrooms in a wood, there was something wonderfully mysterious about the way they suddenly sprouted out of nowhere and something awesome about their unpredictability, whether they would turn out to be nourishing or deadly. And because thoughts changed their shape, blossomed and shrivelled, just like people, she did not want to solve the problems of the universe once and for all, even if it were possible, even though so many great thinkers had believed that it was the way to happiness, justice, peace. Thinking had to be an eternal joy. Being confused, being misunderstood, was part of the process. Perhaps in the next world, misunderstanding would be accepted at last as inevitable, as natural as the mist that always wafted through the light of Paradise. Only then would people not try to force their opinions on others.

As Colopatiron talked, Sumdy grew calmer and settled down more confidently for a long, quiet think. But her thoughts were almost immediately disturbed. The hum of the universe seemed to be growing louder, to change its tone, become more discordant; and then she realised that there was shouting ringing out from all sides of the Tower. She looked out of the window. The idlers outside had become a huge crowd, pressing against the walls. The molehills all around were exploding like bombshells. Souls were rushing out of them, scattering dust as though they were soldiers jumping from trenches to attack an enemy. They were banging at the windows and chanting slogans.

The word had spread that in the Tower of Babel a miracle cure for boredom had been discovered. Instantly the modern souls in every part of Paradise pricked up their ears and trembled with excitement. Hastily packing their tennis rackets, their skis and their football boots, they were rushing to Babylon in frenzy, repeating the rumour to each other as they went, embellishing it, saying that though they had known they could not change Paradise themselves, they had always been confident that one day the angels, whoever and wherever they might be, would change it. No revolution on earth had ever succeeded unless it had some support among those who held power. Governments are not overthrown, they lose their nerve, they abdicate, they betray themselves. The souls in Paradise who were burdened by discontent needed a sign from the angels. It had come.

And yet not one of them dared enter the Tower. Sumdy looked more closely. A Ruritanian uniform, waving pistols in the air, was stopping them. It was the Archduke Francis Ferdinand. He had come with the crowds, because as a customs officer he liked to be present at every migration. But this time he was not questioning their right to enter. Instead, he was warning them, and he had scared them. The Tower of Babel might contain the secret of happiness, but – he knew it for certain – it also harboured a cockroach. They would catch unmentionable diseases if they approached it. Paradise, which so far had been distinguished in the whole universe by its freedom from vulgar illness, would be doomed if they went in. The Archduke had caught up with Sumdy at last. The dead are not so easily defeated. And now the souls were

311

hesitating, debating whether they preferred health or release from boredom.

The alarm bells rang in the Tower. The angels poured down to the ground floor, where the artists were holding their paint-brushes in mid-air, like statues in praise of unfinished art. All agreed that they were not ready to be invaded by these hordes, who might well be preparing one of the great fiascos of all time. They had not finished their thinking, any more than Sumdy had. Thinking is never finished. They too hesitated. If they had unwittingly started a revolution, they did not want to share the fate of so many revolutions, which suffered from not happening at quite the ripe moment. The moment was never ripe. The question was, should they accept that events had to be determined by accident, always accident?

Sumdy was not ready either. She felt she was just on the point of seeing her way to a decision on what she would do, perhaps the most important decision of her life. She could see no reason for moving until everything was clear in front of her. But perhaps that never happened. There was so much more she needed to learn in Paradise. And yet what astonished her most was that the shouting of those desperate souls outside made her realise that she wanted to go back to earth. Their cries were so poignant, so hungry, she was suddenly conscious of how she had felt on earth, of why she had come to Paradise. To be a hermit on top of a tower for all eternity was not her ideal. Her puzzlement about happiness on earth had started her off, and it was still what absorbed her. Perhaps this was the accident or opportunity that would oblige her to return to life.

She realised now that thinking could not be a private amusement, a mere form of gluttony. Thinking that was devoid of compassion was empty. If it was selfish, it was incomplete. It could not end in despair, because it creates despair itself, and so can undo it. In a flash, she saw where her travels in Paradise were leading her: the truth was usually terrible, but it was always possible to squeeze a drop of beauty out of it. That was what thinking was for, to create beauty where there has been none before. And she now knew where to search for that. She must do what no one else could do. But what exactly should that be? It was not where she jumped that mattered, but how she jumped, how she kept her freedom wherever she went, how she spread freedom around her, how much courage she added to the world. She could see it at last. To be an angel was to spread courage and freedom. That was what she wanted to do more than anything.

There was a chance that the whole history of Paradise might be altered by the meeting of the souls and the angels. It would be more than lamentable if a cockroach should be the obstacle that made history stop, just as it was about to start. She announced that she was leaving, and taking Forgetmenot with her.

She began a speech of thanks to all those present, attempting to express her affection for them: she wanted to say she was on their side. What they had said to her had moved her deeply. But she only managed a few words. She embraced Colopatiron, who said nothing to dissuade her. She and the angels were bracing themselves for the inevitable. Sumdy shook as it seemed a thousand hands. Jolly, with his tail now high again, was raring to go, jumping excitedly. Forgetmenot was safely in its jam jar. Sumdy left with tears in her eyes.

The crowd, holding their noses, made a path to let them pass. Sumdy ran to Henry Ford's ferry. He took them back to earth, asking no questions, saying nothing except that it would be no better down there, and if they ever wanted to return to Paradise, he would always be ready to drive them:

313

that was what motor cars were for, to drive backwards and forwards.

Sumdy scribbled a card and asked him to post it. It was to Newton. She said nothing ever turned out quite as expected; she had meant to see him again; he would always be in her thoughts.

The journey took longer than she remembered. Sumdy was so emotional, she paid no attention to Jolly's barking. Her eyes remained fixed on the Tower of Babel in the distance. Gradually Paradise vanished, but the Tower of Babel remained there, as clear as ever, like an apparition that had got stuck in time and could not go away. Then suddenly the Tower began to totter, bits of it fell off, and it crumbled as though she was watching a slow-motion film of a sky-scraper being demolished. When she arrived on earth she could still see the smoke rising from the rubble, mixing with the fumes from Henry Ford's Model T. It was impossible to know whether she was imagining that collapse of the Tower of Babel. In Paradise you see what you want to see.

Jolly was still barking. And now Sumdy saw why. The jam jar was empty. Forgetmenot had disappeared. Sumdy never found out whether the cockroach had decided to remain in Paradise, thinking that the earth was no place for a cockroach, that the friendship with Jolly could not continue there, or whether it had hidden in Henry Ford's car, concluding that ultimate bliss for it was to spend eternity travelling through space in the Model T. She was uncertain whether she was pleased or sad that she might have enabled the Archduke Francis Ferdinand to have something he could chase till the end of time.

EPILOGUE

When Sumdy returned home, the air felt heavy with dust that was rough and prickly, biting her face as though a sandstorm was raging around her. The colours of people's clothes seemed both drabber and more glaring, the dyes artificial; she missed Paradise's peculiar mist of little dots and thought she could see less clearly than she used to. There was more noise than she remembered, out of tune with the wind. When people spoke, their voices sounded too loud and their fetid breath made her recoil. Above all she was overpowered by the smell of sweat and garbage. She never became fully acclimatised again to living on earth.

She found that there had been strange rumours about her. Almost nobody would believe that she had gone of her own free will. Sinister meanings had been read into her letters; it was assumed that when she mentioned Paradise, she was being sarcastic and using a code. Many people were convinced that she had been kidnapped. Her photograph had appeared in the press. Journalists were waiting outside her house. However, when she insisted that she had indeed been to Paradise, and was not going to make any revelations about ransoms or masked bandits, most left in disgust, saying they received hundreds of calls each week from people claiming to have talked with the Virgin Mary and God Himself: that sort of thing was not news. One paper published a paragraph about her reporting that she had returned safely, but in a disturbed condition, from an arduous journey to observe the great bird of Paradise in Papua New Guinea. She knew that she was back on dry land.

This welcome confirmed Sumdy in her resolve that she would not try to tell people what Paradise was like, least of all describe every detail, repeat every word. Each one must go and find his own Paradise. The reward of Paradise, for her, was not the sights she had seen, but the shaking her beliefs had undergone. Each of the souls she had spoken to had given her a somewhat different account of what Paradise was about, which did not fit neatly together like a jig-saw puzzle; and somehow, she found this immensely satisfying, that there was not, that there could not be, a final solution. Paradise had to be infinite. Doubtless she had left at a crucial moment, just when the modern history of Paradise was about to begin. It would always be so.

A doctor came to examine her, to establish what effect her journey had had on her. She told him that she no longer looked on the living as she had once done. She was not sure that he was truly alive as he spoke to her, as he poked into her ribs and looked down her throat, saying Aa; the death of the body and the death of the imagination seemed to her to be separate events; she was now interested more by the problem of how to survive the disappearance of the imagination than that of the body, and how to find nutrition for the imagination.

The doctor wanted to know if she had had a difficult child-hood, a tormented family life. She said her stay in Paradise had made her determined no longer to blame the past, nor to allow the past to be a dunce's cap which she could never take off; she had met too many souls whose existence was turned into

316

misery by brooding on their memories and by resentment that nothing ever happened as they would have liked it to. The doctor seemed to suspect that she might have had hidden suicidal tendencies, and suggested that she should spend three months under observation. She had never been so optimistic, she replied: Paradise had freed her from the desire to find out what was wrong with her. All the souls she had met had something wrong with them. But it seemed to matter much less than what was right with them. What people could do in the future seemed to be more worth noticing than what they had done in the past.

A faded, worried man came to her door, on a warm, sunny day, wearing a faded mackintosh. The spies in the skies, he said, had spotted her going in and coming out of Paradise. Though the interior of Paradise itself was not one of the territories which his department kept under surveillance, because of the objections of the churches, he had his job to do, foreseeing all eventualities, preparing for all possible dangers, supporting the march of progress, so that eventually the secrets of the dead would no longer be concealed from the living. He had come to find out whether Sumdy had noticed any threatening developments in Paradise, any indications of hostility. Sumdy told him that she had never heard a single mention of the government in all her time away. He said of course she was lying; he quite understood that was how their negotiations had to begin; he would be back.

On the Stock Exchange, her name was whispered knowingly. Financiers telephoned her, wondering whether events in Paradise might not be promising new indicators of booms and recessions. Sumdy replied to all enquiries solemnly, saying that the inhabitants of Paradise had great difficulty understanding each other, and growing mutual incomprehension seemed to her to be the most important long-term influence on the future. It was the reason for her optimism.

317

There was a whole new art to be discovered, of how to live intelligently with misunderstanding, of how to cope with the increasing complexity of individuals and the multiplicity of their moods; as individuals became more different from each other, there would be ever more scope for ingenuity and imagination. The Age of Communication had not really arrived yet: there was only talk about it and the Age of Talk was quite different. Advances in technology had not changed most people. In Paradise, preparing for the next world, they seemed to be working on the assumption that an Age of the Imagination had to come first. Her personal opinion was that there was a new renaissance on the way, which would inevitably cause conflicts, protests, disasters. Several important institutions asked on what terms she would be willing to return to Paradise to report on these disasters.

The young curator of one of the country's largest museums wrote to her that he was organising an exhibition of fantasies and dreams. He believed that it was time that these were recognised to be as important a part of history as coins and pots and battle-axes; dreams which never quite came true were as much events, in his view, as well-established facts, which frequently only just managed to happen. Could she contribute anything? She sent him her invisible marble. It was put in an empty glass case, labelled "A Piece of Happiness found in Paradise" and attracted a lot of attention. The usual comments were made, which every exhibition of modern art evokes, that the taxpayer was being made fun of, but this marble was said to be even more of a disgrace, at least objects of art were things, not empty space. However, Sumdy was surprised by the number of visitors who took up the defence of the empty glass case, praising the pleasures of staring at empty space, lamenting how rare it was to find a quiet piece of empty space, and hoping that more museums would try to preserve it. That pleased her, because Paradise had indeed made her

318

notice how much empty space there was in people too.

A school invited her to talk to the children about the history of Paradise and how the famous people she had met there looked. She said it was not how they looked that struck her most, but how her own way of looking changed. She could not be sure that she had seen them as they might appear to someone else. It made her think that there must be many more ways of looking at people, in the present or in the past, and of learning history, than the children were taught. If painters were able to invent new ways of looking at the world, why did historians present history only in a classical style, why did they have no equivalent of Impressionists, and Cubists, and Surrealists, why, if they were constrained by their scientific method, did they cling to such outdated notions of science, of time and of objectivity, why did they borrow their ideas about human nature from dead psychologists and sociologists who may never have lived at all. She told the children that she now felt that she reinvented her history every day, and that history had something different to say every day. If they wanted to know what the famous people of the past were like, they should go and meet some live famous people to start with.

The local television station had a late-night programme about the invisible marble, and Sumdy was interviewed. Did the marble make her happy? Would it work for anybody? Her happiness, she said, was a choice, a faith, which she found more congenial than gloom and worry. Her mind, like everybody else's, had a tendency to dribble, to make a mess, like an infant's mouth, like a nose with a cold, like eyes that shed tears without being able to help themselves; but she did her best to get it to behave. As to whether the marble might make other people happy, she had no way of knowing, it was for them to say.

What ambitions did she have now? For what job had Paradise fitted her? She had come back, she said, feeling that

319

the ordinary ambitions of the world were too limited. One very rarely saw advertisements inviting people to become saints, which was the most noble ambition one could have. Not many people sincerely wanted to become saints. Not everybody sincerely wanted to be happy either. In Paradise, the only worthwhile ambition a soul could have was to give courage to others; and she wondered whether that was not what humans wanted more than anything else, what they owed to each other, an exchange that went beyond charity, beyond even love. They needed courage to put up with not receiving as much love as they wanted, they could never have enough love. They needed courage to seek for beauty where their instincts saw only a frightening strangeness, and courage to accept that even all the lessons of Paradise offered no guarantees, no security, no promise of success. The Five Great Disillusionments of Mankind and the Five Escape Routes did not add up to Ten Commandments. She had seen no one telling others what to do in Paradise, and she had not returned with any desire to do that herself. All she had found there was an invitation to new adventures.

But the courage to undertake them, though present in everyone, easily gets lost. Every civilisation begins as an act of courage; then it closes the gates and becomes afraid to lose what it has. Civilisations vanish, but new ones take their place. From Paradise, the world looked so young, so full of promise. There were so many people who spoke different languages, in every sense, who had never yet met: it was from their meetings, from their curiosity, which is very difficult to extinguish, that she expected courage to spread, very slowly. Perhaps a new Tower of Babel might be built on earth one day, perhaps one in every city, to bear witness that the confusion of tongues, far from being a reason for despair, could be a source of hope and beauty too.